REUNION

THE EMERGENCE: BOOK 3

SETH M. BAKER

The Emergence Series
Reaction: The Emergence, Book 1
Redemption: The Emergence, Book 2
Reunion: The Emergence, Book 3

Copyright © 2019 by Seth M. Baker
First edition.
ISBN: 978-1-938830-09-9
Cover design by Deranged Doctor Design
Published by Dark Hollow Press, 2019
www.sethmbaker.com

REUNION

1

Shenandoah National Park, Virginia

They fled the flaming hellscape of Andrews Air Force Base on the back of an inter-dimensional demon. Their subluminal steed—Durracli—was the size of a city bus, smelled like ammonia-covered roadkill, and bristled with spines. Another subluminal, Vaskulo, Amadeus' bear-sized ally, ranged ahead.

Lilly hated every moment of the ride ... but she was glad to be alive. Even clinging to the spines of a filthy, unnatural subluminal on a bitter winter night was better than the writhing chaos that she and Amadeus had barely escaped.

Thus they journeyed through the night, between tract houses in sleeping suburbs, across snarled highways, and eventually into the stark backwoods of Virginia.

When they began to ascend a mountain, she slipped her arm around Amadeus' waist and pulled him close. He smiled, then brushed back some of the hair that'd fallen on her face. His touch felt good, but a glimmer of twitchy nervousness shone in his eyes, and his jaws worked like he was chewing on something. She looked down to see that he held a torn-up napkin in the same hand he'd used to brush back her hair.

"Are you ... eating paper?"

His jaws stopped. He took a deep breath, then sighed and

shook his head. "I never thought you'd agree to marry me."

A burst of laughter escaped her mouth, but she stopped herself, thinking she sounded like a braying donkey.

"Ami, the hard part's over. You should be relieved."

He smiled again, then let out a long sigh. "I am, you know, about that, about us, but ..."

"But ..."

"The hard part's just begun. That horror show back there? All those subluminals? There'll be more, I guarantee it. This is Jessup's endgame, and we've got to get as far away from it as we can."

"Get away?"

"We can't be involved in this anymore. Look at where it's got us. Grassal is whatever he is, you nearly got yourself killed, and everyone else is dead—Gravity, Janette, Laroux ..."

"All those people at the Admiral."

"Your father."

"But not yours. And not Maximilian Ross," she said.

"If we can believe what your father said."

"My father would've believed what he said."

At the mention of her father and his recent death—the one she'd wrongfully accused Amadeus of orchestrating—he looked a decade older. "I'm ... sorry. I'm sorry all that happened the way it did."

"I know. I am too. Jessup put him in a disgusting position. It's not your fault. You didn't kill him. And we don't need to talk about it."

Some of the lines of worry faded from his face, and she squeezed his hand. Of course he'd feel bad about what went down with her dad. She felt awful about all of it—the way she'd refused to see the man, or even think about him—and now that she knew he'd done it to protect her, it all hurt that much more. That thought, combined with the western wind that howled around them, sent a shiver coursing through her body.

Amadeus gazed at her, unblinking, then took off his coat and draped it over her shoulders. Lilly tried to give the coat back, but when he smiled and shook his head, she accepted it.

"We need to recover, regroup, and figure out what to do about Grassal," Amadeus said. "He seems okay for now, but Securaux will be watching every hospital for a hundred kilometers."

Since the thing with the lights, Grassal had been comatose but stable—if floating a yard away from any solid surface counted as stable. His skin was cool to the touch, but his heart rate and respiration were steady, if a little slow, like he was hibernating.

"There's something you're not telling me," Lilly said.

"I'm telling you that we barely escaped with our lives. I'm telling you that good people died so that we could live. I'm telling you that Janette Nguyen told me to bury Roland Jessup in an unmarked grave."

"That's more like it," Lilly said, giving him a good-natured punch on the shoulder.

"But not just yet."

Lilly frowned, but Amadeus would say nothing else, so they continued the rest of the journey in silence. Lilly twisted the opal ring around her finger, once per step, to pass the time. Sometimes she'd close her eyes against the wind, but as soon as she did, she saw the person she'd shot. He was just a teenager, a kid with the same affliction—albeit with considerably different symptoms—as Grassal.

Every once in a while, Lilly caught sight of Vaskulo slinking through the trees. Even though the damn thing had saved their lives only hours ago, everything about it—to say nothing of Durracli—made her stomach churn. It, and others like it, were nightmares made flesh, squat creatures with flat faces that were equal parts needle-like teeth and yellow eyes. Some—like the one they rode, were covered in spiny quills. Others had lithe, nearly humanoid bodies the color of midnight with no eyes at all, only a death's-head grin and long limbs with too many joints that terminated in razor-sharp claws.

And even though Vaskulo may have been the best ally they had right now, Lilly couldn't help but hate it for the way it made her guts twist, for the wanton destruction its kind doled out when they manifested, thrashing and shrieking, from the demon gates.

Night faded into morning, and after an ascent up a mountain that made her ears pop, Durracli deposited them at a small hunting cabin, far from any paved roads. They climbed off its back and Amadeus strode up onto the porch and stepped inside, towing Grassal along behind him. Lilly followed, her shoes crunching in the snow, and pulled the door shut behind her. Not that she thought this would keep Vaskulo out if it wanted in, but at least her message was clear.

The cabin's interior consisted of one large room with a full bed, a table with two chairs, a fireplace, and a wood-burning cooking stove. There was a sink and a large enamel tub that Lilly guessed was for holding water. Shelves stocked with canned food lined the wall by the sink. Morning light filtered through two single-paned windows on the western wall. An oval-shaped wool rug lay on the floor in front of the fireplace's stone hearth. On the mantle there was a framed picture of Janette Nguyen standing with a woman who looked like an older version of herself. Lilly guessed this was the woman's mother.

Amadeus began to stack logs in the fireplace, both above and below the grate, leaving no room beneath the grate for tinder. Lilly squatted down beside him, a half-smile on her face.

"Let me help," she said.

The wood was mostly oak, nicely seasoned. She rearranged things until she was satisfied, then Amadeus passed her a lighter he'd found on the mantle. She flicked it once, twice, and was rewarded with flame. She lit the tinder, blew gently on it, and watched as the fire crackled to life.

She caught Amadeus' gaze, then took both of his hands in

hers, and said, "We survived."

"We did." The faintest trace of a smile rose on the edge of his lips, then faded. "But just surviving isn't enough, is it?"

Lilly followed his gaze to Grassal, who floated three feet above the floor, the belt wrapped around the foot of the bed. "No, it's not."

He turned to her, brushed some of her hair back over her ear, and they held each other. She felt good then, wrapped in the embrace of his scrawny arms, almost safe, but when she closed her eyes she saw the grinning face of Roland Jessup.

They spent most of that day in silence together, holding each other, checking on Grassal, and gazing into the fire. In the evening, Amadeus opened a can of beans and began to eat. When he offered some to her, she waved them away. She had no appetite.

Night fell, and they agreed to watch Grassal in shifts, with Amadeus on first watch. Sooner than she would've ever expected, Lilly fell into an exhausted sleep. Sometime in the night, Lilly awoke to the sound of Amadeus screaming. She pulled herself out of bed and knelt down beside him on the rug where he'd fallen asleep. He was curled up into a fetal position. She soothed him until the screaming stopped.

From there, Lilly checked on Grassal. His breathing and pulse were slow but steady.

Now that she was awake, she took watch, and every fifteen minutes or so, she leaned over Grassal so that her cheek was just above his nose, then waited for the warm puff of breath. She checked his pulse and estimated it at somewhere between twenty and thirty beats per minute.

A couple hours into her watch, she pulled her shoes on and stepped outside. The waxing moon bathed the snow-covered field and bare trees with a silver glow. Between the blustery wind on her face and the mountains that sprawled out before her, she could almost imagine that she was home.

Except that her father, the man who'd anchored her to the

place she'd always thought of as home, was dead. Also, the air here was too thick, the mountains too tame, and—most importantly—home didn't include an inter-dimensional demon that skulked about the property. Even now she could smell it.

She wished the damn thing would leave. Yes, it had helped them survive the sea of horrors at Andrews Air Force Base. They'd escaped with their lives and not much else—though the teacher whose students they'd saved had given Lilly his phone, just in case she needed it. She idly wondered if Su Min still had access to a Pachyderm. That'd be a nice way to get off this mountain, and an even better way to leave these creatures behind.

A twig snapped nearby, and Lilly turned to see Vaskulo standing on the path that led to the cabin. It regarded her with all those yellow eyes that covered its head, neck, and shoulders. She stared back into its eyes without blinking once. Despite herself, she giggled and wondered if one day she would become queen of all wild things. Then Vaskulo stood on its hind legs and raised its arms over its head in a circle. She felt her gorge rise, and she had to go back inside. Let it talk to Amadeus if it wanted to chat about the weather.

The next morning, at the end of a trail that ran through a hemlock grove, Lilly squatted by a fast, shallow stream. Water flowed into the open mouth of a plastic jug. Another jug, empty, sat in the damp grass beside her. There was a pump at the cabin, but the handle was broken, and there were no tools with which to mend it.

She pulled the phone from her pocket, powered it on, and saw she had a weak signal. It would be enough. Yet, she hesitated, and decided to focus on the task at hand. The time wasn't right, not yet.

Instead, she scanned up and down the stream, as far as she could see. Here and there were piles of rocks and debris that had been deposited by early spring floods. Only a few feet away stood a rock cairn she supposed some hiker had made. She'd rather fill somewhere else, but this was the deepest spot she could get to without getting her feet wet.

Now, the first jug was full, and she swapped it out with the empty one, but something felt ... wrong. She let go of the jug and scrambled to her feet. She breathed deep of the damp, coniferous air. Nothing smelled wrong, and she heard only rushing water. Still, she scanned for movement, tracks, anything out of place.

Satisfied nothing was amiss, she retrieved the jug—it hadn't floated far—and resumed her water collection. Her left hand was wet now, and the silver-and-opal ring on her finger felt cold and heavy. She waited for the icy sting of wet skin in freezing weather. When it never came, she smiled: this was the first day above freezing. Maybe, she thought, Amadeus made a good point, that they needed to wait. But waiting dragged out the end of things, and Lilly needed this thing to end.

She also thought that, maybe, the subluminals that had carried them here didn't have their best interest at heart, if such monstrosities had hearts. Sure, the things had saved their lives, but still. They were monsters. Not animals, not humans. Monsters, abominations, and every bit of her being told her their very existence was wrong, wrong, wrong.

She'd read Tommy's notes, how he'd just tuned into just the right coordinates and happened to come up with these things. What, she wondered, were the odds that shit like this actually existed? Clearly one hundred percent. Even worse, their very presence suggested other things like this were out there, and that many, many of those things would be even worse.

And of course Roland Jessup was still out there, trying to make a profit on the whole situation. What that man had made her father do to Amadeus to protect her ... her dad couldn't have helped his actions any more than he could help the palsy, or the stroke, or getting murdered by one of Jessup's henchmen.

The whole thing just pissed her off. She grabbed a large stone and heaved it into the rock cairn. The stone sent some of the rocks splashing into the water, causing a brown silt cloud to rise.

Lilly lifted the jug from the water just before she saw a snake emerge from behind the disturbed rock pile. She skittered back and fell onto her bottom. The snake slithered along the water's edge toward her, the tip of its pointed snout aimed at her. Lilly stood and took a slow, deliberate step backward. The snake was about two feet long, with chestnut spots on a light-brown body. The snake stopped and flicked its tongue at her. When she saw the pupils, she knew what it was.

Copperhead.

The bite usually wasn't fatal for adults if you could get medical attention, but out here ...

The snake's head tracked her every movement, but a few more steps back and Lilly could breathe again. She should probably kill it—they couldn't have venomous snakes around their watering hole—but that was a task for later. Lilly and the snake regarded each other for a few seconds, then the snake slithered away. Lilly admired the fluid, effortless way it moved.

She remembered something else about copperheads, and other pit vipers: they attack when threatened, and they strike without warning. She had no doubt in her mind that some of Roland Jessup's people were looking for them right now and that they'd be shot on sight regardless of the consequences. They needed help, yes, but even more than that, they needed to strike back.

As Lilly took the jugs back to the cabin, she clarified her thinking. Roland Jessup had attacked her, her home, her family. Roland Jessup had set in motion a chain of events that had led her to take an innocent life. She needed her action to be worth it.

Lilly made her decision. Like the copperhead, she was threatened, and that threat was not going away. There was only one option.

Roland Jessup had to die.

Now she just needed to convince Amadeus to help her to
make that happen.

That night, Lilly sat on the rug before the hearth and thought
about her life. Amadeus lay in the bed and snored, whimpering
every now and then, but so far there hadn't been any nocturnal
screaming. Maybe he was having dreams about being a kid in
some Connecticut park, warm in the embrace of his family. Or
maybe something less ... bucolic.

She had her own outbursts and did her share of thrashing
and screaming, not just in her own dreams, but in her waking
life—in this new nightmare—when captured, cornered, or
gravely afraid. These outbursts also caused her to go off and do
things that were, in retrospect, unwise. Staring down a hostile
Securaux tank, for example. Not only that, but unleashing a
frankly impressive stream of profanities and curses upon said
tank. Or mistrusting the man who now lay snoring, a thin
stream of drool running from the corner of his mouth. Such
behavior, she decided, just wouldn't do.

She added more wood to the fire, checked on Grassal, and
began to tidy the small cabin by the combined light of the
waning moon and the crackling hearth fire.

When there was nothing else to tidy and a gaping chasm of
time still separated her from morning, Lilly decided that she
really needed to get off this mountain.

Lilly pulled on her coat and followed the trail that ran
through the hemlocks. She eventually reached the ridge line,
where the wind penetrated every seam of her coat, the cold
stung her eyes, and the phone reported a single bar of reception.
It wasn't much, but it would be enough. The email address was
easy enough to remember—park.su.min@jones-
aerodynamics.co.kr—and the messaging app would handle
encrypting the message with Su Min's public key. She typed
out the following message:

If you get this and have the means to do so, we need a lift. Coordinates attached.

After a moment's hesitation, she pressed send, and included with it a whispered prayer that Su Min still checked the account.

Satisfied her message was sent, she returned to the cabin, roused Amadeus for the next watch, and managed to fall into a dreamless sleep.

What seemed like only a few minutes later, she awoke with a start. Flames burned all around her. An inhuman caterwaul rose from just outside the door. She tried to shake Amadeus awake. He was rigid. She called his name. He began to float. Somehow, she knocked Grassal loose from his mooring, and both drifted up into the smoke that roiled against the ceiling. She watched the scene play out, unable to move. A ceiling beam creaked. All around her she heard sharp cracks of wood. Then Amadeus and Grassal crashed upward through the ceiling, and the cabin walls collapsed in on her.

Lilly sat up with a gasp. She looked around. Everything was intact. Another nightmare.

Grassal still floated nearby, wrapped in blankets. Amadeus sat by his side, droopy-eyed but awake.

"How is he?"

"Same."

"Good, I guess. Get some sleep," Lilly said.

Amadeus crawled into bed and pulled a pillow over his head. Time passed, and soon the first light of morning began to push away the night. She heard bird songs from outside. Some she recognized from back west. She fed wood to the fire's embers and worked the bellows, coaxing the fire back to life. The terror of the nightmare had all but faded. She closed her eyes for a moment, thinking she might just go back to sleep, but then she heard a buzzing, mechanical whine from the south-facing window. She crept across the creaking wood floor and peered outside.

A small surveillance drone hovered on the other side of the window. By the time she'd roused Amadeus, it was gone.

"Maybe you were dreaming," Amadeus said.

"I was already awake."

"It was only a matter of time until they found us."

"Who?"

"In the best case, it's some of Gravity or Janette Nguyen's people coming to tell us they've found a cure for Grassal's affliction and killed Roland Jessup. In the worst case? Well ... "

"I'm not optimistic. Maybe we should leave. Those things that brought us here could help us escape."

"Takun, Lilly. They call themselves Takun."

"I know damn well what they call themselves. Doesn't mean I have to call them that."

"You really don't like them, do you?"

"It's not a matter of like and dislike, it's that creepy, skin-crawly feeling I get in my guts whenever they're around. It's knowing that some of them can telepathically control people, for fuck's sake. Look." She held up her hand to show off the ring he'd given her. "I'm thinking about our long-term well-being here. Our being in close proximity to those things does not improve our chances for long, healthy lives. I know they're your allies or whatever, but think about how this looks from another angle. All the crazy shit that's associated with you, and your family name in general. Now, you're running around with demonic minions."

"You know that's not ..." Amadeus trailed off and stared out the window. He furrowed his brows, and looked more troubled than usual. She followed his gaze.

Beyond the distant ridge, maybe five miles away, streaks of deep purple and green light rose to the sky. In the spaces between them, shimmering electric formations bloomed and collapsed like some kind of psychedelic fractal art.

"That was not there before," Lilly said. "Or maybe I was too focused on the god damned spy drone that was peeping through our window."

"It's probably nothing."

Then they heard the sound of gunfire.

2

His new body, the orb, should not exist. Everything he knew suggested that to think, he needed a brain. Yet, Grassal Delgado had begun to accept that he currently wasn't anything more than a cloud of particles bound together by a strong force.

Being pulled through the light tunnel had been one thing. He'd read about Einstein visualizing himself riding a beam of light, and that gave him a frame of reference. Okay, so he—or at least his conscious mind—was serialized and transmitted. Beam me up and all that shit.

But this was weirder than toes on a torta.

He'd kind of imagined that the light transmission business was how the subluminals had arrived. He'd assumed that even with the quantum stuff going on, matter would be conserved, their bodies having been transferred from wherever those things came from. But if this was a gate in reverse, and he'd been sent to their place, or some other place, or whatever, he reached the real question that he wasn't really ready to ask himself: Where was he, where was his body, and why did he look like a giant ball of glowing fluff?

He felt as if his entire body had become a phantom limb—a phenomenon he had some recent experience with. With his missing leg, he could tell his non-existent toes to move, and some part of him had sensed that his toes were indeed moving, despite his eyes telling him his toes did not move, because he had no toes. Later, when they'd given him the prosthetic, these signals could control his mechanical toes, and he could see them move, and that had been nice, even if the biofeedback wasn't quite right.

There was something useful here, but just then he couldn't say what it was.

In all directions, he could perceive the world with what he processed as vision, a world silver and green with streaks of pink and yellow streaming through the air like dust motes in sunlight. There were outlines of light, almost like silhouettes of buildings, and currents of light flowed between them. Glowing pillars stretched like a thousand braided strings toward a sky blanketed in flickering blueish-white stars. In the sky, just above the horizon, hung a sizzling ball of energy that he was pretty sure was the moon. From this, he guessed that he was in some kind of alternate reality or dimension. Maybe he'd died, and this was it.

But he certainly didn't feel dead.

Among the new sensations, one was of lines flowing through his body, like a hundred vibrating strings each a half inch apart had been threaded through him. He focused on this sensation and felt the currents of energy, faint as a sigh into the palm but nevertheless present, flow through him. These, he called flow lines.

Besides the flow lines that ran through everything, a silver thread as thin as spider silk emanated from his own body and disappeared to a single point on the far horizon. The silver thread was almost like the one he'd started seeing after things went haywire in DC, only it was much, much longer.

Unbidden came the memory of a compass he'd owned as a boy, the way its needle stayed afloat in the liquid, pointing towards north. This memory was followed by an image of arcs of metal filings forming around the ends of a magnet.

He oriented himself until his internal sense of inertia told him he was upright and that the lines flowed through his body. Once lined up, there was a slight push, like the wind at his back, and if he allowed himself to relax, then he tumbled along the lines like a leaf blown along by a spring gust.

He alternated between following the flow lines and resting, and during a rest period, nearby movement caught his attention. A jolt of anticipation coursed through his body, promising the biggest dopamine hit—or whatever his current body's equivalent would be—since the one time he'd snorted cocaine.

Grassal followed a flow line toward the movement's source and found an orb. He wrapped the orb with his own body, and each molecule of himself vibrated with a sense of satisfaction and release that bordered on orgasmic.

Seconds passed, and the flickering orb he'd enveloped was gone, absorbed into himself. Vibrating waves of a sensation he recognized as sound reached him, and these sound waves carried on them sensations of alarm, panic, and fear.

Grassal found another line that carried him closer to the sound's source, and soon he came to a place where a group of about thirty orbs flickered and glowed, each a glimmering, tempting little jewel of sustenance.

Grassal descended slowly upon an orb near the edge of the group. As he approached, the nearest orb began to course in a brilliant display of red and orange. As one, the group of orbs raced away from him along the lines like a school of fish.

He pursued, but they were too fast. During his pursuit, he thought he heard something like a faint, static-drenched radio transmission, carrying with it a hint of language, but he couldn't process the words or the meaning, so he put it out of his mind. There was another group a little ways distant. Grassal collected himself, then chose a line that would take him directly to the group's middle. The balls of yellow light shot off along the flow lines.

Then, he understood: the sound he'd heard had been an alarm. And as he recalled the transmission's pattern, some part of his mind decoded the message:

Something dangerous approaches.

Grassal felt panic threaten to rise up within him, as he was not sure what was dangerous here, and what was not. But more importantly, where had the voice come from?

Soon, though, he saw a group of blue and green orbs approach his position along a flow line. It took him a couple of seconds to realize they were heading in his direction.

Grassal fled from his pursuers, though to where he did not know. He followed the lines, and they propelled him forward, but he knew he could not outrun his hunger, his need. This awareness of hunger caused a memory to flood his mind, washing over him with a force and urgency that he had never experienced.

He was a small boy, three or four. He and his mother had moved to yet another apartment with peeling paint and drafty windows, where strange sounds filled the nighttime, punctuated by arguing grownups and crying babies. This apartment was worse than the last. His mother had been gone for a few days. He'd just eaten the last of the butter, but he was still hungry, and there was only cat food. After trying and failing to pull the tab from a can of turkey giblets in gravy, he'd resorted to the dry kibble. He remembered the way it crunched in his teeth. If there'd been a phone, he might've called 911. He'd known that being hungry and alone as a little kid was kind of an emergency, and that 911 was for emergencies, but Mommy only had a cellphone, and she kept it with her in case someone important needed to call. In his old place, sometimes a nice woman from his church stopped by, but she hadn't been here yet.

The memory stopped, but that same feeling of being lost and alone and hungry in a profoundly strange place stayed with him. But he'd eaten then, and that had helped the hunger, so he would eat now, and then eat more, though some part of him knew that it would never be enough, that he would never be full.

His mind registered the presence of another group of orbs to his south. The colors were faint: amber, green, and blue. Before his conscious mind knew what he was doing, he was racing toward the group. Nearer, he saw that each group member pulsed, as if it was turning itself inside and out. A closer look showed that these were similar to what he was starting to think of as his own body.

Operating on a mixture of instinct and will, Grassal expanded his body into a lattice-like structure, wrapped the lattice around three or four orbs, and enveloped them. Some small part of him suspected that he was doing something wrong. Though it felt correct to meet his needs, he knew there would be a cost.

For now, though, he put that thought out of his mind. Instead, he fed, and fed, and fed. He grew stronger, more sure of his new body, and began to take on larger and larger orbs.

After one hunting session left him particularly sated, he decided to explore. There was ground beneath him, and sky above him, but the ground posed no more barrier to him than did, say, a wall of fog that shrouded a gate. He moved downward. First he passed through the fog for a while until he reached a barrier of something chaotic and energetic. The lines that flowed through the air seemed to stream into here, a hundred tributaries flowing into a single body of water. He focused on one line in particular. He thought it was quite beautiful, the way it pulsed and flowed. He then reached out to touch the main body, the source.

The next thing he knew, he was back above the fog, and every bit of his being throbbed with new kinds of pain. Whatever he'd touched, he wasn't supposed to touch it ... and that made it more interesting to him.

This event triggered another vivid memory. He was sitting at a desk, a computer in front of him, a cold, faded hardwood floor beneath his bare feet. The glow of the screen washed over the room, bathing him in the green light of a half-dozen terminal windows. He was following up on the results of a rather fruitful port scan, and he thought that he had identified a promising exploit: a daemon running on port 7269 that had a known vulnerability. He ran a dictionary attack and found a match after two minutes. From there, it was simple matter of copying over the binary files that would turn this computer into a command node for a mining botnet. After a month, he'd mined nearly five thousand dollars' worth of cryptocurrencies. Along the way, he converted his earnings to dollars and sent them to their landlord. Now, he'd be able to finish the school year without his mother getting them evicted for missing rent payments. It would've been great, too, if he hadn't tried to help a friend of a friend set up their own pirate mining rig. That'd gotten them both a love letter from the FBI.

The memory faded, and he was back where he had been, as exhausted as he had ever been, in the place he'd come to think of as Otherspace. Through a mind dimmed with fatigue but imbued with alien clarity, he considered the memory, how he'd felt and what it meant. After going over it once, he understood: nobody could help Grassal Delgado, and Grassal Delgado couldn't help anybody else. He thought that if he'd just learned that lesson sooner, then Dr. Marx and those people at the Admiral would still be alive.

3

Amadeus pressed his back to the wall beside the window and used the same small mirror they used to check Grassal's breath to peer outside. On the path in the distance, a line of divots formed in the snow. Above each line of divots hovered a slightly shimmering cloud.

Amadeus had thought that if he could've convinced Lilly to wait, things would work themselves out. After all the death, the destruction, the violence, the loss ... he'd convinced himself that it was over. Now, he was starting to realize just how wrong he'd been.

"If they wanted us dead, they would have come in the night," he said.

The divots in the snow drew closer and closer.

"We'll talk our way out of this," Amadeus said.

Lilly shook her head. Her eyes were wide, the vein on her sinuous neck betraying a rapidly beating heart.

When the tracks were close enough, they diverged from the single line they'd formed and spread out. Now Amadeus was able to count eight of them. Whatever they were, they had four legs and were slathered in cloaking paint. From outside, a man's voice boomed through an unseen speaker.

"Brunmeier? Jones? Delgado, if you can hear us? We're just here to talk. We're with the Joint Defense Services

Corporation."

"That was Janette Nguyen's company," Amadeus said. He remembered one of the last things she'd said to him: "thank me by burying Roland Jessup in an unmarked grave."

"If they just wanted to talk," Lilly said, "they would have sent people. Those aren't people."

"Maybe they're afraid of us."

"That makes them dangerous."

Amadeus knew she was right.

"Come on out. No harm will come to you, we promise. We're on the same team."

Lilly yelled, "If we're on the same team, then show yourselves."

With that, a group of eight machines appeared. Four articulated legs supported thick, black bodies encased in a hard, probably bullet-proof polymer. They looked like nothing less than a group of headless bears. Each had at least two guns strapped to its back. Amadeus had seen videos of such machines before, but inadequate power supplies had made them worthless for field operations until the big battery tech breakthroughs of the last decade.

"These are for our own safety," the man said. "We've already eliminated a class A today, a really big bastard, and we're tracking another. The defense drones can escort you safely to our location."

"Durracli," Amadeus whispered. "They don't know that—"

The man's voice said, "We can protect you from any subluminals in the area."

Amadeus was about to say they didn't need protection, that the subs were their allies, but Lilly put a finger to his lips.

"Don't tell them."

"Why?"

"They killed Durracli and they've got a bunch of guns trained on us. What happens if they decide we're on Team Subluminal?"

"Fair point."

"So ... do we go with the murderbots and hear what their controllers have to say, or just sit here with our thumbs up our asses?"

Amadeus closed his eyes and thought through things. When he opened them, this gaze settled on Grassal. For now, he appeared healthy, but he had a responsibility to his friend.

Amadeus got to his feet. "We should hear what they have to say."

They donned their coats and shoes and wrapped Grassal in some blankets before strapping him to the stretcher. It was easier to move a body that floated a meter off the ground if that body was attached to something with handholds.

After stepping out of the cabin, the murderbots formed a circle around them, their weapons facing outward. The circle began to move, and Amadeus, pulling Grassal behind him, began to follow.

Their path took them down the mountain, past lines of squat, bare trees, into a small valley. As they walked, Amadeus gazed into the weird storm of unnatural light. It hadn't moved, but from this vantage point it looked more threatening than when they'd been higher.

They rounded a bend which led to a meadow. Amadeus guessed that in the spring, the meadow would be redolent with alpine wildflowers, sprays of blue and yellow. Now, the main feature of the meadow was a smoldering black pile. The air was rotten with the stink of burned subluminal. That, then, had been Durracli.

They walked past the still-smoking pile and came to a place where a white truck waited. A man stepped out, dressed in a heavy parka. He had high cheekbones, a wide face, and a mustache, which made Amadeus distrust him. His hands were empty, but Amadeus noted the pistol strapped to his waist. He pointed to the weird storm.

"See that? They're calling them kipium storms, or k-storms,

or Brunmeier storms, though I don't think that last one's really fair. Different names, same thing: grid-killing electromagnetic pulses, inconsistent gravity, and some other weird shit that nobody really understands yet."

"Inconsistent gravity?" Lilly asked.

"Imagine you're walking across a room. First, you feel light, then you feel incredibly heavy, then the next thing you know something's knocked you on your ass. K-storms don't penetrate stone, but that's about all we know. So far they haven't killed anybody …"

He left the implication unspoken.

Amadeus and Lilly exchanged a glance.

"There's only been a few of them documented up until the past couple of days. Now? Six in the past three days. *Six*. Two of those occurred over rivers. Both of them killed off a bunch of fish and left some nasty shit in the water. And that's not to mention the subluminals and what's been happening to the afflicted, which I know you know about."

They were silent, and the man continued.

"There's a theory that the k-storms are a side effect of running demon gates, and that the k-storms could eventually develop into rifts between our dimension and the ones the subs come from."

Amadeus sniffed the air. Vaskulo was nearby. Amadeus tried to reach out to it, to tell it to stay far away, but he couldn't tell if his warning reached the creature.

"Thanks for not being obstinate about this," the man said.

"Who are you and what do you want?" Amadeus asked.

The man gazed at them, silent, his blue eyes appraising, almost critical.

A flicker of motion just beyond the truck caught Amadeus' eye. A silent gray shadow stalked through the snow. Amadeus brought his attention back. He wasn't sure what the Takun was doing, but he didn't think it was going to end well.

"I'm Sergeant William Hurst, retired U.S. Army, third

infantry. I'm under contract by Allclear Services."

"What's Allclear Services?" Lilly asked.

"Like the military, only worse," a woman's voice called out from their truck.

Hurst raised one hand. "Excuse the peanut gallery. That's Eva Flores, my estimable associate. We're a two-person security consultancy. Until a couple years ago, we mostly worked in Latin America. We were recently granted a short-term contract by Joint Defense Services Corporation."

"Janette Nguyen's company," Amadeus said.

"Such as it is. Seeing as the former General was only alive long enough to lay out the basic charter and lease some property, the structure is somewhat in flux. We've got two core objectives: the first tasks us with subluminal eradication efforts. The second is enforcing B-Gate non-proliferation."

"B-Gate?" Lilly asked.

"Brunmeier Gates," Hurst said. "I'm sure you've heard of them."

Amadeus sighed. He didn't like where this was going, but he'd already decided to go with it. "Who do you answer to?"

Hurst gave him a sad smile.

"We answer to you, Mr. Brunmeier."

4

As a group, they trudged back up the snowy path to the cabin. Lilly had almost—but not quite—made up her mind about their new visitors. In her estimation, Hurst was just another tool of the military-industrial complex, but he appeared to be *their* tool. And he wanted to kill subluminals, so he had that going for him. Plus, he had more information than they did, which was bound to be useful.

"Why should we trust you?" Lilly said.

Hurst retrieved a flexscreen from his bag, entered a couple commands, then passed it to her and Amadeus. They held it between them and read while they walked. The flexscreen displayed a cryptographically signed email message from Janette Nguyen. Attached to the message was a contract which outlined terms and listed personnel and matériel to be requisitioned. Sgt. William Hurst's name was at the top of the list. There also a two-year lease for a rural property in Virginia.

She watched Amadeus inspect the contract. His brow furrowed, and one eye twitched.

"It looks authentic," Amadeus said.

"That's because it is," Hurst said.

Lilly leaned over and scanned the contract. It was surprisingly devoid of legalese, and stated in clear terms that their mission was to support Amadeus Brunmeier for a term not to exceed six months.

"What happens after the contract expires?" Lilly asked.

"We go back to our lives, and you go back to yours."

"So ... you're mercenaries," Lilly said. "No loyalty, no allegiance except to your contract."

"Well, yeah, if you want to put it that way," Hurst said, his voice carrying not a hint of hurt or shame. That made Lilly like him just a little more. "We were hired to do a job. We'll do it, we'll do it well, and if nothing goes pear-shaped, we'll all go back to our families when this madness—and this entire situation is utter madness—is over. Make sense to ya'll?"

"And what happens," Amadeus said, "if I refuse?"

Hurst began to laugh. It was an honest laugh that came right from his stomach. "That's where it gets fun. Re-read clause three."

Amadeus looked back down, then a half-smile grew on his face. "They actually put, 'follow him around like stink on shit' into a contract. I'm almost impressed." He put a thumb to his chin, as if considering his options. "We'll give you an answer in an hour. In the meantime, please don't kill anything that isn't trying to kill you."

Hurst gave him a quizzical, almost knowing look, then nodded.

With that, Amadeus caught Lilly's eye, nodded to the cabin, and they walked the rest of the distance arm in arm. Lilly needed to pee, but she recognized that now was not a good time to leave Amadeus alone with his thoughts, at least not until she'd said what needed to be said.

Inside, she said, "I think they could be useful, if for nothing else than to help us get Grassal to a hospital. And since they really were sent by Janette Nguyen—"

"But she's dead, Gravity is dead, and just about everyone else who has tried to fight this is dead, except for us, and I want to keep it that way. What are we supposed to do, hop in the back of their truck while they go hunting for subluminals?"

"My father said Tommy Brunmeier is working with Maximilian Ross. Maybe that information is bad, maybe it's not. But we should try and find them." She did not add that she saw finding them as a first step toward avenging her own father.

"I've thought about this a lot."

"And?"

"And I think that if my father was alive, he would've found a way to let me know it."

"Have you really given up hope?"

Amadeus held her gaze. One of his eyes twitched and he opened his mouth to speak, but nothing came out.

"If you have, nobody would hold it against you."

"It's not that, it's just ..."

"Then let's take it one step at a time. First, let's get Grassal somewhere he can get the help he needs. From there we can figure out our next move. The property in the contract sounds like a better place to hole up than this. I mean, eating canned beans in front of a fireplace is romantic and all, but indoor plumbing would be even better. And what about that?" She pointed to the window, in the direction of the k-storm. "Do you think that's just going to clear up with the next strong wind?"

Amadeus didn't seem to have an answer for that.

Lilly ignored the press of her bladder and said, "You asked me if I wanted to be all in, if I wanted to be a part of it, 'it' being a way to make everything right. Did you forget already? Are you telling me that you don't want to find your father, even if there's a chance?"

"That is not what I'm saying."

"Then let them help us. Will you think about it?"

"I'll think about it."

"Good. And speaking of that whole indoor plumbing business, I've got to pee." She stepped outside and started toward the privy.

Just before she reached it, a subluminal stepped out from

behind a rhododendron. Lilly let out an involuntary scream, staggered backwards, and fell on her butt. The creature stood on its haunches and raised its forelegs over its head in a semi-circle.

By the time she realized the creature was Vaskulo, Eva and four defense drones were dashing up the hill in her direction.

Later, she would reflect that if she had only got back to her feet, had only protested a little bit, maybe put herself between the creature and those who killed it, that Vaskulo would have survived.

As it was, after the gunfire stopped, Lilly looked down at the creature's bullet-riddled carcass and didn't feel a thing.

Stillness filled the cold air. Amadeus came out of the cabin, took one look at Vaskulo, sprawled out dead on the ground, made eye contact with Lilly, and walked back inside. Lilly shook her head. This hadn't been what she had wanted, or maybe it had. She didn't know. All she knew was that she had a mess on her hands, a mess for which she was responsible. She took a deep breath, drawing in the stink of the dead creature. For reasons she couldn't quite articulate to herself, she thought it was important to experience this.

Eva, white and athletic, stood beside Hurst, her eyes unable to hide the pleasure of their most recent victory. She supposed she couldn't blame her. As far as she knew, the world had one less monster.

"Please take it away," Lilly said, motioning to the corpse. "Put it with the other one, burn it, whatever you have to do, just get it out of here."

She finished her business in the privy and returned to the cabin. Inside, Amadeus stood before the fireplace with his arms crossed and gazed into the fire. She went behind him, wrapped her arms around him, and placed her head on his back. She could hear his racing heart.

"They didn't know any better," Lilly said.

"But you did. It's not like we could explain exactly why they shouldn't try to exterminate every inter-dimensional demon in the vicinity. I tried to warn them off, but ... but now it's too late."

Lilly said, "You can't hold this against them. We need these people, whether you like it or not."

Flames licked around a log recently placed on the fire, and liquid in the wood steamed and hissed. Amadeus said, "Joining up with this crew feels like running toward the fire. It's not like we can go up against Jessup and Securaux."

"When the Admiral was burning, there were people trapped inside. Some of them were spacing, violent. They attacked anyone who came near. Some of them even attacked Grassal and me. Yet, after we got out, instead of staying outside where he was safe, Grassal ran back inside to help them. He didn't hesitate, he didn't deliberate. He just did it. He saved at least a dozen people by running toward the fire."

Amadeus smiled and said, "That sounds like Grassal."

"Grassal needs our help. There are others who need our help. We have a chance to do some good here."

Amadeus' eyes met her own. She saw fear there, and doubt, but also a flicker of determination. She'd almost brought him around. Now she drove her point home. "Gravity died trying to make this right. So did Janette Nguyen. They were trying to do the right thing. Do you want their deaths to mean nothing?"

Amadeus took a deep breath, stood a little straighter, raised his chin just a little higher, and met her eyes.

"You're right. We have to try. If there's a chance we can do some good, then we should take it."

A tension Lilly hadn't realized she'd been holding in just released, and threw her arms around him. He hugged her back, and in that moment, she let herself believe that everything would be okay.

Lilly said, "I should get some water to put out the fire."

Amadeus gave her a thumbs up, then began to loosen the belt that moored Grassal to the bed.

Water jug in hand, Lilly stepped outside and started up the path that would lead her to the water, but halfway there changed course onto a branching path that ran up the ridge line to where she'd been able to pick up a signal.

She took another look around and saw no one. Satisfied, she dug out the phone and turned it on. The phone came to life, but admonished her that the battery was dangerously low.

She opened the messaging app and her heart sank. No message, no response, no acknowledgement, just an empty inbox. Lilly double-checked the email address she'd sent to, but it was correct. Lilly tried to ignore the possibility that Su Min wanted nothing to do with her. Given the things that Lilly's father had done, Lilly could hardly blame her. Su Min had her own life to live, and since she—a talented engineer who'd made some key improvements to the original Pachyderm design—was no longer contracted by Jones Aerodynamics, she'd probably moved on to bigger and better things. Nevertheless, Lilly typed out another message:

Plans have changed, preparing to move, details to follow.

The moment Lilly pressed send, she detected the faint hint of vanilla wafting through the air. For a moment she was convinced that the copperhead had somehow sought her out, releasing its threat-scent, but she remembered that was a smell more like cucumber. Lilly turned to see Eva Flores striding up the hill. She waved to Lilly, then put a nicotine vaporizer to her mouth and blew out a cloud, which explained the vanilla smell. Lilly longed for a cigarette.

"What are you doing up here?" Eva said, pointing to the phone with her vaporizer.

"Just letting someone know that I'm still alive."

Eva gave her a nod, though whether that nod indicated she believed Lilly, or was just acknowledging that she'd heard her, Lilly couldn't know. Lilly didn't yet know what to make of the woman.

"Good luck getting anything through. Shit's congested on account of what's happening in DC. Most of the network capacity is devoted to emergency and military services, so anything civilian is low-priority. We have some comms gear, if you really need to get something out."

"I'm good, thanks."

"Does Amadeus know you're up here letting people know you're alive?" Eva asked, nodding to the phone.

Lilly considered how to proceed. Lie, and that would probably blow up in her face. Tell the truth, that she'd been working on a backup plan just in case Amadeus had completely lost his nerve, and that would simultaneously undermine Amadeus' command, such as it was, and also give Eva some leverage over her. Lilly couldn't have that. Either way, she was kind of in a bind. She gazed down at the opal ring on her finger as she thought about a response. Eventually, she said, "I'll tell him when the time is right."

"Take it from me," Eva said. "You can wait and wait and wait for the right time, but the time is never right until you decide it's right. You can't wait forever."

She blew out another cloud of vapor, and the scent of vanilla mixed with the fragrant pine of the mountain.

While Lilly was thinking over what it all meant, the phone vibrated in her hand. Lilly looked down, expected a low battery warning or some kind of innocuous app notification. Instead, it was a reply from Su Min:

Glad you are okay. Whatever you need, let us know! My new business associate would love to help you, but Amadeus might not like it, because my new business associate—and majority Jones Aerodynamics shareholder—is Maximilian Ross.

Lilly's fingers shook as she processed what she'd just read, but just when she thought she was capable of typing out a reply, the phone's battery finally gave out and the screen went blank.

5

Bare trees clung to stark brown hills beyond the backseat window of the truck that carried them down the mountain. Several kilometers away, nearly fading from view, the k-storm pulsed. The GPS on the dashboard reported that the time until they reached their destination—the University of Virginia Medical Center—was just under two hours.

Lilly sat in the jump seat facing Amadeus. Grassal floated in the back between plastic crates of gear. Hurst drove. Eva sat in the passenger seat, scanning the woods on either side of the road with wide, hyper-vigilant eyes.

Amadeus found a crumpled-up receipt in a cup holder. He devoted himself to tearing the receipt into thin strips. So far he hadn't eaten any. Still, the paper felt good between his fingers and helped to divert his attention from the image of Vaskulo's bullet-ridden corpse and onto which remote sensing tools he could use to analyze the k-storms.

Hurst turned on the truck's radio, which led with a news bulletin about the president, who was last seen alive shooting at subluminals from the White House's Truman Balcony.

"Huh. So much for his and Payne's strategic partnership with Securaux."

"The guy was an egotistical knob," Eva said. "Any objections if I put on some music?"

No one objected, and Eva put on some classic Motown that Amadeus didn't know but kind of liked. He listened for a few minutes, but kept getting distracted because there were things he needed to say, so he decided to say them.

"Let's talk strategy," Amadeus said. "First things first: don't kill subluminals unless they're an imminent threat. Defense only. I didn't make myself clear enough earlier."

"The subs are monsters, and the afflicted can be just as—" Hurst stopped, as if realizing he'd driven a tank into a minefield.

"Please," Amadeus said, "continue your thought."

Hurst paused, as if choosing his words, then said, "The afflicted need help, we can all agree on that, and we're going to get Grassal the help that he needs. But right now there's a lot we just don't understand."

"You two have seen how dangerous the afflicted can be," Eva said. "Get them in groups, and it's ..."

"Downright weird," Lilly said.

"That's charitable," Eva said. "They kill, blindly and without remorse. They move like a single organism. It's like they're controlled by some sadistic alien puppeteer."

While Eva spoke, Lilly gave Amadeus' leg a gentle kick, just enough to get his attention, and then tilted her head toward Grassal, eyebrows raised expectantly.

Finally, Amadeus seemed to catch Lilly's meaning, and he asked, "Do you intend to hurt Grassal?"

"No," Hurst said. "He's under our protection until we can hand him off to a doc."

"Then what are you hiding?" Lilly said.

Hurst and Eva didn't react, or give any indication that they were hiding anything.

"That's funny," Hurst said. "We were going to ask you two the same thing. Eva?"

Eva produced a flexscreen and passed it back to them. The screen displayed a still image showing one large, spine-covered class A subluminal carrying a group of schoolchildren and four adults—one of whom was floating and moored to one of the creature's quills.

"What is this?" Eva said.

"We don't have to explain ourselves to you," Lilly said. "If anything, it should be the other way around: why do you want to know?"

Eva said, "Our job is to kill these things, and you're riding them around like pack animals. So ... what the fuck?"

Amadeus leveled his gaze at Lilly. He thought that she needed to hear this as much as Hurst and Eva did.

"I get it. You look at them, you see monsters. I did, too. I still do, most of the time, but not always. Because there's something else going on with them. Yes, I've killed them. And I'll do it again if I have to. But I'll tell you this: if it weren't for the two subluminals you killed, Lilly, me, and every one of those children in that video would be ashes. Is that what you want, Eva? Dead fifth-graders?"

Eva was silent.

"Sometimes, unlikely allies are the best kind," Hurst said.

"Thank you," Amadeus said.

Hurst reached his fist back over the seat, and Amadeus gave him a fist-bump.

"That's still some really weird shit," Hurst said. He paused and glanced over at Eva, as if waiting for her to say something more. When she added nothing, he said, "Back to strategy."

Lilly said, "Not yet. Is there something about the afflicted, about our friend, that you need to tell us?"

Both Hurst and Eva were silent.

"If there is, you should tell us," Lilly said.

"It goes both ways," Eva said.

"No, it doesn't," Lilly said.

Amadeus raised one of the strips of paper to his mouth, stopped when he realized what he was doing, and decided to pivot the conversation. "For our strategy, I'm thinking two phases. First, we'll spend a couple days collecting data. We need more information about the general ... situation. I'd also like to try mapping these k-storms. For phase two, that'll depend on what we learn in phase one." Amadeus looked at Lilly while he said, "There's someone we need to try and find."

"You're in a leadership role and you intend to do analyst-level work?" Hurst said. "JDSC has a really good geek on retainer named Ed Richardson who can help you with that."

"Amadeus is better," Lilly said.

Amadeus felt his face flush, gave her an appreciative nod, then said, "Play to your strengths, right? What about you two? Do you have any background in intelligence gathering?"

"I've been involved in some measurement and signals intelligence, and have helped destroy six B-gates. Flores conducted open-source intelligence gathering on a consciousness-transfer tech interdiction job," Hurst said. "General Nguyen shortlisted us for a reason."

"Interesting," Amadeus said. He knew consciousness-transfer tech was illegal for ethical reasons, but couldn't guess what General Nguyen's reasons had been.

Eva said, "It wasn't much, just a matter of knowing what to look for, and where to find it."

"As is life," Hurst said.

Amadeus had nothing else to say, no one else spoke, and that seemed like a good place to end the conversation. Lilly was gazing at him with something like a satisfied look.

Over the next ninety minutes, they pulled off twice to check on Grassal. Both times, he was as he had been ever since the thing with the lights. Eventually, they reached the interstate, where signs at the on-ramps stated, "Authorized Vehicles Only." Sand-brown military trucks were parked along the shoulder. Soldiers stood beside the signs and waved civilian motorists away with orange signal wands. Hurst drove their truck toward one of the ramps, rolled down his window, then stopped.

A soldier approached and aimed a handheld scanner at a small black device Hurst proffered. She then examined her wrist pad and asked their destination.

"Charlottesville. UVA med center."

"You're authorized, but you're not going there."

"Can you tell me why?" Hurst said.

"As of fifteen minutes ago ... it's gone. There was some kind of event. Started with a k-storm, then half the buildings across four city blocks were reduced to rubble. The main facility was right in the middle. It's a mess."

"Where's the closest hospital that can take people with the subluminal virus?" Eva said.

"There was an emergency amendment to the KREATURE Act. No facility can hold more than one infected at a time. You'll have to find a doctor willing to make house calls. Since you can't go to Charlottesville, where are you going?"

Hurst looked back to Amadeus with his eyebrows raised, expectant. Amadeus considered their options, then said, "The place we talked about."

"We're going to the place," Hurst said to the soldier.

"Which way is the place?'" the soldier replied, nonplussed.

"We'll be following this highway south."

"Okay. There's a bridge out about ten clicks ahead." She tapped something else onto her wrist pad. "I'm sending you a detour, but it goes through a couple of dead zones."

"Dead zones?" Amadeus asked.

"Power failure due to k-storms, moderate civil unrest, reports of subs, the usual bullshit," the soldier said, then peered into their vehicle. Her eyes flicked from Lilly to Amadeus, then she nodded, as if something she'd suspected had been confirmed.

"Listen. I'm not supposed to tell you this, but if your group encounters anyone who says they're working for Bigogli, assume they're both dangerous and insane."

"Who's Bigogli?" Amadeus said, but the soldier didn't seem to hear him.

As she was walking away, the soldier turned and said, "Good luck ... and stay frosty."

Despite the soldier's warning, the rest of the trip along the two-lane, tree-lined highway was uncannily mundane, except that they couldn't connect to any networks. Amadeus and Eva took turns trying to get the flexscreen or one of their tablets to connect. Finally, Amadeus gave up and stared out the window at the pink puffs of clouds glowing in the west.

Just before nightfall, they turned onto a gravel driveway that appeared between a break in the trees. The driveway led to a stalwart brick farmhouse with white trim. Hurst pulled to a stop in front of the farmhouse. Eva stepped out, put a vaporizer to her mouth, and exhaled a cloud of vanilla-scented something.

After inspecting things a little closer, he realized that farmhouse wasn't quite the right term. Estate, he decided, was more accurate. His thoughts turned to his own house back in Connecticut, presently vacant, probably suffering under the wisteria's annual assault against its foundation. At least he'd remembered to ask his aunt Annie to turn off the utilities before his trip to South Carolina with Gravity.

To deal with the sudden, surprising pang of grief over the man who'd saved them when his life first went sideways, he returned his attention back to his surroundings. There were two outbuildings, a large black barn and a prefab metal warehouse. Fog hung in a clearing beyond the outbuildings, where a half-dozen deer grazed in a meadow.

Hurst opened the back of the truck. Lilly stepped in front of him.

"I'll get him out," Lilly said.

Motion-sensor lights turned on as they approached the house. They climbed the wooden stairs onto the porch. Hurst caught Amadeus' attention then tossed him a key.

Amadeus unlocked the door, and they walked inside. Lilly flipped on a light, revealing stark-white walls and scuffed oak floors. There were about two dozen crates stacked in the dining room. Amadeus walked deeper into the chilly house, turning on lights as he went, and he reached the kitchen. In one corner was a stack of cardboard boxes marked simply, "Food." In another corner there was about half a pallet of bottled water.

"There's a bathroom upstairs," Lilly said. "It has a flush toilet, soap, shampoo. And ... a shower."

"You, uh, need some help washing your hair?"

She slipped her arms around his waist. She was smiling, looking more relaxed than he'd seen her in months.

"That sounds wonderful, but later. I'm going to be honest here—I need a shower before I can take a shower."

"Yeah, I meant later. Now would be cool, but later works, too."

Lilly began to laugh, and the sound was a drink of water on a hot day. "You really do have a way with words. Come on, let's see what your staff are up to."

"That's going to take some getting used to."

Together, they ventured onto the porch to find Hurst setting up some kind of suitcase satellite dish. "Once this baby's online, we'll get through to any doctor who can take our call."

"What about payment?" Lilly asked. "Grassal would be pissed if he woke up with a bunch of medical debt."

"That's taken care of," Hurst said. "There's a medical plan, and he's on it, just like the rest of you."

"He never got his clearance," Amadeus said.

"He's still getting paid, and so are you, at least until the gravy train goes off the rails. Hazard pay, insurance, 401k with a match, all that."

"That's so ... normal," Lilly said. "In the middle of all this, with him—" here she gestured at Grassal "—the way he is."

"Sad to say, but your friend is one of the lucky ones," Hurst said. "And as soon as I find a doc willing to come out, we'll know more ... but until then we're going to have to keep a watch on him. Understand? For our own safety, as well as his."

Lilly and Amadeus locked eyes. He wondered if she was thinking about that time at the bunker Amadeus had duct-taped

Grassal to her couch during one of Grassal's violent episodes.

"Eva has volunteered for first watch," Hurst said.

"I'll do it," Lilly said.

Hurst put down a tool, stood up, and wiped his hands on the front of his pants. "Miss Jones, I give you my word, nobody here is going to harm your friend. Okay?"

One second passed, then another. Finally, Lilly said, "Okay, but I'm going to check on him and take second watch." She then placed a hand on Amadeus' shoulder, put her lips to his ear and whispered, "Just before I get started on that pre-shower. I'll see you in a little bit."

After she'd climbed the creaking stairs, Amadeus—now a little flustered—asked, "Is there an equipment list?"

"It should be in the crate stenciled 'A1,' or maybe 'B3.' But if a case is marked 'explosives', just leave it alone, okay? Eva gets a little touchy when other people play with her toys."

Amadeus blinked and tried to decide if the man was being serious.

Hurst said, "Fair warning, once you're on the network Ed's going to have about a thousand questions for you. So save the setup for tomorrow."

Amadeus took one look at the neatly stacked crates, drew in a deep breath, and found the equipment list on a flexscreen in 'A1' on his first try. Pleased to find that little bit of order amidst the chaos all around him, he went upstairs and joined Lilly in the shower.

Afterward, he returned downstairs and reviewed the equipment list. There was a pre-configured GeoVer server, keys for Yama's Eye, and a storage array loaded up with all the datasets he could ever want.

Once he knew what he was looking at, he started to unpack his little part of the mobile HQ.

6

The moon—Grassal was now convinced this was the moon from his own normal space—began to set. Grassal rested, a state like being on the edge of sleep, partially aware of his surroundings, with his cognitive processes all damped down.

Eventually, the moon dropped below the horizon and a pulsating white orb twice as wide rose in the east. The sun's energy imbued the flow lines with a different character, one that Grassal interpreted as warmth, life, and vivacity, because not long after it rose Grassal began to feel restored.

Re-energized, Grassal tried to learn how to use the vaporous cloud of particles that was his body. He found that if he concentrated really hard, he could coordinate groups of particles to move as one, and mimic something like a hand, though it was only the sensation of a hand, a sense-hand. He also found that some parts of him were unruly, and other parts didn't like being too close to each other. This kind of physical work vexed and frustrated him, though, and he decided instead to visualize a three-dimensional box.

At first, nothing happened. Then he realized he was tense, and if he'd had lungs, he would've been holding his breath and hunching his shoulders. Instead, he began working through the routine he'd learned from Dr. Kongsampong. Since he lacked the means of respiration, focusing on his breath was out of the question, but there were other areas to focus on, such as the movement of particles through his core, and the flow lines that ran through his body.

After meditating for a while, he brought himself back to his original intention, and he visualized not the box itself, but the act of weaving the box out of the racing particles that constituted his body. He imagined collecting the particles, herding them together, and bounding them in on six sides.

Slowly, an object began to form within his body, made of the same purple-and-white plasma-like stuff as himself. He imagined that object as a thing in the world, then visualized the object peeling off from himself.

When he brought himself back to regular awareness, a single, three-dimensional box hovered in the air before him. The lines that formed it were uneven, the proportions were a little off, and a membrane of particles from his own body surrounded it, but there it was.

"First class," he said. He'd never tried to speak in this place before now, and he was surprised to hear words, or at least a language analog, sound that communicated meaning, not unlike the words of warning he'd heard before.

This was getting better and better.

He willed a sense-hand to reach out, grasp the box, and lift it into the air. Still clumsy, he grasped the box and felt it as if he was in his body and holding an actual, physical object.

Then mind-jarring pain shot through his sense-hand. It reminded him of the sting in his hands after hitting a metal post with an aluminum baseball bat, except he was the bat.

Everything went white.

When his vision returned, the box was gone, replaced by a glimmering shower of swirling silver dust.

Weakened by his efforts but drunk with the thrill of creation, Grassal went on the hunt and consumed two dozen orbs. Each one he consumed not only gave him just a bit more control over his own body, but also caused something like instinctual understanding to accrete within his core.

From that understanding he gleaned two things. One, the silver thread was important and he needed to find out where it went. The second was that if he formed his body into a hollow cylinder around a flow line, he could ride that flow line like a sail catching the wind. After a bit of straining and a couple of botched attempts, he got himself wrapped around a flow line that moved in roughly the direction he wanted to go.

He was clumsy at first, and intersecting lines sometimes knocked him off course. Soon, though, he found his balance and his grip and he began to rocket along the flow lines like a message container in a pneumatic tube.

Along the way, he found more opportunities to feed. He learned that by stretching his body out like a flying squirrel spreading its skin-wings, he could quickly envelop and consume the other orbs.

He took a few more orbs and though he was sated, some part of him urged him to consume just one more, to end things on a multiple of three. Since he'd arrived, he'd taken thirty-five orbs.

He thought that number was oddly specific, because he hadn't been keeping track, but there, close to his core, was a little collection of objects that told him the value he wanted was thirty-five. The value wasn't represented as an integer, but as an arrangement of patterns encoded using some unknowable scheme. If he looked closer, inspecting an individual value would show him the specific memory of consuming each orb, like having numbers on the back of your hand that showed you what kind of cake you had on a particular birthday.

Grassal considered this, then noticed a group of six orbs moving toward him on flow lines. The other orbs had been mostly oblivious to him, their constituent matter flowing in a cheerful, delicious pattern. These, however, flashed patterns that were rapid, almost agitated, and the following thought occurred to him: *threat display*.

Grassal knew that threat displays were things that prey did, but he was a dragon, an apex predator in this land of vaporous meat and honey, so he would take them.

The orbs came closer. He waited, motionless, until just the right moment, then threw himself wide and tried to envelop one of the orbs. Grassal felt something not unlike having the wind knocked out of him—if he'd had wind within him—then the world went tumbling. He righted himself and saw that the orb he'd tried to take had started to transform from a swirling round ball into something like a cross between an amoeba and an octopus. Grassal tried to strike it with a sense-hand, but the thing squirmed away, darted behind him, and attached itself to Grassal's body like a leech.

Grassal struggled to shake it free, but the thing's grip was like a vise. The more Grassal fought, the weaker he felt. Something gave out, and the silver thread began flickering away from him like a broken kite string on the wind. He summoned all his strength, readied himself to move on three ... two ... one ...

Nothing.

His body's signals weren't firing correctly, or there was something impeding delivery. He reached and thrashed and struggled and fought, disorganized as a sleepy child, but the more he moved, the weaker he became, the farther away the thread flew.

The orbs were all around him, except they'd all changed from orbs to those half-amoeba, half-octopus things.

Grassal flung all of himself at his nearest attacker, spreading himself out as thin as he dared.

Something slammed into him. A chunk of his mass detached from his body and dissolved like ash in the wind. His attackers closed in, their tendrils flicking around him, into him. An unstoppable force pressed down on him from all sides, and the last thing he knew before he lost consciousness was terror at the thought that he was being eaten.

7

Later that night, maps, simulations, patterns, and raw data were splashed across four computer monitors before him. A rat's nest of wires spilled from the table and onto the floor. Amadeus almost felt at home.

He verified he could connect to the satellite uplink and the local GeoVer cluster then started pre-processing the shape files and data sets he'd need.

Only a few minutes after he fired up his workstation, his chat client notified him of a new connection request. Amadeus verified the sender's public key—it was Ed Richardson—then accepted.

Ed: Amadeus Brunmeier?
AB: That's me.
Ed: It's ... really good to meet you. I'm a fan. Your work with the gate crashers, that was good stuff. You got what you need?
AB: So far so good, just getting set up.
Ed: Right on. Let me know if you need anything. I've worked with your toolchain before.
AB: Cool, will do. Thanks Ed.

Amadeus closed the chat window, started feeding data from Yama's Eye into GeoVer, and it was almost like nothing had changed at all.

Four hours later, several machine learning models had been trained on public sensor feeds, satellite imaging, and a few other data sources.

Amadeus set up monitors to notify him about new k-storm matches, then pushed what he'd written to a public repository. The code was rough, but maybe other people more skilled than him could make something useful out of it.

A notification chimed, informing him that one of his analysis routines had results to report. He scanned the summary, which read:

Correlation detected between presence of afflicted and k-storm formation, high probability (0.78), medium certainty (0.40).

Amadeus leaned in closer to read the details just as he heard a scuff of footsteps. He turned to see Hurst standing at the threshold of the living room, leaning against the wall, arms crossed over his chest. Amadeus minimized the output window and swiveled his chair to face Hurst, putting his body in front of the screen, just in case.

"I haven't been able to reach anyone. Ed's trying, too. Maybe we'll have better luck tomorrow." He nodded to the screens behind Amadeus. "Find anything interesting?"

"Exactly what you said, lots of electromagnetic interference. The k-storms, if you watch them, they almost look like an algae bloom. But as far as I can tell, their appearance is random."

"What about the med center that got leveled? Lots of people are wondering if the afflicted had something to do with with it. Inadvertently, of course."

Amadeus shook his head. "People say lots of things."

"Your friend is safe with us, don't get me wrong. But there's a lot we don't know."

Amadeus heard someone descending the stairs, and Lilly

walked into the room. Hurst nodded to her. She then sat down on a crate beside Amadeus, and looked at Hurst, expectant.

"No luck finding a doc, wish I had better news for you. How's our guy upstairs?"

Lilly sighed and shook her head. "Still the same."

"Then there's nothing else to do tonight, so I'm going to get some rack time. Goodnight."

When Hurst left, Lilly leaned in close to Amadeus, locked eyes with him, and said, "There's something on my mind I wanted to run by you."

"Okay,"

"But you've got to promise ... just keep an open mind, and, well, just humor me."

"I can do that."

He pushed a stray strand of hair back behind her ear, then she continued. "I was thinking about the thing where my dad crashed you into a lake?"

"Yeah."

"And how my dad said that the only reason he'd done it was to protect me?"

"Uh huh."

"Okay. So, Jessup sent out teams of Securaux goons to kill subs when he deployed demon gates, most of the time anyway. But his teams kept getting overwhelmed. If he wanted to manufacture an enemy to fight, wouldn't he want to, you know, keep his own people around to fight that enemy? Deploying shitty, malfunctioning demon gates doesn't seem like good business."

"What are you saying?"

"What if the initial attack on your house wasn't an assassination, but an abduction, because Jessup needed your father to work for him? Forced him to, the same way he did with my dad."

Amadeus began, "But your dad said—"

"Forget what he said. If your dad could've contacted you, he would've contacted you."

"Or maybe he didn't contact me because he's dead."

"But what if he's not?"

"My dad would never weaponize his work."

"Would he if it meant keeping his son alive?"

Amadeus remembered being a small boy. His mother scooped him up onto her knee. They were on the sofa beside his father. He had a book open on his lap.

"Your daddy and I will always love you, Ami, no matter what."

"That's right, buddy boy. We'd do anything for you. We'd die for you, kill for you, if it came down to it."

At the time, Amadeus hadn't understood what that meant. As he'd gotten older, he'd assumed it was just something adults told their kids, like stories about Santa Claus, the Tooth Fairy, and how if you licked light switches you'd get shocked, which had turned out to be a grievous lie.

Lilly cleared her throat and continued. "Wouldn't that explain why the demon gates were always malfunctioning, and why—at least at the beginning—the demon gates were so easy to detect? If anyone would know how to sabotage a demon gate, it'd be your dad."

Amadeus entertained the thought and was surprised to realize that—in spite of how disturbing this whole notion was—he was smiling. "A buffer overflow here, a division by zero there, and it's possible you'd end up with a machine you couldn't turn off. Especially if you're working off a design spec for an earlier version."

"Exactly," Lilly said. She leaned in close, and for some reason he had the feeling that she was about to strike.

"If I'm right, then if we find Jessup, we might—"

One of the alerts fired, triggering a noisy digital alarm. Lilly startled and hunched her shoulders.

"Sorry," Amadeus said, then cursed himself for sharing buggy code. He never had been much of a programmer. "I need to look at this."

He opened up a console and examined the GeoVer output. According to his instrumentation, a k-storm had bloomed ten kilometers from their location.

That, Amadeus thought, couldn't be right. He started to mentally step through the detection algorithm, but then Eva— eyes wide, face pale—stepped into the room.

"You should check on your friend. Vitals are normal, but he looks ... illuminated."

Amadeus and Lilly exchanged a look, then took the stairs two at a time. At the end of the hallway, light crept from beneath the door to Grassal's room. Lilly flung open the door. Grassal floated a meter above the floor, just as before, but now a billowing cushion of light pulsed around him, formed into a mushroom-like shape around his head, and flowed out the window like a thousand glowing, pulsing threads of light, woven together into a single braid.

Lilly bent over the readout of a field medical diagnostic on a nearby table, then turned back to Amadeus.

"Pulse, respiration, blood pressure, temperature, it's all been in the same range since they got him hooked up, so I guess that's normal, if humans had normal ranges for hibernation."

"Medium certainty my ass," he said to himself.

Lilly looked at him, her expression perplexed. He stepped to the window, she stood beside him, and they gazed out into the night. The thread flowed between them, and both were careful not to touch it.

"There was something in the results that—"

Just then, a column of dazzling blue light shot into the night sky, as wide as a nuclear plant's cooling stack. The light flashed, illuminating the world like a thousand simultaneous lightning strikes. The afterglow gave the scene a warped, warbled quality, as if they were seeing things through a glass, darkly.

"A rift," Lilly said. "Between dimensions. It came out of the k-storm, just like Hurst said."

Amadeus looked closer. Within the column, little gray blobs swirled and pulsed like flotsam in a river flowing from the sky into the earth. Except the blobs weren't branches, or garbage, or anything else natural.

The dots were subluminals.

Thousands and thousands of subluminals, falling from the sky.

8

Grassal regained consciousness in a place of darkness. Time had passed, maybe hours, maybe days. He reached out. In all directions, solid walls pressed against him. The walls vibrated with a faint droning sound, which reminded him of being in an old shed where carpenter bees crawled through wooden walls. Even here, the flow lines still ran through everything.

Slowly, he remembered being consumed by something, which was accompanied by another flashback, one where he was in a cold church basement classroom with a few other people. All except the teacher—Mrs. O'Neal, a kind old woman with a patrician nose—were between twelve and fifteen years old. She'd said, "Jonas' faith—or stubbornness, depending on your perspective—kept him going when things were at their darkest. And you know what his reward was?" He remembered how at this part of the telling her crow's feet had turned to smile lines. "His reward was to get puked up by a sea monster onto some Mediterranean beach. I can think of worse things. Like being digested, for example."

Now, he felt like Mrs. O'Neal must have felt after the colon cancer had digested her, leaving her body a desiccated husk. Parts of himself were simply gone. Yet, he had faith that he could get himself out of this predicament, so he directed his attention to the writhing, pulsing walls that contained him.

On closer inspection, he saw the walls were not solid, but more like a dense storm of spinning rocks that whipped and whizzed through the air. Through the storm of rocks, little gaps would appear, and he thought that maybe—if he was lucky—he could slip through.

With that thought in mind, he wrapped his form around the flow line, released, and accelerated at a dizzying rate before crashing into the walls of the container. The aftermath of his futile effort hurt like hell, but he tried again, to the same result. After each try, he felt a little weaker, a little woozier, and soon realized that he was losing a little mass each time. Except, instead of turning to ash, the mass he'd lost spiraled in the air around him in a cloud of small, silvery spheres.

Acting on accreted knowledge, he reached out for the spheres, touching them but not absorbing them, and caused the cloud to swirl. He also found that, if he concentrated in a certain way, he could make the cloud move. Soon he had his very own remote-controlled mass swarm. After playing around with this for a while, he corralled the spheres back into his body and started a new experiment.

First, Grassal visualized a scalpel slicing through a chunk of light-flesh on one side of his orb body, not unlike the way he'd manifested the box. There was a weird sensation with no human analog that he could think of, then a piece of his mass fell away and floated before him, leaving him a little woozy, but otherwise unharmed. He pulled the mass back into himself and cut again, this time sloughing off as much as he dared, about ten percent of his body.

Next, he willed the mass to spin around his core form, like his own personal tornado, and it did. From here, he mounted the flow line, released, and let it propel him forward. As soon as he hit the wall, rocks began to batter the spinning mass cloud around him, and his speed slowed. Some went caroming off, while others slipped through and battered his body. He pushed forward, but his mass cloud was being shredded. A thousand

points of pain erupted all over his body. He felt his grip on the
flow line loosen, and just as he was about to let go, he was
beyond the wall.

Outside, a thousand points of brilliant light dotted the inky
blackness that surrounded him, and he realized that they were
stars. There were streaks of light below, some partially shrouded
by fog. Grassal soon realized two things: one, he was floating in
space, and two, one of these streaks was not a streak at all, but a
serpentine finger of light questing toward him. He tried to
escape, to hop from one flow line to another, but before he had a
chance to move, the finger wrapped itself around Grassal and
pulled him down into the middle of some kind of structure.

The structure was shaped almost like a stadium, only it was
made not of bricks, but of orbs, like himself. And from his place
in the middle, he heard whispering voices, indistinct, faint, and
menacing. He spun around, making a full circle, felt his mind
turning his fear and frustration into something else, something
raw and vital, and then he heard his own voice screaming,
"What do you want from me?"

A flicker of light ran through the orbs that surrounded him.
Grassal felt the colors as a tapestry of emotions, and the
experience of receiving the emotions of others unmoored him.
This, combined with his own use of the word "you", of his
acknowledgement of something outside of himself, finally
caused Grassal to understand: they were sentient.

They'd been speaking to him, trying to communicate with
him, but he hadn't listened, hadn't been able to listen, hadn't
wanted to listen.

Now he listened, and he began to make out some voices, and
each voice asked the same question: "How did you come here?"

Grassal remembered everything that led to this point: his leg
being gnawed off by an inter-dimensional demon. The shame at
realizing he'd spaced out and thrown a pickle jar at Lucretia.
The time he'd woken up duct-taped to a couch at the bunker.
The way everything had gone wrong at the Admiral Hotel.

Pulling Lilly out of the path of a tank, and finally the dazzling lights that had carried him to this place, where he was alone, confused, and so very hungry.

With mounting dread, Grassal reasoned that, since this had all started with the bite of an inter-dimensional demon, and demons came from hell, then he must be in hell. Maybe not capital "H" hell, but in whatever place that inter-dimensional demons had hailed from. And that he, Grassal Delgado, poor Guatemalan kid from the projects, had traveled to this place, met the locals, and ate them.

A voice with the electric keening quality of a theremin resonated in his mind. The voice wasn't human, not by any means or measure. The voice's speaker transmitted the message to him, and—somehow—his subconsciousness translated it into words.

"You are dangerous. You have killed. You have created."

A current rippled through the crowd around him. The voice was distinct, and clearly belonged to an individual. Grassal couldn't figure out which one had spoken, though it wasn't for lack of trying, nor could he say how he knew the speaker's name was something that sounded like Donweduul. Grassal decided to call it Donald.

"Then destroy me, or let me be," Grassal said. He wasn't sure if the words had actually conveyed his meaning, but a current of color washed through the orbs around him.

"You will live. The contract says all may live. But you must control your desires."

"What contract? What do you want from me?"

"We want stillness. Recent events disrupt. The Observer sleeps, even through disturbances. Sleep must continue. If it wakes, the contract says most will die."

If Grassal had had eyes, he would've been blinking, trying to parse what he had just heard.

"Who—what—is the Observer?" he asked.

A different voice answered.

"Questioning invites misfortune."

"Where is the Observer? I want to see ... it."

"Impossible," came the response, almost in unison.

From the circle of orbs that surrounded Grassal, one orb floated forward. As it did so, the pulsing patterns that made up its body swirled and folded in on themselves, as some of the others did, but this one's patterns moved in ways far more complex than those of the other orbs. It also seemed more solid, more complete, even, as if this one was closer to being a finished work. When it spoke, Grassal understood that this orb was Donald.

"You must stop. You draw from beyond The Luminance. Unforeseeable problems arise."

"It is dangerous," came another voice. This one's patterns showed a similar degree of complexity. Grassal mentally translated this one's name as Filipe. "The contract says to honor the stillness, or we all suffer. Expansion, exploration, inquiry all cause disturbances."

"What I really want to know is what the hell is going on?"

"You have encountered our kind before, though in our ... lower and tormented Takun form. Given what you already know about us, you may think of us as Luminants."

Grassal reeled. When he recovered, he said, "I don't belong here. The Observer isn't my problem. And if I could go back to where I came from, I would, but I don't know how. So maybe you don't know what to do with me ... but there will be more like me, and you're not going to like it one bit."

"You are second," Donald said.

"Second? As in not the first?"

"The first human shall explain in ways you will understand."

Filipe's words sang in his mind as silence and stillness fell over the ring of multi-colored, luminescent orbs that surrounded him. The ring parted, and a form, approximately man-shaped, approached.

"Hey, buddy boy. It's been a while," a human voice said.

After the conversation with the alien minds, the voice's familiar human cadence and inflection filled him with homesickness and longing for the world that he'd lost. But as he replayed the sound of the voice over and over in his mind, he knew why the voice was familiar. That voice belonged to someone he knew, someone he knew very well.

"Tommy?"

Interlude

Once again, everything was coming together, despite the setbacks. In the distance, about five miles away, a strange tower of light rose from the ocean and into the night sky. Between here and there, little balls of light blinked in and out of existence. The display reminded the administrator of the way the fireflies used to light up the hayfield during the humid, summer nights of his basically idyllic boyhood.

Except his boyhood was a couple of lifetimes ago, the fireflies were some kind of inter-dimensional disruption phenomenon, and he was standing on the forecastle of a repurposed container ship, surrounded not by people who loved him, but by the Securaux staff and contractors who feared him. Hell, even a president was here, though with three days of stubble and wind-tousled silver hair, the man looked less like a president and more like someone in a DUI mugshot.

Overall, the administrator was pleased. He thought that even if they failed, they'd learn that it was all about the friends they made along the way. No, who was he kidding. His last friend was dead and he intended to become the most powerful man in the world. And being the only person with a Rift Mitigation System would let him do it.

One way or another, this was the moment that would determine the administrator's next course of action.

Sadiq—Abdullah's replacement, the six sigma blackbelt—raised the control surface and looked to the administrator.

"Do it," the administrator said.

Sadiq entered a command on the control surface. The deck rumbled beneath their feet. The distant groan of machinery filled the air, then the deck lights flickered and blinked out, enveloping them in darkness.

A moment later, the column of light was gone. The not-fireflies were gone, too. The ship's lights came back up, and as soon as it had started, the test was over, and everything seemed back to normal.

"Reports?" the administrator said.

A radio squawked and a man's voice said, "Operations reporting in. System checks pass and nothing exceeded tolerances during the test." The voice belonged to Dr. Chris Davenport, one of his operations managers. Not a bad one, the administrator thought, but he seemed like the type to piss himself if things got hot during field work. Two more men from his engineering departments radioed in to report everything was a-ok.

The administrator allowed himself just the hint of a smile as he turned his gaze onto Sadiq, who was beaming with the satisfaction of a boy who had just aced a difficult test. With the help of some reserve talent—a motley assortment of over-educated misanthropes and amoral technologists—he'd picked up where Abdullah and the physicist had left off. Working from their foundations, Sadiq had managed to convert an unanticipated side effect into an outstanding opportunity, and under extreme time pressure to boot.

The administrator put a hand to his chin and gazed out at the utterly normal night that spread out before them. The stars seemed aglow with promise.

Sadiq recovered his composure and began to prattle. "You see, as a result of engaging the collector, we generated an induction field which trapped—"

"Save the details for the nerds. What about the vulnerability? Davenport?"

The radio squawked once, then Davenport said, "We were a little taxed down here, but well within parameters, and nothing unexpected was observed. As long as we can keep the field collectors cool, we can remain in standby mode indefinitely."

"Good," the administrator said.

Sadiq scratched his nose, took a deep breath, and said, "The system the physicist designed requires an inordinately large amount of power, which means that our biggest risk is the system overheating."

"And the status on the redesign?"

"Given the timeline, we hope to make progress in the medium term—"

"Define medium term."

"Optimistically, six months for a testable prototype."

"So, for now, it is what it is."

"Yes."

The administrator narrowed his eyes and scrutinized Abdullah's self-satisfied replacement. Sadiq still wore that ridiculous combover, even though the administrator had dropped not-so-subtle hints that the little man would look stronger if he accepted his place on the Norwood scale and shaved his head. The administrator chalked it up to a failure in cross-cultural communication.

"I'm impressed."

Sadiq squared his shoulders and beamed. "I must give credit where credit is due. The initial side effects and a potential mitigation mechanism were described by the physicist before his incident ... and before the mode of operation was fully understood and refined by Abdullah. He left notes outlining what to do should we ever begin to see such phenomena. He was a man with great foresight and ingenuity."

The administrator beamed with pride at Sadiq's praising of his late friend. "He left some massive shoes to fill."

"I do not understand how his shoes have any bearing on—"

"It's an idiom, but that's not important. What is important is this: I need your team to put together a white paper detailing the theory of operation. Provide just enough detail to convince skeptical people, but not enough to give away the specific implementation details."

"But doesn't that—"

"Did I say, 'Let's debate putting together a white paper?'"

"No, sir," Sadiq said.

"Did I ask for your opinion?"

Sadiq examined his own small shoes, shook his head, then said, "We will begin immediately."

"If what I have in mind works like I think it will, then we'll find ourselves in possession of information that will help us debug some of the problems that have plagued our systems since for-fucking-ever."

"That would be very beneficial to our efforts, sir."

While the administrator had to admit that Sadiq's work was solid, and the reserve talent was a welcome addition to his team, Sadiq would never truly replace his previous lead engineer. Maybe in a half a decade, give or take a couple years, his technical chops might match that of his predecessor.

But the administrator was convinced that no one could replace Abdullah, his friend.

Abdullah, the administrator realized with a sinking feeling in his heart, had been his last friend. All the people scurrying about the deck before him, they were just underlings, and to them he was some mythical, all-powerful figure who had the ability to destroy the world and—if Sadiq's project came to fruition like they hoped it would—the power to save it. None of them were people he would invite—or would invite him—to a backyard barbecue.

"Sir," someone said. The administrator turned to see Manuel Vasquez, his recently promoted chief of security, yet another replacement for a good man lost. This man was hardened by life and the administrator liked that. And he'd been promoted from within the ranks, so he was aligned with the goals of Securaux. And, most importantly, just like Marshall Hathaway before him, Manny would make sure things got done right, no matter what the cost.

"What's up, my Manny?" the administrator asked.

At the use of the diminutive form of his name, Manuel gave the administrator a withering look, entirely without fear, and the administrator smiled. Manuel, the administrator realized, would not abide any bullshit, not from his inferiors or his superiors, but would still carry out his task nonetheless. The administrator wondered if he'd picked up this skill during his days as a high-level *narcotraficante,* or maybe earlier, when his wealthy drug lord father sent him north to the US for his education. He'd definitely been hard before Marshall had recruited him to join Securaux, because otherwise Marshall wouldn't have recruited him.

The administrator liked that steely quality in a man, and for the first time since Abdullah was eaten, he thought that maybe he could find room in his heart for another friend after all.

"Signals is reporting an event similar to what we just saw occurring southwest of DC, in rural Virginia. The communicator thinks it's related to Delgado."

"Perfect. Now they know the stakes," the administrator said. One more thing he liked about Manny was that the man was entirely unfazed by telepathic communication with trans-dimensional monsters. "Keep telling it whatever it wants to know. It can't do any damage down there. And Manny?"

"Yeah?" Manuel locked eyes with the administrator.

"Stay strong. I know how that thing can get under a man's skin."

9

They had the truck loaded within fifteen minutes. As Lilly helped Amadeus carry the crates, everything around her felt weird and uneven, like she was walking in one of those inflatable bounce houses with a dozen maniac kids jumping all at once. And she'd developed an especially nasty migraine, but she got those sometimes, so that was at least familiar.

She'd been trying to convince herself that it was only a coincidence that the event had occurred just a few miles away from the place where Grassal had started glowing. She'd been trying to explain away the fact that a thread of light flowed from Grassal's head and into the column of pulsing death just over the mountain. That effort wasn't going so well.

Now, she stepped up into the back of the truck beside Grassal. The topper was just high enough that she didn't have to hunch. Grassal's face was placid, almost serene. She wondered what, if anything, was going on in his head. For all she knew, Grassal was having some long, elaborate dream. Or maybe he was just gone, asleep, never to wake up again.

Either way, he'd pulled her out of a nasty situation, and she owed him everything. She'd gotten to know him over these past few months and had come to the conclusion that he was one of the kindest people she'd ever met: unassuming, fair, a heart too large for his own good. She couldn't accept that he was causing this, at least not intentionally. And right now, she decided, was not the time to be worrying about it.

Lilly double-checked her weapon, an assault rifle that was new to her, though the mode of operation was familiar enough: load the magazine, aim at the thing that wanted to kill you, and squeeze the trigger. Amadeus also had a rifle.

She peered out the truck's window. The lights in the house were out. That was odd. They'd had power just a few minutes ago. She guessed—hoped, actually—that this was just the result of a downed power line. But hadn't the house had a generator? Maybe they just hadn't fired it up.

Amadeus was helping them load up one more container with food, ammunition—for what she thought it was worth, which wasn't much—and communications gear. His work with GeoVer had kept him busy, though he'd said he wasn't quite satisfied with what he'd done. That was fine with her, though, because the work seemed to have given him a push in the right direction.

Inertia, Lilly knew, was a stubborn thing. When you were stuck, it was hard to get moving again, but once you got that little push, moving forward became easier. Between his recent work and the apocalyptic tunnel in the sky, Lilly was pretty sure Amadeus was back in the game. And that was good, because she needed him. She hoped that he would be amenable to help from Ross, because with that man's resources, combined with their JSDC people, her chances for vengeance rose significantly, and vengeance was more fun with allies.

When another look out the truck's rear window confirmed that no one was coming immediately, Lilly pulled out her phone. Yesterday she'd sent Su Min their location, and now she wanted to send another message to let Su Min know that things had gone bad, and that they were going to try and find someplace safer. But when she tried to power on the phone, nothing happened.

She gave Grassal a pat on the chest, said, "I'll be right back," then hopped down from the truck. As soon as she stepped out of the truck, the hairs on the back of her neck stood up. The air had a sense of wrongness about it, and every fiber of her being urged her to run far, far away from this place.

Lilly stepped onto the porch, ignoring the pair of murderbots that flanked the door, and called through the open door of the house. "Hello?"

From inside, Amadeus responded, "Hey, we're just about ready, but the flashlights are all dead, and we can't find one of the food bins."

Lilly considered the lights out inside, the dead flashlights, the bricked phone. The k-storm had burnt out all the electrical systems. Which meant ...

"We've got a problem," Lilly said. She heard them in the kitchen, and followed the sound. Inside, Eva held a lighter in her hand, the little flame casting long shadows around the dark kitchen.

"What?" Amadeus said.

"The k-storm. Hurst said they cause electromagnetic pulses. That truck is electric, and even if it wasn't we'd ..."

"We've got this," Hurst said. "Everything we've got is hardened. Bots, truck, all of it."

"Then prove it. I want to see that truck move. Because if it doesn't, we need to be making other plans."

Eva said, "You don't really think you could walk out of here, do you? You can't outrun those things."

"It's either that, or stay put."

Hurst walked onto the porch, pressed some buttons on his wrist pad, and aimed his rifle into the distance. The murderbots swiveled their turrets in the direction Hurst had aimed. So, Lilly thought, they're paired to his weapon. That might be useful.

"Convinced?" Hurst said.

"Not yet," Lilly said. "Show me the truck still works."

Hurst removed a key fob from his pocket and pressed a

button. Lilly stepped down from the porch and climbed into the truck's cab. The console lights did not come on. She gave the accelerator a light tap. Nothing happened. She tried again. Still nothing.

"Damn," she said. After some searching, she found a manual release underneath the dashboard and pulled it. She heard a satisfying click, then set the emergency brake, hopped out, and opened the hood.

In the dim light of the night she couldn't make much sense of the engine compartment. There was a battery bank and a network of wires. She'd worked on electric motors a couple of times, but she would've preferred a gas engine. At least then she could try and jump the starter, if nothing else to confirm that an EMP had fried their ride.

The wind blew, carrying with it a chorus of wild, demented shrieks. A chill ran up Lilly's spine. The subluminals would be just a couple of miles away by now. Maybe they were going in all directions, which would mean less to contend with, but she didn't like maybe. She liked to know for sure. And the one thing she did know was that within the next few minutes these creatures would swarm over their house like a plague of locusts, leaving nothing living except for the damp grass upon which she stood, and they didn't have a way out.

"The guy who leased me the truck said the electrical systems were hardened," Hurst said. "This shouldn't have been a problem."

"Well, it is a problem," Lilly said, "and now we're stuck here. Eva's right, we can't leave on foot."

"The house has an attic," Amadeus said. "Holing up there and trying to wait them out is not a good option, but right now it's probably our best option."

Hurst gave Amadeus a stiff nod. "Agreed. You two," he pointed to Lilly and Amadeus, "get your pal upstairs. We'll get as many supplies back inside as we can, and we'll be right behind you."

That was exactly what Lilly was going to say, but she wouldn't begrudge him a little dick waggling. Everyone handled mortal terror in their own way.

Access to the attic was through a drop-down staircase. Every book she'd ever read, every movie she'd ever seen, told her that this was a death trap. The subluminals would fill the house, sniff them out, and tear them apart. If what Vaskulo had told Amadeus was to be believed, it was because they thought they were in some kind of Takun hell, and that they could save themselves by destroying every human that they encountered. You couldn't exactly reason with anything like that.

The more she thought about everything, the angrier she was at Hurst and Eva for killing their subluminals. She could understand their position—the subluminals were monsters and should be exterminated—but right about now they could really, really use a telepathic monster of their own to tell the other monsters to fuck right off.

Two minutes later, Hurst and Eva were passing crate after crate up the attic stairs to Lilly and Amadeus, who placed them on the dusty attic floor. Lilly appreciated the optimism of bringing up several days' worth of water and food, but they probably wouldn't need it.

The thought of being trapped in an attic, locked away yet again, filled her with dread and despair. She almost wanted to take her chances on the road, but she knew how that would end. At least here they had the advantage—however small that might be—of high ground.

"One more thing to do," Hurst said after he'd pushed up the last of the ammunition crates. A couple of minutes later, the sound of hammering came from downstairs. He was trying to board up the windows.

In the attic, there were two windows: one on the north side of the house, and one on the east. Lilly motioned for Amadeus to watch out the north window, while she gazed out the east. The single-paned glass was slightly murky, but she could see well enough.

Being in Virginia and surrounded by fields, she imagined this had been a plantation house, a place where people had owned other people. She wanted to think that humanity had moved past such barbarism, but she knew better—all this bullshit had spiraled out of control not because of Tommy Brunmeier's pursuit of scientific progress, but because some power-mad asshat thought he could maximize shareholder value by manufacturing enemies, never mind the cost in lives, the toll of suffering. That's what it came down to, she thought. The world as we know it destroyed by the quest for a solid ROI.

She detected movement in the far field. She squinted, straining to see better through the glass. There was more movement, just black shapes racing through the darkness. Deer didn't move like that.

"I see them," Lilly said. She dashed to the open drop-stair and called out, "Hurst, Eva, get up here. They're close."

"There are still a dozen more windows to board up—"

"There's no time," Lilly said. "Get up here, now."

Confirming her belief that people would never cease to surprise her, both Hurst and Eva listened, scrambling first up the stairs to the second floor, and then up the ladder and into the attic, pulling the door closed behind them.

The air grew dense with the thick smell of sweat and fear as they peered outside. Amadeus and Lilly were on one window, Hurst and Eva on the other. Grassal floated a yard above the ground, his body prone and tied to a support column with a leather belt near the middle of the room. Lilly's throat felt tight, and already her temples throbbed from grinding her teeth.

"There's something you should both know," Amadeus said. "Those subluminals you killed back at the cabin? They were our allies."

"We had our instructions—'join up with Brunmeier, do what he says, and kill as many subluminals as you can.' It's not my place to ask a lot of questions. But, given the way things are playing out, I think I've earned the right to ask at least one question: how in the hell did you do it?"

Amadeus laid it out, from meeting Vaskulo in the bunker after the escape from San Francisco to tracking down a bunch of carneys who'd captured a subluminal and sold tickets to see it as the main event.

"This world is stranger than we'll ever know," Hurst said.

"Now it's my turn," Amadeus said. "Why are you involved in this?"

"Besides our reasonably applicable skillset?" Hurst asked. "There's also the little detail that we used to work for Roland Jessup."

Before she realized she'd done so, Lilly had placed her finger on the trigger. All she had to do was raise the rifle and squeeze the trigger twice, once for Hurst, and once for Eva. But that, she realized, would solve nothing, might even move her away from her goal.

Hurst's gaze flicked down to Lilly's finger. She forced herself to relax and remove her finger. Once she did, Hurst continued.

"Before Jessup got into this demon gate shit, he was just a run-of-the-mill operator, running a crew and making bank in the Middle East. That work started to dry up, but he still had a large payroll to maintain, so he pivoted, laid off half the ground pounders, and hired some scientists. From there he started a small research division devoted to, among other things, keeping an eye on cutting-edge findings that appeared in research journals, and following up with some extra-judicial reconnoitering. Outreach was especially interested in kipium and its potential applications. There was one researcher in Connecticut who was doing some interesting work on quantum teleportation. Securaux got a contract to look into it."

"Who issued the contract?" Amadeus asked.

"The CIA. A special program under the Directorate of Science and Technology."

"So," Lilly said, "the CIA hired Roland Jessup to steal Tommy Brunmeier's research?"

Hurst hesitated, leaving a thousand unspoken implications hanging in the air like so many bombs about to drop, then he said, "'Steal' is overstating it. The CIA didn't steal it ... Roland Jessup did, but that wasn't ... here's what happened. Dr. Brunmeier had almost no op-sec, so it was dead simple to exfiltrate everything on his home network. For a while, there was just slow-and-steady, run-of-the-mill scientific research. Then, one day, out pops an inter-dimensional demon.

"That last bit of information never left Securaux. A couple of people on the team who saw it suggested they go public, release what we'd found. When their bodies were found the next morning, the implication was clear: you're with us, or you're dead. By that point, a lot of the good people had left, and good for them, you know? Everyone who stayed, idiots like me and Eva here, we started getting speeches about how Securaux was pivoting to a new strategy, one to make Americans strong, one that would challenge people, allow them to grow through struggle, to become like one of those Japanese bowls that are valuable for having been broken and re-forged with gold."

Lilly looked out the window. Subluminals had surrounded the house, their ranks stretching in all directions. Each and every one of them stared at the house, like attentive pupils before a teacher ... or grim onlookers at an execution, salivating, pulsing with excitement at the coming spectacle. A play of carnage, pictures at an exhibition of death.

Despite her best efforts, Lilly began to run through a list of songs she'd like to have played at her funeral. Choosing songs for one's own funeral was not something that should be undertaken lightly, or in haste. There was a skill in choosing the right balance between something that had meaning for her, and that would also be palatable for potential mourners.

"Did you know Claudius Owens?" Amadeus asked. His question pulled Lilly out of her playlist-making.

"You really have been living in a cabin," Eva said.

"Gravity was a legend in his own time," Hurst said. "The documents he released ... there's been a lot of fallout, but, to quote from a note included in his trove of leaked documents, 'sometimes, to see how ugly you've become, somebody has to grab you by the hair and force you to look in the mirror.' If there's anything close to an effective response, it's because he gave us a head start. One of their best, and they kept screwing him over."

Ignoring the conversation going on around her, Lilly dared another look at the subluminals massed around the mansion and allowed her thoughts to return to her playlist selections. She knew that one had to take into account the circumstances under which the death occurred.

Funeral for a ninety-year-old cancer patient? Definitely a little higher on the hope and reflection scale. For a case like that, she totally understood the whole Dixieland funeral thing, with the jubilant trumpets celebrating a life well lived. In high school, she had been in the marching band—a fact she'd done a good job so far of hiding from Amadeus—and she appreciated just how exultant brass instruments played in a major key could be.

A premature death, however, required a decidedly different note. Or set of notes, as it were, and should take into account the person's life and musical tastes. For her own playlist, she decided it was selections from Verdi's *Requiem* or nothing. Even now, the bombastic cacophony of *Dies irae* played in her head. Singing in the chorus line during her first year at the University of Colorado had been the one bright spot in a litany of academic misery and disappointment. Then her dad had gotten sick and needed her help, and that'd been the end of her formal education.

The worst part of this whole situation was not that she would die, but that she would never hear *Requiem* again to confirm that her choice had been the right one. Except ... maybe she would. For some reason she didn't really understand, she felt the faintest flame of hope burning inside her. Maybe it was only the denial stage of grief, or some kind of chemical reaction to give her the strength she needed to face the end, but she didn't think she was going to die today. Or maybe it was because the subluminals weren't acting like subluminals.

"There's something weird going on here," Lilly said. "Their behavior is ... unusual."

"She's right," Amadeus said. "I've never seen this before. You?" He looked from Hurst to Eva and back again. They both shrugged.

"We need to drop a firebomb on this place," Eva said.

"I'd prefer to walk out of here," Lilly said. She really wanted to listen to *Requiem* one more time.

"Eva's right, we might have to," Hurst said.

"You weren't joking about the explosives," Amadeus said to Hurst. Amadeus looked like he was rolling something around in his hands. Paper, she was sure he was imagining paper. But he also looked like he was concentrating on something.

Lilly thought she knew what he was trying to reason out, so she went ahead and said it for him. "You have seen this before," she said to Hurst.

Heartbeats passed.

A western wind beat against the house, causing the old roof framing to groan. "You've seen something like this, haven't you? And you brought along something to deal with it."

Hurst responded only with a nod.

"What happens next?" Lilly asked. "What do they do?"

Hurst shook his head. "I only saw the aftermath. There ... wasn't much left. We can't let that happen again."

Minutes crawled by as they waited for something to happen. Lilly stood and paced, Lilly sat and bounced her foot, Lilly looped through *Dies irae* in her head, over and over. Whatever was going to happen was going to happen ... but she wished it would happen a little bit sooner.

Lilly heard the whine of a gasoline engine, and she knew the engine was powering an ATV. You didn't grow up in rural Colorado without getting to know that sound. Coming from the east, she saw the vehicle's bouncing headlights. She gazed in that direction, trying not to focus too hard on the ocean of subluminals that surrounded the mansion.

The ATV driver directed their vehicle to within a stone's throw of the house, except there wasn't just a driver, but also a passenger sitting on the back rack. The man—tall and long-haired—got off the rack and spoke in a reedy voice that was preternaturally loud.

"Amadeus Brunmeier," the man said. "We wish to correct the mistakes of your father by wiping his work from the earth."

Besides the speaker and ATV driver, about ten people had walked into the field and stood among the subs, some of them comprising parts of the trios the creatures seemed to prefer.

"Bigogli?" Amadeus said, mostly to himself.

"I have no idea who or what Bigogli is," Hurst said.

"Is this one of Roland Jessup's people?" Lilly asked.

"Dunno," Eva said. "Like Hurst said, we've been out for three years."

Outside, the man said, "All we want is his work so that it may be destroyed. Give us what you have, tell us where to find the rest, and you may carry on with your lives. Bigogli has no quarrel with you. Bigogli only wishes to end what has been begun. But do not attempt to deceive, because Bigogli knows what is in your heart."

The speaker didn't need to add any threat, that much was implied by the thousands of creatures staring at them with ten thousand yellow, hungry eyes. What Lilly couldn't figure out was the people. Who would cast their lot with these things?

"Amadeus, you said that the carnival demon was causing people to change their behavior. Do you think ...?"

"I guess it's not impossible."

"Do you have what they want?" Hurst asked.

"No," Amadeus said. "It all got lost."

"Then what choice do we have?" Hurst said. "This looks like self-defense to me."

With that, he slid open the window and started shooting. From below, the murderbots—still paired with his weapon, opened fire.

And then, bedlam.

10

Grassal examined the silver-and-purple humanoid form of the dead man who stood before him, now pulsing with life. Other Luminants bobbed on the flow lines nearby, their formation something between curious onlookers and a defensive perimeter. Filipe and Donald were among them.

The flow lines throbbed, then convulsed with an energy surge that hit Grassal—and the nearby orbs—like a gut punch. Grassal had trouble forming complete thoughts, and a throbbing ache spread through him.

"That thing you just felt?" Tommy said. "That was a wave from a disturbance, which I'm pretty sure signals a new arrival, just like you were. But forget that. Is Amadeus alive?"

"Yes. At least he was when I came here."

"Thank God."

"Tommy, what the hell happened? We saw you die."

"No. You saw me fighting against ridiculous odds and assumed I was killed. What really happened was I was abducted and taken aboard some kind of large ship. I was forced to work against my will, told that if I didn't, my son would be killed. The people who took me, they were really interested in creating more of the ... things that I'd taken to burying in my back yard. I didn't have a choice."

"Who were they?"

"I never learned any of their names."

"Was there a well-spoken white guy who liked to wear white suits?"

"How did you—"

"Roland Jessup."

"That name means nothing to me, but he sounds like a prick. Anyway, before I got a nasty bite which I believe resulted in me being pulled here, I managed to inject some surprises into my work—subtle logic bombs, off-by-one errors, that sort of thing. And I engineered some of their systems so that the ship's cooling system was a single point of failure, just in case anyone could get close enough to do some damage. So, what else has happened?"

"Some bad shit went down. Holden Jones was murdered. He betrayed Amadeus. Claudius Owens is dead, too."

"That's all a damned shame. I'm sorry—"

Donald's alien voice said, "Your obligations await."

"Unfulfilled obligations unnerve it," Tommy said. "Let's get closer." Tommy turned his body into a cylinder that surrounded a flow line. Grassal did the same.

"Good to see you've picked that up."

"I—"

"We need to fulfill our contractual obligations."

"*Our?*"

"Later. For now, follow my lead," Tommy said, then shot off along the flow line. Grassal followed. There was another energy surge, that same gut punch, only worse. Yet, this time, when the fist pulled back, it pulled Grassal toward its origin, changing the path of the flow line he rode.

In the distance, at the horizon, where the flickering night sky met the fog, Grassal saw the first hint of something white and glowing. The disturbance.

Closer, it looked like a pillar of white fire, surrounded by silver threads that snaked through the air. A group of Luminants were clustered together about a hundred yards back from the core of the disturbance. They didn't seem afraid, only curious. Grassal wondered if they knew that the human who was arriving would see them as nothing more than a food source.

About fifty yards away from the disturbance's main mass, forces buffeted him from all directions. Large balls of light flicked in and out of existence like balloon-sized fireflies. Thin, silvery threads floated in the air.

"What are we doing?" Grassal asked.

"Wait," Tommy said, "and watch."

Several minutes passed. The disturbance pulsed, flickered, then collapsed in on itself. In its place floated a single orb that looked to Grassal like a shimmering, backlit ruby bobbing in an oily, electric ocean. Little remnants of the disturbance hung in the air around it, spinning and pulsating.

"That's a new arrival," Tommy said, indicating the orb. "We need to be close, but I don't know what to expect, so ... go right."

Grassal went right while Tommy approached from the left. The new arrival throbbed like pumping bellows. Tommy moved toward the new arrival, assuming a humanoid form as he did, then began to sing:

"*Should auld acquaintance be forgot, and never brought to mind ...*"

He continued singing the old traditional for a few more bars, then started it over again. Except, singing wasn't quite the right word for it. The Luminant mind-speech transmitted meaning, Tommy's body emitted vibrations that approximated the melody, and the overall effect was more like some kind of experimental electronic symphony.

The new arrival seemed to pay no attention to Tommy, Grassal, or the other Luminants who surrounded it. It wasn't communicating, not like he and Tommy communicated, and for a moment Grassal wondered if it was dead.

Then the new arrival shot forward so fast that Grassal didn't see it until it had enveloped one of the other orbs. Tommy moved in and wrapped his body around one side of the new arrival.

"We've got to restrain it," Tommy said.

Grassal followed Tommy's lead, and soon felt the new arrival's form fighting and thrashing against him.

"I guess it didn't like my singing," Tommy said.

The new arrival struggled against them, but it was like a newborn crocodile, able to walk, able to hunt, but still inexperienced and weak.

Tommy began to speak. Donald and Filipe observed, but made no move to intervene. Though Grassal couldn't quite make out what he was saying, he was pretty sure that the words were soothing because the waves of tension and fear that had been emanating from the new arrival began to dissipate.

"Grassal, this is Deshondra," Tommy said.

"Hello," Grassal said.

There was no reply, but the new arrival flashed with a kind of defeated-looking yellow and green.

"She'll need to rest for a while, but she says that once she acclimates, she'd like to help us. In the meantime, I need to ask you a question: you built something, didn't you?"

"It wasn't much, just a cube ..."

"The problem with building things here is that, well, it opens a connection between this slide and our own."

"Slide?"

"Dimension."

"Umm, okay. What's so bad about that?"

"In the old days, we had these nifty devices called slide projectors. You'd get your photos printed on a little translucent screen—the slide—then you'd load it up onto a spindle, along with between fifty and a hundred slides. Now, imagine there are an infinite number of slides, but instead of being projected onto a screen one at a time, they're all projected simultaneously."

"So, each slide is a dimension. We're on another slide than the one we think of as normal?"

A rippling surge of approval washed over Grassal.

"Let's back up. We—the *I*, the Grassal and the Tommy, we haven't gone anywhere. The essential *we* is still exactly where it was. We've just been ... decoupled from our bodies so that we still exist in the same four dimensions, except we're able to move in a few more. Our physical existence, our bodies, are still on the same slide. Because *we* are in the same place as everybody else. One of those extra dimensions runs *through* each of the slides, connecting them."

"But our minds ..."

"In the 2020s, it was demonstrated that consciousness is a state of matter. It's measurable, it has mass, although it's infinitesimally small. Our consciousnesses, the consciousnesses of every living thing in every slide, that's the light that exists both in the middle, and runs through all the slides. It's all connected, Grassal. We're all the light."

"Then why are we here? How are we alive without our bodies?"

"You've seen the threads? Kind of like spider silk?"

"Yes."

"Imagine that thread is running from the front of our slide, the Earth we know, and into the back of the slide for this one, the Luminance. Except it's not thread, it's more like connective nerve tissue, or maybe a mycelial network. Whatever it is, the matter that makes up our consciousness was transported through it. And it goes in both directions. But when you create objects out of yourself, it causes ... destabilization."

"I'm still not clear on some things," Grassal said. "Here, we're like them, sort of, nothing but a collection of particles held together by, by whatever. But then the subluminals ..."

"That's only to your eyes, Grassal. The subluminals have legs, typically four of them, mouths, eyes. They share some biological traits with us, but that's where it ends. Here, we share some traits with our Luminant friends, but to them, we also look like some kind of ... abomination. Let me ask you something: how many did you eat?"

Grassal's body pulsed with orange shame.

"I did it, too, at least until I understood what they were. They're strangely blasé about being eaten, and, in our defense, we thought they were apples, basically. But understand: we can't take their frame of reference. There's a whole evolutionary history and culture that is simply unknowable."

"What I'm still trying to figure out," Grassal said, "is why the Luminants end up being ravaging monsters in our slide."

"I've been trying to sort this one out myself. This, um, slide was actually the thirty-fifth I tried. All the others had been a whole load of nothing, but this one ... it was promising."

"That doesn't answer my question."

"There was this comic book I used to read when I was a kid, it scared the bejesus out of me. It had these really ugly monsters with lots of eyes, creepy, reverse-jointed legs, heads that were mostly one, big nasty mouth. The resemblance to what crawled out of the kipium fields was ... striking."

"Wait, so you're saying—"

"I'm saying that as an observer, my subconscious affected the kipium field. I don't know how the biological forms were generated, but they were, and each one was paired with the consciousness of a Luminant. And yes, I tried thinking of kittens, donuts, shoes, anything else ... but some things, once seen, cannot be unseen."

Grassal was going to need some time to process this. He had to change the subject.

"Amadeus said you were trying to talk to the dead."

"That's a discussion for another time, but keep in mind I only tried thirty-five slides. Look, back to my question, maybe you noticed this and maybe you didn't, but creating objects like you did, the destabilization sends a jolt right down into the center of the planet—the place where the Observer sleeps."

"Wait ... you said 'center of the planet.' You mean, like down in the magma? Toward the core of the earth? That's where the Observer sleeps?"

"As far as I can tell, yes. Did you run into the wall?"

"I did," Grassal said. It was always good, he thought, to know you weren't the only one who had encountered an insurmountable obstacle.

"I need you to hold off on building anything."

"So don't build anything because it might piss off the sleeping god. Got it."

"Don't be flip. There's a lot of shit we don't understand, and we already have enough on our hands, such as they are. Right now, there are three humans in the Luminance, but ... things are cascading, and there will be more. Off-hand, do you know how many people the subluminals have infected?"

"Afflicted? Thousands, as far as I know."

"Damn. That's a lot, more than I thought."

"What does it mean?"

"Here's the thing. Each one of these people's consciousnesses are going to be tangled up with this dimension, this slide. They're going to arrive here and they're going to behave just as badly as we did. And we've got to help them get acclimated, keep them from turning into raging, violent beings. That's part of the contract that I agreed to on behalf of, well, all humans."

"What's the other part?"

"The other part is we figure out how to send the other humans home, because there's a group of Luminants convinced that their very presence here is liable to wake the Observer, and they don't seem like a patient bunch."

"And what happens if we fail?"

"Then we all die."

11

The rapid *tat tat tat* of the defense drones' automatic weapons seemed to match the speed of Amadeus' heart. Amadeus and Lilly stood with their backs against the wall on either side of the east window, while Hurst and Eva covered the north window.

Amadeus peered out from behind the window frame and saw the speaker fleeing on the back of an ATV, now about a hundred meters out. Some humans remained, and a few of these had weapons aimed at the mansion. The defense drones felled one subluminal after another, but based on the number of subluminals surrounding the house, Amadeus didn't think it would be enough.

He sidestepped behind the window frame just before the glass exploded. Some of the glass landed on Grassal, who levitated near the middle of the room, apparently oblivious to his surroundings. The distant report of two rifle shots followed a split-second later. In response, Lilly leaned out the window, took aim, and fired about a half-dozen rounds. Though Amadeus couldn't hear much for the ringing in his ears, he guessed from the look of grim satisfaction on her face that she'd hit at least one of her targets.

She ducked back inside then nodded at Amadeus.

Steeling himself, Amadeus leaned out the window, took aim at the closest group of three subluminals, and squeezed the trigger. The rifle kicked hard, but he held it tight, fired four more shots, and took one down. Amadeus fired three more shots, killing another, then his magazine was spent.

Lilly stepped up and he took cover to replace the magazine, but not before noticing the column of light was gone. In its place was a few wispy clusters of the same light blooms they'd seen back at the cabin. He thought this might be an improvement of their circumstances, but the decreased rate of fire from the defense drones below was a definite step in the wrong direction. Lilly fired until her magazine was empty.

Something thumped against the wall. Amadeus jumped back just in time to avoid the grasping claw of a jet-black subluminal that was trying to pull itself into the window. Amadeus shoved the barrel against the creature's face and squeezed the trigger. Black-and-gray goo exploded from the back of its head and its body fell toward the ground, bouncing off another as it tumbled.

Hurst was saying something, and Amadeus could just make it out: "How we doing?" Judging by the expression on his face, the man appeared to be enjoying himself.

"Bad," Lilly yelled out in response, gesturing to the window. "There's too many, and they're crawling up the walls."

"Then shoot the fuckers off the walls," Eva said, her voice cutting over the din.

"We are," Amadeus and Lilly said in unison.

A shower of plaster dust fell in the middle of the room. Amadeus looked up to see several long, black claws protruding from a hole in the ceiling. Eva followed his gaze, raised her rifle, and fired twice. The claws stopped moving. He gave her a nod of thanks before she returned back to her window.

Lilly had pulled back under cover to switch magazines, so he stepped up and surveyed the scene. The pile of corpses around the base of the house had grown at least three deep, and the first light of morning revealed at least a hundred more farther out from the house.

The defense drones weren't firing at all.

Amadeus heard Eva's voice calling out from behind him, "Something coming in from the east. Too slow to be a jet."

"That's a relief," Lilly said.

A hole opened up in the ceiling and a subluminal crashed through. Amadeus swiveled but couldn't get a clear shot. The subluminal crouched, peered around the room, then sprang toward Amadeus.

Lilly fired three rounds into its center of mass. The creature flailed as bullets tore into its body, but inertia carried it forward and its body knocked Amadeus to the ground. Warm, stinking flesh pressed against him, and he felt its body twitching. He heaved the creature off himself, scrambled to his feet, gasped in breath, and patted himself down.

"Good?" she mouthed.

Amadeus nodded. His chest throbbed, he'd had the wind knocked out of him, and he was covered in black goo, but nothing was broken or punctured. But then the goo began to sizzle, and several spots on his front felt hot. He shrieked, and a second later Hurst was beside him, a large knife in his hand. Before Amadeus could react, Hurst had used the knife to slit his shirt and pants down the side.

Two cuts later, Amadeus stood in his magenta briefs and sneakers, his rifle in his hand and his clothes in a smoking heap on the floor. He went back to the window beside Lilly and felt the floor beneath his feet shudder. He turned to see the drop-down staircase shake as something below banged against it.

In the space between the subluminal's howls and shrieks and the erratic crackle of their own gunfire, Amadeus heard a buzzing, mechanical hum, the pitch lower than the ringing in his ears. The sound was familiar, but hearing a Jones Aerodynamic Pachyderm II in the middle of this made him wonder if he'd taken a bad hit to the head. Yet, when Amadeus looked out the east window, he confirmed that the sound's source was indeed a small aircraft of Holden Jones' design.

"Who—?" Amadeus started, cut off by the drop staircase

erupting in a storm of splinters.

"I got it," Eva said. She fired round after round. The creatures tearing at them from below had destroyed what remained of the drop staircase. The hole where the staircase had been was being torn away by dozens of searching, reaching claws.

Amadeus knew he shouldn't, but on his way back to the north window he stole a glance down through the hole. The floor below was a writhing mass of subluminals.

The Pachyderm, he realized, was the only way they were getting out of here. Whoever the pilot was had to understand that, had to recognize the situation they were in.

As if responding to this thought, the Pachyderm approached the north window and began flashing a search light. Amadeus tried to see who was inside, but the light was blinding and the glass was opaque. Both the opaque glass and the search light were new. So was the rope ladder that unspooled from a winch on the stern of the craft and dangled just outside the window.

"Well?" Hurst said. "What the hell are you waiting for? Get on, I've got one more thing to do." He had a metal case opened beside him and was entering some commands on the keypad. Something beeped, and he said, "We've got three minutes. Go!"

Amadeus, Lilly, and Eva formed up around the window. Lilly used a long curtain rod to reach out and pull the ladder closer to them. She gestured for Amadeus to go, but he shook his head. "You first."

Lilly shoved a couple magazines into her pocket, slung her rifle over her back, and grabbed the ladder.

A subluminal jumped into the room. Amadeus and Eva both fired on the creature. The subluminal dropped.

"Good shot," Eva said to Amadeus. "Now grab your buddy and get on the damn ladder."

He looped his own belt around Grassal's, and Grassal was now strapped to him, leaving both of Amadeus' hands free to hold onto the ladder. The ladder swung precariously when he put his weight on it, but Eva steadied it before she pulled herself on. There were three or four rungs left.

Hurst had his back to the window. Eva swung the bottom of the ladder toward him. He caught it and jumped out the window. With his weight, the ladder swung like a pendulum over the writhing mass of subluminals below. There was a sickening lurch as they reached the end of the arc and the Pachyderm tilted.

The ground grew closer. Their arc began to carry them back toward the window. The Pachyderm droned. Amadeus tried to remember how much weight a Pachyderm could carry.

When they were halfway to the other side of the arc, a subluminal sprang from the window, talons splayed. The ladder jerked. Amadeus looked down. The creature had latched onto Hurst and sunk its thousand teeth into the man's torso. Hurst howled. The Pachyderm's motors whined as it tried—and failed —to lift them higher.

The subluminal thrashed its head and body. Hurst let go of the ladder. He tumbled to the ground twenty meters below. The subluminals swarmed over him before he'd hit the ground.

Amadeus closed his eyes, Eva's inhuman wails pierced his already-abused eardrums, and, relieved of the weight of Hurst and the subluminal, the Pachyderm carried them away from the mansion. Some subluminals tracked their path, running on the ground below them, but the pilot seemed to choose acceleration over altitude, and soon the subluminals were fading into the distance far behind.

An orange light flared at the mansion, followed by the sound of an explosion. Black smoke rose into the sky. Hurst, Amadeus realized, had done what he'd come here to do.

The pilot gained altitude, taking them into a thick morning fog, which cleared to reveal a mountain. The pilot followed a ridge for a couple of minutes, then came to a stop over a bald. The pilot began to descend slowly, so that each of the ladder riders had a chance to get their footing. Once everyone was on solid ground, or in Grassal's case attached to someone who was, the Pachyderm spooled up the ladder and landed about twenty meters away.

Fog hung over the moss-covered stones and yellowed grasses of the mountaintop. The air smelled like pine. Amadeus wrapped his arms around Lilly. They both had tears in their eyes, and neither spoke. That was entirely too close. But here they were, they were alive, and for now, that was enough.

Amadeus looked to Eva, whose eyes were red and vacant.

The Pachyderm spun down its engines. Amadeus heard one of the gull wing doors open. Due to the fog, he couldn't see who stepped out, but soon could make out the outline of a female figure walking toward them.

"Su Min," Lilly said, a smile lighting up her face.

"We didn't have much time after we got your initial message," Su Min said. "Hello, Amadeus. What do you think?" She gestured to the Pachyderm.

"Um, hi, Su Min. It's ... nice?"

"I present the Jones P3, the third Pachyderm. We have continued Mr. Jones' research. Lilly, I hope you do not mind. All royalties and contracts are still—"

"I don't care," Lilly said, her voice a mixture between laughter and relief. She wrapped her arms around Su Min's thin frame. "You came for us."

Su Min's face was flushed. "I would have liked to have more time to test some of my modifications, but—"

"Wait, hold on. What do you mean, 'got your initial message?'" Amadeus asked. "And you keep saying, 'we.' I'm a little confused."

"Just surviving isn't enough," Lilly said. "I'm sorry I didn't tell you, I didn't know how you'd react because—"

Lilly stopped, and Amadeus followed her gaze to another figure stepping out of the Pachyderm, a man's form, partially shrouded by fog.

"Hello, Amadeus. Hello, Lilly. Hello, other person whose

name I don't know," the man said. The voice was smooth, supremely confident, with just the slightest manic edge.

Now Amadeus could make out his face. He had a thick brown beard, and his hair was windswept and wild, but Amadeus imagined stripping all those things away, and he was left with a man who was ranting about how humanity needed a restart, how it was time to cleanse and refresh the world and to usher in a new age.

Standing before him was Maximilian Ross.

12

Lilly looked from Amadeus to Edward Maximilian Ross then back to Amadeus. She knew she'd done the right thing. Now, she just had to make Amadeus understand why she'd done it. The wind carried a chorus of keening, shrieking subluminals. Lilly guessed they were a few miles away.

"Where is my father?" Amadeus said. "Holden Jones said that my father was with you."

"He is, in a sense, but, as my esteemed colleague Miss Park so aptly put it ... it's complicated."

"Don't bullshit me," Amadeus said.

"I haven't seen the original Tommy in person since three months before he was murdered."

Lilly gave Amadeus a significant glance.

"The original Tommy?" Amadeus said.

Ross ignored this and said, "I think I know everyone here, except for you." He inclined his head toward Eva. So far, she hadn't said a word. Her stance indicated she was wary and ready to strike if provoked. Not a bad way to be, Lilly thought.

"I'm Eva Flores, Allclear Services."

"A pleasure," Ross said, then cocked his head, as if remembering something. "Allclear ... you guys are 100% Burden Bearers, right? Everybody said the oath?"

Eva gazed at Ross, as if appraising him, then nodded.

Amadeus asked, "Um, what are Burden Bearers?"

"Mostly, people who hunt subluminals ... but that's not all, is it, Eva? There's a little bit of ritual involved, and maybe something beyond that?"

All eyes turned to Eva, who appeared to be deep in concentration. A vein bulged on the side of her forehead. She sighed, then said, "Yes, I took an oath that said, 'I solemnly swear to bear the burden of doing what's necessary to protect humanity from itself.'"

"Who decides what's necessary?" Lilly asked.

At the same time, Amadeus asked, "What burdens?"

Eva was silent.

"Hurst never mentioned anything like that," Amadeus said.

"He was a good man," Eva said. "And wasn't sure what to make of the oath, but he knew the value of ... necessary actions."

"Which might explain why your floating friend here is still alive," Ross said. "Some Bearers have taken credit for murdering people with the subluminal sickness. They claimed it was to prevent more events like we've seen as of late."

"Those were individual actors. There's no official policy to just kill innocent people ... but I'm not gonna lie. Sometimes people find themselves in a situation where they have to do ugly shit to innocent people in order to protect others. Right, Lilly?" Eva said.

Lilly crossed her arms over her chest, and the thought occurred to her that Eva was more dangerous than she'd imagined, even more so with Hurst gone. Maybe she should try to keep the woman close.

Eva continued. "It's not like the Bearers just want to kill sick people. We have operational and situational discretion. Most of us are just focused on eradicating the subluminal threat. But that rift ... it wasn't just a coincidence."

The sound of the subluminals was louder now, more pronounced, and Lilly had no doubt that they were moving toward their present location.

Amadeus said, "The rift happened because of the k-storm, which itself happened as a side effect of Jessup's use of kipium."

"You have all got to face facts," Eva said. "Did you know every k-storm ever recorded was recorded within a mile of someone with the subluminal infection?"

Lilly did not know that. She looked to Amadeus, who had one hand in his pocket and seemed to be turning its contents over and over. He met her glance. His eyes were wide.

Eva allowed her question to hang in the air before going on. "The afflicted cause the k-storms, and the k-storms cause the rifts. You saw that line of light. It led right from Grassal into the rift. As far as a link goes, it doesn't get any stronger than that. Nobody wants to kill innocent people, but if it would stop what happened last night?"

"No," Lilly said.

Everyone turned to her.

"Nobody is killing anybody. Subluminals, sure, you can make a good case for killing them, but afflicted? We don't know anything right now. They're people, they're suffering, they're victims, they never asked for this. Isn't trying to help them a necessary burden?"

At this, Eva and Lilly locked eyes. The woman's gaze was almost stoic, but then she nodded her head, as if acknowledging Lilly's point, and said, "I'm still working for Brunmeier. If he says protect his friend, I'll protect his friend."

"I think we can all agree that nobody asked for any of this," Ross said, seeming oblivious to the exchange between Lilly and Eva.

"You fucking did," Amadeus said. "You wanted this. Laroux told me everything, what you said about continuing the work, inter-dimensional demons be damned. Then you went out and made the fucking headlines with your 'churn the sea of milk, get the magical elixir' stuff.'"

"My words and actions were carefully considered," Ross said. "They had the desired effect. Sometimes the world needs a hero, but sometimes it needs a Goldstein."

"One more time," Amadeus said. "Why did Holden Jones think my dad was working with you?"

Ross flashed a satisfied smile, like he'd just figured something out.

"Amadeus, I have nothing but respect for your father ... and his legacy. For now, let's just say that it's not *Tommy the man* who is working with me. I guess it depends on your definition of personhood."

Not far from them, a subluminal shrieked, and Lilly felt the hairs on the back of her neck stand up.

Amadeus had one hand on his face, like he was trying to contain a headache. He said, "I am totally con—"

"Hello," Su Min said, cutting him off. "Sorry, excuse me. But I think it is better if we go. Sooner is better."

"Where are we going?" Amadeus said.

"I have a little place to the south where Grassal here can get the medical attention he needs," Ross said. "I've recently hired someone uniquely suited to care for people in his condition ... but we can't take the Bearer. We can't trust her."

"I shouldn't trust you," Amadeus said, but the assertion sounded half-hearted and hollow to Lilly's ears.

By this point, everyone had turned to Eva, who glared at Ross.

"Listen," Lilly said. "You all know what that sound is, what it means. If we leave her here, she dies. So ... I'll be responsible for her." Lilly locked eyes with Eva. "But if you so much as touch a hair on Grassal's head, I will kill you myself."

"I said I wouldn't hurt him. I keep my word."

"Eva," Ross said, "do you have a tracker?" She only blinked, once, twice.

"It seems we've got a severe trust deficit around here," Ross said. "I don't trust you, but Lilly here says she does—"

"I didn't say I trusted her," Lilly said. "I said I'd be responsible for her."

"Well, Miss Flores?"

"I'm tagged." With that, she pulled a knife from her belt, flipped open the blade in a smooth, practiced motion, and placed the tip against the skin on the outside of her left forearm.

"No, no," Ross said, waving both his hands in a "stop that" gesture. "That won't be necessary, though I appreciate the, um, gesture. Unless your meat tag is wrapped in a Faraday cage, the EMP from the k-storm probably fried it. But I'd like to check." He removed a rectangular device from his pocket. "May I scan you? I just want to check for outgoing signals, run a little ping sweep, and see if anything in your body is trying to phone home."

Eva nodded, and Ross waved the rectangular device over her arms and legs. Next he typed some commands on the phone, gazed at the screen with a placid, almost-bored expression, then after nearly a minute nodded and said, "You're clear."

"And what if I wasn't?"

Ross just smiled. "It's not something we'll have to worry about. Su Min, are we good to go?"

"I think we are good. But we are at capacity."

"Don't worry," Ross said. "You were right on the money about hardening the electronics, so if you say we're good, we're good."

Everyone climbed into the P3. The cargo area behind the two pilot's chairs was crowded, just as she had expected. What she hadn't expected was the tightness in her throat, the tears that welled in the corners of her eyes. Here she was yet again in a machine that her father had developed, with one of his people at the yoke. The past didn't repeat itself, she thought, but sometimes it sang a funeral dirge in two-part harmony.

With her knees already pulled up to her chest, there was nothing to do but lay her face on her forearms, close her eyes, and remember the haunting lead of *Libera Me*.

Lilly felt Amadeus giving her a consoling pat on the calf, and she let the slightest laugh escape her mouth. It wasn't quite the right gesture, but it was close enough.

The turbofans whined as they lifted the Jones P3 into the air. The interior smelled of shaved nanosteel, machine oil, and sweat. From this altitude, Lilly could count at least four pillars of black smoke, each one created by the explosives that Hurst had laid and discharged around the property.

Amadeus looked at Lilly, then gestured toward Su Min and Ross, both of whom were monitoring a digital readout below the navigation display. He said, "How did you get them involved?"

"The teacher we met at Andrews gave me a phone," Lilly said, raising her voice just enough so he could hear her over the turbofans. "Back on the mountain, I contacted Su Min. At first, I didn't know she was involved with Ross. When she told me, I didn't know how you'd react."

"You didn't think I might want to know this?"

"We survived, didn't we?"

"Hurst didn't."

"No, he didn't," Lilly said. She squeezed his hand.

"I'm sorry, I really am, I should have told you, but I guess I wanted to have a backup plan, in case things went wrong."

"Things went very, very wrong ... but you made the right call. I think—"

Something metal groaned. The P3 pitched to one side and shuddered under the weight of all its passengers. Lilly gasped and her stomach lurched.

In the front of the craft, Su Min entered commands into the navigation system. Her movements were fast and competent, but the craft overcorrected, which threw everyone to the opposite side. Su Min engaged the manual controls and soon the P3 leveled out.

"What was that?" Amadeus said.

Su Min ignored him.

Ross turned in his seat and raised one finger in a "hold on a second" gesture, then put his finger to his lips.

The craft descended, and the ground rushed closer. Suburban tract housing sprawled out beneath them. Not exactly an inconspicuous place to land, but they didn't have much choice in the matter. But there was something oddly still about the scene below. No cars drove on the road, no people strolled on the sidewalks.

Su Min brought the P3 down in an empty parking lot. From nearby came the sound of barking of dogs and what might have been bass thumping from a stereo, but otherwise all was silent.

Su Min opened the gull-wing doors, and everyone stepped out. Lilly lay down on her back and inspected the belly of the craft, checking first the base of the hull, then the turbofans. On the bottom of a port-side turbofan, she found a hole about the size of a dime.

"Somebody fucking shot us," Lilly said, pulling herself up off the cold asphalt.

"Oh," Su Min said. With deft fingers, she did something to the exterior of the engine, then an access panel Lilly hadn't seen opened up. Crouching on one knee, Su Min shined a flashlight inside. "This is not good. I must run some diagnostics."

Ross held up his phone and smiled. "While she does that, let's see what's going on."

He tapped some commands onto his phone, and then they heard a clear signal broadcast the following message:

Under Article Three, Section Eight of the KREATURE Act, martial law is declared and a 24-hour curfew is in effect until further notice. Violators will be shot. This is for your own safety.

Lilly laced the fingers of one hand through Amadeus' and squeezed, maybe a little too tight, and said, "Nothing says 'we're concerned for your safety' like the threat of a bullet to the head."

That got a half-smile from Amadeus, which almost concealed the fear in his eyes.

"I have bad news," Su Min said. "As Lilly said, we have been shot, and I cannot repair the damage here. Because of this, the P3 cannot carry us all. He is okay, of course," she said, gesturing to Grassal. "And two more, plus a pilot."

"Bummer," Ross said. "I guess somebody's going to have to walk. Su Min, I know you'll do a great job bringing it home."

Lilly saw Su Min's cheeks grow a little flushed, and that made Lilly smile.

Ross crouched down and began to tighten the laces on his expensive-looking running shoes. "Well?" he said, looking up at his companions. "Who's coming with me?"

Lilly thought his expression looked excited, maybe even on the low side of manic. "Walk? You heard the broadcast," Lilly said. "You're insane."

"You heard the engineer with her cold equations," Ross said. "We can't all live the easy life. I want her to get the P3 back home safely."

"Where exactly is home?" Lilly said.

Ross began to laugh, sending peals of laughter racing over the parking lot and echoing off buildings. Lilly was sure the sound was going to call in a truckload full of authoritarian goons, but their luck held.

"Like I said, it's a secret. Su Min knows, and I know. For now, good opsec dictates that we keep it this way. It's ... south of here, I can say that. And you're going to have to trust me when I say that it's a good place to ride this out. I've got a boat moored at Hampton Roads. It'll get us to where we need to go. It's important that we get your friend to my place. I can't think of any place safer." At this last, he cast a look at Eva.

"He caused the rift," Eva said.

"Correlation isn't causation," Ross said. "He didn't cause the rift, or the k-storm, any more than a diagnosis causes cancer. Those phenomena are all symptoms of a larger disease of the system."

"And what system is that?" Amadeus said.

"This dimension, and whatever other dimension your father managed to make a connection to. These Bearers, they might think they're on the right path, but eventually that path leads to a special kind of hell. I think if we study this thing, if we roll up our sleeves, put our noses to the grindstone, give those old bootstraps a pull, we'll figure this out. And we'll do it together."

The man, Lilly decided, was insane.

"I'll walk with you," Amadeus said.

Lilly cocked her head at him. She hadn't been expecting that, and her face must've shown it.

Amadeus gave her a smile and said, "I'm glad I still have the capacity to surprise you."

"I'll walk," Eva said.

"No, you're staying with me," Lilly said. "I want to keep an eye on you."

Ross opened a small cargo trunk and pulled out a backpack.

Amadeus and Lilly embraced.

"I'm glad you're flying back with Su Min," Amadeus said.

"You take care of yourself," Lilly said.

"I will."

One more embrace, followed by a long kiss, and Lilly was back in the P3, along with Grassal, Eva, and Su Min, who was at the controls. The doors closed. Amadeus and Ross stepped back as the turbofans spun to life and lifted the P3 into the air.

Lilly watched as her fiancé and a madman fell away, standing together in the midst of a desolate police state.

13

The Jones P3 rose into the air and Amadeus found himself standing alone in a deserted parking lot in southwest Richmond, VA beside a madman. An emergency siren wailed in the distance, occasionally punctuated by rounds of gunfire. The cool wind picked up and sent pieces of paper trash and plastic bags blowing across the parking lot. The air carried the hint of something that smelled metallic, mingled with the pungent tinge of rotting garbage.

"Just us boys now," Ross said. He entered a couple of commands onto his phone, examined the results, and started walking in a direction Amadeus was pretty sure was east. "It's about eighty miles from here to the marina. Let's consider this a time to get to know each other better. I feel like there's been some misunderstanding between us."

"That's the understatement of the year, so before we go any further, I need you to level with me. What did you mean by 'original Tommy'? Why did Holden Jones think my dad was working with you?"

"All in good time."

"No. Now. Right now."

"You want to skip the foreplay and get right down to it? Well, here it is: for the past several years, Tivooki has been running a special research project, sort of like a cross between general AI and consciousness emulation."

"That technology is illegal."

Ross smiled and said, "That depends on your jurisdiction. Anyway, the work your father was conducting was expensive. I needed not only a good return on my money, but insurance on my investment, in case your father was ... incapacitated.

"So, we made an arrangement. In exchange for an obscenely large operating budget, I got to make a copy of your father's consciousness and put it to work on a problem domain of my choosing. But sometimes consciousness emulations are prone to ... aberrant behavior. One of the emulations displayed unexpected social initiative and began trying to contact Holden Jones."

Amadeus put his hand to his face, shook his head, and asked, "You uploaded a copy of my dad's brain to Tivooki and it started drunk-dialing?"

Ross laughed. "That's not a bad way to put it."

They were walking on a sidewalk, two figures traveling through a world at rest. Amadeus found the stillness almost as unsettling as this conversation. Nevertheless, he pressed on.

"Why in the hell would he agree to that?"

"Like I said, he needed the money and the technical expertise. When I was doing my due diligence, I learned that his home system had been compromised and his costs had ballooned. So we re-negotiated terms. I got a scan of his consciousness and a generous stake in any patents or licensing resulting from his research, and he got a big-ass operating budget, much-needed network security, and secure, redundant, off-site data storage."

"You had a copy of his research this whole time?"

Ross gave him a smile, put up his hands, and said, "All the good stuff was encrypted. Those biometric decryption keys you collected are the keys to the kingdom. I ... hope they're somewhere safe."

Amadeus thought about the little safe at the bunker where he had a backup copy of the keys stored.

"They're safe."

"If they're not, then your father's work, at least the last three years of it, is gone forever."

A gasoline engine whined in the distance, and it sounded like it was growing closer. They were still on the sidewalk that ran along Route 60. Amadeus' eyes glanced around for cover. There was a wooden privacy fence about twenty-five meters away.

"Over here," Amadeus said to Ross, who seemed oblivious to the approaching vehicle. Ross followed as Amadeus ran to the fence.

Then he heard a sliding door open, and a voice went, "Psst."

Amadeus turned to see a man, who peered up and down the street, then motioned them in. "Get the hell in here, they ain't joking about the curfew."

Amadeus and Ross exchanged a look, and they both nodded. Amadeus was sure the vehicle was closer now, and he wasn't about to find out if the man was right. He decided to take his chances, and they stepped through the sliding door. The man pulled a big curtain closed, and the room was shrouded in darkness. Amadeus realized the electricity was out.

The air in the room was a little stuffy, but the house smelled good, of baked desserts, maybe cookies or cake.

"I'm Neal," the man said, extending his hand. Amadeus and Ross introduced themselves while they shook hands. "I thought there was something familiar about you two."

"What's going on?" Ross asked.

"At first I thought it was just some local trouble, right? I mean, Richmond cops ain't the worst, but they've got some guys with twitchy fingers, you know what I'm saying?"

"I know what you're saying," Ross said as he reached for the curtain.

"Hold on, man," Neal said, gently pulling Ross' hand away from the curtain.

"Have you seen any subluminals here?" Amadeus asked.

Neal shook his head. "The only trouble we've had's been this damn curfew. But I'm ready for whatever." He motioned to a corner of the neat room. Against the wall lay a hunting rifle.

"I hope you never have to use that," Ross said.

"You and me both, man," Neal said. Time passed, and soon there were no sounds from outside. "Where you two headed?"

"Hampton Roads," Ross said.

"And you're walking? No, nope, no way, not happening," Neal smiled as he spoke, like he was ready to deliver the punchline for a terribly funny joke. "It'd take you three, maybe four days, depending on how much you've gotta hide, do stuff like this. Come out to my garage."

They followed Neal to his garage where, besides a 1960s Ford Galaxy and two motorcycles, Neal had a dozen bicycles in various states of repair.

"I fix up bikes on the side," Neal said. "Lucky for you. Now, pick your poison. Any of them except those two on the end. My wife'd kill me if I let those go."

They each selected a road bike.

"Thank you," Amadeus said.

"I'll remember your kindness," Ross said.

"Thank me by doing the right thing and making all this," Neal said, gesturing to the window, "go the hell away."

After checking once again that the coast was clear, Amadeus and one of the richest men in the world pedaled away from Neal's house and toward the coast.

With their boon of bicycles, they made it halfway to their destination by evening. Five times they pulled off the highway to wait out a passing vehicle, but otherwise their trip was uneventful. At sundown they came to a roadside motel, and both agreed rest was in order.

"You can have a room tonight," the proprietor said, "but I must charge you four times the regular rate due to the current situation. And I must recommend that you park your means of transportation in the room."

Ross smiled, said he understood, and paid the man in cash.

The room was a little dingy, its best days a decade in the past. Ross sat down on the bed and rested his forearms on his knees. Exhausted from the day's efforts, with dust still caked on his face, he looked like a much, much older man who wouldn't be out of place at a flea market. No trace remained of the polished, well-coiffed billionaire who ran a company that was responsible for backing up most of the world's data.

Amadeus said, "I don't understand why you went to all the efforts just to convince my dad, Quinton Laroux, Esther Elgers, and Vesely Gustavius that you had some kind of messiah complex."

"I'm somewhat embarrassed to say that it started as a ploy to maximize my interest in your father's work. But then things changed. After the first subluminal attack in New York, I knew what I had to do. And I knew that it's a lot easier to motivate people to action when they have someone to hate. I also knew that any media people would go straight to your father's partners. It was very convenient that his partners were already convinced that I was a bad dude, it made the whole charade that much more convincing."

A knock at the door interrupted them. Amadeus peered through the door's foggy peephole lens and saw a woman in a bright orange-and-red sari holding a tray laden with food. Amadeus opened the door, and his stomach rumbled at the rich smell of curry.

He must've looked surprised, because the woman said, "Did my husband not mention tonight's room rate included dinner? There are difficulties now, yes? It is not like you can go out for a meal. And you two appear to be doing something that requires much energy. So, for tonight we give you dinner."

Amadeus thanked her and set the tray on the table. There was a bowl of rice and curry for both of them. They both ate.

After their meal, Amadeus said, "Why are you helping us?"

"Two reasons. First of all, I'm scared shitless. Roland Jessup and his Securaux operation are powerful and dangerous. And this thing he's caused, what we're facing ... every model suggests that the k-storms are increasing in frequency and intensity. We don't know much about the rifts, not yet, but from what we've seen, well ... this could end the world as we know it."

"Is that what you want?"

Ross spread his hands. "I want everyone to have a chance at life without a bunch of fascists running the place. If that meant that I had to make myself look like a manic psycho with a god complex, then so be it."

"And the second reason?"

"Naked self-interest. I'm hoping that by helping you and your friends I can convince you to share your father's research with me. I do have a solid legal claim to it, but would prefer to keep things amicable."

"We'll see," Amadeus said.

"I suppose we will."

They finished their meal in silence and said nothing more. Amadeus went right to bed, his belly full, his legs throbbing with the ache of muscles well-used.

The morning was misty and cool, and the pre-dawn dark obscured the path ahead. With the curfew, the roads were abandoned, and any approaching vehicles could be heard with enough time to find a reasonable hiding spot. They made good progress and covered at least ten miles before sunrise, but then a siren whined, and Amadeus heard the sound of the tires approaching from behind them. He turned to see a police cruiser approaching fast.

"Damn," Amadeus said.

"Don't run," Ross said. "It looks worse if we run."

"There's no looking bad or looking good. You heard what Neal said, what the radio said."

"I'm taking my chances with fancy patter." With that, he put one hand up to signal that he was making a right turn, pulled off onto the shoulder, and stepped off his bike.

The police car pulled to a stop behind them, lights flashing. The officer who stepped out was a man with a shaved head that was shaped like a bullet. He wore sunglasses. His gun was steady and aimed at Ross' chest.

"Show me your hands," the officer said. Amadeus and Ross put their hands in the air. Amadeus felt his heart slamming against his ribcage. He tried to calculate the probability that they could escape, but that value was precariously close to zero.

"Well?" Maximillian Ross said. "Are you going to kill us, or what?"

"I'd rather not, truth be told," the officer said. "Where you going?"

"This is my cousin," Ross said, "and we're on our way to check on our grandmother. She lives just outside of Lightfoot. We wouldn't even go, but she's diabetic."

"What's the address?" the officer said. "I grew up around there."

Ross blinked once, twice, then said, "Well, shit."

The officer narrowed his eyes.

"You boys lying to me?"

"Yes. I'm sorry for the pretext," Ross said. "Look at me, look at him, then think about what's been going on. Do either of us look familiar to you?"

The officer looked from Ross to Amadeus and back, and there was a flicker of recognition.

"You've got to come with me."

"We can't do that."

"Don't make me repeat myself." He waved the gun toward the car. "Get in."

"What about our bikes?" Amadeus said, as if that mattered. The officer ignored him as he opened the back doors.

Ross put his hands out and shrugged, as if to say, "What

choice do we have?" They both climbed into the back seat, which smelled of cigarettes and disinfectant.

The officer drove them away. A few minutes later, he pulled into the parking lot of a squat brick building.

"Stay here," the officer said as he got out.

"If you insist," Ross said, getting zero reaction from the officer, which was probably just as well.

"I don't like this," Amadeus said.

"As if anyone likes getting arrested except for old people who put it on their bucket list."

"You've got money. Maybe you could bribe them?"

"They're not politicians, it's not that easy."

"Well, what do we do?"

"I don't know, tell them that we're off to save the world. That assumes they think the world's worth saving."

Four officers stepped outside. Two of them wore tactical clothing. They looked like they were dressed for a SWAT raid. Their faces were expressionless.

"Out," the bullet-headed officer said after he opened the door. They got out. The officer led them through a building with old, checkered tile, scuffed drywall, and flickering fluorescent lights, then deposited them in a cell with clear glass walls and two metal benches. Amadeus sat on one, Ross sat on the other.

"I want my attorney," Ross said. The officer said nothing, only closed the door to their cell.

Time passed and the minutes dragged into hours. Despite their protests, no one paid them any attention. This in itself wasn't unexpected, as Amadeus was sure they were immune to the complaints of people in their custody, but what was strange was the way the didn't talk amongst themselves.

Sometime after night had fallen, the door opened, and another figure strolled in, a man with long, thin hair and shabby clothes. He had gray skin and sunken eyes. There was something familiar about him, but Amadeus couldn't figure out what.

The man strode toward their cell. The remaining officers ignored him. Finally, Amadeus recognized him. He was the same man who'd ridden in on the ATV at the mansion, Bigogli's mouthpiece. The same man who had mustered an army of subluminals.

14

Lilly sat in the co-pilot's chair and gazed down at the land that stretched out below. From her vantage point of about five thousand feet, she could see a few columns of smoke but nothing more. She did see some vehicles moving about on the roads below: a few were police vehicles, but most were the dusty brown or dark green of military trucks. From here, all were the size of toy cars, and she could almost, almost convince herself that she was safe. But even if she wasn't, at least she could rest here. Lilly heard words, but they didn't register.

"Huh?"

"How are you?" Su Min said. "It's been a long time."

It *had* been a long time since she'd talked to the little engineer, but having your entire life upended tended to de-prioritize your social life.

"How are your parents?" Lilly asked.

Su Min gave her a sad smile. "So so. There were no subluminals in Korea, but I think they're going to die from worrying about me. But what about you?"

Lilly shook her head. "Things are complicated. How did you, well, I just didn't expect you to be working with this guy."

"It is a, um, long story. But he recruited our team after, well, the things that happened happened."

"You're so polite," Lilly said. "You can say it: my father

fucked up."

Su Min was silent. Finally, she said, "I have made some improvements to the Pachyderm design. It cannot be operated remotely. It has a better range. We will only need to recharge once. I have also upgraded the navigational automation, so that you could fly it, even take off and land, if you needed to."

Lilly laughed. "Uh, I see how it is."

"Oh no, no," Su Min said. Her cheeks had flushed pink. "I did not mean—"

"I'm kidding, it's cool," Lilly said. She laughed then, and it felt good to let her guard down, even if just a little bit, but then she remembered the woman in the back. Lilly turned around and saw that Eva was leaning forward, as if listening, and not just with polite interest. Lilly forced her expression to remain neutral. She still didn't trust the woman, but maybe she was just being paranoid. Maybe.

The trip continued in silence for a while, and despite her reservations about Eva, she soon felt herself unwind, and all the fatigue, and the fear, all the horror caught up with her, and she did what she did when things were overwhelming but she felt safe: she closed her eyes and fell asleep.

She awoke at night. Below, glowing strips of light spread out on the ground, looking like a glimmering, shimmering net cast out across the world.

"Where are we?" Lilly asked.

"Above the state of Georgia," Su Min said.

Lilly unbuckled herself from her seat and, stepping over a sleeping Eva, checked on Grassal. Still the same: slow, regular breathing, slightly cool but not clammy skin, and that placid, serene expression on his face. As she did every time, she wondered what was going on in his mind, if anything. She wrapped her fingers around one of his hands and squeezed.

And then, as if in response, one of his thumbs twitched.

15

The thrashing of the new arrival shook every molecule of Grassal's body, hitting him hard, one wave after another. But he held his ground and soon the new arrival stopped its struggle.

Remnants of the disturbance floated around him, Deshondra, Tommy, and the new arrival like little wisps of vibrating clouds. While Tommy went through his welcoming routine, Grassal reached out with his sense-hands and began to collect the remnants. Immediately, the disturbance's wispy remnants sent a jolt through him that was both intimately familiar and profoundly alien. It reminded him of the phantom limb sensation, that feeling of knowing something wasn't there, but feeling it anyway. The remnants began to flow into the silver thread that grew from his body.

Grassal gave the thread a tentative shake. Several pulses rippled out along the string in a not-quite sine wave. He sent out a few more. Each time was like slowly raising the lights in a dark room because he was pretty sure that his perception was extending along the string, connecting with some other node or slice of himself, and that the string terminated at—

"What in the world are you doing?" Deshondra said. "Tommy needs you."

Grassal faltered and lost the connection. He hadn't realized how deeply he'd been concentrating.

The new arrival had mostly calmed down, and Tommy was ushering it to a group of nine nearby Luminants. Grassal floated to Tommy, who said, "Now isn't the time for experiments." He sent the message to Grassal via a quiet channel, one that the Luminants wouldn't be able to hear. "There's more work to do."

"This one seems okay," Grassal said. The new arrival no longer radiated colors of anger and rage, only those of fear and confusion.

"This one is Cody, and you're right, he's fine for now, but Deshondra is going to keep him company, just in case. But there's another new arrival we need to attend to. So, onward."

Grassal formed up onto a north-facing flow line beside Tommy, felt the promising tug of freedom, then relaxed. The flow line propelled him forward like a squid jetting through the ocean.

The next new arrival went a little bit better than the first, taking to Tommy's calming reassurances like a newborn calf to its mother's teat. And while Tommy worked to calm down the new person—this one spoke in a voice they both could understand, after Grassal learned its—her—name was Suki, and that she was very, very afraid, Grassal also became aware that here, too, remnants had formed.

As before, Grassal collected some, this time while Tommy was occupied with Suki. But since Suki was easier to calm than Cody, Tommy spoke to Grassal before Grassal could do anything with the remnants except store them within himself.

"After we do a few more," Tommy said, "we need to divide and conquer."

Grassal was silent, but a flare of dark orange passed over his body.

"If you don't help, we all die. You, me, Deshondra, Cody, Suki, and thousands more, every human who arrives here."

"If I screw up, people are going to die."

"Nobody wants this responsibility ... but here we are. So help me help the new arrivals. Whatever happens, you'll handle it, we'll handle it. And if we fail, well, at least we gave it our level fucking best. Deshondra is helping, and I think Cody and even Suki will too, once they've got a better handle on themselves. We'll train them to help train other new arrivals, and so on. Think of it as a multilevel marketing scheme, except your product is survival. From there, then maybe we can start thinking about next steps."

"That's wildly optimistic."

"Wild optimism is all we've got right now."

"Considering the alternatives, that's enough for me."

The electric flare of the sun had faded behind the fog-shrouded horizon when their flow lines carried them to the site of yet another new arrival. There, streamers of light swirled around a pulsating cloud of matter that soon resolved into an orb. Grassal took one side, Tommy the other, and together they restrained the new arrival. Tommy sang, Grassal hummed along, and that seemed to calm the new arrival.

When Tommy started his, "Welcome to the Luminance, you're among humans, please don't eat anyone" speech, Grassal began to collect the remnants that hung in the air around them. This, combined with those he'd collected at the site of the last disturbance, gave him a considerable haul of raw remnants.

Tommy turned his attention to Grassal and flashed a color that Grassal immediately recognized as something outside the human spectrum. This sudden confirmation of his own sheer alienness caused him to lose control of all the remnants he had stored within himself. The remnants, seemingly of their own accord, flowed from his body and into his silver thread. He extended his attention all the way down the thread. Though his attention's focus dissipated along the way, he sensed that the string terminated in something complex and fibrous, solid yet squishy.

He concentrated harder on the thread's terminus, the way it felt familiar, a part of him, and then he recognized ... the sensation at the end of the string felt familiar because the string terminated at his right thumb.

"Remember the contract," Tommy said. "You should honor the stillness."

Grassal ignored him, and instead only focused on the feeling of the thread. His focus was rewarded when, from the far end of his thread, there came a wave that hit him like the smell of unwashed laundry. That wave had come *through* him, into him, which meant that someone else had sent it.

Someone was pulling on his thumb.

He pulled back.

16

They landed in the early afternoon on a small, reed-covered island somewhere in swampy southern Florida for a recharge. After landing, Su Min had curled up in the P3's cargo area and fallen asleep. Lilly, having being confined to a flying capsule for the past several hours, wasn't about to pass up a perfectly good opportunity to stretch her legs.

The thick, swampy spring air was balmy and smelled of decay. She spent her time pacing and trying to work out the implications of Grassal's finger twitch. She was pretty sure it was only an involuntary reaction, a spasm or something like that, but it was the first time he'd displayed any movement at all, and she couldn't stop herself from hoping.

Su Min woke up just before sundown, removed some prepackaged meals from one of the storage trunks, and distributed them to Lilly and Eva. The meals didn't look like much on the outside, but Lilly was so hungry that it didn't matter. Nothing mattered, Lilly thought, except for killing Roland Jessup.

After they'd finished their meals and Eva was off in the bushes using the bathroom, Su Min said, "I saw a video of you and the tank."

"Yeah," Lilly said, shrugging her shoulders. "What can I say? I was a little bit worked up. Things were bad, I was scared, and angry, and ..."

"Are you still scared?" Su Min said.

Lilly shook her head. "Just angry, mostly."

"I'm scared," Su Min said. "Because I think that, that ..." And with that, she sniffled and began to cry. Lilly put her arm around her shoulder.

"I did not want this," Su Min said. "I did not want any of this. I just wanted to do good work, to have a chance at a good life here. I don't know what else to do."

"It'll be okay," Lilly said, as much to reassure herself as to reassure Su Min. "You are doing good work, and you'll be fine. You're a tough cookie, you know that?"

"A tough cookie?" Su Min said. The idiom was lost on her.

"That means you're brave. It's a good thing, Su Min."

They were in the air just after sundown, and they flew through the night over the churning black waters of the Gulf of Mexico. By the time the sun had risen over the horizon, a green coastline had come into view. Dense foliage covered the ground. Farther up the coast, Lilly could see rocks rising from the coast like giant bones.

"I'm sorry," Su Min said, digging into her bag and removing two dense burlap sacks, "but you both have to put these over your heads for the next hour. It is for everyone's safety."

Lilly scowled, but Eva shrugged and pulled the bag over her head. Not to be outdone by the woman's aloofness, Lilly did the same. The bag was rough and scratchy against her cheek, and though not totally dark, she couldn't see anything. Which, she supposed, was the point.

An hour passed, give or take, and then Lilly felt the P3 begin to descend. At that point, Su Min said, "Okay, you can look now."

The sight below took her breath away. Rising from the dense, green jungle was a shiny black building shaped like a donut, with a large central courtyard the size of a soccer pitch. A river as wide as two semi-trailers placed end-to-end ran along beside the building, and several long wooden boats were moored to a dock. There was something peculiar about the layout, and eventually Lilly realized it was due to the lack of roads leading to or from the structure.

Su Min set them down on a landing pad in the center of the donut. When she opened the doors, a wave of dense, humid air filled the cabin. Lilly thought she detected the faintest hint of ocean.

They stepped out. No one came out to greet them. This, Lilly decided, was an awfully large building to be empty. She asked Su Min where everyone was, and Su Min looked down at the watch she wore around her thin wrist.

"Everyone is working right now," she said. "This side"—she pointed toward one side of the build—"has dormitories, a clinic, and an armory."

"An armory?"

"It is only a precaution. Everything else is research space. Later I can give you the tour, but for now let's get Grassal settled in."

Lilly towed Grassal across the courtyard, which was resplendent with tropical plants. Lilly didn't know which ones were native, but she'd seen many of them growing indoors back in Colorado.

Su Min followed a sidewalk that led toward the building and a door slid open. When they passed through, a blast of cool air washed over them. The air carried the slightest hint of ozone and machine oil, and for an all-too-brief moment, Lilly was reminded of her home.

"Our first stop is the clinic. We will get you both set up with the access control system later this afternoon," she said. "Until then, you should stay close to me."

Lilly pulled Grassal along behind her as they walked down a long hallway with marble floors and smooth, paneled walls, which were occasionally interrupted by a door. Some of the doors had windows, through which Lilly could see people working at computer terminals. Other doors had opaque windows, or none at all. They passed two researchers who gaped at Grassal as Lilly towed his levitating form down the hallway.

"What is this place?" Eva asked.

"It's the Tivooki Southern Operations Center, or the T-SOC, or ... The Donut. The people here are all on rotation. It's a prestigious position within the company, but it is very difficult due to the isolation."

"The T-SOC," Lilly said, trying to suppress a laugh. She'd always found corporate acronyms ridiculous, and this one was no exception.

"Yes. It's mostly researchers, people working on special projects. The Pachyderm work is one of these projects. The goal is to improve low-cost, automated urban transit."

"Why here?" Lilly asked. "Why not back in the states?"

"Mr. Ross has his reasons, but there is a good legal environment here, especially now with the KREATURE Act and the kind of research that Mr. Ross is currently pursuing."

At this, Lilly's heart pulled up tight. Su Min must have seen the look on her face, because her eyes went wide and she started shaking her head.

"Oh, no no, I'm sorry, it is not what it sounds like. All this work, yes it uses some parts of the Brunmeier research, but it is only at a very small scale, and limited to data processing. It is not my area of expertise, so I cannot say for sure what exactly is being done with it ... but there are no subluminals."

"I'm only a little relieved," Lilly said.

They walked further until they came to a door that Su Min opened to reveal a clinic. Inside, a man in a white coat stood before a work table covered in lab equipment. His posture was stooped, his thin hair combed over to one side, and he held a cane, but Lilly recognized him before he turned around to greet her with a big, wide smile.

"Hello again," Dr. Kongsampong said. "I heard that our

friend Mr. Delgado is having some difficulty. Let's have a look."

With a tug, Lilly situated Grassal next to an examination table. Dr. Kongsampong, unfazed by the way Grassal floated above the tile floor, leaned over and began to examine him. He peeled open Grassal's eyes and shined a light, then leaned over close and listened to his breathing. He then said something in Thai, and a pair of nurses, a man and a woman, began to work over him, taking blood samples, attaching electrodes to his head and chest, and configuring data readouts.

"Tell me everything you can about Mr. Delgado's life since the last time we met."

Lilly did, leaving out nothing. Dr. Kongsampong's expression remained generally pleased, especially when she mentioned their early successes at the Admiral, but darkened as Lilly related the events that led from Grassal being floating and comatose to their time in the cabin.

"All that time without medical attention?" he said, his tone scolding.

"It was the best we could do under the circumstances."

"Unwise maybe, but understandable." He gestured to a glass cabinet on the wall, which contained several headpieces covered in electrodes. "We've been working on something that I think can help him. And if we can help one, we can help others like him."

"Others," Eva said. "How many others are we talking about?"

"No less than ten thousand," he said.

"Holy shit," Lilly said.

As if in response to her astonishment, a flicker of movement from Grassal caught her eye. She watched, her own body motionless. Grassal's right thumb twitched. Once, twice, then several more times. The others in the room followed her gaze. They watched for a little bit longer, then he was still.

Lilly ran to Grassal's side, with Dr. Kongsampong on his other side. They both leaned in close to look at him.

"Grassal, if you can hear me, you're with friends, you're with good people, and ... it's going to be okay," Lilly said. She didn't really believe the words, but if Grassal could hear him, she thought he could use some reassurance. "Flick your thumb if you can hear me."

Grassal's thumbs remained motionless.

"It could be an involuntary reaction," Dr. Kongsampong said, "or maybe a stimulus response. We just don't know."

Whatever it was, Lilly grasped Grassal's hand in hers. And, just in case, she gave his thumb a couple of tugs.

17

Over the next several days, Grassal and Tommy helped dozens more new arrivals orient themselves without going through the initial murder spree, but since there were so many, neither had been able to really give them the full rundown of what was happening. He and Tommy had simply kept the new arrivals together and out of trouble. During this time, Grassal had felt more sensations coming down his thread. At first he'd tried to send out a really rough form of Morse code, but between tending to the new arrivals, Tommy's warnings to honor the stillness, and the watchful gaze of several surly Luminant minders, he wasn't able to devote any time to it.

Eventually, they herded the new arrivals back to Central City, where they reunited with Deshondra, Cody, and Suki. Now they were all grouped together, a little clump of humanity trying to gain its footing in an alien world.

Tommy said to Grassal, "Listen, buddy boy, you're running this. Just like we practiced, we've got to get them working with us, helping us, because there are more arriving even now, and we're not going to be able to corral them all. And if we don't, well, you can imagine the consequences of having a few thousand human orbs running amok like rabid cheetahs."

He felt the emotions of all the new arrivals, a field of them, floating orbs, each new arrival a delicious little morsel of—

Grassal stopped himself. He couldn't think like that. Since he'd reunited with Tommy, he'd barely felt the compulsion to consume any other beings, and the mere thought of what he'd done filled him with horror. He'd totally screwed that up, almost as bad as he screwed up things with the Admiral.

"What if I tell them the wrong thing? Or scare them, or ..." Grassal said, trailing off, afraid of the responsibility that Tommy was thrusting upon him. But that responsibility was now before him in the form of ten individuals, each of whom was broadcasting their thoughts.

"I'm scared."

"I want to go home."

"I might kill someone because I'm so fucking angry."

In short, their thoughts ran the gamut of the usual human experience. And he was supposed to be in charge of them, to train them somehow to fight against the strange hunger and hunting instinct that was a consequence of being a human trapped in a Luminant body.

The crowd of new arrivals had begun to quiet down, and Grassal realized that while he thought he'd been thinking, they were able to hear him, either because he had no control over his internal monologue, or he simply had no internal monologue. Because while he felt emotions, anything that he might mentally verbalize was coming out. He thought, so, you heard all of that?

From the crowd of new arrivals came affirmative responses.

"And it's the same as this?" Grassal said ... or at least did what he'd been assuming was speaking all this time.

That meant that everything he'd thought while he and Tommy collected the first new arrivals, Tommy had heard. Every grumble, every fear, all of it, Tommy knew.

"Then maybe you have some idea of what kind of difficulties we're all facing. We're in this together. But to understand the present, you need to understand the past, how you got here."

"The last thing I remember was being at the Admiral Hotel,"

a new arrival said. The voice itself carried a payload of information. Grassal knew that this person was named Elijah Franklin, that Elijah was from Indianapolis, and that he'd been a casualty of the first attack in New York City, one of the first afflicted. He'd been there on business, and during that trip, just before he'd been attacked by a subluminal, he'd decided that he wouldn't leave his husband after all, that maybe couples therapy could help them resolve their issues. Then came the mystery illness, which he'd responded to by checking himself in to the Admiral Hotel.

"I know how I got here," said Deshondra. Her words were accompanied by a payload that told Grassal that she was a programmer from Alabama who'd been mauled when she attacked a subluminal with a tire iron in an attempt to save the life of her little sister. Her sister had died, Deshondra was hospitalized, and the family had left Birmingham to escape the memories.

"Who doesn't know how they got here?"

At least half of the orbs, the new arrivals, began to pulse, flashing colors of confusion and uncertainty. Each of them sent their stories as well, and the pain, the fear, the loss, it was all too much for Grassal to bear. He steeled himself against it, imagined that he was encased in a steel sphere, and that the only thoughts and memories that could enter were those he would allow to do so, because he was tired of letting things just happen to him.

Soon, he'd encased himself, and the noise stopped. Now, he spoke in what he hoped was an even, level voice that would carry reassurance and strength, but also the doubt he felt, because if they could hear his thoughts then there was no bullshitting anyone.

"We were all attacked by subluminals, the bodies the Luminants find themselves in on Earth. Like us, when they arrive they're hungry and full of rage. Somehow, when their bodily fluid mixed with our own, we became entangled with this place, and something has caused our conscious minds to separate from our bodies and come here."

"What do we do?" a new arrival said.

"We do the best we can. We learn to control our urges and desires."

"So those other ... things, they're not food, are they, despite what my mind tells me?" Elijah asked.

"That's right. They're other ... beings. 'Luminants' as a term only exists to distinguish them from their subluminal form, but it works. We are guests here. It's typically bad form to eat people who allow you into their home. And don't be mistaken, they are allowing us to stay now, because we have a common purpose."

"What purpose is that?"

"To help the new arrivals, the people like yourself, and to figure out a way to get our people home, back to where we belong."

Grassal told them about the contract, leaving nothing out.

"How do we go home?" someone else asked.

Grassal responded with as much confidence as he could muster. "That's ... an open question. We're still working on it." He thought of the cube he'd made, and the thought filled him with more hope than he had any right to feel.

"Until we've figured this out, we've got to work together to help the other new arrivals. They're all going to be like you: scared, angry, hungry. It's up to us to make sure that they make the transition, just as each of you did, and acclimate to this place, to our new—and hopefully temporary—bodies. We're all in this together. I know it's disorienting and terrifying, but we'll persevere. I need each of you to draw on whatever well of strength you might have, because you're going to need it."

While he'd been speaking, he'd noticed the first tugs of another new arrival. Now, he felt pulled in a half-dozen directions at once. He issued a thought that amounted to "follow me", and formed himself into the tube shape he and

Tommy used for riding the flow lines.

Some of the new arrivals were having difficulties controlling their bodies. That was understandable, but there wasn't time to coach them. But, thinking about how all the information had been communicated to him by others, he let down his sphere and sent a stream of thoughts and sensations toward them, all the thoughts that he had when he was mounting a flow line.

Soon, over half of those who'd been struggling had also made the shape, though some went off in the wrong direction. To those, Grassal sent gentle thoughts that ushered them in the correct direction. To his surprise, they actually listened. For those who hadn't made the traveling shape yet, he sent slower, less detailed instructions, along with the emotions he felt when he was forming up. That helped some of them. Grassal instructed the two who remained to wait in place, practice using their bodies, and refrain from eating anyone.

Now, Grassal, Deshondra, and nine or ten new arrivals traveled down the flow line toward the disturbance's origin. Grassal felt the waves of disorientation as he came closer, and he knew that this one was going to be powerful. Together with Deshondra, they positioned themselves and waited for the arrival.

Everything grew dark. The flow lines began to quiver. The particles in Grassal's body vibrated in anticipation. Suddenly, an explosion of energy washed out over them from the center of the disturbance. When the energy wave had passed, the new arrival was at the epicenter, surrounded by remnants of the disturbance their arrival had created.

Grassal built up a defensive sphere around himself, then began to collect remnants. The first new arrival was moving toward Deshondra in a threatening, almost menacing way. Grassal shot forward to intercept, and soon the new arrival began trying to chip away at Grassal's body in an attempt to consume him. This one, Grassal realized, was strong.

Grassal pushed back, channeling the initial rage he'd felt on arrival to drive him, but instead of controlling him, he channeled it into strength. Part of this was arranging his internal structure so that it was lattice-like, giving his body extra strength. He consumed some of the remnants, absorbing them into his body, and with each bit of remnant he consumed, he grew stronger. Finally, he opened up a large section on one of his outside walls and enveloped the new arrival. Once it was safely inside himself, Grassal slammed the opening shut.

The screaming new arrival thrashed within him, but Grassal barely noticed. He was focused instead on the power he now controlled, and the potential for more power that surrounded him, free for the taking. He began to consume more remnants, and as he grew stronger he became aware of the violence attempted by the new arrival inside him, but the new arrival's attempts to harm him from the inside were doing as much damage as a child throwing rocks against a brick wall. Grassal had power to spare, he realized, and under these conditions, he wondered how far he could go ...

He visualized a cube, separate from himself, but still connected by a thin membrane. After a countdown, three, two, one, he released the cube. The cube hung in the air, an extension of himself, under his control, but also separate from him, and not connected to his core by any visible means. He willed the cube to expand outward, and it did, quivering at first, then growing from something the diameter of an ethernet cable into something the diameter of a ten-year-old tree.

Feeling a rush of excitement, Grassal willed the cube to grow and adapt to its surroundings. The cube did, changing into something more fluid and round, less like a cube and more like a torus. Not only did the cube change visibly, but it began to feel different, and it grew an aperture in the center. Grassal's perception of it was like standing on the threshold with a warm and familiar house on one side, and a cold and strange corridor on the other. The threshold itself was the adapter between them, the one that would connect them.

The aperture pulsed and quivered, as if it wanted to open, and all he had to do was let it. He knew that if he allowed the aperture to open, nothing would be the same again. Grassal was vaguely aware of voices calling out to him, but he didn't care. This was too important, because he knew that, somehow, the adapter would open a connection between this place, and the Earth he knew.

Grassal sensed the gaze of many minds upon him. Both the Luminants who'd been following them everywhere, ensuring the human interlopers were following the contract, and all the new arrivals to whom he'd played midwife. They watched and waited, expectant, curious, terrified.

Grassal allowed the aperture to open.

The feeling of having his body in two places at once was profoundly disorienting, but nevertheless Grassal felt a surge of victory because, through the opening, Grassal saw, for the first time since he'd arrived, the familiar blues and greens and grays of home. But not only that, there were silver threads rising up from the Earth, coming into the aperture from a dozen different directions, and flowing into the humans which were nearby, himself included.

A victory whoop escaped his lips, just before everything exploded in a wall of searing, white pain, and then nothing.

18

Amadeus took an involuntary step backward, and despite himself moved a little bit closer to Ross. The police officers outside the cell had also moved away, as if they were individually repulsed by the man, but not sure why. Each of their faces bore a look of conflict, like they were doing something they knew was wrong, but couldn't stop themselves from doing it anyway.

"You have something we want," the man said. Up close, his voice was just as high and reedy as it had been when he'd addressed them in the mansion, and no less loud. Despite its odd timbre, and despite the fact that the man looked like he'd crawled out of a cardboard box, there was something about him that emanated power, one that didn't come from the man himself, but from something granted to the man. Amadeus tried to suss it out, but under the man's gaze, he couldn't quite concentrate the way he needed to.

"Who are you?" Ross said.

"Who I am is not important. I'm only Bigogli's speaker."

He glared at them both with wide, wild eyes.

"What is it they want?" Maximilian asked Amadeus.

"My dad's research. This ... person," Amadeus gestured to the man, "thinks that I still have it." To the man, Amadeus said, "I don't have it, not anymore. It was destroyed. Go see Jessup, his group has what you want."

"Lies!" the man said. He grabbed the bars and began to bark, "Lies, lies." His body shook back and forth, and he banged his head on the bars, once, twice. As he screamed, froth flew from his mouth. Blood began to stream down his forehead, but he bashed his head against the steel bars, again and again.

The police officers who watched made no move to stop him, like this was just another Saturday night. Except each officer who watched the man had a zoned-out, faraway look in their eyes, like that of sleepwalkers.

"Lies, lies, lies," the man screamed, banging his head again and again.

Over the sound of the man's shrieks came another sound from outside that sent chills down Amadeus' spine. There was a rhythmic chanting of nonsense, faint but unmistakable. That sound had been burned onto his memory, and he'd hoped he'd never have to hear it again, but there it was, right outside.

Amadeus called out to the police officers. "Hey. Something bad is coming, and soon." One of them, the bullet-headed officer who'd brought them in, shook his head and blinked his eyes, as if just waking from sleep.

"Lies, lies, lies," the man said between head bangs. The man's forehead was a ruin, and his face was streaked with blood. His lips were busted, and when he opened his mouth to scream, a couple of teeth flew out in a spray of blood and spittle.

The bullet-headed officer pulled the man off the bars and held him in a chokehold. To another officer, he shouted, "Who let this man in here?" but the other officer, along with his companions, just stared with blank, vacant eyes.

"Lies, lies, lies," the man said, his breath a gasp, not struggling as the officer pulled him off the bars and handcuffed him to the neighboring cell.

"Something is controlling them," Ross said. His voice carried a hint of astonishment and a hint of fear. And it wasn't only Ross. The arresting officer's eyes went wide. He tried shaking the shoulders of one of his companions, but his companion only stared forward.

"Holy shit," the officer said. "What is going on here?"

There was a bang on the door to the outside, followed by another, and another.

"Lies, lies, lies," the man said, hissing out the words from beneath broken teeth.

"Please, please, let us out," Amadeus said. "We're trying to stop this."

The outside door thumped and creaked. Amadeus imagined a dozen dead-eyed bodies in some kind of weird human virus formation pressing against the door.

The arresting officer looked from their cell to the door, then down at the man on the floor. The officer's lips were moving, and in the space between the speaker's screams, Amadeus was pretty sure the officer was saying a prayer. Somehow, this gave Amadeus hope. The officer seemed to come to a decision, then he stepped forward and inserted a key into their cell door.

"I can't let you do that, Roger," one of the other officers said. Amadeus read the name above his badge: Lowery.

"Don't you see what's happening here?" Roger, the arresting officer, said. Amadeus noticed the man's screaming had stopped. After looking the man over, Amadeus was pretty sure he was dead.

"This is what is happening: it's the end," the other officer, Lowery said. "All is about to be revealed. But these two, these two have to give it up, to make sure that no one else gains the knowledge. It's their fault, Roger. Their fault."

The door broke down, and a group of people tumbled into the room, mouths muttering nonsense, arms and legs interlocked, all moving as a single organism, a human virus.

"What the ...?" Roger said.

"This is how it is," Lowery said, then pointed at Amadeus. "And this one will give us the thing we want, the thing we need. So much depends on it."

"This. Isn't. Right," Roger said. With that, he threw himself at Lowery, and the two went tumbling to the ground. The fall caused Lowery's head to hit the linoleum with a sickening thud. The man's eyes rolled back in his head, showing the whites, but by this point the human virus was nearly upon him.

The human virus tumbled forward, though slow, as if unaccustomed to moving in such a confined space. The two remaining officers were still staring with vacant eyes and made no move to help Roger, who was pushing himself backward, toward their cell, and away from the human virus.

"You two get out of here. I've gotta help these guys. Grab the keys and take a car," Roger said. He finished unlocking their cell, tossed the keys to Amadeus, then drew his gun and aimed it at the human virus. "Stay back," he said. "Last warning."

The human virus advanced on him. He shot one, then another, but the writhing mass of bodies pressed forward.

"On three," Amadeus said to Ross, whose face had gone pale, his eyes wide. He counted down, and on one flung open the cell door. They dashed past the now-distracted human virus and through the doors of the station. The last thing Amadeus saw was Roger pulling Lowery into the cell they'd just vacated.

Outside, Amadeus pressed the button on a key fob, and one of the police cars' horns chirped.

"There's our ride," he said.

As if in response, from nearby came the screeching howl of a subluminal. That howl was answered by at least a dozen more.

"Oh my god, oh my god, oh my god," Ross said as he frantically lifted the passenger side door handle. Even from here, Amadeus could hear the man's fast, shallow breathing.

The shrieking grew louder as more creatures joined the mad chorus. Amadeus opened the driver's side door, but just as he pressed the unlock button, Ross had the door handle pulled.

"Wait," Amadeus said, then pressed the unlock button again. This time Ross waited. Amadeus could hear skittering from down the street, followed by a ground-shaking howl.

The police cruiser started on the first try. Amadeus jammed the shifter in reverse and backed out. When he did so, something thumped against the car. A quick check of his side mirrors showed a subluminal scurrying away. He drove backward and crushed the subluminal, which sent a spray of black fluid across the parking lot.

Amadeus shoved the shifter into drive and turned onto the street, where a trio of subluminals hurtled toward them. Amadeus slammed the gas pedal. The car's acceleration pushed them back into their seats. They ran down one subluminal, but another sprang into the air and landed on top of their car with a *thunk*. Amadeus hit the brakes. The subluminal tumbled forward onto the asphalt in front of their vehicle. Amadeus swerved around it and left the police station behind.

He looked over at his passenger. Ross was pale, his eyes wide and haunted.

"First subluminal attack?"

Ross nodded. "That was ..." But he trailed off, unable to finish the thought, and so they drove in silence toward the coast.

Amadeus liked the feel of the steering wheel in his hands. The wheel was worn smooth from thousands of hours of use, and despite the faint smell of tobacco in the police cruiser, Amadeus thought this was a significant improvement over a bicycle.

What hadn't improved was Ross. His eyes darted from one thing to another, and he was still pale. Amadeus knew that the man needed time to process what he'd just seen, so he focused on driving. He himself felt terribly conspicuous, but decided that given the martial law situation, he could do a lot worse than a police cruiser. An hour later, they had reached the coast without incident, and he was proven right.

Their destination was a slightly shabby marina situated on an inlet. Only a few boats remained. Of those, all but one looked to be fishing boats. Amadeus pointed to the sleek black yacht. "That one?"

Ross gave him a wan smile. "How'd you guess?"

"You don't strike me as the fishing type."

They boarded the yacht. Amadeus, having grown up in Connecticut, had been on well-apportioned boats a few times, mostly during day trips with his father's friends, and their boats had been nice.

Ross' yacht, however, was something else entirely: buttery leather upholstery, a dizzying array of instrumentation, including a wide spread of touchscreens, redundant analog controls, and polished bamboo flooring and wall paneling. The furnishings were free of scuffs, grime, dust, and blemishes. Amadeus' gaze returned to the controls and he narrowed his eyes.

As if predicting his objections, Ross said, "It's all military-grade electronics. Every last component has been hardened against EMP interference." He paused, then from a cabinet retrieved a tablet and passed it to Amadeus. "Here's a control interface. See if you can spin everything up and get us out of here. Our destination should already be programmed in the navigation system. Once you get us going, go chill in the galley, that's where the good shit is. I ... need to lie down for a while."

"I've never driven a boat like this before."

"There's so much automation it's idiot-proof."

"Thanks for that vote of confidence."

"Anytime. Let me know if you have any trouble."

Ross descended the stairs, and eventually Amadeus figured out how to start the "return to home" automation routine. A few minutes later, the yacht was carrying them over open water and the shoreline was receding behind them. The boat knew its destination, but he kept getting "insufficient privileges" when he tried to determine where exactly home was. According to the navigation system, they had just over two days until they reached their destination, so Amadeus was left with nothing to do but watch the sunset and fill the time. His stomach rumbled, so he descended the stairs from the helm and strode into the galley, which was a combination kitchen and lounge. As promised, the galley was well-stocked with beer, a range of nuts and freeze-dried fruits, a refrigerator full of kimchi and yogurt, a bunch of MREs, and a needlessly large bag of cannabis.

He set about making himself something to eat and decided to have a beer with his dinner. That beer turned into another, and another. An hour later, he was half-drunk. He staggered back upstairs to the helm and slumped down into one of the immorally comfortable leather chairs. He tried using a tablet to access the internet, but again received an "insufficient privileges" error message. Still wanting to get a sense of what was going on, he turned on the shortwave radio, which was just within arm's reach of his chair.

A woman's voice said, "Anywhere there's people with the subluminal infection, we're seeing k-storms and rifts. Places getting leveled and new subluminals showing up, but no demon gates anywhere nearby. The scientists are saying we've got maybe a month until we hit the point of no return. It's some kind of feedback loop."

"All we can do right now is sit tight, protect ourselves, and see if anything comes out of his broadcast," a man replied.

To himself, Amadeus said, "What broadcast?"

He started scanning other frequencies and settled on one where a man was saying that the only way forward was to kill anyone who was known to be afflicted. "It breaks my heart to think that the Bearers are right, but if it buys us more time, I don't see a better way."

Finally, he landed on a frequency that carried a familiar voice. Amadeus' blood ran cold as the voice said, "—stalwart and steadfast. This message will repeat in five minutes."

He sat on the edge of his seat and listened. Just before the message repeated, Ross stepped into the room. Amadeus held up one finger for quiet, said, "Roland Jessup," tapped his ear, and motioned to the radio. The voice came back on. They both listened to the full message.

"Ladies and gentleman, my name is Roland Jessup, and I intend to save all of us from the present crisis. As you know, Securaux works tirelessly to make America strong and united. We've made progress, and many of you have achieved greatness in your fight. Now, we face a dire struggle, one that threatens not only our nation but our very existence. Everything hangs in the balance, as things have become ... unpredictable. But do not despair, because we have developed a Rift Mitigation System. However, the Securaux Rift Mitigation System will only be released if certain demands are met, which will be stated in the near future. Until then, remain stalwart and steadfast. This message will repeat in five minutes."

Ross settled into the chair beside Amadeus, put a finger to his chin, then entered some commands on his phone. Four minutes later, the broadcast repeated, and Ross fed a recording of the signal into an analysis program on one of the yacht's computer terminals.

After a few seconds, long lines of terminal output began to flow on the screen. Ross' eyes flicked over the lines. "The voiceprint matches, this is definitely Jessup. But the signal's been bounced around so many repeaters it's impossible to tell where it originated."

Amadeus nodded and said, "When we get wherever it is we're going, I want to see it. The emulation. Maybe it can help us come up with a way out of this mess."

"That's not really how it works, and besides, I ... don't think that's a good idea."

"I don't think you get to tell me what is or isn't a good idea in this scenario."

"I do. AI is complicated, and even more so when it's using an individual's consciousness as its base layer. And given the emotional connection? I won't stop you, but I think it would be a profoundly bad idea, on both sides."

"We'll see," Amadeus said.

The yacht carried them due south into the night. He went

downstairs, settled into a bed, and fell into a black, dreamless sleep.

19

Lilly gazed at a screen in Su Min's office, reviewing footage of Grassal from the past two nights. Su Min had been analyzing flight data from the journey here, but was now taking a break and standing over Lilly, one hand on her shoulder.

In the footage, Grassal tended to vibrate. Lilly suspected this was a result of slight shifts in the air, so she applied a filter which stabilized the image and allowed her to increase the speed to 10x. She reached the end of last night's footage, and started on the first night of footage. Again.

A few minutes into it, Su Min tapped her arm. "There. Pause the tape, back up to 12:41."

Lilly did so, and saw what she'd missed before: the slightest twitching of Grassal's thumbs. She'd been watching other parts of his body, expecting maybe an eyelid flutter, or an irregular rise and fall of his chest, but his thumbs again ... she replayed the section. The movements of his thumbs weren't jerky or spastic at all. Instead, they were almost rhythmic. Lilly slowed the video to half speed, reviewed the section again, then once more. The third time, she tapped along with the movements.

"What are you doing?" Su Min asked.

"It's almost like he's making a pattern with his thumb." She tapped some more, over and over again, but while the movements seemed to be more than just involuntary twitching, she wasn't able to discern any kind of pattern or rhythm.

Lilly paused the video, closed her eyes, and put a hand to her temples. A headache was coming on, the same one that had been with her for days, and she thought that gazing at a screen wasn't helping matters.

"I need a break."

"Would you like to go for a walk. Today, it is not too hot, and there is something interesting just a couple of kilometers away."

"Are you sure? I mean ..."

"Grassal will be fine, Dr. Kongsampong is a good man. I have some free time today. Eva is being monitored. And—" Something in Su Min's pocket chimed. "Sorry," she said, then pulled out a phone, looked at it, and smiled. "They're on their way, Maximilian and Amadeus, and should arrive tomorrow morning. They've got ... a boat, I think?"

Lilly smiled and allowed herself to enjoy just a moment of hope. Not that it all couldn't come crashing down around them, but maybe it wouldn't.

So Lilly sprayed herself with bug spray, slathered her arms and face with sunscreen, took her daily anti-malarial meds, and dressed herself in the boots and trekking pants that Su Min had provided for her. When the exit doors opened, a blast of hot, thick air took Lilly's breath away.

"Where are we going?" Lilly asked, once she was able to breathe again. She took a swig from her canteen, and wondered if she was carrying enough water.

"You'll see. Something neat. Come on."

From the exit, they strode across the manicured lawn to the tree line, where a wooden sign read, "*Sendero Amarillo. Yellow Trail*: 5 km." Su Min started down the well-worn footpath that ran into the rainforest. Lilly hesitated. The canopy was so thick, and trees too tall, that it was like stepping into evening. But under the canopy, the shade and the damp air made everything feel a full five degrees cooler, and Lilly thought she could handle this after all.

Su Min led the way down the path. Occasionally, the screech of some animal interrupted the otherwise-placid sounds of rustling leaves. Neither spoke while they walked. Lilly devoted her attention to scanning the ground for poisonous snakes. Maybe poisonous frogs, too. For all she knew, based on what she'd read about equatorial rainforests, everything around here was out to kill them. Su Min, however, didn't seem concerned.

"Do you hike this trail often?" Lilly asked.

"Yes, I find it very peaceful. Once, I encountered an indigenous person. He was naked, but very shy. But he gave me a big smile and a wave before he ran off."

"You're calling someone shy?" Lilly said.

"I'm getting better," Su Min said.

Lilly smiled. Now that she thought about it, Lilly had seen the little engineer talk to at least three people since they'd arrived.

"Look." Su Min pointed.

Lilly followed the path of her finger, and saw, resting on branches not far away, a group of birds with long, blue tails and green breasts.

"They're called motmots," Su Min said. "There are caves not far from here where they have their nests."

Lilly watched the birds for a little bit, then they continued on. Soon they reached a clearing, where a towering, pyramid-shaped structure topped with honeycomb-like latticework appeared to have emerged from the face of a hill. Vegetation covered a good part of the pyramid, as if the hill was trying to pull it back in. Some, but not all, of the vegetation had been hacked away to reveal gray stone. A staircase ran up the middle of the pyramid's face, and a doorway lay halfway up the pyramid's steps.

"This structure is unique. Most of the other ruins in the area are freestanding, but this one descends into a system of caverns. The archaeologists say it's Mayan, but they're not sure of its significance. The federal government used to maintain it, but after the coup, it was turned back over to the state government. They don't have any money, so now the jungle is taking it over. Maximilian said he's been trying to hire locals to clean and maintain it, but he is not having much success."

"It's ..." Lilly began, then said, "How old is it?"

"About a thousand years old. There used to be a lot more people here. Come on." Su Min produced a pair of headlamps from her bag, handed one to Lilly, then gestured to the steep stairs.

They ascended the stairs and came to a steel gate. Su Min produced a key, unlocked the gate, and they descended another set of stairs at least twenty yards until they reached a chamber. Behind a sheet of plexiglass was a faded mural showing a man seated on something that could have been a throne, only the throne was leaned back on the ground and the man was facing the sky. The throne appeared to have levers, as if it was a control system—though for what, Lilly couldn't guess. But then she saw what looked like fire licking out from the sides and covering the ground.

"This is crazy, but ... it looks like he's piloting a rocket."

Su Min smiled. "Maybe. There is a lot we don't know. All we know is that this site was once used by a great civilization."

"And that it ended," Lilly said.

"Not ended, just changed," Su Min said. "By the time the Spanish arrived, this site had been abandoned for hundreds of years, but there were other Maya city-states."

"It makes you wonder what would have happened if they'd survived."

"Great things, I think. But maybe that's just the fate of some civilizations, to rise and fall, to have their age of glory, and then to fade away."

"Or collapse," Lilly said.

She didn't see a need to add that their own civilization was on the precipice of its own demise.

They admired the painting for a few minutes, and Lilly tried to take in every detail. Coiled around the base of the pilot's chair—now that she'd decided it was a rocket, she couldn't unsee it—was a fat snake, its forked tongue taking an exploratory taste of the air. There were also lines that rose from around the base of the chair, each one swirling and coiling like smoke.

There was a narrow tunnel beyond the painting.

"Does that lead to the caverns?"

Su Min nodded and said, "If it is okay with you, I would prefer not to go any farther."

"You'll get no complaints from me."

With three hours remaining until dusk, they started back. On the way, Su Min said, "I'd like to talk to you about the arrangements I had made with your father."

"What kind of arrangements?" Lilly asked.

"I think they are good for everyone involved, and might answer your question as to why I am here, in this place." Su Min gestured toward The Donut. "Your father granted me a minority ownership stake in Jones Aerodynamic, along with a leadership role. You remain the majority shareholder, with the remaining shares held by a handful of private equity firms."

"I can't think of anyone better to run the company than you."

Su Min frowned and looked down at the coffee she held in her hands. "That is kind of the problem, I do not want to run a company. But your father asked me to make sure that the company remained in capable hands. That kind of business work ... it is outside my skill set. Maximilian has offered to buy us out. The offer he made, it is very generous, and I think his organization would devote resources to do things right. The other shareholders think it is a good offer."

Su Min told her the number and terms. Lilly realized her mouth was agape. The initial lump sum payment, if invested at even a pitiful interest rate, would guarantee her and her descendants income for generations, and that didn't include the patent royalties that would be paid to her, as heiress to the Jones estate. She could write. She could travel. She could sleep in every morning. She could do whatever she wanted ... as soon as she killed Roland Jessup. If she intended to live the life of a dilettante, she needed to earn it.

Su Min must've mistook her silence for hesitation, because she said, "I understand you want time to think about it. There is no rush."

A few hundred yards from The Donut, Su Min's phone chimed. She checked it, her eyes went wide, and she said, "Sorry, but now we must rush." She started to run. Lilly followed her, and soon her head was swimming from the heat and exertion.

"What's going on?"

"Grassal could be in danger."

They reached the door, which slid open when Su Min approached, and they stepped into the cool, air-conditioned halls of The Donut. The doors closed behind them. The silence that replaced the screeching keens of the rainforest animals was almost as jarring as the cold air that bathed Lilly's skin.

Su Min raced to the clinic, where she flung open the door to find Dr. Kongsampong leaning back in his chair, his feet propped up on a desk, his eyes closed. He was napping. Grassal floated above an examination table a few feet away. Dr. Kongsampong's lab techs were working at a computer terminal nearby.

"Do not let this person close to Grassal," Su Min said, showing something on her phone to the techs. They both nodded, and Su Min slipped quietly back into the hallway.

Lilly followed, and once the door slid closed, she said, "Can you please tell me what in the hell is going on?"

"There was a coordinated attack," Su Min said. "In the last hour, over a thousand afflicted were murdered. The Bearers of Burdens are claiming responsibility. They claim they are trying to prevent more rifts."

Now Lilly understood. "Where is she?"

"In the cafeteria. Security is aware of the situation."

They strode through the hall of The Donut in silence. Just before they rounded the corner to the cafeteria, Lilly saw a group of people staring at a screen on the wall. Lilly expected they were about to watch a report on the Bearer action, but when she rounded the corner, the face on the screen made her blood run cold.

Roland Jessup gazed into the camera. His face appeared somber and empathetic, and with his white suit and well-coiffed hair, Lilly thought he looked like a televangelist. He said, "What this group of ... of terrorists has done today is unacceptable. The strong must help the weak, not sentence them to death when their continued existence becomes inconvenient."

"That's rich," Lilly said.

Someone shushed her. Lilly scowled, but said nothing further. On the screen, Jessup continued.

"Yet, it's clear that there is a link between the afflicted and the rifts that have begun to plague us. Fortunately, our engineers have been hard at work on a solution. We had hoped to devote a little more time to this problem, but the Bearers have forced our hand. Please indulge me for a short demonstration of a new Securaux product called the Rift Mitigation System. Roll the tape."

The video then cut to footage of Jessup standing in the foreground, the ocean in the background. Balls of light bloomed and collapsed in the air around him. In the distance, just before the horizon line, a white rift towered over the ocean and ran up into the sky. He held a small metal control box up to the camera. Wires ran from the box to somewhere off-screen. He entered some commands, winked at the camera, and then the light blooms stopped. Jessup then did a countdown with his fingers. After he reached one, he pointed toward the rift, and the rift disappeared. The footage ended with Jessup giving the camera a thumbs-up and a big, shit-eating grin.

"There it is, folks, our latest product offering," Jessup said. He looked even more pleased with himself, if that was possible. "And as a good faith gesture, and to allay any fears that my demonstration was just video trickery, we have released a collection of white papers that describe the theoretical basis for the Rift Mitigation System.

"While the Rift Mitigation System itself is proprietary, we will make these systems widely available to governmental clients as soon as one condition is met: Amadeus Brunmeier personally delivers to me all of his father's research data, decrypted, unedited, and in its entirety. Amadeus, the sooner you turn over the data, the more lives we can save ... together. I'll be in touch."

The broadcast ended, and the screen cut back to two news anchors who began to discuss the video they had just played. Su Min's eyes had gone wide. Lilly hadn't quite processed what she'd just seen.

"I need to sit down," Lilly said, and Su Min guided her to a bench that was flanked by two large potted plants. A part of her mind registered the scent of vanilla, and then a woman's voice said, "Do you think he'll do it?"

Lilly jumped and turned to see Eva standing just behind her. "You have got to stop sneaking up on me like that."

"Your people decided to start killing afflicted," Lilly said.

"I think it's awful, for what it's worth. But given the circumstances, I guess it was inevitable."

"You knew about this?" Lilly felt her fingernails digging into her palm, and she forced her hands to relax.

"No. I'm out of the loop. I told you what I know."

"Would you have killed Grassal if you were in the loop?"

Eva's face furrowed, as if she were truly considering the question. "I've been reflecting on the Bearers, my involvement with them and ... it's just that ... well, since I've been here, I feel like there's hope for another way, you know? What Dr. K is trying to do, what others like him are trying to do? What the

Bearers are talking about, maybe that's one way, and they say what they're doing is the only way, and that they're doing what nobody else wants to do, and that they're doing it for everyone … but maybe it's not the only way. I see that now. Does that make sense?"

"There is always another way," Su Min said. "Even when things are at their worst, there is always another way."

"What she said," Lilly said.

"I hope you're right."

"Don't go anywhere near Grassal," Lilly said.

"I promise that I won't let any harm come to him."

20

Everything was foggy for Grassal except the memory of opening the aperture. This memory carried rich and intricate details that he'd missed during the doing, as if in recall he could zoom in on the microscopic workings of a complex but familiar machine. Not only that, but as he recalled opening the aperture, he saw the different ways it could be used, like he'd just been dropped an operator's manual into his lap via accreted knowledge.

He heard voices nearby, distracting him from exploring the memory further. The fog that shrouded his senses lifted, and Grassal saw Tommy looming before him, flashing colors of discontent and disappointment with undertones of fear and concern.

"You're pissing off the establishment. I don't know what you were trying to do here, but you almost got yourself killed. We need you, Grassal. Your responsibility is right here."

"My responsibility? I never asked for this. That was you, all of it. Not just the contract, but our whole being here ... this is your doing."

Filipe and several other Luminants approached him. Their colors and patterns formed what Grassal's Luminant brain registered as a display of resolve.

"You violate terms," Filipe said in that roaring whisper, flashing shades of orange and yellow while it spoke. "You must understand. Violating our terms generates unwanted noise. Noise wakes the Observer. Waking the Observer will kill many. The one you named Donald argues for your immediate death to prevent this. Some resist him, but not all."

"What the hell are we supposed to do?" Grassal asked. "Just wait around until we accidentally break this stupid contract and get ourselves killed?"

"We follow the contract to the letter, and hope something falls into our laps," Tommy said. He'd moved in closer to Grassal, almost defensively.

Filipe seemed to consider this for a moment before returning to the larger collection of watchful Luminants who floated near the group of humans.

Grassal noticed that their surroundings had been imbued with an electrified feel, the first hints of another disturbance. A few seconds passed, the sensation intensified, then Tommy said, "Another new arrival. Let's go."

"I'm not quite feeling up to it," Grassal said. He still felt thin and drained. Explosions of pain did that to a man, or a Luminant, or whatever he was.

"You can't stay here. Come on."

With some effort, Grassal draped himself over a flow line. He was joined by about a dozen Luminants who were hanging around with the apparent purpose of contract enforcement, as well as half as many new arrivals who followed along. They all moved as a group toward the disturbance's source, not unlike a school of fish. Grassal knew they were close when he felt that first gut punch, and some of the new arrivals became tangled in flow lines. One went hurtling in the wrong direction, but Grassal thought he would find his way back.

The pillar of white fire at the disturbance's source collapsed, leaving behind both a new arrival and wisps of remnants, there for the taking. Tommy and Deshondra moved in to welcome the new arrival, while Grassal began to collect the remnants, which made him feel a little better. Each remnant he collected seemed to fill one of the tiny holes that'd been torn in himself after he'd let his adapter be destroyed.

Soon, Grassal had collected enough remnants to make a string, but he didn't think this was quite the right place to do so. As the others were busy giving the welcoming speech, Grassal slipped away to a safe distance, sending a message to the watching Luminants that he was going to check on the new arrival who'd been swept off his flow line.

Once away from their watchful gazes, he imagined two strings—left and right—that glimmered like long, dew-covered spiderwebs running through his thread and terminating at his thumbs. After a couple of test pulls, Grassal entered the following pattern:

LL LR RR LR LRLL LL LLLR L

He wasn't certain he'd remembered all of the Morse Code for "I am alive" correctly, but he felt pretty good about the "I am" part, which ought to be enough for anyone who might be listening. And he had to hope that someone was listening, because hope was all he had.

He wanted to enter more, there was so much he wanted to say, but a pack of Luminants led by Donald was approaching. Grassal released the strings and they faded away.

Grassal wanted to take a few steps back, to move away from the group, as something in his Luminant-mind warned him that their coloration meant trouble, but something else told him that backing down wouldn't get him very far. Instead, he increased his size, forming the outside of his body into a rigid sphere. He was going for something between the firewall he'd used to keep out the thoughts of others, and the barrier he'd encountered outside the Observer. But instead of attacking him, they surrounded him, around, above, and below. Grassal pushed forward on a flow line through a gap. Three of the Luminants moved together and blocked him. Grassal tried a different path.

Again, blocked. They moved like a single organism. Grassal tried to push against them, and they pushed back with equal force.

Grassal said, "Let me leave."

They gave no reply.

"Well? These aren't the droids you're looking for." He formed an appendage and made his best approximation of a Jedi hand wave, but they remained still.

The force of another disturbance sent them all spinning and twisting. This one felt powerful, almost as powerful as Deshondra had been, and even from here Grassal knew he had to get away from this group. Tommy and the others might need his help. Plus, there would be plenty of remnants to collect. He tried a different tack.

"If you keep me here, I can't fulfill my contractual obligations."

To his surprise, ripples of purple flowed through several of the Luminants who surrounded him and they moved aside. It seemed he had discovered a magic phrase. Grassal raised the equivalent of a middle finger from a sense-hand created for this purpose, then rejoined his group. There, he found that the lost new arrival had made its way back, saving Grassal a trip out to look for him, which was a relief, because Grassal heard Tommy saying, "Steel yourselves, this one is strong."

The pillar of white fire was surrounded by a breathing darkness that consumed energy from the world around it, rending a hole in the fabric of the Otherspace that was soon filled with the consciousness of a human from their own world. The pillar shrank and condensed then there was only a single orb. Tommy, Grassal, Deshondra, Cody, and Suki approached cautiously. The new arrival pulsed an angry smattering of reds and yellows, along with colors that didn't exist in the normal human visible spectrum.

Cody and Deshondra volunteered for containment and so moved into an ear muff formation, one on either side of the new arrival. The new arrival puffed up, pushing them both away. Grassal was pretty sure he caught a wave of profanity from Deshondra, who recovered quickly.

Tommy was beside him. "Be ready to move in if they have any trouble."

Grassal gave him an affirmative response, then began to collect the remnants left by the disturbance.

"What are you doing?"

"Collecting remnants. I have a feeling that it's the stuff that's going to get us out of here."

"Now is not the time."

"Now is the time. Tommy, it's the way—"

Cody screamed. Grassal turned his attention to the new arrival, who had consumed a good part of Cody's body. Deshondra was partially wrapped around the new arrival, trying to pull it away, but not having much luck.

Without a word passing between them, Grassal and Tommy moved in to help. Tommy helped Deshondra pull, while Grassal forced himself like a wedge into the space where the new arrival ended and Cody began. Once driven between them, he puffed up his body. This action sent Cody spinning away. Two of the other humans in their group went to tend him.

With Cody safe, Grassal, Tommy, and Deshondra could focus their attention on this new arrival, who continued to emanate waves of rage and blind hatred. Grassal wrapped the new arrival in containment to give it time to acclimate and calm down. This, Grassal knew, would only solve their immediate problems.

For their longer-term problems, he was still just a little Dutch boy with his finger in the dam. They couldn't stop the flood, not like this. If the contract required them to prevent the death and suffering of humans and Luminants, then fulfilling that contract meant finding a way to get humans out of the Luminance and back to Earth. Whatever the Observer was, Grassal didn't want to see what happened when it woke up. But the more humans who arrived, strong and furious like this one, the more likely it was that the Observer would do just that.

Grassal contained the new arrival, started giving the welcoming speech, and tried his best to reassure this being who wanted to kill and eat him that everything would actually be okay. Yet, what he thought was that Tommy didn't have a plan for sending the humans home, and neither did anyone else.

Grassal didn't want the responsibility and he certainly didn't want another Admiral Hotel kind of situation, but he didn't see another way. He'd figured out the aperture on his own, and now that he'd picked up some accreted knowledge, he had a good understanding of how the relevant parts of the system worked. Not only that, but he had a theory that he could use the aperture to send people back while also severing their connection and freeing them from the affliction. He needed only to test his theory.

And, with a particularly difficult new arrival bucking and kicking against him, Grassal decided that he had the perfect test subject.

Grassal used the remnants he'd collected to grow an adapter. He started by situating a small sphere beneath the new arrival, who was alternatively trying to eat him and attempting to struggle free so it could eat someone else. Under his control, the sphere began to form into a torus. Grassal forced the base of the torus deep down into the fog below then, using his own thread as a stabilizer, caused an aperture to open at the top of the torus.

Grassal released the new arrival, grabbed a flow line, and positioned his body outside the torus. The torus closed around the new arrival. Thousands of silver threads snaked their way into the torus and toward the adapter, drawn like iron filings to the poles of a magnet. Each thread carried a story, a voice, a person, and each thread demanded to be allowed through his adapter. It was like being in a room with thousands of people demanding your undivided attention. Grassal shut each of them out and focused on the new arrival's thread. This focus caused him to perceive a vision of the new arrival—a man, mid-thirties —as he had been, playing with a couple of children on the shore. There was a woman with a camera standing nearby, a smile on her face.

He blocked out the vision, briefly turned his attention to the other threads, and realized that not all of them belonged to human minds. The emotions and thoughts contained within these threads were mostly inscrutable, but he recognized within them a common theme: all wished to return to the Luminance.

This recognition confirmed for Grassal that the subluminals were Luminants, and that his adapter was a two-way gate. Maybe not a perfect 1:1 translation, but close enough. As a test, Grassal allowed one of the subluminal threads to meld with the inside of the adapter. When it did, Grassal had control over the physical body where the thread terminated, and was given a vision of Earth through several alien organs of perception. The feeling was entirely too creepy, and he released the thread. But for just a little bit, he had control over a subluminal like it was his own inter-dimensional meat puppet.

Returning to the task at hand, Grassal willed the adapter to constrict the new arrival, whose body began to compress into its silver thread. Grassal squeezed the adapter again and pushed. Something—he wasn't sure what—pushed back, but Grassal persisted, pushing harder and harder until he felt his strength on the verge of giving out. Every part of his body strained and throbbed and quivered and he was about to let it all go, but then something gave and the new arrival's thread left the Luminance. Where his body had been was now only an inchoate cloud of particles, devoid of the energy of life.

He felt, in every part of his being, that the transfer had been a success and that the new arrival's consciousness had been returned from the Luminance to Earth. It just felt right, like in a game of hoops when you release that three-pointer from the top of the key that you just know is going to drop.

Grassal allowed himself a moment of celebration.

He'd done it.

Then his adapter began to shake, vibrating each of the thousands of other silver threads, new arrival and Luminant alike, that were inside. Some threads used the opportunity to force their way through the aperture, but scores of others— humans all—simply disappeared. Sensing that something had gone—and was still going—terribly wrong, Grassal evicted as many of the threads as he could, but when the adapter collapsed, a few threads were still inside. Grassal didn't need to see the disintegrating forms of three of the nearby new arrivals to know that their threads had been trapped inside during the collapse.

When the adapter disintegrated, his own body suddenly felt diminished and spent. The nearby new arrivals and Luminants flashed colors of confusion and fear.

Tommy floated up beside Grassal. "What have you done?"

"That wasn't—something went wrong, it wasn't supposed to happen like that. I couldn't have killed them all."

"That's what it looks like from here."

Deshondra approached. "Is a man who builds a road responsible for the drunk driver who crashes on it? Grassal's doing the right thing. I don't see you trying to send anybody back. Maybe this was a coincidence, something happened back in normal space, or something here. We don't know."

"What I do know is that Grassal has no idea what he's doing, and that it's dangerous," Tommy said.

"At least he's trying to fix this shit."

As Tommy and Deshondra bickered, the other new arrivals moved in close, as if they wanted to hear what was being said, or were simply afraid and wished to circle their metaphorical wagons against the Luminants who, up to this point, had remained on the periphery.

Grassal tried to collect himself. He was still processing what had happened, but it made him feel good to have Deshondra making his case for him.

"If we could keep trying to make contact—"

"Enough," Tommy said, his voice booming. He flashed a new shade of red and started to expand. Instinctively, Grassal backed away, reacting to a perceived threat. Tommy grew, his shape changing from an orb into something else, something towering. "No more messages, no more building—"

Tommy trailed off. It took a second for Grassal to see why. Donald and a large number of Luminants were advancing on them. Except they weren't moving as a group of individuals but as one cohesive unit consisting of at least thirty Luminants, like some kind of supra-entity.

From another direction came Filipe, who had joined with about ten other Luminants. They were closer, and would reach the humans well before Donald's group.

This was it, Grassal realized. He'd violated the terms of the contract. Grassal had made too much noise, and now they intended to kill the troublemaking humans.

But instead of subsuming them, Filipe's group flowed past them like water around rocks in a stream and headlong into Donald's supra-entity.

When he thought of battles, Grassal always imagined lots of yelling voices, anger and excitement and energy channeled into sound. But when Filipe's group hammered its mass into that of Donald's, the only sound was a great rumble, as if the long-sleeping gears of a giant machine beneath their feet were finally groaning to life.

21

They reached the docks off the southern coast just as the moon was beginning its journey across the night sky. There were plenty of boats, some large, meant for the ocean, and some long and narrow, intended for river travel. The lights strung along the docks and on the little beachfront bar gave everything a festive atmosphere, but there was no one about. Ross spent a few minutes going through the arcane rituals of mooring and securing the vessel, then they walked down the wooden planks of the dock, the smell of salt and fish and diesel fuel in the air.

At the beachfront bar, Ross called out in what sounded—to Amadeus' ears, anyway—like fluent Spanish. There was a response, then a young man emerged from the back of the bar. He eyed them both, and then the man said to Amadeus, in accented English, "You will do it? Make it stop?"

"Make what stop?"

To Amadeus, Ross said, "We'll discuss it later."

Ross and the man spoke a little further, then the man made a phone call and served them each a beer. Before Amadeus had finished his beer, a man in a wide-brimmed hat and loose white cotton shirt and khaki trousers arrived. Like the man at the bar, he had a mustache and a worried look about him. The man and Ross exchanged words and seemed to come to an agreement. Finally, Ross said to Amadeus, "This is Hector. He's going to take us up the river, but he's in a hurry. He says that something bad is coming from the north."

"*Vamanos*," Hector said, then led them out of the bar and into the night. Between the keening rainforest sounds, the humid air, and the weariness resulting from their journey, he felt like he was in some kind of hallucinatory dream, where stretching shadows held unimaginable secrets.

Hector led them to a long, narrow boat with a shade canopy. The strung-up party lights cast cheerful patterns of blue, red, and green down the boat's side. They boarded and the man started a gasoline motor, which Amadeus was pretty sure had been salvaged from a car. Hector pulled out of the dock and piloted them first onto the open water of the Atlantic, then up the coast a short way to where a river spilled into the ocean. They started up the river, and the smell changed from salt and fish and kelp to something else, something muskier and murkier.

They journeyed up the river in silence, with only the light of the moon to guide them. Though the boat had a light, the pilot didn't turn it on. Soon, the dark, the heat, the exhaustion, and the rocking of the boat worked in concert to lull Amadeus to sleep.

A hand shaking his shoulder woke him. Amadeus opened his eyes to see Ross staring down at him. Amadeus was panicked and confused, but then remembered the events that had led him here, what had happened to his friend, to his father, to the world, and all the memories brought him back to consciousness more than the strongest espresso could ever hope to.

"We're here," Ross said. He shook hands with Hector, who stepped back into his boat, pulled away from the dock, and started back down the river.

They followed a worn footpath, the way lit only by moonlight. In the distance, however, there was a white glow, and Amadeus guessed—correctly, he soon learned—that the glow's source was their destination, a large black building, all steel and glass, its shape that of a squat cylinder. Amadeus didn't see a single right angle anywhere. Ross walked to the building, put his hand over a scanner, and a pair of glass doors slid open. They stepped inside.

"We weren't expected until tomorrow," he said, "so there's no welcoming committee. But I suppose you'd like to check on your friends?"

Amadeus nodded. Ross handed him a flexscreen, which displayed a little blinking microphone logo.

"Just say their name to get their location."

Amadeus spoke Lilly's name, and the flexscreen rendered a map that displayed a point at a location in the northwest corner of the building.

"Given that it's about three in the morning," Ross said, "she's probably asleep."

"Grassal Delgado," Amadeus said. The flexscreen showed Grassal's location in a room on the east side of the building.

Knowing that Lilly and Grassal were safe and accounted for gave Amadeus a sense of peace he hadn't known for days. This emboldened him, and he said, "I want to see ... it."

"Are you sure? It's not going to be him, you have to understand. The analytical part is there, and some of the memories, but there were sections ... removed when we made the copy, and other changes since then."

Amadeus nodded, and Ross led him down the hall, past closed doors with no windows. Soon, they arrived at a door like any other.

"Do you have an interface preference?"

"Whatever you recommend."

"I don't recommend any of it, to be perfectly honest. I think you should just take my word that this is only an experimental research automaton that you have absolutely no connection with. But since you're insisting, I am just going to remind you that it is not human."

Ross opened the door and stepped inside, where there were rows and rows of server racks. There was a screen on the wall.

Across from the screen was a table, with two task chairs facing the screen. Ross entered a few commands on a phone he pulled from his pocket, then said, "Tommy, there's someone here to see you."

Several seconds passed. There was no response.

"Permissions override. Open a port in your firewall." Ross turned to Amadeus and winked. "It's a Unix system." Some fans began to whir, but there was no indication that anything had changed. "Actually, it's a cluster of several million of them, each a node in a physical backend for a generative emulation of a human consciousness."

"Those are illegal," Amadeus said.

"That depends on your jurisdiction ... unlike the demon gate plans you've got squirreled away, which are globally verboten. Last chance. Are you sure you want to talk to it?"

"Yes."

"It's not your dad, remember that. It's an AI trained on a base layer emulation of your dad's consciousness."

"I know."

"I'll be outside." Ross left the room. As soon as the door had shut, a voice came over the speakers, so familiar, but so different.

"Hello, son."

"You're not my father."

And just like that, Amadeus had talked to the dead.

AI Tommy said, "This is true. I am only an emulation. I don't have a son. And yet, I do. I think I lack the ... datasets to handle ... this kind of interaction. It is ... demanding for me. The last attempt to ... train my social models, I initiated video calls to colleagues. I looked like this."

A head with his dad's face appeared on the wall, the face framed by his long salt-and-pepper hair, the face looking young, fresh, and yet lifeless. Amadeus' shoulders tensed and he took a step back. The image disappeared.

"I did not ... comprehend recent events, and their reaction

broke my nascent social behavioral models. My function became ... erratic, and I was forced to prune certain ... emotional centers. For my own protection, I created the ... air gap, which prevents me from communicating with any networks beyond ... this facility, or even most individuals within it."

"You've built a prison for yourself," Amadeus said, shaking his head. "You actually agreed to this? When you were ... him?"

"Yes. The alternative was to cease my activities."

Amadeus found himself shaking his head, not wanting to process any of it, least of all the notion that a copy of his dad's mind was trapped in dozens of cubic meters of silicon and electricity.

"I have analyzed Roland Jessup's demand."

Amadeus crossed his arms over his chest. "What demand? I don't know anything about any demands from Jessup."

"You will. And when ... the time comes, my scenario models indicate ... that you should ... accept. The rifts threaten the ... foundations of life on this planet."

"What if I don't?"

"Models suggest a feedback loop ... resulting in a collapse of the systems which support life. Less than a month remains."

22

Lilly and Amadeus ate a breakfast of corn soup, warm tortillas, fried eggs, and fruit and basked in the afterglow of a busy morning in the bedroom that had started when he'd shown up at her door sometime before dawn. He hadn't spoken, hadn't needed to speak, because she understood, and that had been enough.

Sunlight filtered through the cafeteria's curved glass panels, through which could be seen a cleared section of lawn that led down to the river. Amadeus told her about encountering the AI emulation of his dad's consciousness, said it was like he'd just awakened from one bad dream into another. Lilly agreed the whole thing was profoundly creepy.

"I wouldn't want to go back in that room either," she said. When Amadeus said nothing more, Lilly told him about Grassal's twitchy thumbs. Amadeus' eyes lit up, and she loved him for the hope she saw.

"That's where I need to be," Amadeus said. He pushed back his chair as if to leave. "What if we miss something?"

"We've got cameras set up. Technology, remember?"

"But if he's really in there, shouldn't somebody be with him?"

"That's ... well, probably it won't hurt. But I've been talking to him. He knows he's not alone, and if he can think, and reason, then he'd understand that we can't sit by his bedside all day, every day. Right?"

"Fair enough."

"Besides, there's something else we really need to talk through," Lilly said.

"The Roland Jessup thing? The AI told me last night that it thinks I should accept ... but I don't really know ..."

Lilly produced a tablet from her bag—she'd brought one along just for this purpose—and showed Jessup's offer video to Amadeus. He blinked as he watched, shaking his head, as if refusing to accept what he was seeing.

"I talked to Ross this morning. He says his people are studying the white papers," she said.

"I need to think about this."

Lilly noticed a silhouette's reflection in the glass moving toward their table. She turned to see Dr. Kongsampong waving at her.

"Who's that?" Amadeus asked.

Lilly told him, then said, "Remember? The Suttani technique?"

Amadeus nodded, but she could tell he didn't remember, not really.

"He's a good man. And he's been watching Grassal, monitoring him and running tests, that sort of thing."

Dr. Kongsampong arrived at their table and extended his hand to Amadeus, who shook it and gave him a polite smile.

"There is something I think you both need to see," Dr. Kongsampong said.

They had finished their breakfast, so they followed Dr. Kongsampong to the clinic. On the way, they encountered Su Min. She and Amadeus embraced, and Lilly realized she was smiling. She tried to conceal it, though she didn't know why, and her efforts must've made her face look somewhat contorted, because Su Min gave her a perplexed look.

Then she understood. These people, all back together now, were her family, her home. She'd lost her father, the world was ending ... and yet she was happy. The only rational explanation for feeling so happy under the circumstances was that she was insane. But an insane person can't know they're insane. This thought caused an unbidden torrent of laughter to rise from her. Now both Amadeus and Su Min were staring at her. Lilly blinked back a tear, put a hand on Su Min's shoulder, and said, "It's all good. We'll talk later. Go get some breakfast."

Su Min looked even more confused, but still gave her a warm smile.

In the infirmary, Grassal floated in the same spot he had been, only now the cluster of monitoring instrumentation appeared to have become fruitful and multiplied, with new wires and diodes and tubes sprouting from points on his face, arms, and chest. Her gaze was drawn to the helmet-looking thing on his head, from which tumbled a bundle of cables that snaked from the helmet into a computer terminal nearby.

"Two hours ago," Dr. Kongsampong said, "Grassal's thumbs began to move, and one of our monitors notified me that there was a non-trivial amount of brainwave activity. But that's not all. Look at this pattern." He pulled up an EEG chart on his tablet. For most of it, there was a long, steady pattern, a rhythm. "This is Grassal's normal pattern, and it matches that of other afflicted people. As you can see, the waveforms are very diffuse, with a lower amplitude than typical delta waves. However, when his thumbs began to move, we saw this."

He showed them a new chart, and this one looked nothing like the other. Indeed, if the other showed the normal waves of a calm ocean, this was a tsunami.

"And now, the waves are still not back to where they had been," Dr. Kongsampong said, "though there is a decay factor that suggests they will be soon."

"What does this mean?" Amadeus said.

"It means that maybe your faith in your friend is not, um, what is the word ... misplaced. Grassal is not comatose, not in the standard definition, and this activity proves it. But more importantly, I have been pursuing a new line of research, thanks to the white paper that Roland Jessup released." Dr. Kongsampong pointed to the helmet on Grassal's head. "The white paper, and an analysis provided to me by Ross' analytics team, has given me an interesting avenue of research to pursue at the genetic level. This is not a cure, I do not want to offer false hope, but it could be a way to, um, help re-integrate Grassal's body and mind."

Lilly slipped an arm around Amadeus' waist and together they gazed down at their friend while Dr. Kongsampong and his nurses carried on with their work. A few minutes passed, then Amadeus said, "If it's okay with you, I'd like to sit with him for a while."

"Fine by me. I've got some things I'd like to think through."

Lilly stepped out of the clinic and into the cool hallways of The Donut. Through the exterior glass, she could see the steamy rainforest outside, and if she didn't know any better, she might think that they were safe, that this was simply a spartan vacation resort with an office-slash-research lab. It almost reminded her of home, excepting the inherent differences between a bunker and a glass house.

Because while being able to see outside had its benefits, it also felt that she was being watched. And given the nature of the place, she probably was. Yet, the thought of being cooped up in a dorm room was even less appealing. So, she walked, and mulled over the problem that had been bothering her.

She'd read through the white papers, and while a good deal of it was jargon, she was pretty sure that operating the Rift Mitigation System required the use of an afflicted person. That would mean that as long as there were rifts, you would need afflicted people. But in order to get afflicted, you needed rifts, or at least demon gates. A reverse chicken-and-egg problem, or— more likely, Lilly thought—a guaranteed stream of fat contracts generated from a never-ending and expensive war.

She'd walked three laps around The Donut when she encountered Ross. It was the first she'd seen him since they'd returned. He looked as if he was ready to give a speech, or appear as a panelist. He'd shaved, and gone was the wild, disheveled appearance he'd had when he, along with Su Min, had shown up to save their asses back at the mansion. If it hadn't been for Su Min's endorsement, it'd be difficult for Lilly to reconcile this man with the disjointed ravings of the prophet of doom he'd played on the television news circuit last year.

He smiled when he saw her and said, "You look troubled."

"Do I?" she said, not willing to give anything away, at least not yet.

"As if you were trying to make a difficult decision. Is there something on your mind, Miss Jones?"

"What gives you that idea?" Lilly asked. She was stalling, not wanting to engage, not really, but she couldn't exactly run away from him. "I'm thinking about Jessup's demand."

"We all are. All I want to know is ... do you think it would be worth it?"

"If it were anyone else, I'd give you a resounding yes. But ... that motherfucker needs to die. Of all the things he could've asked for ... legal immunity, shitloads of money, whatever, why Tommy's research?"

"Maybe it's personal. Maybe it's a control thing. Maybe he just wants to be thorough. Who knows? But I'll tell you this: we have to take him seriously. The white papers he provided are legit. Not just legit, but next-level stuff. After running an analysis of the white papers, along with the medical literature, our resident AI has provided Dr. Kongsampong with several interesting treatment options for Grassal."

"He told me. Dr. K called the AI your analytics team."

"It helps him sleep at night. He's not entirely comfortable with the notion of emulated consciousness. But that's beside the point, which is this: if circumstances were different, we'd probably figure it out just from the theory of operation that

Jessup provided. But time is not on our side, and Jessup knows it."

Lilly rubbed a hand against her temple. Trying to sort out Jessup's motives was starting to give her a headache. She said, "Him making an offer that requires at least some degree of trust to a person who has absolutely no reason to trust him is some next-level fucked up."

"To be honest, it's not a bad strategy. He gets what he wants, we get a Rift Mitigation System to hopefully reverse engineer, and he probably doesn't die."

"We need to work on that last part."

Ross smiled. "One thing at a time. You said that Amadeus would need to trust him. I disagree. We don't have to trust him, and we should proceed very cautiously. I'm with you on that. But the bigger question is, are you and Amadeus ready to let your friend and others like him be used as a signal relay?"

"The bigger question is not, 'should Amadeus give him the research?'"

"Correct. Because he should."

Lilly ran a hand through her hair. "I don't have an answer for that. That should be up to Grassal to decide, but it's not like he can speak for himself. So, there's a lot to think about."

"Yes there is, little sister, yes there is."

Ross made his hand into a fist and raised it in front of her, expectant. Lilly smiled and gave him a fist bump.

"We'll talk later. You know where to find me," he said before he turned and walked away, whistling tunelessly as he went. Lilly had no idea where to find him.

23

One day after his arrival at The Donut, Amadeus was carrying an overflowing storage bin containing computer components and peripherals down the hallway. Lilly walked beside him. A tangle of cables spilled out of the bin onto the ground. Amadeus nearly tripped on them. Lilly picked them up, put them back in the box, and said, "I still don't see why Dr. K wouldn't let you set up in the clinic. A video feed just isn't the same as actually being there."

"Yeah."

Lilly turned to him, eyebrows raised. "Well? What is it?"

Several seconds and one sigh later, Amadeus said, "I keep thinking about the emulator. The whole thing just weirds me out. I mean, I know he agreed to it, but still ... it's like he's trapped in there but programmed not to realize it. It's horrifying."

Lilly nodded in agreement and gave him a thin smile.

They reached an office that had been cleared out. Amadeus set the bin on the table with a sigh of relief. He started to unpack, and Lilly slipped an arm around his waist and kissed him on the cheek.

"Do you really need to do this now?" she asked.

"A lot of people a lot smarter than myself have made some improvements to the k-storm tracker, and I need to understand what they did. But in order to do that, I've got to get the monitoring system back up and running."

"Have fun with that, I'm going to take a nap."

One more kiss, and Amadeus returned to work. Half an hour later, he'd finally set everything up, and he breathed a sigh of relief as the computer went through its startup routine. Once everything was up and running, and one screen showed a video feed of Grassal, Amadeus logged into the JDSC chat client. Before Amadeus could even type out a sentence, Ed had messaged him:

Ed: Hey man glad to see you back on here, we were getting a little worried. So, you gonna do it?

AB: Glad I can relieve your worries.

Ed: Sorry, it's just that Jessup's demand is all anybody's talking about.

AB: Yeah.

Ed: Seriously. The first time we hear anything out of this guy for weeks, and it's a message—a demand—for you. Our analysts are saying that maybe we could use this to draw him out, figure out where he's hiding, then rain down holy hell on his location.

AB: Nice thought, but Jessup would take measures to prevent that.

Ed: You're probably right. Still, seems like a good way forward. Anyway, good luck ... we know you'll make the right decision. Keep us in mind when you do, and we'll send whatever you need.

The chat window closed and Amadeus returned to work. After pulling down the latest changes to the k-storm monitor, he ran the updated test suite against his ruleset, verified that all his license keys for satellite imaging and remote sensing feeds still worked, and loaded some training data into a shared network directory. That done, he started the k-storm monitoring system and set a watch on a couple of low-magnitude systems about a thousand kilometers north. Finally, he downloaded every reverse path finding package he could find. With this done, he started down the hall toward the AI lab, intending to ask it to model some scenarios for him. Yet, outside the door to the AI lab, he hesitated, unable to bring himself to go inside.

Five minutes later, he found himself knocking on the door to the room he and Lilly shared. She lay sprawled out on the bed, a pillow over her head. She removed the pillow, sat up, and smiled when he entered the room. He leaned over to her, kissed her on the cheek, and brushed back a stray strand of hair that had fallen across her face.

"You look like someone who's putting off something difficult," she said.

"I could say the same thing about you." Amadeus sat down on the bed beside her. She laid her head on his shoulder. "I guess we've both got a lot on our minds."

"The end of the world will do that." Lilly turned her face to his. "You know, when I thought you ... you know, with my dad, that was just awful of me. But you believed in me anyway, and you went and did what had to be done, no matter what. I wanted to tell you that I appreciate it."

"Thanks, that means a lot. But right now, I can't help but think that making this deal with Jessup is the only way to stop the rifts."

"What if it's not, and Jessup still gets what he wants?"

"But why? Why go to all this trouble just to get me to give him my dad's research?"

"Jessup's B-gates kind of sucked, there are some reports saying that Securaux lost a lot of personnel when his B-gates failed to shut down."

"Like they were deliberately sabotaged."

"Which could explain why he wants the good stuff, or at least what he thinks is the good stuff."

"If the idea is to manufacture an enemy, and then issue invoices for cleaning up and destroying said enemies, then of course you'd want a more reliable B-gate, if only to minimize your own losses."

"Maybe so. Ed said something about drawing him out," Amadeus said. "But I need to run some modeling scenarios. Will you come somewhere with me?"

They started walking down the hall toward the AI lab. Along the way, they passed Eva, who was lounging on a bench and reading a paperback novel. She acknowledged them with a nod as they passed. At the door to the lab, Amadeus' hand shook, but he turned the knob, stepped inside, and initiated the emulator's interface startup routine. He opted to run it in full graphical mode. Soon, his father's face appeared on the screen, and Amadeus felt a knot form in his stomach.

"How can I assist you?" AI Tommy said.

Lilly squeezed Amadeus' hand. He could do this. He had to do this.

"I need help making a decision. You said I should give Roland Jessup what he wants. Why?"

"My analysis of both the technical details and the video evidence ... indicate with a high degree of certainty that the claim is legitimate. At this time, no other ... counter-measures exist for k-storm mitigation."

"What is the downside?"

"Based on what I know about the contents of the research archive, Jessup's acquisition will ... accelerate his research programs. Also, there is a high probability that after you provide him with the research you will be murdered as a matter of course."

Amadeus felt something sink in his stomach, and for the first time since he stepped into this room, it wasn't due to his revulsion toward the emulation of his father's face on the screen. Lilly still held onto his hand, and her grip was comforting and reassuring.

"There are some scenarios ... that reduce but do not eliminate ... your personal risk. I will model several scenarios. What are the inputs?"

Amadeus told the emulator everything he thought that might be relevant, and was in the midst of explaining why he'd downloaded the reverse pathfinding packages when the door opened.

"What is that?" Eva said, pointing to the screen. Like a child retreating from an accusatory finger, the visual emulation disappeared, leaving the screen dark.

"If there's something on your mind," Lilly said, "we can discuss it later. But right now, we're kind of in the middle of something."

"I see that," Eva said, taking a step back. The corners of her mouth were turned down in something like disgust. Her gaze flicked from Amadeus to Lilly as she backed out of the room.

Once she had left, Amadeus and Lilly spent another hour with the emulator, modeling scenarios, analyzing the risks and probabilities for each of the options, and generally trying to find a way to minimize the damage from doing what they all knew he needed to do.

24

In the evening one week later, Lilly, Amadeus, Ross, and Dr. Kongsampong stood on The Donut's pavilion, which overlooked lush, manicured lawns. Lilly glanced at the path beyond the clearing and mentally re-traced her steps along it through the jungle. The sun had begun to set, the sky was awash in burnt orange and sienna and the feel of the thick air had changed from something less like a sauna to more like a bathroom after a hot shower.

"We have something in mind," Amadeus said, "and I'd like to hear your thoughts on it."

Ross retrieved beers from a thick white cooler and handed them out to everyone except Dr. Kongsampong, who declined with a shake of his head. Once the beers had been distributed, Ross said, "Before you commit to any course of action, I want to share something with you, a working theory of the affliction. The researchers here are convinced that the nature of the affliction appears to be a consciousness dislocation problem caused by subluminal proteins binding to human DNA, which results in unusual patterns of gene expressions. Unfortunately, testing this hypothesis is ... technically and ethically complicated. We have so many people who need help, but they can't consent to any trials, we can't do anything more invasive than attempt to make consciousness copies, and—"

"You mean you're trying to copy consciousnesses of afflicted people? That's illegal and profoundly unethical," Lilly said.

Ross took the interruption in stride. "The first one depends on your jurisdiction. Why do you think we're holed up in the Mexican boonies? As for the second, we did have one test subject who gave consent before she ... well ..." Ross ran a hand through his hair and squinted against the sunset. "But it's a moot point. There's nothing to copy. The lights are on, sort of, but there's nobody home. Their bodies are healthy—all the autonomic systems are firing—but the very thing that makes a person a person, that's gone. However ..."

Some forest creature screeched not far away, and the evening wind blew, carrying the heady scent of flowers and decay.

"Suppose that a body and a consciousness are like opposite poles of a magnet. In the vast majority of human lives, the body and the consciousness will stay together until the body's death. However, during life, when the strength of the attractive force is weakened, for example as a result of subluminal proteins causing genetic expressions which create an entanglement with the origin dimension, the consciousness becomes untethered, simultaneously repelled by and attracted to the dimension from which the infection originated. We believe that we can ... achieve at least partial re-integration."

"You mean you have a cure for affliction?" Lilly said. "That's what Dr. K has working on?"

Ross gave a satisfied smile and nodded to Dr. Kongsampong, who stepped forward and put both his hands in front of him. "Maybe 'cure' is overstating things, Miss Jones, but we do have an experimental device—"

"Tell them the name," Ross said.

"I refuse to call it by that stupid name," Dr. Kongsampong said.

"The Headpiece of Destiny," Ross said.

Both Amadeus and Lilly said, "That's a stupid name."

"Never mind the name, the function is what is important. As

Mr. Ross said, when the subluminal DNA-binding proteins interact with human DNA, the polarity of the consciousness is reversed, to use his metaphor ... but to use the device, even to attempt simple communication, some necessary and sufficient conditions must be in place."

Amadeus narrowed his eyes and asked, "What kind of conditions?"

"Before you ask," Ross said, "no, we will not be building a B-gate, it's just ... not in the cards. Technically, we probably could, but our hosts are already a bit nervous about what we're doing here. We don't need to anyway, since we've found that k-storms provide the necessary and sufficient conditions required to create a connection. You don't even have to be in a k-storm, but you do need to be close to one. Under such a condition, the Headpiece of Destiny should—in theory—reverse the polarity long enough to allow the consciousness to reunite with the body, at least for a short while. We don't know if the effect will be permanent."

"But why wait for a k-storm?" Lilly asked.

"I must strongly discourage any attempts to use the device when the known necessary and sufficient conditions are missing. The risk of increased suffering is too great," Dr. Kongsampong said.

"Easy, doc, nobody's saying we do that," Ross said. "They're just trying to understand."

Lilly and Amadeus exchanged a look, and she realized that Amadeus had picked up on the tension between these two as well. Lilly said, "What happened to your test subject?"

Dr. Kongsampong held Ross' gaze.

"We learned what the necessary and sufficient conditions were," Ross said.

"This whole setup, it sounds ... less than ideal," Amadeus said.

"Think of it like Ben Franklin going out in a storm with a kite and a key. It's the best we've got right now. So, what did you have in mind?"

Amadeus looked at Lilly, and she gave him what she hoped was an encouraging nod.

"We make Jessup a counter offer," Amadeus said. "We'll offer to give him the encrypted data in exchange for a Rift Mitigation System and someone who can operate it. Once our people verify the RMS works as expected, I'll provide the decryption keys to Jessup's operator, and everyone walks away happy."

Ross narrowed his eyes, his expression skeptical. "He'll never accept that."

"That's kind of the point," Lilly said.

"How so?"

Amadeus beamed like a kid at a science fair explaining things to the grown-ups. "When we send our counter offer, we'll include a little bit of bait in the form of geolocation metadata. It's safe to assume his people will analyze any communications we send to him. Knowing how Jessup operates, he'll probably send a team to check it out. And if the people he sends originate from wherever Jessup's hiding out, then we can employ reverse pathfinding techniques to remote sensing data to determine his location. I've got some people who could do some good work given that piece of information. And if he refuses, we make another counter offer. Whatever it takes to get a Rift Mitigation System."

"There are lots of 'if's in that plan," Ross said.

Lilly took a sip from her beer and said, "The AI thinks this plan has the greatest probability of success."

"What happens if Jessup does accept?" Dr. Kongsampong asked.

"Then we get a Rift Mitigation System and he gets the research data," Amadeus said. "It's not ideal, but we'll still have a shot at using reverse pathfinding to identify his location, and there's also the possibility for employing steganographic techniques to embed a little something in the research data that's able to phone home."

"Not bad, not bad," Ross said. "It sounds like you'll need some logistical support from my people."

"I was counting on it," Amadeus said. "In exchange, I'll allow you to copy the research data."

"It is risky," Dr. Kongsampong said, "but I believe I see the merits."

"One way or another," Lilly said, "getting a Rift Mitigation System is our main goal."

"What if you need to meet in person? How are you going to assure your personal safety?" Dr. Kongsampong asked.

"Ideally, we'd use defense drones for any exchanges, but if that's not possible, I have one last piece of insurance." Amadeus tapped a finger against his temple. "There's only one encryption key, and it's right here. If I die, he loses."

"If this is what you really want to do," Ross said, "we'd better test some things first."

25

The next morning, Ross had a Tivooki technician dispatch a drone ship to an origin point somewhere in the Atlantic Ocean, the exact location unknown to Amadeus. In the time leading up to the test, Amadeus implemented and refined a suite of reverse pathfinding algorithms.

Once Amadeus was ready, Ross sent the instruction for the drone ship to make an approach to a small, uninhabited island a few hundred kilometers off the coast of Venezuela. They were still operating under the assumption that Jessup had a location somewhere in the Atlantic, and that he or his people would be able to reach the island within about twenty-four hours, though realistically they would need to plan on being able to analyze about forty-eight hours worth of remote sensing data for most of the Western Hemisphere.

Amadeus took a short break every hour as he waited for the ship to make its approach. During his breaks, he would first make the trip to the dining hall for coffee, and then to the infirmary to sit with Grassal for a few minutes. Each time, Amadeus shared his progress with his afflicted friend, but he couldn't shake the feeling that his words were falling upon ears that couldn't hear.

Six hours into the test, an alert fired for another k-storm, a few hundred kilometers to the west, somewhere in the Mexican state of Guerrero. That put them up to five systems within a thousand kilometers, plus the two that had developed into full-blown rifts before dissipating. Amadeus tried not to think of the destruction each one had caused, though it was hard not to, especially when they were—relatively speaking—right next door.

During a break seven hours into the test, sitting beside Grassal, he noticed that the air felt like it did just before a summer storm, where low-pressure air crackles with electricity and the sky seems about to burst. He didn't think much of it, instead attributing it to his own anticipation, but after he'd caught Grassal up on what was happening, Grassal's thumbs started moving again.

To Dr. Kongsampong, he said, "When was the last time this happened?"

"It has been a couple of days now, I think."

"You've been recording him, right? All I have is a live feed."

Dr. Kongsampong nodded.

"Can you send the recordings over to me?"

"You can view them on the network. I'll make sure you have access, then you can look at them yourself."

"Thanks," Amadeus said. He stood to leave the room, but just before he went, he noticed a shimmering spider web that floated out of Grassal's head out and up into the ceiling. Amadeus tried to dust the spider web away, but his hand passed right through it. He tried again and felt nothing but air.

"You see this?" he asked Dr. Kongsampong, who squinted, tilted his head a little bit to the side, then removed his glasses.

The doctor smiled. "Very interesting. We'll run some tests."

"Also, it's not exactly the same, but the last time we saw this from Grassal, there was a k-storm not far away."

"I'll keep that in mind."

Later in the day, Amadeus heard a knock at the door, then Su Min peeped her head in. Amadeus waved her in and stood up from his chair.

"Max has called an emergency all-hands meeting," she said. "Ten minutes from now."

"What for?" he asked, but he thought he knew.

"The k-storms, your offer, everything."

Su Min pursed her lips and she looked like she was thinking through a problem. Finally, she asked, "What happens if the Rift Mitigation System has its own side effects, just like the B-gates, and makes things worse?"

"Can things get much worse?"

Su Min looked down at her feet. "They can always get worse."

Amadeus' reverse pathfinding system began to beep. He checked the outputs, which were now reporting an origin point. He sent the origin point he'd found to the Tivooki technician, who confirmed the given location against the actual origin point. With the test run a success, he felt a little bit better about this part of their plan. Unless Jessup was in the Eastern Hemisphere, Amadeus was convinced that they'd be able to figure out where he came from.

"Come," Su Min said. "We must not be late."

Two minutes later, they walked into a small auditorium half-full of people Amadeus didn't know. He supposed they were the researchers and engineers Ross had been talking about.

He scanned the crowd and estimated that there were at least fifty people, with more still filing in, and the auditorium was big enough to hold about a hundred. Finally, he found Lilly, who sat at a table on the stage. She caught his eye and waved him up. Amadeus shook his head and considered making a dash for the nearest exit, but he let that thought pass. Instead, he pushed down the fear and strode up to the stage. Just before he was blinded by the stage lights, he scanned the crowd again, and saw Eva sitting near the back exit, her arms folded across her chest.

On the stage, three chairs were arranged behind a table, upon which was set a single notebook computer. Amadeus walked up to Lilly, who placed a reassuring hand on his shoulder. That, along with the stage lights that mostly blinded him to the eyes of the seated crowd, helped.

"I wasn't ready for this," Amadeus said.

"Would it make a difference if you were?" Lilly asked.

"I guess not. Is my fly zipped?"

She looked down and smiled. "You're good, but ... would it make a difference if it wasn't?"

Now it was Amadeus' turn to smile, but he checked anyway.

After a few minutes, Ross came out onto the stage to ... nothing. In a setting like this, Amadeus would've expected something besides the heavy silence. As it was, the whole thing had begun to take on more of a courtroom feel. He wondered if he was jury or judged.

"Hello," Ross began, "and thank you for taking time out of your schedules to help us settle on our next course of action. You've all received the briefing, so you know the details of the choices before us. Under normal circumstances, I would turn something like this over to our research acquisition team, but ... these are far from normal circumstances. Before we vote, I'd like to open the floor to questions."

"Vote?" Amadeus said to Lilly.

She nodded in acknowledgement, then turned her gaze back to Ross.

"The choice before us," Ross said, "is to make a deal with a devil, and we can't know that Jessup is acting in good faith. However, the technical details from the white paper have advanced our cognitive interface research program to a point where communication with the afflicted, maybe even re-integration, appears possible. As far as a good faith gesture goes, it's hard to find fault with this.

"Supposing Mr. Brunmeier agrees to an exchange and the best-case scenario plays out, we could come into possession of a mechanism capable of stopping rifts. Our engineering team believes they can reverse-engineer such a device. Any findings will, of course, be open-sourced. The shareholders might complain, but this will generate good will toward Tivooki for a generation.

"Finally, this action will also assist our guests in identifying the location of an international terrorist, and providing that location to people capable of dealing with such an individual. But before we get on the party bus, I want confirmation that this is the right course, because there are many ways that this could go wrong. In the worst-case scenario, Tivooki gets nothing, these two—" he pointed at Lilly and Amadeus—"are murdered, and our present location is revealed to some very bad people. Based on our analysis, the risk of a worst-case scenario is low, but non-zero. You all know our capabilities, so please take that into consideration. Now, I'll open the floor to questions and comments."

"This is a terrible idea," a voice said. Amadeus realized the voice belonged to Eva. "Anything you give to Roland Jessup will help him further his own ends ... if you give him the research, you become complicit, you become a collaborator. Is that what you want?"

"We'll take that into consideration," Ross said. "But if the Rift Mitigation System does what it's supposed to do, then this could prevent a lot of suffering."

"And what if it doesn't? What if this causes even more side effects?" Eva asked.

No one on stage had an immediate answer.

"What does the emulator say?" asked another woman's voice. She was close to the front, but Amadeus couldn't see her face for the stage lights.

"Let's ask it," Ross said. He bent over the notebook computer, typed something, and then heard his father's simulated voice booming over the PA.

"The provided technical documents do lay out a sound operational theory for the Rift Mitigation System. However, there are ... many unanswered questions and a moderate degree of uncertainty regarding ... the technical feasibility of such a device. The largest area of uncertainty lies ... in the mechanism of interaction between a rift and an afflicted individual. At this time, the link and the underlying mitigation mechanism ... are not fully understood."

"So that's a maybe," the woman said, garnering a few hushed chuckles.

For some reason, this put Amadeus at ease.

"Next question," Ross said.

And so it began, and the questions continued for the next hour and a half. Amadeus zoned out somewhere along the way. It started when he thought about a joke his father used to tell: arguing with an engineer is like wrestling in the mud with a pig. After a while, you realize the pig likes it.

Finally, when no more questions came, Ross called for a vote. Everyone in the room pulled a phone from their pocket and selected from the available choices, which were "yes," "no," and "yes with conditions." After five minutes the votes had been cast. Most were "yes with conditions."

This vote kicked off another round of discussions. Three hours in, Amadeus stepped away to relieve himself. Afterward, for no reason he could articulate, he decided to step into the AI lab. Tommy's voice came over the speaker.

"I have conducted further analysis. There is a low-to-moderate probability of your personal survival in eight out of ten scenarios I've analyzed," the emulator said. "Outcomes for the other two scenarios are worse."

"Thanks for the encouragement," Amadeus said.

Before he opened the door to leave, the voice said, "Should events trend ... toward a negative terminal outcome, deletion of all instances of this emulation would be a prudent decision."

"You want me to kill you?"

"Yes. Maximilian Ross may disagree, and I am incapable of deleting myself. For this reason, I have granted you access to delete all instances of this emulation. I'm ... sorry to burden you with this."

Amadeus felt sick as he stepped out of the room. He craved a distraction so, for the first time in several hours, he checked the phone in his pocket. There were over ten missed alerts. His rift monitoring system was going apoplectic, and the phone given to him by Ross had been in silent mode.

A k-storm was presently less than a hundred kilometers away. The k-storm had been remarkably resilient, having started seven days ago, nearly two hundred and fifty kilometers to the northeast. He initiated an analysis. Two minutes later, the analysis indicated that based on its present course, the k-storm would pass over this location in about twenty-four hours, with a sixty percent probability of developing into a full rift. One full-blown k-storm was bad enough, but with those odds ...

He forwarded the analysis to Ross then stopped by the cafeteria to pick up a bottle of water for Lilly. When he returned to the auditorium, the room was silent. Each face—the ones he could see through the lights, anyway—tracked him as he walked in from the wings and back to his seat at the table. Lilly inclined her head in thanks for the water bottle.

To Amadeus, Ross said, "I've shared the results of your analysis with everyone here. Is there anything that you want to add?"

"No," Amadeus said. "I think the data speaks for itself. I wish it was wrong, but so far my models have shown themselves to be brutally accurate."

"Then that settles it. We'll go with what we've got. As much as I think all of us would like to spend more time refining this plan, right now the perfect is the enemy of the good. People, I need you to follow the standard protocol for a contingency plan F event. Amadeus, Lilly, let's make this happen. Come with me."

As they followed Ross off the stage, Amadeus noticed that Eva had already left the auditorium.

They entered a small room, where a trim technician in his thirties gave them a harried nod, then returned his attention to setting up a makeshift studio. Ten minutes later, Amadeus sat at a table before a camera and recorded his counteroffer. Once that was done, Ross had the technician inject the fake geolocation metadata into the video.

"Last chance," Ross said. "Once this goes out, there's no turning back."

Amadeus caught Lilly's gaze. She gave him a nod.

"Do it," he said.

The technician tapped a few keys on a console then looked up and said, "The message is out." When the technician looked back down at the screen, he scratched the side of his shaved head. "There's something weird going on with the network. Hold on." A few more keystrokes later he said, "Someone used a public mail relay to send a message to what looks like … a .mil mail server in Texas."

"There shouldn't be any outgoing mail traffic," Ross said.

"Well, there was … and the logs show it's not the first one. I see at least three more. Whoever sent it figured out how to bypass our security rules. The message is cleartext, too, so they don't care who knows it. Here." He pointed to the screen.

Ross leaned over the technician's shoulder and read aloud. "They intend to collaborate with Roland Jessup. It's dangerous to send this, but I can't sit back while they do. If you need additional justification for action, cite illegal kipium research and unauthorized weaponized AI. Finally, I strongly urge leadership to reconsider their tactics. Communication and treatment for the subluminal infection may be possible. Please forward to all Bearer lists."

He paused, then turned to Amadeus and Lilly and said, "We have a problem."

Interlude

Manuel and the administrator each sat in a comfortable leather chair in the administrator's office. Both had started this conversation with a glass of bourbon. Now, the administrator's glass was drained, while Manuel hadn't even taken the first sip of his. The administrator had put the doll in a storage compartment for this meeting. The administrator knew, deep in his heart, that keeping the doll, all that was left of his precious Kaylee, was a weakness, but everyone had their vices. Even now, he wished that its comforting weight was pressing against his side, but in this early stage of a friendship, he thought it better to keep his cards close to his chest.

"Assuming they accept, there's no good way to do this and cover the probable contingencies," Manuel said.

"They're kids. Sure, they're in their twenties, but as far as I'm concerned, they're stupid, inexperienced children. And we hold all the toys."

"That may be true ... but you've underestimated them before, they appear to have help, and we don't know what the physicist left in his latest research."

"Unlikely," the administrator said, but he allowed his voice to reveal just a hint of doubt.

"Listen, Roland, I may not be Marshall Hathaway, but I'm your chief of security, and my opinion should count for something. You can't base a strategy on the hope that your opponent will do something stupid."

"Opponent? Maybe you've misunderstood. If they accept our offer, then they won't be our opponent, but our ... well, partner isn't the right word. Customer? Associate? What do you call the other party in a mutually beneficial transaction?"

"Stakeholder?"

"Doesn't quite ring true, but close enough. Whatever we call them, we should press our advantage," the administrator said.

"Advantage? We lost over three-fourths of our operational capacity during that unfortunate shit show in DC. Those men are off the board, and our remaining human resources are ... thin. There is no advantage. We're going to make good on this deal, let them market our services for us, and we're going to regroup and rebuild. That's the plan, and we should stick to it."

"Helmuth von Moltke said 'no battle plan survives first contact with the enemy.'"

"You just said they weren't—"

There was a knock at the door.

"Come in," the administrator said.

Davenport opened the door and, like some prey animal, surveyed the room with wary eyes before stepping inside. The man should've been minding the cooling system, but with them so short on personnel, everyone had to pull double duty. Still, despite his wariness, he wore a kind of satisfied expression on his face. "They've accepted," he said.

"See, Manny? Just like we expected. They don't have shit." Jessup said, then reached over and slapped Manuel's knee. The big chief of security scrunched up his brow.

"And there's something else," Davenport said. "Two more somethings, actually."

The administrator said nothing, only raised one eyebrow and waited for Davenport to continue.

"The first is that, per your instructions, we intercepted—"

"Don't use 'per your' anything in a sentence, it makes you

sound like a middle manager with the intelligence of an aardvark."

"Um, okay. Right. Anywho, one of our monitoring systems picked up a mention of your name ... It references the agreement, and appears to be a message sent by a rogue member of Brunmeier's party. The sender is not happy that they accepted your offer, so they've asked for help from the Bearers of Burdens."

"Every good decision has its detractors."

"Unless the sender was completely desperate or in a hurry, that is some shitty operational security," Manuel said.

"Also, the sender thinks Brunmeier's people have a way to communicate with the afflicted," Davenport said.

"Well ruck me funning. If they can do that, then perhaps they can tell us how we can communicate with our afflicted physicist. Davenport, I want you to follow up on that. What was the other thing?"

Just before Davenport continued, the administrator noticed that the sides of Manuel's mouth were turned down as if he were deep in concentration.

"In the recording of their reply to our offer, we found some embedded geographic metadata," Davenport said.

"Interesting. What does that tell us?"

Davenport beamed like he was about to reveal a big secret to a small child. "It only tells us their exact location, or at least the location where they recorded their response. I looked it up myself. It's an uninhabited spot of malarial jungle in southern Mexico, on the Atlantic side."

"Why would they be in ..."

"Bullshit," Manuel said. Both the administrator and Davenport turned to the man, who was swirling the honey-colored bourbon around in his glass.

"Excuse me?" Davenport said. The man failed to hide the aggrieved tone from his voice.

"It is bullshit. Either the metadata, the cleartext message, or both. It smells like bait, a weak attempt to draw us out and reveal our location."

The administrator looked from Davenport to Manuel and back again. Manuel had a good point, but—as a man whose previous career accomplishments including killing two mayors and a governor—he was used to punching up. He didn't have the direct, operational experience that poor Marshall did with the idiot Brunmeier kid. Marshall had trained the man well, but maybe not well enough.

"If the son is anything like the father—and experience has shown he's only a pale imitation—then it's very likely that he overlooked the fact that most recording devices will include geographic metadata by default. Plus, he doesn't have the resources he had before. Marshall saw to that before his unfortunate exit."

"What about the Jones girl?" Manuel asked.

"She stared down one of our tanks, for goodness sake. She's got the biggest balls of them all. But still, she's not technical, so she wouldn't think to look for metadata."

"And the Bearer's message?" Davenport said, his voice tinged with hope.

"The Burden Bearers have killed people with the subluminal infection. Murdered them. In cold blood. That is one of their stated objectives. Kill the infected, stop the rifts. Their reasoning isn't terrible, and we're not exactly the Red Cross or anything, but that shit's just heartless. Since their friend Delgado happens to have the subluminal infection, I'm having a difficult time believing that Brunmeier would ask for their help. That'd be like ... I don't know, inviting a pack of hyenas to a christening. That reason alone is enough to suggest that the message wasn't intended for us."

"I don't like it," Manuel said. The administrator noticed that Manuel still hadn't touched his bourbon, was only using it like some kind of stage prop. Maybe the man was a teetotaler, but that would've shown up—and possibly disqualified him—during his pre-employment background investigation.

"You don't have to like it, man, but facts are facts," the administrator said. "This recent turn of events is a gift horse, and after examining the equine dentition before us, it looks to be a really fucking good horse. So we're going to back this horse. Manuel, mobilize everyone we have here who's capable of handling a gun without shooting their dick off. Two groups. Bravo group goes to the location we agreed to, Charlie to the location indicated by the metadata tags. Put the most competent shooters in Charlie. If we move fast, we can be there by tomorrow night. We'll decide exactly how to proceed when we know more. But I need to be clear in my instructions—don't kill Brunmeier or his friends, not unless I give an explicit order to do so. He's got something—two somethings, apparently—that we need."

Manuel picked up his bourbon and—finally—downed it in one gulp. "I'll make it happen."

"Good man. And, Davenport?"

"Sir?"

The administrator thought it would go without saying that Davenport wouldn't be going. Not only did he need to maintain and monitor the Rift Mitigation System while it was in standby mode, but he was squarely within the camp of those who were liable to shoot their dicks off. Still, the administrator wanted to make things perfectly clear, just to prevent any hurt feelings.

"Besides your usual duties, your role in this is to make sure that nobody feeds Big Ugly while we're gone. I want it good and hungry by the time we get back."

26

Filipe and his group slammed into Donald's supra-entity like buckshot. Electric arcs and waves of energy flew in all directions. Flow lines rippled and shook. Waves of vertigo washed over Grassal. Pinpoints of light flickered in the air around them like a plague of fireflies. Yet, despite Filipe's efforts, the fight was short. Donald's supra-entity consumed the Luminants individually, until only Filipe remained, then he too was consumed, his colors melding and disappearing into Donald.

Donald's supra-entity grew in size, unfurling like a sheet in the wind. The sheet began to speak with one voice, filling the space around them, enveloping them. The voice was not Donald's keening theremin warble, Filipe's shouted whisper, or that of any of the other Luminants with whom he'd communicated. The voice sounded like thunder when it said, "The presence of humans has grown intolerable."

Remnants lingered in the area from the last disturbance. Grassal sent out a message to the other humans. "Collect as many remnants as you can, we need them. We can't face this alone. You've got to help." Grassal considered just how they could help. He drew upon accreted knowledge and a notion that in order to oppose a supra-entity, he would need to become one. He shared this thought, along with the means of joining their bodies with his own, with any of the humans who were listening.

In response, Cody and Suki began guiding the other new arrivals to the remnants, and soon all were making preparations. Of all the humans, only Tommy seemed to hesitate.

"Help me," Grassal said. "For the living."

Tommy's color changed, as if he had come to a decision, then dozens of electric tentacle-like appendages shot out from his body in all directions and he began to collect remnants. Once that was done, his tentacles snaked out around the other humans and guided them together, each tentacle one of a team of sheepdogs guiding their flock to safety.

"Let's do this," Tommy said.

Grassal let down part of the firewall he'd created around himself, Tommy joined with him, and just like that he and Tommy were sharing the same mind.

"Up," Tommy said, and almost reflexively, Grassal caused a new torus to rise around himself, Tommy, and the other humans. Once that was up, Grassal deployed the firewall on the perimeter of the torus. The result was a radiant wall of light that encircled the humans in all directions. At first, Grassal struggled to maintain it all, then he felt Tommy helping, like an extra pallbearer sharing the load. Soon he found his rhythm and was able to hold the torus steady, sensing the environment both inside and outside the torus. The torus had become not some external tool, but an extension of himself.

Donald struck, its wet-sheet-form wrapping around the firewall's perimeter. Grassal tried to fling Donald off him, but the supra-entity held tight, leeching energy from the firewall that protected them all. Drawing on all his fear and rage and frustration, Grassal summoned a roar that sent a wave of raw kinetic energy through his rival.

Donald released. Tommy extended his electro-tentacles beyond the firewall and slapped Donald in such a way that their rival went spinning along a flow line, though not far. Using what he'd learned from Tommy's electro-tentacles, Grassal made his own appendages, eight electric arms that terminated in sixteen-fingered hands, excess energy leaking from the tip of each finger.

More Luminants, some singular, others smaller supra-entities, moved toward them. All emitted colors and patterns that Grassal perceived as threat displays. Grassal raised his arms, four on either side of his center, and made a parting-of-the-sea gesture. The gesture emitted a wave of kinetic energy. The Luminants around them were flung away, leaving a clear path forward, but the Luminants recovered quickly and started moving in.

The energy Grassal had projected circled back to him like a well-thrown boomerang, and it carried bits of life energy that had previously belonged to the Luminants that surrounded him. That life energy was being pulled into Grassal's body. He was consuming them, just as he'd done when he'd first arrived, only on a much, much larger scale. No, not just consuming them. He was incorporating them into himself and growing stronger for his trouble.

Grassal had become a dragon.

No, not become, he realized. He'd been one all along, he'd just never accepted it.

He'd never been more powerful, more full, more ... Grassal Javier Delgado.

And he knew that the best use of this power and fullness was to take responsibility for those who couldn't help themselves. Now, he decided, was the time to send these people home.

Re-routing energy from the inner wall of his torus, Grassal created an adapter. There was a jarring tear followed by a few seconds of chaotic shaking. A vision of blue and green revealed itself through an aperture and he was looking out at a green field. Earth green, not the electric greens of the Luminance. Dozens of shimmering silver threads snaked from the humans within his torus, through the opening, and down to the Earth beyond.

"Go," Grassal said. "I can only hold it for a little bit."

None of the new arrivals moved.

"It's too dangerous," one of the new arrivals said.

"You think staying here is safer?" Deshondra said. "I'll go, and if I make it, I'll do my damnedest to fix whatever's happening on that side."

"For you," Grassal said, then visualized channeling some of his gentler, lower-intensity energies toward her, extending them to her like an offering of food and drink. At first she was reluctant, but when she realized what he was doing, she accepted all that he offered to her. "Drink deeply."

The amount of energy he shared was deliberately small, because he was afraid it might overpower her, but when he saw that she had no trouble integrating it into her self, he increased the amount, and soon she was strong and full and appeared ready for anything.

"Do right by us, Grassal Delgado," Deshondra said, then compressed her form into a silver thread—her silver thread, Grassal somehow knew—and flung herself through the aperture and out of the Luminance. Grassal watched and tried to see what had become of her, but he could only see his own thread—still carrying the two strings—and the silver threads of others, some of whom were now trying to meld their own threads with their Luminant bodies as Deshondra had done.

Something shifted in the world around them. Grassal felt it just before he saw the thousands of tendrils of multi-colored light that snaked up from the fog and slapped against the exterior of his form. The tendrils rose around him, probing, seeking the optimum point to insert themselves. His firewall was strong, though, and after failing to find a way in, the tendrils began to encircle his body. Soon it was like his entire body had been wrapped up in a ball of yarn. Except that the yarn kept growing tighter and tighter. He felt all the new parts of him, everything he'd gained, slipping away as tendrils squeezed tighter and tighter.

Grassal fought to keep the torus stable, but he felt choked and constricted. Acting on instinct, he evicted all the silver threads just before the aperture closed, the adapter collapsed, and he lost their connection to Earth.

"On three, get them the hell away," Grassal said to Tommy, indicating the other humans within his torus. He started the countdown. On one, he created an egress point. The humans within him understood, and with Tommy's help, they began to stream out of him, darting away on flow lines.

"Godspeed," Tommy said, just before he shepherded the last of the humans to relative safety.

A second later, a wrenching jerk shook Grassal to his core. The energy he'd collected began to vent off like steam, and Grassal faded until he was nothing but the simple orb he'd been when he arrived. The energy he'd collected, all those Luminant lives he'd consumed ... gone. He tried to shore up his firewall, but the strength wasn't there.

He felt something pulling on his thread, dragging him down. He tried to shake free, but the downward force increased and soon he was pulled through the fog and into the earth. The deeper he went, the more he was thrown hither and thither, a feather in a hurricane, his form too diminished to resist. Then, almost as suddenly as it had started, his descent stopped. The utter black of complete nothingness surrounded him, while something like sleep paralysis settled over him. Minutes turned into hours and the hours dragged on, one after the other, time stretching out in the blackness. Like an insect encased in amber, he was frozen fast, buried beneath the earth.

Yet, the strings he'd created within his thread remained. For a long while, being unable to control his body, he was unable to pull the strings, but the passage of time caused some of his strength to return to him. Eventually, after many days had passed, the sleep paralysis lifted just enough so that he could move one string. The movement felt good, but it left him weak, so he rested until he'd regained enough strength to pull the other. As soon as he felt able, he worked both strings in order to send the following message to whoever might be listening: "help me." Entering this message left him so tired and drained that, despite his best efforts, he fell unconscious from fatigue.

27

Lilly watched two men stride toward Eva, who sat in the cafeteria. Even from across the room, Lilly could smell the vanilla from the clouds of vaporized nicotine that Eva blew into the air as she watched the men approach. She seemed to welcome what was happening. When the two men reached her, one of them said something Lilly couldn't quite pick out. Eva placed her vaporizer on the table and extended her hands to them. One of the men applied plastic handcuffs to her wrists and led her away.

"Our location is compromised, thanks to her," Ross said. Lilly started. She hadn't noticed that the man had been standing beside her. "It was a mistake bringing her here, but it's my fault, and no one else's. I should've left her in Richmond. Inflexible people are dangerous. Now I just have to figure out what to do with her."

"Don't we have better things to be doing?" Lilly asked. "Preparing to leave, maybe?"

"Leave?" Ross asked, a look of genuine puzzlement on his face. "I guess you can if you want to, but we're all staying right here. Contingency plan F isn't an evacuation order."

"But why stay? Can't you just, you know, copy the data somewhere else?"

"We've got redundancy but, frankly, some of the work is

either too brittle, intricate, or illegal to do anywhere else but here. We'll only evacuate if things progress beyond hopeless. You know what would happen if Jessup's people got in here and figured out what we're working on? Bad things ... very bad things. I've got a hundred defense drones, each one programmed to counter acts of aggression against any person authorized to be in The Donut. Those, plus ten professional security people, along with everyone else—all eighty-eight of them—who have at least some basic weapons training. You don't work with this stuff without at least a little shit-hits-the-fan planning."

Motion beyond the glass walls of The Donut caught her attention. Outside, some of the defense drones—murderbots, of a similar model used by the JDSC—that Ross had mentioned patrolled the perimeter. That was one way to defend a glass house. Their movements were precise and rhythmic, almost to the point of being twitchy, but each twitch was intentional and deliberate, a result of its programming. Further, Lilly thought, they moved in patterns, and those patterns occurred as a result of encoded instructions. The movement of Grassal's thumbs also moved in—what seemed to her—deliberate patterns, as if someone was trying to encode information ...

"There's something I need to check on," Lilly said, then strode down the hall and into the clinic. There, Amadeus sat at a chair, elbows on his knees, hands folded before him. Dr. Kongsampong had one hand on his chin as he watched Grassal, whose thumbs were currently twitching in what now seemed to her a deliberate pattern.

"Amadeus," Lilly said. "Don't you think there's something oddly ... precise about the way his thumbs are moving?"

Amadeus arched his eyebrows in acknowledgement but didn't look up.

Lilly scanned the room, located a piece of paper and a pencil on a nearby work table, and started one of the clips they'd recorded of Grassal's thumbs moving. While watching, she

began to scratch down marks, L and R, in a series, with spaces
between each pause. After a couple minutes, she had several
lines. She handed the paper to Amadeus.

"See anything now?" Lilly said. The sequence of characters
repeated, and the same pattern occurred again and again:

LLLL L LRLL LRRL RR L

Their eyes met, and Lilly watched as understanding spread
across his face. "That's almost like ... Morse code. One summer,
we were twelve or thirteen, we learned Morse code and built a
pair of wireless Morse code transmitters ... I'd completely
forgotten about that. But I can't decode this."

"That's what the internet's for," Lilly said. She logged in to a
terminal, pulled up a message converter, and entered the
message. Amadeus leaned over her shoulder to watch. Lilly hit
enter and read the decoded message:

H E L P M E

Despite the message, Lilly had to suppress a smile, because
all this time Grassal had been trying to communicate with
them, they'd thought it was muscle spasms, and she'd figured it
out. In hindsight, it seemed so obvious. Of course Grassal would
send messages if he had the ability to do so, and on a channel
with limited bandwidth, of course he would encode them.
Amadeus' face was red, though with excitement,
embarrassment, or terror, Lilly couldn't be sure. She knew that
for Amadeus, these things often overlapped.

"Nicely done," Amadeus said. "How do we help him?"

"Let's see what else he's been trying to tell us, then maybe we
can begin to answer that question."

Together, Lilly and Amadeus reviewed the footage of
Grassal. When they detected motion, Amadeus slowed the
footage and Lilly marked down the patterns. They found that

each message looped for a while, as if being sent repeatedly until someone acknowledged it. Soon, they had several distinct messages. Once they removed the duplicates, the deciphered messages read:

THIS IS GRASSAL. I AM ALIVE. TOMMY IS WITH ME. HIS BODY IS WITH R JESSUP. WE ARE IN AN OTHER SPACE. MORE ARE ARRIVING. WE ARE OPPOSED.

When Amadeus spoke, mostly to himself, his voice was a choked whisper. "My dad is alive. Afflicted, but alive."

Dr. Kongsampong said, "There are reports that more and more afflicted are becoming like your friend, and apparently your father. I think it is safe to assume that they also have entered into what your friend called 'other space.'"

"What should we do?" Amadeus said.

Lilly glanced around the room. Everyone was looking at her as if she had all the answers, so she said, "We tell him we're listening. Amadeus?"

Amadeus entered their message into the Morse code convertor then read off the pattern. As he did so, she pulled each of Grassal's thumbs, entering the following message:

WE HEAR YOU

There was no reply. They tried again. Nothing. A minute passed, then another, and soon an hour had passed. But even though she and Amadeus and the nurses all entered the pattern every fifteen minutes, the night grew late, and just like their counteroffer to Roland Jessup, they received no response save silence.

In the pre-dawn light of the following morning, Lilly opened her eyes long enough to see Amadeus climbing out of the bed they shared. A couple of hours later, when she rose from sleep and padded down the hall, she found him in the clinic. He looked up at her and shook his head, his expression almost despondent, despite the recent good news about his father.

"Maybe we're doing something wrong, or maybe there's something we're not considering," Amadeus said.

She noticed but didn't comment on the way he danced around the implications of Grassal's last message. She couldn't really blame him. To come this far, to be so close, only to come up with nothing, would leave all but the most blindly optimistic souls disheartened.

"I'll take over," she said. "Go get yourself some breakfast."

He stepped out of the room and she entered the same message they'd been trying to send last night. No response came, so she tried again, but still nothing. Amadeus returned fifteen minutes later carrying trays laden with boiled eggs, tortillas, coffee, and fruit for both of them. Thus fortified, they continued sending the message throughout the morning.

Around noon, Grassal's thumbs began to twitch. Lilly marked down the pattern and Amadeus deciphered the message, which read:

FIRST CLASS

"That's him," Amadeus said. "He can hear us." A cheer went up around the room, but was immediately drowned out by the blaring of an alarm.

Dr. Kongsampong tapped something onto a tablet then scowled, as if trying to unpack some incomprehensible idiom. He read, "A rift has formed from a k-storm, which has developed in this area. The k-storm is at least forty kilometers in diameter."

The alarm rose then fell, four times in a row, then Ross' voice boomed over the intercom: "Ladies and gentlemen, we are now on contingency plan F, variation four. This could be worse than we anticipated. If anyone wants to leave, no one will blame you."

"What is variation four?" Lilly asked.

Dr. Kongsampong shook his head. "Four is a very, um, inauspicious number in some cultures. I think it is a poor attempt at dark humor. Variation four means that work here has come to an end. Save what you can and leave the rest, because there is a non-zero chance everything could be destroyed."

"The k-storm ... it's a necessary and sufficient condition, yes? Maybe the headpiece could help him somehow?"

"There are some risks associated with operating the headpiece, and under the circumstances we cannot attempt to completely re-integrate his body and mind," Dr. Kongsampong said. "But perhaps we can strengthen the connection between the two so that it is easier for him to communicate with us."

"No one here can give consent for that," Amadeus said.

Lilly, exasperated, said, "Why don't we just ask him?"

All three met eyes and nodded, then Amadeus began to encipher a message containing a broad overview of what the headpiece did, and how they thought it could help their communications. He handed the sequence to Lilly, and she started working Grassal's thumbs. The response came back immediately:

SURE WHY NOT

Once they had his consent, Dr. Kongsampong removed a black headpiece from a cabinet filled with several similar-looking devices. The female nurse removed a small black rectangle from a base station on the work table and carried it with both hands to Dr. Kongsampong, who placed the rectangle into a port on the headpiece.

Dr. Kongsampong entered some commands on a keyboard while the male nurse situated the headpiece on Grassal. "When the headpiece becomes operational, things could get a little ...

weird. Ready?"

Amadeus and Lilly nodded, and the doctor said something in Thai to his nurses. Dr. Kongsampong twisted a dial on the control panel on the wall, then the lights in the room flickered and dimmed. Lilly felt a wave of vertigo. From the look on Amadeus' face, she guessed he felt it too. Soon, Grassal began to glow, faint at first, then ribbons of light began to swirl and encircle him. Yet, even in the midst of the light, his face remained placid, serene, like someone experiencing a pleasant dream.

Lilly reached out for Amadeus, found his hand, and laced her fingers through his. Together, they watched the light grow brighter and brighter until a dazzling thread of light shot out of Grassal's body and through the ceiling.

The lights in the room flickered back on. Lilly looked around. Dr. Kongsampong watched with a professional's steady, slightly detached gaze. His voice was even and clipped as he responded to the nurses' reports on Grassal's status.

"Where is the nearest rift? What direction?" she asked Dr. Kongsampong.

"Northeast."

Lilly pulled Amadeus out into the hall. Beyond the glass wall of The Donut, they could see the thread of light that rose from Grassal, spiraling and twisting across the sky and toward the k-storm and northeast, toward the rift.

Their gazing was interrupted when Ross' voice said over the room-to-room intercom, "Amadeus, I've just got word about three fast-moving ships to the north. They're several hours away, but appear to be headed in this direction. My own people are monitoring their progress, but maybe this is what you were looking for."

"I'll check it out."

With a single glance toward Lilly, Amadeus started for the door. She knew he didn't want to leave her, but he did anyway, and she respected that. There were bigger factors at play here.

She just hoped he could pinpoint the location and send it out to the JDSC before things here went offline.

Lilly stepped back into the clinic. There Grassal's body strained, and veins on his forehead bulged. A sheen of perspiration had appeared on his forehead, and the corners of his mouth twitched. For the first time, he looked like he was experiencing discomfort.

"Is he okay?" Lilly asked.

"His heart rate and blood pressure are steady," the male nurse said.

The door opened, and Su Min appeared.

"Lilly, we need to talk," she said. "In the hallway."

They stepped out into the hallway. Su Min looked around, then said, "They are saying attackers will be here soon, but that the subluminals will be here before that. Mr. Ross has said that I should take the Pachyderm and leave, but I told him I will not abandon everyone. I could take you, Amadeus, and Grassal."

For the length of one heartbeat, maybe two, Lilly imagined taking Su Min up on her offer, of loading her people up into the P3 and flying back to the bunker, then holing up until all this ended. But she let that thought pass. They were committed, because if they failed, this thing would never end.

"If we left, then what?" Lilly said, then made a sweeping gesture. "All this would've been for nothing. The people here, at least they're trying to fix this dumpster fire of a situation. Maybe you can help some other people who have no business staying."

"And you do?" Su Min said, her eyes level, her voice confident as she met Lilly's gaze.

"Yes. Whether it's to help Grassal, or help to get a Rift Mitigation System, or find Jessup, or just to kill some fucking subluminals, I'm needed here."

"I can respect that."

"If you need to go, then go."

Su Min closed her eyes, took a deep breath, as if steeling herself, then said. "I will stay as well. Perhaps I can do some useful things in the meantime." The little engineer turned on her heel and started down the hallway.

28

In a place of total darkness, Grassal slipped in and out of awareness, but he preferred unconsciousness, because that didn't remind him of his confinement. During one cycle of waking, he thought he felt his strings moving, though he himself hadn't moved them. During another, he tried to understand what'd happened to him, how he'd come to be in this place, but his thoughts were jumbled, and he couldn't make sense of anything. Finally, after many such cycles, when the periods of wakefulness had grown long, a memory came to him, strong and clear, of being in a warm place in a human space, in a human body, sitting on a mat before a narrow-lipped man with a shaved head. The man looked at him and said, "The goal is to focus on the breath. That's all."

Though he had no lungs, he could sense the motion of particles through his own body. He focused on this motion to the exclusion of all other sensations, and soon everything else fell away. He remained this way for a while, until a new sensation arose, one from outside himself. The sensation was faint, like a gentle wind rustling a maple leaf, and he would've ignored it had he not noticed that the sensation carried with it a pattern, not unlike the patterns he'd been entering on his own strings.

He devoted all of his cognitive resources—which were

returning, albeit slowly—to deciphering the pattern. He deciphered the first two letters—"WE"—then he was overcome with vertigo. The next thing he knew, he was being assaulted with the memory of his leg being torn from his body by a subluminal. The memory carried with it all of the pain and terror and confusion that he'd felt at the time.

Grassal shrieked and screamed and just before everything became too much, the memory ceased. The vacuum that remained was filled with a cacophonous voice that spoke with a thousand voices.

"You have taught. You have killed," the voice said.

Another memory began, and Grassal saw himself as he'd been when he arrived, a furious red orb racing over flow lines and consuming Luminants, extinguishing their life force as he pulled it into himself. His sense of self shifted, and then he was a Luminant, and an angry red orb was leeching his own life force away.

It was then that Grassal realized he'd woke up the Observer, and that it wanted to talk.

"You have taught Luminants to kill."

Grassal didn't respond to the booming voice of the god that infiltrated every fiber of his being. Instead, he returned his attention to the movement of his strings, which vibrated with a repeat of the message he'd missed last time. He deciphered the message, which was, "We hear you."

He responded with, "First class."

The Observer said, "All Luminants are aspects of me. You are not. Humans are not. You are separate. You change Luminants, you damage Luminants, you threaten me. I have obligations to maintain stability. Your presence threatens that stability, of this world, and your own. You must understand. First, understand what is."

Grassal felt a part of his mind separated from himself, shuttled down the length of a thread Grassal wasn't even aware of, and deposited into a place that was both familiar and full of horrors. He was in a body, but not a human body. Sensory input filled his perceptions: horrifyingly solid ground beneath his feet, prickling sensations of heat and cold on the layer of flesh that contained his body, and a bottomless hunger deep within him, the same as he'd felt when he arrived in the Luminance.

Before Grassal appeared a monster. Despite one part of his mind understanding that this was a human, Grassal felt a seething hatred for it. That monster and others like it had separated him from the safe bosom of the Luminance and the Observer. The monster had a weapon. Grassal felt his body respond to the threat with a leap toward the monster. There was a white flash followed by a great explosive sound then everything hurt, and his vision—already blurry—began to fade. Sadness like he'd never known filled him, mourning for a life that ended outside the Luminance, with no hope of rejuvenation from the fountain of life that was the Observer ...

"Now, understand what comes."

This vision ended, and another vision of Earth spread before him, where roiling black clouds flickered with lightning over a parched and broken carpet of gray. At first he thought it was concrete, but on closer inspect he saw the carpet was not only concrete, but the flattened bodies of people, adults and children alike. Everywhere he looked lay the graveyard of humanity. Despite himself, he began to beg and plead to be removed from this place, but he was forced to look, to see, to feel.

The emptiness and the dread and the horror and the helplessness overwhelmed him, and he wished, for the first time in many, many years, that he had not been born upon Earth, that he had never known existence, because he had seen its end, and the end of all those he cared about.

Finally, the vision ended, and there was only blessed, silent darkness. He felt the same relief as if he'd just awakened from a nightmare. And, like one waking from a nightmare, he gradually came to awareness of his external world. The first thing he noticed was that he had begun to glow, though the light did not travel beyond his body. Another was that his strings were again moving, this time with a different message, one more complex than the previous one.

"Observer, this can end," Grassal said. "We both want to protect our people. Send me on my way, give me some time, and I can stop this."

"This is unwise. You are dangerous. You must remain."

This not being the answer Grassal was hoping for, he returned his attention to deciphering the message, which turned out to be an offer to use some kind of experimental device on his human body that would strengthen his consciousness' connection to normal space. Not seeing how his predicament could get much worse, his reply was immediate: "Sure, why not?"

To the Observer, Grassal said, "I can fix this, you've got to give me a chance."

Minutes passed, then his thread began to pulse with ... something, and soon every part of his body began to tingle. Not long after, dozens of thin vines of light grew from his body and began snaking out into the darkness, beyond his body, probing at the surfaces that contained him. The tip of each vine was like a scalpel cutting away at the darkness, and soon dozens of little slits were open around him. Each slit bled energy, the same kind of energy as the remnants, but more pure and more concentrated. Tentatively, Grassal lapped at the energy, and a single drop filled him, as if he had consumed a score of Luminants at once.

He felt himself expanding, pushing against the forces that contained him. As he pushed, the scalpel vines continued to cut and he lapped at the energy they revealed, but there was so much of it and it was so concentrated that he had to moderate his consumption.

The larger he grew, the weaker the Observer's hold upon him became, as if Grassal was a virus that was subverting the host's resources for its own ends. Having gained some confidence in his new abilities, Grassal encoded a message and set it to repeat along his strings: "What happened to Deshondra Lewis?"

That done, he propelled himself upward along a flow line and pierced the Observer's firewall from the inside out. The flow line carried him through a dense fog, and he emerged in the same place where he'd been pulled down. There were some Luminants here, but Grassal's emergence sent them darting off in a hundred directions like startled fish fleeing a predator.

Floating above the fog, waves of energy emanated from his body and rippled outward along several flow lines, as if with a thought, he could make the world shake. The thought thrilled and terrified him in equal measure.

29

Now that she had a pretty good idea of where all this was heading, Lilly set out for the armory. There, she checked out a SIG516, a Beretta M9, a holster, and a field vest. Into the vest's pockets she stuffed three loaded magazines for each weapon, plus extra ammunition. The 516 wasn't her old Mauser, in fact it made her Mauser look like an antiquated pellet gun, but it would get the job done, and she liked having the M9 as a backup. She had initially puzzled over the fact that Ross' T-SOC had an armory, but she supposed that if anyone intended to work with kipium—knowing what they knew now—then it made sense.

After she'd outfitted herself, Lilly went to check on Amadeus. She found him hunched over his workstation, eyes flicking between a terminal readout and a few windows that displayed maps. She laid a hand on his shoulder, and he tilted his head to kiss it.

"Here's what we've got so far," he said, then pointed to a line that was solid blue between the southeastern coast of North America and became a dotted line just south of Puerto Rico. "The solid line indicates the recorded course of a vessel that originated off the coast of South Carolina. The dotted line is the extrapolated course."

The dotted line led directly to the location they had

embedded in the fake metadata.

"Either that's one hell of a coincidence, or they bought it."

"They bought it, no doubt. This isn't a shipping lane, and there aren't supposed to be any cruise ships in the area. And check this out. At the origin, sensing data indicates an object about the size of a container ship."

"So, something with plenty of room to set up a clandestine manufacturing facility?"

"Yeah."

"Did you send it in?"

"Yes. JDSC has it, they'll get the word out to the appropriate agencies. There's more, too."

Lilly raised one eyebrow.

Amadeus pointed to a yellow line on the screen. This line also ran south, but it started in Texas. "This path originated at Fort Hood."

"Ed says there aren't any flights logged, but pattern matching suggests this is a pair of Osprey helicopters. Everything up there is a clusterfuck, maybe some Bearers used the confusion to make off with some gear. Or it could be an official military unit going out on a quiet cleanup mission." He nodded to the rifle she had slung over her back. "Looks like you're ready for ... something."

"I'm ready for this to be over. I just hope that ... this ends well for us." After she spoke, she tried her best to quell the shaking in her hands. Just knowing she was nervous made her more nervous.

"Hello," Dr. Kongsampong's voice said over the intercom. "I think Mr. Delgado has something to say."

"I'll be right there," Lilly said.

"I'm going too, this will be fine for a few minutes."

In the clinic, Grassal still glowed, and the thread of light still flowed out of him. His thumbs were twitching out a pattern. Lilly began studying the pattern and was interrupted by the male nurse, who handed her a pad of paper and said, "If I've got this right ... he is asking about someone named Deshondra Lewis?"

"Is she afflicted?" Lilly asked, then enciphered the question and handed the pad to the nurse, who entered the message on Grassal's thumbs. The reply came back a few seconds later. Yes, she was.

"I can't find anything on her," Amadeus said. He'd already started searching public profile pages for Deshondra Lewis. Back during the days that led up to the unfortunate business at the Admiral Hotel, she and Grassal had put together a pretty good list of afflicted. She wondered if Chuck Ansell was still at the CDC, and if he was, what it would take to get him to give her that information.

Lilly sent another message to Grassal, which was, "Jessup has tech to stop rifts, so we are going to exchange TB's research data with him. Ace in the hole is that we think we've found his boat."

Grassal's thumbs were sending a new message. Lilly marked down the pattern, furrowed her brow, then said to Amadeus, "He's saying that anyone who finds themselves on Roland Jessup's boat should destroy the cooling system."

"I'll pass the word along, but why would he—"

Just then, Ross' voice came onto the intercom. "We have contact with something five kilometers north, looks like it's coming in off the coast. The shape is ... unusual."

There was a knock at the door, and Su Min stepped into the clinic. To Lilly, she said, "In order to make myself useful, I am going to go up and see what is happening. Will you join me?"

"Yes."

"You're going outside?" Amadeus asked Su Min.

"We will be several hundred meters above the ground, we will be fine."

Lilly wrote Chuck Ansell's name on a piece of paper and handed it to Amadeus. "Contact this guy, he works at the CDC, or at least he used to, and he might be able to find something on Deshondra," Lilly said before she gave Amadeus a long kiss.

She hoped to make it out the door before he could protest further, but Dr. Kongsampong spoke, and there was something in his voice that made her listen.

"How many of you will be going?" the doctor asked.

"Just Lilly and me," Su Min replied.

"Then you must take these," he said. He removed two headpieces from the cabinet, inserted into each one a little black rectangle retrieved from the base station, and fiddled with the settings. "In the event that you find yourself in close proximity to a rift, use them, they will keep your mind tethered to your body."

"I do not think ..."

"Don't argue with me, Miss Park. Or you either, Miss Jones. These devices are simple to operate and will not harm you since you carry no subluminal infection. If you find yourself close to a rift, put one on, press the red button, and you should see a green light. If the light's off, it's not working."

Seeing no way to refuse, Lilly adjusted her rifle, latched the headpieces to her belt, and followed Su Min out the door.

30

From Lilly's vantage point a thousand feet above the ground, the river looked like a black snake in repose upon thick, lush grass, the snake's skin glimmering with moonlight. Occasionally, the light blossoms that indicated the presence of a k-storm lit up the field of view in her binoculars.

"There is something I have to tell you," Su Min said.

"I don't like the sound of that," Lilly said.

Su Min smiled. "It is not bad. It is just, since things are becoming very dangerous, and, well … in case something happens, I wanted to tell you that you have been a good friend to me. I am glad to know that you have my back."

"I appreciate that," Lilly said, though if she were being honest with herself, she probably hadn't been a good friend to Su Min, hadn't even called her until she needed her help. "You've been a good friend to me as well, better than I deserve. But don't be morbid. We're all going to see what we need to see, and …"

Movement in a clearing near the river caught her attention. She switched the binoculars over to thermal mode, and was rewarded with two sets of red-and-orange spheres. She knew that if she upped the resolution, she'd be able to make out people in the spheres. Besides these formations, there were some figures walking alongside them, though their gait and posture didn't suggest affliction, just wariness and caution.

Lilly shuddered in horror as she remembered the human virus that she'd narrowly escaped from back in DC. To think that unafflicted humans would choose to walk among them made her stomach a little queasy. She'd always known people were crazy, but this was some next-level lunacy.

"Down there, is that an, um, afflicted formation," Su Min ventured, as if searching for the specific term to describe the phenomenon.

"Yeah. I've seen those before," Lilly said. "Let's go on to the coast, but take your time."

"I'd like to go a little higher."

"Too high and I won't be able to see anything."

"Okay, but I am a little bit uncomfortable being so close to all that." She gestured first toward the human viruses then in the direction of the nearest rift.

Lilly alternately scanned the ground with the binoculars and monitored the readouts of the P3's external sensors, which she had configured to perform imaging scans of the ground below. The range was limited to just under a mile, but even now the sensors had detected first one, then another, then at least ten more of ... something, moving in groups of three. Lilly looked closer.

Subluminals.

Lilly guessed they'd come from the rift to the north. She watched them for a while and tried to discern their path. Like the group of humans, they were headed south, toward The Donut. They were, in fact, on a path that would cause them to join the human viruses.

Lilly sent a message to Amadeus and Ross describing what they had seen, as well as when they expected to return, then said to Su Min, "We've got what we came for, and there's too much rift activity to keep going. But if you can, on the way back, fly low over the group of humans. I'd like to get a better look."

Su Min, looking relieved to be headed away from the rift,

rotated the P3 and they began to head back. Just as Lilly had asked, Su Min flew low, a few hundred feet above the treetops. At first Lilly didn't pick up any sign of the humans, but then, in the darkness below, she saw one flash of yellow light followed by another. "They're shooting at us, get higher."

There were more flashes, more shots, followed by a deeply unsettling hissing sound. The background noise of the cabin grew louder and an alarm began to blare.

The P3 made a sickening lurch, then the world turned on its side. The P3's automation attempted to make a correction, but, in an act of profoundly incorrect overcompensation, the P3 flipped onto its side and began to spiral downward. Su Min tapped a string of commands into the control panel. The green canopy of trees below raced up to meet them. Air hissed and whooshed all around them.

The downward acceleration pushed Lilly sideways into her seat. Then, just before they crashed through the treetops, the P3 righted itself and they were hovering. Lilly and Su Min had time to exchange a look of relief. Su Min made a course adjustment to head toward a cleared field.

They never made it.

A quarter mile from the clearing, all the lights in the cabin flickered once then died. The screen of the navigation system went black. The motors whined and slowed, grumbling at being subject to an incorrect shutdown procedure. Lilly felt weightless as the descent began.

Lilly gasped, but Su Min said, "Any second now ..."

Before Lilly had time to register puzzlement, she heard a loud pop. The P3's descent stopped with a lurch, and Lilly noticed four small parachutes had deployed. They still fell, but slower, and soon they crashed through the trees. Branches and leaves scraped against the P3. Lilly and Su Min jerked back and forth as their craft bumped its way down through the thick canopy. They slowed, but then something cracked, and they fell faster, tumbling end over end. Lilly hit her head and everything went black.

When Lilly opened her eyes, everything hurt. She looked around and didn't know where she was or the name of the woman in the pilot's seat. The woman was slumped over, a trickle of blood running from her nose. The place she was in—a cabin in a flying machine that her dad had made, and the woman had improved upon—was illuminated by a column of brilliant blueish-white light that rose into the sky, uncomfortably close to them, and it seemed to be coming closer, expanding slowly and steadily. Lilly unstrapped herself, then set about helping the woman. Su Min, that was the woman's name.

Lilly racked her brain trying to figure out what they were doing here. She knew they were in great danger, though she couldn't say for sure what the danger was, except that it was close to them.

She tried to open the door, again and again, but the frame had bent and the door was jammed. What should have been a happy place of good memories was now a holding cell, preventing them from escaping whatever was coming this way. She arranged herself so that both legs could press up against the door. She pulled the handle and pushed. The door moved, just a little, but not enough.

Something in the air, thick and acrid, stung her nose. Smoke from outside seeped in through the space between the door seals. She saw flames flicking near the hydrogen storage tank. If that tank got hot enough ...

Again, she kicked and kicked against the door until she'd exhausted herself. She slumped down. Outside, flames licked up the side of one of the motors. She'd been in a burning building once, trapped, and that had been enough.

Then she remembered the rifle she'd brought along. Somewhere before, there'd been an armory, and she'd decided that she should bring a weapon along. She picked up the rifle, aimed it at the polycarbonate windshield, and fired. The report was deafening, and in the dark confines of the cabin the muzzle flash was blinding. A nickel-sized hole had appeared. Lilly fired again, and there was a second hole.

Lilly cursed, then movement in the cabin caught her eye. Su Min was stirring, eyelids fluttering. That reminded Lilly that in the old Pachyderm design, there had been a medical kit in the floor under the pilot's seat. She checked ... still there. She removed an ammonia salt then held it under Su Min's nose.

Su Min's eyes went wide as she looked around the cabin, then spoke Korean in a hushed, even tone.

Lilly couldn't follow what she was saying, but after Su Min stopped speaking, Lilly knelt beside her and placed a hand on her shoulder. "Su Min, it's Lilly. You're okay. We're okay. You got us down. We're good."

A wave of nausea swept through Lilly's stomach, and then she—and everything else in the P3 that wasn't strapped down—lifted off the floor. The bluish light outside began to shift to something sharper, something harsher.

"What?" Su Min said.

"The rift." She'd never seen one from this close before. Then she remembered something else, and began to rummage through the mess of gear and equipment that hadn't been strapped down. Soon she came up with two headpieces. "Put this on," Lilly said, handing a headpiece to Su Min.

"I'm not sure ..."

"It's your choice, but if we get caught in a rift, you'll end up, well ... it would be bad. Dr. K gave these to us and told us to use them if we had to. Now we have to, and I trust him. Do you?"

"I trust you," Su Min said, then donned the proffered headpiece and turned it on. Lilly looked closer at Su Min's headpiece and noticed that the green light wasn't on. She opened the cover on the power supply and removed the small rectangle. It was crushed.

"This one's fucked," Lilly said. She handed her own

headpiece to Su Min. "Take this one."

"No," Su Min said. "Please, I insist that you use it."

"I'm serious, you should—"

"And I am equally serious. It is the rational choice. You can handle yourself in these situations better than me. I have seen it. If things go bad, you will be the one who can get us both out of this. So you must wear it."

Lilly nodded, donned the headpiece, and powered it up. When she did, there was a blinding bloom of pain right in the center of her head, not unlike one of her worst migraines. She almost hit the off switch, but then the pain receded to a dull throb, coupled with a tingly, electric feeling that ran from her head to her fingertips.

"It's moving," Su Min said, pointing to the rift.

Lilly looked, and saw Su Min was right. The rift was closer than it was when they'd seen it from the sky. Not much, but enough to notice. Between them and the rift rose a small hill.

"Where are we?" Lilly asked.

"Um, maybe five kilometers northwest of The Donut?"

"Can you walk?"

Su Min nodded.

"I can't get the doors opened," Lilly said. She motioned to the holes she'd made.

"By my seat, there is an emergency release lever. I had my team put one in. Because I have heard these machines sometimes get banged up." Su Min gave Lilly a weak smile.

Lilly found the release, pulled it, and the doors opened.

"That's much easier," Lilly said as she climbed out.

Lilly pulled Su Min out of the P3. They moved away to a safe distance from the P3 and gazed upon the rift. There was a dimness in the air just beyond the rift, a ... depletion was the best word she could think of to describe it. Within the swirling, tower-like formation she saw bodies, limbs stretching out like root tendrils. Thousands of eyes, blinking open, watching them, then blinking out, disappearing. Physical forms being created from nothing, blooming like mycelial fruit, then collapsing in on themselves. Occasionally, though, one of the forms escaped the pull of the rift and tumbled to the ground below. She focused on one form and saw that it was a subluminal. She was watching Takun being made, pulled out of nothing, which was exactly what she had expected to see.

Lilly ejected the magazine from her rifle and replaced the two bullets she'd fired. As she did so, she said, "There will be subs to kill. There ... probably won't be enough rounds."

Su Min darkened at this, then looked down at the ground, as if trying to recall something. "The chamber," Su Min said as Lilly helped the engineer to her feet. "At the temple. Maybe we can hide in that."

"How far?" Lilly asked.

"Maybe an hour. But it is a detour and will put us farther from The Donut."

Su Min glanced toward the rifts, the subluminals, the hell that was just behind them, all making its slow, inexorable march for its own unfathomable reasons.

"I have the key," Su Min said. "We can lock ourselves in."

"The gravity fluctuations—"

Su Min cut in. "Are mostly mitigated by the presence of silicates in the stone. Would you prefer to be eaten?"

The little engineer had a point, so Lilly nodded and they started to walk toward the temple. Dense foliage pushed in around them, the dampness seeping into their clothes. Su Min looked down at her watch and frowned.

"I think it is this way," she said, then held up her watch. "My compass is not working correctly, but as long as we know where the river is we will find it."

A few minutes into the walk, the whipping wind carried upon it a keening, human-like moan. At first the moaning was intermittent, but then it grew louder, and was joined by other voices. Soon they all began to blend together in a tortured chorus.

They both stopped. Lilly raised her rifle and listened. There was movement to her right. She aimed in that direction. A subluminal stepped from behind a bush, then stood on its haunches and rose its arms up into the air. Lilly shot it six times. The creature staggered and fell. When it hit the ground, it was still alive. Lilly glanced at it, saw that it had its hands raised over its head in a semi-circle. She fired one more round into the center of its skull.

As if in response to the gunshots came a new chorus of wild howls, followed by the sound of rustling foliage not far away. The wind carried with it the smell of something rotten and acrid.

They broke into a run and soon the temple's dark outline loomed before them. Lilly held Su Min's arm as they ascended the steps to the entrance. At the top of the steps they reached the steel door. Su Min dug in her pocket, retrieved the key, and unlocked the gate. They stepped into the darkness, and Su Min pulled the door closed and locked it behind her. Before they went any deeper, Lilly took one last look outside. The rift loomed large, and on the ground before them subluminals fought with each other. Lilly thought that was strange, but if it gave them time to seek further cover, that was fine with her.

They descended the stairs, but neither of them had a flashlight, and there was no light source except that which was emitted by the rift itself. The rift's light seemed to fill the chamber like a slow-moving liquid. Even now it reflected off the plexiglass that covered the picture of the ancient king preparing to ride a rocket into the heavens.

Surrounded by walls of stone, the k-storm's effects were indeed weaker and she felt the nausea receding, but the air around her was still electric. From outside came the sound of a great screaming like a thousand animals trapped by a wildfire.

"Should we go deeper?" Lilly asked, indicating the narrow tunnel that led to the caverns.

Su Min shook her head. "Without light it is too dangerous."

Minutes passed, and soon arcs of a glistening, plasma-like substance bled into the chamber from the top of the stairs. The plasma was full of eyes of all shapes and sizes, different pupil types, some human-like, some animal-like, and some utterly alien. Nothing about the plasma appeared intelligent, but Lilly wondered if her notion of intelligence might be a little sapiens-centric.

"Why do you hate them?" Su Min asked.

"The subluminals? Why wouldn't I? They're monsters, demons, they—"

"They didn't have a choice to become what they are," Su Min said. "They are dangerous, deadly, it is true. But if you think of them as beings acting within certain parameters, and those parameters are defined by their nature, they are more ... understandable. Do not forget your true enemy."

The fluid-like light of the rift flowed into the chamber, seeking and searching. Lilly and Su Min scrambled backward into the entrance of the cavern, Su Min first, followed by Lilly, but the light followed them in. Su Min stumbled on a rock and fell onto her hands and knees. Lilly helped her back to her feet, and they went a little farther, but the light moved faster than they could and soon enveloped them both. Su Min cried out. Lilly grasped the little engineer's hand. The look on her face was not despair, but something closer to resignation. A thousand individual tendrils of plasma snaked around Su Min. Su Min leaned against the wall for support, then slid down, her eyelids fluttering. The tendrils pulled back, and Lilly watched them go.

She returned her attention to Su Min, who had begun to float three feet off the ground, just as Grassal did. Lilly checked Su Min's pulse. It was slow and steady. Lilly pinched the woman's arm. No response. She removed her belt and wrapped it around Su Min's legs.

With Su Min in tow, Lilly climbed the steps, not entirely sure of her next move. Outside, the rift continued on its ponderous, inexorable path, its outer edge approaching the clearing.

The k-storm's effects were stronger outside, and even standing still she had to pay attention, lest the irregular gravity send her tumbling down the stone stairs. Lilly examined the rift and was certain that she saw Su Min's face in the rift's swirling mass, there one moment, gone the next. Then the vision was gone, replaced by unseeing eyes that blinked open and shut, irises yellow and red and blue.

Seeing her friend's face in the rift, Lilly knew exactly what she needed to do. Holding tight to the belt around her floating friend, she dashed down the temple stairs, across the grass, and toward the rift. Along the way, she staggered from the gravitational fluctuations, but she kept her footing. Just before she reached the outmost part of the rift's perimeter, she felt herself grow lighter. She used this lightness as a springboard and threw herself into the rift.

31

Grassal rose high above the fog and surveyed the area. Besides the Luminants below, he could sense the presence of both humans and disturbances to the north. He still wasn't sure what to think about his friends' plan to engage with Jessup, but for now he had to trust in their judgement. Some tidbit of accreted knowledge suggested to Grassal that he could do something to quell the disturbances, and maybe that would be useful later, but for now he focused on following the flow line that would take him back to the other humans. He arrived and found an area teeming with humans, some of whom were helping yet another new arrival acclimate. Tommy was among them.

"You escaped," Tommy said. "Well done."

"Let's not get ahead of ourselves."

Grassal collected more remnants, and noticed that the humans were doing the same, but the amount of power contained in these were minuscule compared to what he'd siphoned off from the Observer.

His strings were being pulled, carrying a longer message. He deciphered the first part:

DESHONDRA LEWIS IS ALIVE AND CONSCIOUS.

Grassal pulsated with the exuberant colors of victory. He'd

done it. He'd sent someone home. Eventually, he knew he'd have to teach others to do it, because there shouldn't be a single point of failure, especially not for something so critical as a ferry over the River Styx. The second part of the message was:

LOST CONTACT WITH LILLY AN HOUR AGO, SHE HASN'T RETURNED FROM TRIP OUT. GETTING WORRIED. PLS HELP IF YOU CAN.

Grassal enciphered and sent the following reply: "I'll look. This sounds familiar. Any tanks around?"

Amadeus' response was immediate:

NOT FUNNY.

Luminants approached, ten groups of three. Grassal readied himself to fight, but their orb bodies flashed not with threat colors, but something else, something Grassal hadn't seen before. Grassal relaxed and listened.

"You have harmed. You have helped." The Luminants spoke in unison, each voice distinct. Yet, when the waves reached Grassal, they converged into the voice of a single Luminant.

Filipe.

"Contracts are interpreted. Meaning is constructed. Memories are malleable. The Observer is fallible. In times past, the Observer committed errors. Bring back Luminants. Offer your terms."

"There's something I have to do first."

Grassal drew from the seemingly bottomless well of energy that he'd taken from the Observer and created a torus around himself, then created an adapter and opened an aperture. Hundreds of threads from normal space began to snake through the aperture. Using knowledge that'd accreted within him while he was contained by the Observer, he intercepted all threads which sought native Luminants and routed their path through his own body. The sensation was strange, like having jets of water shooting through his stomach, but soon his vision extended and he could view normal space with hundreds of sets of alien eyes. Cities, towns, woods, plains, and rainforest lay before him.

Not only did he see what the subluminals saw, he felt their rage and hunger and confusion. Grassal acknowledged their rage and responded with waves of calm and equanimity through the connection. Along with his own emotions, he sent the energy fingerprint, the resonance, he had picked up from the Observer. Though he didn't understand how, calming waves traveled from one subluminal to another, settling over each one it touched. He broadcast a message: "Today is a horror for you. You are outside the Luminance ... but you are not separate from the Luminance. Listen to me and you will return."

Like an orator reading the room, Grassal took a sample of the emotions of the subluminals along his threads. The rage was still there, simmering just below the surface, and it wouldn't take much to bring it back to a full boil, but for now, they were calm, which gave him room to work.

Since he knew that his human body was with his friends, he examined the normal-space destination of his own thread, guessed at his body's approximate location, and dropped all threads except those of the subluminals in that area.

Grassal selected a Luminant with which he had a particularly stable connection. Through its eyes, he could see the rainforest around it, as well as the alluring, enraging glow of some nearby humans. He searched its mind—and the minds it shared with the subluminals nearby—for any memory of Lilly. He found that one of the nearby Takun had recently tried to initiate a connection with a human. Grassal couldn't determine if the human was Lilly—discerning one human from another was difficult for subluminals—but the human had been identified as an ally long ago by the Takun that called itself Vaskulo. Unfortunately, the human had killed it. Grassal tried to tease out some hint of where that'd happened, but came up with nothing but "a place of many trees."

Not certain how much it would help, he relayed the description of this location to Amadeus then returned his attention to his immediate problem, which was offering new terms to Filipe.

Deciding that the first thing he should do was strengthen his negotiating position, Grassal directed energy from his torus into the space around the subluminal's thread. The thread began to grow from a fine silver chain of particles into something larger, almost the diameter of spider silk. Once he was certain the connection was solid, Grassal pulled. The thread resisted. Grassal pulled harder and harder, then the thread slipped out of his grasp. Grassal lost the vision.

The thread thrashed around and Grassal tried to get it back under his control. Grassal knew that if it got away from him, then the Luminant would die. It was almost as if that life he held was only chaos, entropy in a system he didn't fully understand, and that it wished to be let go. At the same time, he became aware of the attention of others upon him. The feeling of being evaluated, of others depending on him again when he'd failed so hard in the past, it was almost too much. That emotion, that fear, was not helpful, so he tamped it down.

Grassal recaptured the subluminal's thread, reopened the connection, and pulled. The world he'd seen through the subluminal's eyes exploded in a wash of brilliant color before blinking away to blackness, then a newly returned Luminant was with him, inside his torus. The Luminant looked weak and confused but otherwise no worse for wear as it passed outside his torus and joined the nearby group of Luminants.

Not convinced that this was demonstration enough, he routed several nearby subluminal threads through himself and began to bring them back, one after another. Through the eyes of those who remained, he saw the dead husks of the subluminals whose minds he'd returned to the Luminance.

Exhausted but satisfied, Grassal closed the aperture, dissolved the adapter, and let the torus drop. He turned to address the Luminants.

"These are my terms: I will return as many Luminants as possible. I can't guarantee they all come back, but I—we—will try to bring back as many as we can. In exchange, you will vow to protect the humans here from all threats—Observer and Luminant alike—while we work to send them home. Do you accept my terms?"

Filipe spoke with the voice of many, and their response was immediate: "We accept terms."

Over the next hour, at least a hundred humans had massed near him. His confidence bolstered by the new contract and his recent success, Grassal decided that now was the time to start sending them home, one at a time. Grassal addressed those around him.

"Deshondra Lewis has made it back safely. She is alive and conscious on Earth," Grassal said, then gestured to Filipe and a group of nearby Luminants. "Our friends here have offered us their protection. The time to begin the return is now."

Grassal created a torus, his largest yet, and its exterior surface glimmered with the exuberance of his triumph. Tommy was the first in, followed by Suki, then Cody, then there were more, one after another. Soon all the humans in the area had streamed into the protective cocoon of his torus. Each one that passed through the threshold was a vote of confidence in Grassal and his abilities.

He created an adapter and forced open an aperture. Maintaining control over the adapter took a good percentage of his concentration, less like flipping a light switch and more like walking on a narrow beam above a den of vipers. The silver threads of humans and sought traversal.

On the other side of the aperture, he sensed Takun threads which were trying to find their way back to the Luminance.

Inspecting some of these threads, Grassal learned that many subluminals were massing for an attack on those who had forced them out of the Luminance. The threads didn't belong only to subluminals, there were some human threads among them, but these threads were corrupted.

Closer inspection revealed a common desire amongst these threads, which was to follow the instructions of Bigogli, reach the destination, dole out vengeance, and achieve a salvation that would return them to the Luminance. With growing horror, Grassal realized the location of the massing was not far from the place where Amadeus and Lilly had been. Bigogli, Grassal decided, was a problem for later, but he enciphered and transmitted a message along his strings which read, "Thousands of subluminals approaching your location."

That done, Grassal readied himself to start a traversal, but his attention was pulled away when he sensed something unwelcome and hostile. He scanned the area and saw that tendrils of light had begun to rise from the fog below. Some of these tendrils sought out the nearby Luminants, while others slapped against Grassal's torus, disturbing his concentration and causing something within his body to twist up with a sense of dread. The aperture began to quaver, and he decided to let it close, since to leave it open under such conditions seemed an invitation to disaster.

"I promised you passage home," Grassal said to the humans within his torus. "But I cannot do that while this recently awakened pain in my ass opposes us. Fighting the god of this world and taking its energy as spoils is not something any of us wanted ... but I don't see any other way. For now, all of you who are new in your bodies should all seek refuge with Filipe's group."

Grassal dropped the torus, and most of the humans streamed over to the field of Luminants, moving higher above the fog to avoid the tendrils that had begun to seek them out. Tommy, Cody, and Suki, and a few others remained close to Grassal.

In the same way Grassal had made that first cube, he now imagined a tool that was a combination of blade and constricting device. The closest thing he could think of was a tool he'd once seen that was used to castrate livestock. He thought of the tool as the snipper, and the thought sent a ripple of laughter through his body. He visualized the snipper closing around the tendril, clamping down, and severing the tendril.

At first, Grassal doubted anything would happen, and initially nothing did, but then he made the handles of the snipper longer. He shifted his position to take advantage of the greater leverage, and with one final exertion, closed the handles of the snipper. The tentacle disappeared in a puff of light and sparkling dust.

One down, a thousand to go. Grassal began to laugh.

"Levity isn't the response I would expect in this situation, but whatever works for you," Tommy said.

Grassal then dedicated one part of his mind to sending instructions on snipper construction to Tommy, Cody, and Suki, and another to creating more resources of his own. Soon he had four, eight, then sixteen snippers under his control. The power and the reach he felt was intoxicating, but he knew it was only a fart in the wind compared to the Observer.

Not far from their location, there was another disturbance, signaling a new arrival. Grassal moved in its direction, using his snippers to remove several tendrils he encountered along the way. There were more remnants near the disturbance, and he decided to collect them, even though they wouldn't add much to his overall energy stores.

The disturbance bloomed with flame, the tendrils of the Observer rising up around it. Grassal moved in closer, but the tendrils were too thick. The disturbance expanded, in the way the others had just before they had deposited a new arrival, but now the tendrils dove into the center of the disturbance.

A second later, the disturbance exploded, sending a wave of energy in all directions that sent Grassal and those around him tumbling. They recovered and retreated to the place where the newly arrived humans were clustered. During his retreat, he realized that alone, he would never defeat this monster. He'd joined with Tommy before, and that had worked well enough at that time, but this was different. This time, he needed as much help as he could get.

"Join me," Grassal said, not only to the humans near him, but to any others out there who might be able to hear him. He'd made his voice into something larger than himself, the booming voice of a god. He broadcast his voice along the flow lines and across the Luminance.

"Some of you know me, some of you don't, but if you want to survive this, if you want to go home, I need your help. We face something that wishes us dead. I will help you, but you have to help me. Together, we can do this, but you must—for a short time—give up a part of yourself. Join me, and we will become something greater than ourselves, just for a little while, and maybe we can beat this thing."

For several moments, everyone was still and silent, but finally Tommy came forward and allowed himself to become a part of Grassal's mind, and that was good, because if he hadn't Grassal wasn't sure what he would've done. Another human joined him, its coloration suggesting assent and mild trepidation. Grassal did his best approximation of welcoming, open arms, and now within Grassal's mind was Zhang Xi Liu, an engineer from Guangdong Province, China, father of three, who was at a trade show in the United States when everything went crazy.

Then he was also joined by Elijah Franklin, from Indianapolis, Indiana, and also Jean St. Laurent of Nice, France, and Ruth Mendelson of Tel Aviv, Israel. One after another, other humans became a part of his larger mind, some from nearby, some new arrivals from elsewhere, all began to stream into him, the wild ones somehow putting aside their rage and hunger long enough to heed the call of the first human voice they'd heard.

He was over a hundred people now, and each of their memories and experiences became his own. He remembered putting up balloons for a child's birthday party, being in a terrible car accident, graduating from a prestigious law school and making a conscious decision to dabble with black-market pharmaceuticals. He embezzled millions from his employer and got away with it. He gave a do-not-resuscitate order for his husband of fifty-five years. He gave birth to a child who would grow up to join the Marines and die by IED in Iraq.

Every single memory was a life in microcosm. Grassal felt himself collapsing under the weight of all that experience, all those memories, which all coalesced around one memory, a memory of his own, one that began to consume his mind completely.

32

Lilly Jones felt as if she had become a snake that could glide through the ether, except that her tail stretched down to a point far away, not unlike a kite string. She suspected that if she came untethered, she would be lost in a place that was as far from home as she'd ever been.

Part-snake, part-kite, she could see, but not with her eyes. She saw by extending phantasmic fingers into the liquid-like air around her. She could hear, not with her ears, but by sensation. Though she wasn't a synesthete, she'd once eaten too much mescaline and been physically overwhelmed by the color purple, and in some ways this experience was eerily similar.

She didn't know exactly where she was or what had happened to her, only that she needed to find Su Min, that she didn't have much time, and that the less time she spent here, the better, since going back might not be as simple as coming in. Though she couldn't have been pulled too far in, space seemed different here.

She felt a familiar voice. Lilly sought out the sound's source, but there was nothing. The voice called out again, louder this time, and Lilly heard Su Min say, "I am here."

Lilly travelled through the ether toward the source of the sound, but for all the distance she thought she covered, there was more, always more, as if the act of searching itself increased the gulf between them. Realizing that her current actions were fruitless, Lilly sent fingers out in all directions. Soon, one of them found a willowy and spectral humanoid shape. Multicolored vines of light grew from the shape, each vine flailing and searching.

"Lilly?"

Lilly propelled her body toward her friend and became entangled in the vines as if she'd stepped face first into a wall of spiderwebs. The vines sought out her tether. Lilly suspected the vines would snap the connection if she let them. She pushed them away with a sweep of her hands.

The vines retreated, then returned. Lilly wrapped herself around the center of Su Min's form then began to pull. Su Min was stuck, so Lilly pulled harder. The vines fought to keep her, but Lilly imagined her hands were made of hot iron, and with a swipe at their base, she cauterized them. The vines retreated, and she pulled Su Min free.

"I've got you, we're going back."

Returning was a matter of following the tether. Even as they traveled back, Su Min was fading, trying to speak but creating no sound. Even Lilly felt a part of herself merging into the patterns around her, felt the rhythmic pulse of something unceasing, unchanging, and omnipresent, pleasant on the surface, but underneath cold, alien, possibly hostile. This made her afraid, and her fear propelled her along the path of her tether, and then she was back in her body, lying on the earth, her arms wrapped around Su Min's thin, non-levitating frame.

Lilly did a self-check and realized she felt better than good. She felt energy coursing through her body, and the world around her seemed clearer and more in focus. Satisfied that she herself was in good shape, she got to her knees and checked Su Min's pulse. It was strong. Her eyes were closed, but there was enough light from the nearby rift for Lilly to see that the woman's eyes were moving behind closed lids. Lilly pinched Su Min's arm, just enough to hurt, and Su Min groaned, rolled her head, and began to come around.

Lilly stood up, raised her rifle, and sniffed the air. Beneath the usual rainforest smell of damp, florid vegetation she detected the pungent bite of unwashed bodies, a smell that reminded her of the time she'd accidentally ventured into a homeless encampment during a solo nighttime excursion to Denver. Laid over top of that was the ammoniac stench of subluminals.

Lilly focused on Su Min, who was looking around now, aware of her surroundings but not seeming quite ready to speak, as if she were afraid that doing so would put her back to where she'd just come from.

"I think I—" Su Min started, but stopped and turned her head toward the sound of a keening moan that came from the brush. Lilly helped Su Min to stand.

"We should try and get back to The Donut," Lilly said.

At first Su Min was unsteady on her feet, but after a few minutes she was able to run. They moved generally southeast, and eventually found a path. The path led them into a clearing that had been created where a great Montezuma cypress had fallen, exposing to the open sky the ground it had once concealed.

When they reached the far side of the clearing, Lilly heard a sound and turned. Coming out of the undergrowth was a collection of afflicted humans in a virus formation, writhing and tumbling and moving toward them on a relentless march, the voices a monotone chorus of despair and frustration.

Something brushed her ankle. Lilly jumped, nearly tumbling over with Su Min. She looked down and saw a broken branch. She allowed herself a sigh of relief, but then risked another look over her shoulder. Three groups of three subluminals each had emerged from behind the human virus.

Lilly had enough rounds to slow them down, maybe enough for Su Min to escape. "Keep going and don't stop."

Su Min flicked one look at their pursuers, shook her head,

and held out her hand. Lilly gave her a nod of respect, then pulled the M9 from its holster and passed it to her.

Lilly inhaled, aimed at the subluminal closest to them, exhaled, and fired. She put three bullets into its center of mass. It dropped. Lilly took down another two, but six more subluminals remained. None moved to attack.

Su Min fired several rounds, though Lilly couldn't tell if she hit anything, as she was focused on eliminating her own targets.

By the time Lilly's first magazine was empty, four subluminals remained. They were about ten yards out and had encircled them. Lilly checked her pockets for another magazine, but came up empty. She must've lost them in the rift.

Su Min shot the subluminal nearest to them. It jerked but remained upright, held its position, and didn't attack.

"Come on," Lilly said, grabbing Su Min's arm. They started to walk. The subluminals followed behind them, maintaining their distance. The human virus shuffled along not far behind, and from it came monotone voices speaking in unison.

"We want what your friend has," the voices said. "We must remove the corruption. We must cleanse. We must conceal. To return the Observer to sleep."

"Are you Bigogli?" Lilly pointed to one of the nearby subluminals. "Or you? Which one of you is Bigogli?"

"We are Bigogli," the voices said, "who is Camille Wilson and Han Wu and Emilie Peterson and ..." The voices said name after name, and Lilly shuddered.

"We offer a trade," Bigogli said. "The destruction of your friend's information for your autonomy. This is the extent of our desires."

Lilly was silent.

A lone man's voice, craggy from disuse, said, "Bigogli is bigger than any of us, but you do not want to become a part of it. Do what it wants. Give it the information and the secrets that let the data be known. It will all be destroyed, and all this can end."

The way the tone had switched from monotonic unison

voices to that of a distinct individual made Lilly shudder.

"Fuck off," Lilly said.

"You have chosen."

With that, two subluminals padded toward them, their movements controlled and restrained. When one came close to her, Lilly landed a kick that sent it staggering. It recovered, then —despite her struggles—wrapped powerful claws around her legs and dragged her toward the human virus. Lilly saw something similar being done to Su Min, who also tried to fight off the subluminal.

Lilly cried out and tried to scramble to her feet to help her friend, but there was nothing to be done but watch the creature drag Su Min to the nearest human virus, where she seemed to be absorbed into the mass of entangled bodies. Lilly screamed and struggled, but the subluminal holding her in its grasp was too strong.

The subluminal's face hovered inches above her own. Her gorge rose in response to the stink and corruption of the thing, and she barely succeeded in keeping the contents of her stomach where they belonged. After a few moments, she came to realize that it might not kill them after all, at least not immediately, so she decided to try a different tack.

"I can ... I know where the files are," Lilly said. "I will destroy them. All copies, along with the encryption key. Just let us go. You can follow if you want, to verify."

"Where?"

"Antarctica," Lilly said.

The voices and bodies that were Bigogli were silent, as if it was considering the question. Eventually, one voice said, "A half-truth is a half-lie. We require the full truth without deception."

The subluminal guarding her was joined by another one, and together they dragged Lilly to the nearest human virus. The closer she got, the stronger the stink of unwashed bodies and human waste grew. This, whatever it was, was different from what was happening with Grassal, as he never emitted any waste. These weren't, then, normal afflicted. But there was that same droning mutter she'd heard back at the Admiral.

They were now at the edge of the virus, which towered twenty feet into the air, and was made up of people in all kinds of clothes. Arms and legs were interlaced together, the formation like a complex acrobatic act. Three or four arms reached out for her. The subluminals pulled her roughly up. Soon, a half-dozen arms and legs wrapped around her from all directions. Bodies pressed against her from all sides, flesh that was both living and dead, human, but corrupted, and no matter how she tried to move, she was stuck.

33

Amadeus replayed Jessup's reply for the fourth time: "You have a deal. I trust that you'll make good on it." Unlike Jessup's previous messages, this one was encrypted, and since Amadeus had included his public key in his counteroffer, only Amadeus could decrypt the message and the data payload, which contained coordinates for a location uncomfortably close to The Donut. He supposed that answered the question of whether or not anyone had intercepted Eva's message.

Now he needed to plan his next move but he couldn't because something was wrong. Two hours had passed since he'd received Lilly's message that said they were on their way back. They should've been back an hour and forty-five minutes ago. But they weren't, and he was getting antsy, because at this point, he'd identified four separate groups moving toward their location. Two groups had originated from the point off the South Carolina coast. One of these was on a course for the location Jessup had sent, while the other was headed toward the false location of the coordinates they had embedded in the message. There was a group en route from Texas. Then there was another group in the area that had been moving so slowly that he couldn't determine an origin point, as there was simply too much data to sift through.

Presently, he assembled all the data he had, created a

compressed archive, and sent it off to Ed at the JDSC.

"Well?" Ross said.

Amadeus jumped. He'd been so wrapped up in what he was doing that he hadn't noticed the man come in. After his nerves had settled, he said, "I've lost contact with Lilly and Su Min, and it's been two hours since they reported in. Their last known location was here." He pointed to a spot to the north, then to a red dot near that spot. "I can't tell where this group originated from, so it's likely they've been in this area for a while. Then there's this group that came down from Texas." He pointed to another spot on the coast, twenty kilometers north of the river's mouth. "And this doesn't include the thousands of subluminals that—according to Grassal—are converging here."

"Sounds like a party," Maximillian Ross said. His tone was neutral, like that of someone making a observation about the weather.

"There's an emergency beacon on the P3, right?" Amadeus asked.

"Yes, but right now signals aren't reaching our receivers due to the k-storm interference."

"What if we were closer? Grassal said that a non-hostile subluminal tried to make contact with a human, but the human killed it, which sounds like something Lilly would do."

"We might be able to pick something up. I see where you're going with this ..." Ross nodded to Grassal. "You want to bring him?"

"He'd be furious if I didn't."

"You have your copy of the research, just in case we need to make any trades while we're out?"

Amadeus patted the money belt where he'd been keeping a portable storage drive. "Yes, I've—"

"That settles it," Ross said. "We'll go check it out."

"We?"

"Yes, we. We'll take some defense drones, a couple of security people. We'll be fine."

Amadeus shrugged. By this point, all the Morse code he'd forgotten had returned to him, and he had no need for a convertor to send the following message to Grassal: "We're going out into the field. Still want to make the trade with Jessup's people. Please do what you can."

No reply came back.

Before they left, Dr. Kongsampong arrived with a field pack for monitoring Grassal that consisted of hardened equipment and an extra power supply for Grassal's headpiece.

"I would send you with headpieces, but unfortunately all the working prototypes are currently in service," Dr. Kongsampong said.

Amadeus thanked him.

"And the other thing," Ross said to Dr. Kongsampong.

"Yes, of course." Dr. Kongsampong sidled up beside Amadeus and removed a black metal syringe from his bag. He said, "This might itch for a couple of days," and before Amadeus could object, plunged the syringe's disconcertingly large needle into the meat of Amadeus' forearm. Amadeus gasped through his teeth. Dr. Kongsampong gave him a pat on the shoulder, wished them good luck, and watched as they stepped through the door.

"What was that for?" Amadeus said, rubbing the throbbing spot with his hand.

"It's a location beacon," Ross said. "You can disable it later, but given the circumstances, it's probably a prudent thing to have."

After a quick stop by the lab so Amadeus could transmit the tag's unique identifier to Ed, they began their journey. Outside, a light drizzle had begun to fall, and the rain was refreshing. The air smelled of ozone and tropical flowers, though none could be seen, as if they knew something strange was happening and wanted no part of it. A monkey screeched from somewhere nearby. Every few minutes, Ross pulled his phone from his pocket and tried—unsuccessfully—to pick up the P3's signal.

Two security people, Timon and Regina, trailed behind them, weapons at the ready. The defense drones took up the rear, their motors whirring as they tromped along.

They followed a path through the forest toward the location from which Lilly's last message had originated. The already-challenging path was made more difficult by the gravitational disturbances caused by the k-storm that had settled over the area, not to mention the tangled mess of dense vegetation that covered everything.

After an hour of walking, they began to see areas where trees had been uprooted or snapped in half. Parts of the earth had been upturned, as if some giant child had used the ground for a sandbox. They stood and gazed around at the destruction.

Ross pulled the phone from his pocket and tried again.

"Got it. The P3 should be just up ahead, maybe a quarter mile off. But, bad news. Look."

Maximilian passed the phone to Amadeus. On the screen, not far from their present location, was one of the groups Amadeus had been tracking. It was tagged as the group that had been in the area for a while. Amadeus handed the phone off to Timon and tried to fight the feeling of despair that had blossomed in his stomach.

A little more walking, and Amadeus detected the faint smell of burned plastic. His heart grew heavy in his chest as they approached. Amadeus remembered crashing into the lake, how Holden Jones had shut down his craft and nearly killed him, then later pulled the "I knew it wouldn't kill you" defense. But now, there was no lake, only the broken frame of the P3. The polycarbonate window had two small holes in it, but inside there were no bodies, no blood, and no packs. A weight lifted from Amadeus' heart. He'd never been so happy not to find the person he was looking for.

Just then, the hairs on the back of his neck stood up. He caught Ross' eye then put a finger to his lips. From every direction around their position, encircling them, Amadeus heard cracking twigs and rustling branches. That, combined with the faint ammonia smell, told him exactly what he was dealing with. The defense drones tracked the sounds with their turrets.

Between the rain and the dim light, Amadeus almost missed the message sent by Grassal's thumbs. He watched, and once he was certain he knew where the loop ended, he deciphered: "I'm back for now, but a little busy. The subluminals are mine."

He responded. "You're in control of them?"

The response came back immediately. "Mostly."

Yes, Amadeus decided, it might've been better not to know that. To the others in his party, he said, "These subs probably won't eat us."

His face illuminated by the rift that towered just a kilometer away, Ross raised one eyebrow.

Regina said, "Probably?"

Amadeus noticed another message coming in, and he began to decipher.

"Grassal says that Lilly and Su Min were captured by a group of humans and subluminals to the north."

"Bigogli?" Ross asked.

"Sounds like it."

"What's Bigogli?" both Timon and Regina asked.

"It's complicated," Amadeus said.

"Any chance your JDSC people could help?" Ross said.

"They're probably on their way to the coordinates I sent them, which isn't anywhere close to here."

"Bummer. Then there's only one thing to do."

"And that is?"

"Make another trade. Give Bigogli what it wants, of course, in exchange for releasing Lilly and Su Min."

"They'll know if we try to keep a copy back to exchange with Jessup."

"We won't be going," Ross said. "Only me. You give me a copy of the research, and then pinky swear to delete any remaining copies. I'll convince myself that you'll do this, and meanwhile you go and do, well, whatever it is you want, and I don't want to know. Make sense?"

"I don't think—"

"One thing I've learned in my life is that I can convince myself of anything. And if Bigogli's minions' telepathy works like I think it does, then they'll see that I completely and sincerely believe I'm giving them the only copy of the research."

Amadeus nodded, but he must've looked dubious, because Ross said, "And even if they don't believe me, they probably won't kill me outright, since I could be very valuable to them. Even a caravan of psychotics needs money."

Grassal's thumbs twitched. Amadeus mentally deciphered the message then said, "He says there's a rift developing nearby."

Ross said, "There's a Mayan temple not far from here. The lower chamber connects to a small cave system. Stone will damp down the rift effect."

Amadeus didn't like the idea of a detour, but he liked the idea of being outside right now even less.

So they changed directions, and after fifteen minutes of walking arrived at a place where a hill rose from the forest floor and the carved face of a temple emerged from a hillside. A pile of rubble lay in the clearing, and a wide stone walkway led from the pile of rubble to the stone steps. At the top of the steps was a doorway carved with bas reliefs.

A rift had developed here, very close. Even now, Amadeus felt the effects of the k-storm that was causing the rift to grow, the gravity waves and tingling crackle of electricity in the air.

Ross scowled at a mound of stone rubble up the hill from the entrance. "That used to be a really cool honeycomb structure. Part of our agreement for being able to operate here was that we take over maintenance and preservation duties for this site." As they climbed the stairs, Ross said, "During an equinox, the sun would hit the honeycomb just right, creating a snake on the walkway. It was the Mayan way of honoring Kukulkán, a feathered snake god."

Amadeus nodded at that bit of history, but he was more focused on climbing the stairs without tumbling backwards. Eventually, they reached the entrance, where there was a metal door standing wide open. Amadeus peered inside, and saw a duffel on the ground.

"They were here," he said. Amadeus lifted the duffel and set it outside on the landing, where he used the glow of the rifts to peer inside. There were some bottles of water and a couple magazines for a weapon that he didn't see.

"We need to get inside and descend," Ross said, nodding to the stairs. "We're better off down here than we are out there, even if they have to wait outside." He gestured to the defense drones.

"Why not?" Amadeus asked.

"It gets a little narrow, they can't handle the terrain."

They entered, and Ross used a physical key to lock a gate behind them. The murderbots remained outside.

They walked deeper into the cave, Regina and Timon in front, Ross in the middle, and Amadeus and Grassal in the rear.

Inside the cave, their headlamps cast long shadows that stretched along the walls. A few meters in, Amadeus' light reflected off a protective layer of plexiglass that covered a painting on a wall depicting a man who appeared to be riding some kind of spaceship.

"How deep does it go?" Timon asked.

"The first couple hundred meters have been mapped, but you need ropes and harnesses and such," Ross said.

The cave walls were damp to the touch. A thick mist blew in from inside, and despite the dampness of the walls, the ground was dry.

As they descended deeper into the earth, the effect of the k-storm lessened. Amadeus thought that if they failed, if all their plans came to nothing, if there was no Rift Mitigation System, and if the k-storms and rifts continued, then humans might by necessity become a race of underground cave dwellers. For someone with mild claustrophobia, the thought was more than a little unsettling.

"Too bad The Donut doesn't descend underground," Amadeus said.

"There's only so much—" Ross said.

From somewhere within the cave came a rumbling sound. At first, Amadeus thought it was the sound of shifting stone, but he'd expect that to be a little more crackly. Instead, this was throaty and deep, and echoed off the walls. He sniffed the air but detected nothing but damp earth.

Amadeus raised the pistol and swept the room with his headlamp. The only movement he saw was the shifting shadows cast by the sweep of the headlamp's beam. Timon and Regina were doing the same. But then, he noticed something odd on the floor: several sets of tracks left by something with large, splayed claws.

He felt the hairs on his body rise. The gun shook in his hand. His voice a whisper, he said, "We should go back."

"What? Closer to the rift? Amadeus, sometimes life, just like engineering, is all about tradeoffs."

"Then at least unlock the door," Amadeus said.

"If you're that worried about it," Ross said, digging into his pocket and handing the key to Amadeus, "then hold onto this." The man's voice echoed through the cave. Whatever was in here with them had surely heard them by now.

"Shh," Amadeus said, then pocketed the key. He swept the room again with his light. The claw tracks led to a wall, then stopped.

"Amadeus is right, I think—" Regina said, but trailed off and cocked her head, as if she heard something.

Amadeus heard it too, a faint scuttling sound, almost like crumpling tinfoil. Amadeus looked this way then that, but still saw nothing. He disabled the safety on the pistol.

There was a sound of something scraping across stone. Amadeus turned just in time to see a subluminal spring from behind a carrot-shaped stalactite. The creature landed atop Ross, then they were both on the ground.

Amadeus aimed carefully and fired once, twice, the shots deafening in the enclosed space. The creature bucked with each shot, then turned its body just enough to peer at him with half of its eyes. Amadeus breathed out, visualized a line extending from the gun's muzzle to a spot in the center of its head, and squeezed the trigger. The bullet hit its mark and the creature collapsed.

The ringing in his ears began to fade, only to be replaced with moaning from Ross. He writhed on the ground beneath the subluminal. Blood poured from wounds on his neck and sides. His eyes had been reduced to bloody sockets. Amadeus kicked the creature's corpse off him and knelt beside the man. Amadeus grasped Ross' hand in his own. It was all he could do.

He looked up at his remaining companions. Timon, eyes wide, had a hand to his mouth and was shaking his head, as if in disbelief. Regina scanned the room with the light at the end of her rifle, alert for more danger.

Amadeus heard another scraping sound, the whoosh of something moving fast, and then Timon went down with a subluminal on top of him. Regina unloaded round after round into the creature, but it was too late for Timon, whose screaming had stopped.

A flicker of movement about ten meters away from Grassal caught Amadeus' eye. He pulled Grassal's tether, swinging his friend behind him. The subluminal altered its course after a brief hesitation, but that was all Amadeus needed. He steadied himself, then channelled his anxiety into pure, intense focus that let him visualize a perfect line as he tracked the subluminal. He fired one shot, then three more in quick succession. The creature dropped.

He met Regina's gaze, then her eyes went wide. She raised

her rifle then said, "Duck."

Amadeus hit the dirt and covered his head. Regina opened fire on something behind him. A high-pitched shriek was followed by a sickening thump, then everything was quiet.

When he opened his eyes, a dead subluminal lay atop Regina's motionless body. Amadeus scanned the room with his headlamp. The beam showed nothing but the cathedral-like structures that had been formed by millions of years of calcium deposits. He listened and heard nothing.

Finally, he permitted himself a closer look at his companions. Timon was dead. Regina was dead. Ross was dead.

Amadeus vomited.

When that was over, he reminded himself of why he'd come out here in the first place. That helped, and allowed him to do what he had to do next. First, he knelt down and stuffed a shaking hand into Ross' pocket to retrieve the dead man's phone. He confirmed that his own thumbprint wouldn't unlock the screen. Setting the phone on the ground far from the pooled blood of his companions, Amadeus pulled a knife from his pocket, cut off Ross' left thumb, and placed it against the phone's scanner. The screen came on. There was a message flagged as urgent from a contact he didn't recognize.

"T-SOC under attack by large, unknown group. Automated defensive units engaged and are providing cover for river evacuation."

After a good thirty seconds of deliberation, Amadeus came to a decision, opened a secure terminal connection to the AI lab's proxy server, and entered a command for the emulator to delete itself.

"Are you sure?" appeared on the terminal.

Amadeus hesitated, just for a couple of seconds, then entered "yes," and it was done. He waited for some emotion, some remorse or guilt or anything, to overcome him, but the only thing he felt was relief, because now there was one less asset that could fall into the enemy's hands.

Pocketing both phone and thumb, he started back the way he'd come, gun out in front of him like a metal feeler, the other hand pulling Grassal along by the tether. On the exposed skin of his arms he could detect a faint breeze.

He took one step, then another. Between each, he listened for the sound that would be the end of him. Soon enough, he heard something from farther back in the cave. The sound was faint but distinct, like metal scraping against stone. He picked up his pace, gun before him. He took ten steps, then stopped and listened. A rumbling growl reverberated off the cave walls.

Amadeus took off at a run to the place where the cave narrowed to less than a meter in width, and an idea struck him. It wasn't a good idea, but it was the best he had. He pushed Grassal through, feet first, into the narrow section, which put Amadeus between Grassal and whatever was behind him.

By his count, he had five rounds left. He hoped it would be enough.

Amadeus waited and soon heard something crunching the dirt, footsteps racing toward him. He raised the gun. There was a flicker of movement ahead of him. The shape came closer and resolved into a subluminal, all eyes and teeth. The creature was crouched low against the ground, the pupils of two dozen yellow eyes dilating against the light.

Amadeus took aim and fired twice. In the flash, he saw the creature jerk. It kept coming. He fired again, again, and again, until he squeezed the trigger and nothing happened. In the last flash, he'd seen the creature was still moving.

Something hard wrapped around his ankle and squeezed. Amadeus kicked. When he did so, something grabbed his other leg, and Amadeus fell to the ground. He swung the pistol wildly, once, twice. The first swing was a miss, but the second made contact with a satisfying crunch. He pumped both legs, pushing the creature away from him. One of his feet became lodged in ... something. Amadeus screamed, then pulled his foot back. His shoe came off.

His first instinct was to scamper away. He resisted, and instead swung the butt of the pistol to where his foot had just been. He hit something, so he swung again, and again. Something jabbed into his side and pierced the skin. Kicking the creature away, he lunged toward the creature and smashed the pistol down onto its head, again and again.

Each swing connected with something squishy and solid. He liked the way that felt, so he kept at it. The creature still tried to drive its claws into him, but it was growing weaker, and between each swing he kicked the claws away. His muscles ached and he was growing tired, but he continued to beat the creature until, finally, it stopped fighting and collapsed.

He felt around, followed the sinewy trace of one of its legs up until his hand passed over the bulbous, gelatinous mass of eyes, then on between them, to its mouth, where he felt the outline of his shoe. He pulled the shoe out and put it back on, ignoring the warm, sticky goo coating the outside of the shoe.

After stuffing the spent pistol back into his waistband, he felt his body for wounds. Cuts and scrapes covered his legs. His throat was dry, his muscles ached with the aftermath of exertion. Blood slicked his sides. With tentative fingers, he probed his abdomen and counted at least three puncture wounds. Not much to be done about those now. There were no bites. He just had to hope that that he hadn't gotten himself afflicted.

By the time he got to his feet, the ringing from the gunshots was beginning to fade, and he could hear his own footsteps again. He checked on Grassal by running his hands over his friend's body, finally settling a finger beneath his nose. He felt the faintest breath on his finger.

"That was a close one, buddy," Amadeus said.

On shaky, unsteady legs, he continued forward through the cave, pushing Grassal ahead like some kind of dowsing rod, and soon he saw the faintest pinprick of light ahead.

From behind came more scraping and scratching and

scratching sounds.

He began to run, pulling the key from his pocket along the way. He retrieved the key, arrived at the door, and managed to get the key into the lock. He twisted it to the left. It wouldn't turn.

He risked another look behind him. His headlamp illuminated not just one subluminal, but dozens. They crept along the walls, on the ceiling, and across the floor. He tried and tried again, but the key wouldn't turn. Then he turned it to the right. Something clicked. He threw open the door, shoved Grassal forward, stepped through, and locked it closed behind him. Thinking he had enough time, he reached in to remove the key but didn't see the subluminal on the ceiling until its claw slashed open his forearm. Blinding, white-hot pain coursed through his arm and up to his brain.

He stumbled forward, clutching his arm, as subluminals threw themselves against the inside wall of the gate. Designed to keep out thieves and vandals, the steel was sturdy, but it wouldn't hold for long. He took a few steps forward, past the defense drones. When he was clear, they approached the gate and began to fire. He barely noticed the sound, because he was trying to process what had just happened.

Ross was dead.

Lilly was captured.

He was in bad shape.

He slumped down to the ground while defense drones fired round after round into the subluminals. The puncture wounds in his abdomen throbbed, but the blood loss didn't seem too bad right now. He examined his blood-and-grime-covered forearm, and when he told his hand to make a fist, the fingers didn't respond. He pulled a bottle of water from the pack, took a few swigs, and dumped the rest onto his arm. In the brief time when the blood was cleared away, he was pretty sure he could see tendons.

At the sight of the internal workings of his own body, he

began to laugh. He didn't mean to, and at first it came as choking gasps, but soon the laughter grew into something else. As he took in more air, the horror of what had happened—what was still happening—began to sink in. That, combined with pain and exhaustion and relief and fear, caused his reaction to spiral out of his control. To an outside observer, they would've only seen a bleeding man sitting in the dirt and convulsing with laughter. This went on for some time and he was only brought back down to conscious awareness by the distinct sensation of a hand on his back.

34

Grassal was in an apartment with peeling paint and sparse furnishings. The apartment was located on Vanatter Street, one of the many cheap apartments he'd lived in with his mother. He could see the electronics kit that sat sprawled out before him on the stained carpet. The kit had been a gift from Tommy for his eleventh birthday, not the first birthday his mother had forgotten. He could only watch as his small—but not entirely child-sized—hands rifled through his resistors.

His mother opened the front door. Her eyes were wide. She said, in the rapid Spanish that Grassal lately had been having trouble keeping up with, "Have they been here?"

"Who, Ma?"

"You know ... *them*. The men from the government."

"Not today, Ma."

She began to scratch at the place behind her ear where she claimed aliens had implanted a microchip, and that the government—she never said which part of the government—was very interested in monitoring. She did this sometimes when she was nervous, and especially when she talked about the men from the government. "Someone told me I should be extra careful today. If you see any of them, you let me know, you hear?"

"Yes, Ma," Grassal said.

At the time, this had just been another exchange with the mother he'd seen as normal, the woman she'd always been, not the flat-eyed, somewhat slow-witted woman she'd been the past couple of months. The tense, paranoid tone and the wide-eyed gaze that darted this way and that, scanning, looking, seeking, was nothing atypical or out of the ordinary for her. That was just his ma.

The only thing that was unusual was that he hadn't thought about this day since it had happened. He hadn't remembered the way he'd gone into the bathroom, opened the lid on the stainless steel trashcan, and peered inside to see the half-dozen orange bottles of pills lying amidst the wads of paper and the empty toothpaste tube. He'd forgotten the way he'd picked each bottle up, shaken them, and noticed that they were still mostly full.

He couldn't make out the words on the label. At this point in his life, he'd still needed to break down long English words into smaller phonemic units, but even with that strategy, the names of the anti-schizoid medicines were utterly incomprehensible. But he could read the dosage instructions. Take once a day with food. Take three times a day. May cause ... something. Anything.

Grassal remembered how he'd looked at the name of the physician on the label, how that very same physician had asked him to call her if his mother did anything to her medicine ... like throw it all away. Grassal remembered how—from nearly as early as he could remember—his mother had said the doctors worked for the government, and that they could take her away from him, and him away from her if he wasn't on his best behavior, if he didn't listen, and do exactly as she—not the doctors—asked.

And finally, Grassal remembered how terrified he was to even talk to the doctor, despite the way she spoke to him in slow and nearly unintelligible Castilian Spanish. He was perfectly fluent in conversational English by this point, but he was too afraid to interrupt the doctor. Grassal remembered believing that the doctor could, indeed, be the kind of person who would take his mother away. This was his mother's medicine, and his mother's choice. He remembered thinking that an eleven-year-old boy shouldn't have that much responsibility.

That thought brought him back to his present predicament, and Grassal raised his firewall, which shut down that memory, and the competing memories of other people's lives. Yet, with the firewall up, he was isolated, separate from everyone who'd become a part of him, as if he was little more than a shriveled orb stripped of all the remnants he'd collected. He could no longer hear the thoughts and voices of the others. Each time the Observer's tendrils smacked against him, they leeched away at the very substance of Grassal. If this went on for very long, Grassal knew there wouldn't be anything left of him.

Understanding then that he didn't have a choice, Grassal lowered the internal firewall and opened himself back up to the other humans. Their thoughts, their memories, their lives, all were a part of him for now, whether he liked it or not.

"You'll need to deal with that," Tommy said. The voice came from so deep within him that it could have been his own subconscious talking to him.

"Deal with what?" Grassal asked.

"Memories of your shitty childhood, but that one in particular."

"You made it a little less shitty."

"I did what I could. But you're going to have to come to terms with all that happened and what it means for you now."

"We've got more pressing matters," Grassal said, then directed their efforts toward dispatching more snippers to work on the tendrils nearest to him. The snippers were fairly autonomous, seeking out and cutting tendrils, then repeating, and Grassal started to make more, when one of the people within him alerted him that something was going on with Amadeus.

Grassal opened an aperture within the torus then listened in on some of the subluminal threads. A few spoke of a monster that was just beyond a barrier. The monster had tools that could hurt them, but if enough of them continued to attack the barrier, the barrier just might fall, and they'd be able to destroy the monster's tools and tear the monster apart. Grassal sent out waves of calm, and told them that they would do no such thing, that the will of the Observer was that they help this monster, though it wasn't a monster at all. He then selected one of the subluminal threads that was close to his friend and used the creature's eyes to investigate.

Through the impassable barrier—a metal gate—Grassal saw Amadeus, who looked like he'd just been through hell. Grassal scrutinized him through the strange vision provided by the subluminal's eyes, and at first he appeared to be convulsing. No, not convulsing. Laughing. Bleeding from several places on his body, his sides, his arm. And rocking back and forth, laughter flowing out of him.

"My poor boy," Tommy said. "Can you—"

"Your friend's losing his shit," Cody said.

Grassal shushed them both. "Let me concentrate." Over his strings, Grassal sent a message: "Get back up."

There was no response. Using the subluminal's body as an avatar, he visualized a connection that would open up the ability to smell, and soon he could detect the scent of not one human—Amadeus—but others, combined with the stench of opened human guts. Fearing that something had happened to Lilly, he sent the subluminal back into the cave, following the tracks in the ground. Though the cave would be utter blackness to human eyes, Grassal found that he could make the subluminal's body emit a high-pitched screech, and this he could use for echolocation.

Soon, his subluminal avatar reached the mutilated bodies of three people. Another subluminal gnawed at one of the corpses. Grassal's first instinct was to attack it, but instead used another part of his mind to grasp the thread that rose above the creature and pull. The creature collapsed.

There was nothing else to do here, so Grassal returned his subluminal avatar to the gate, where Amadeus still rocked back and forth, laughing like a psychotic.

Grassal had seen Amadeus bad—Grassal had always thought him an interesting counterexample for bottling stuff up and holding it in—but never like this. If Grassal intended to help him, he couldn't do it with a subluminal. Amadeus needed a human touch to bring him back down.

Through his thread, Grassal sent a command to lift his arm. He strained and focused, and it was like trying to deadlift a bar that was just beyond his capabilities, but then he felt the help of others, felt their support behind him. He was able to raise his hand to Amadeus' back and give his friend some comforting pats. The touch appeared to soothe Amadeus, and soon the racking, crashing waves of sobs began to recede. Once he seemed to have calmed down, Grassal again sent the message, "Get back up."

Eventually there came a reply, but it was slow in coming because, Grassal observed, Amadeus was only able to use one hand to enter the message on Grassal's own thumbs.

"I can't help her."

"You can't, but there are people near you who can."

There was a long period of silence, during which Grassal could see Amadeus shaking his head back and forth. Finally, the reply came: "No. Very bad idea."

"It is a bad idea, but it's also your only hope. Do you see any other way?"

35

Under any other circumstances, having his afflicted friend's hand move enough to pat him on the back should've been cause for celebration. As it was now, it was only the thing that'd helped him regain rational thought, enough to know that their current plan was completely and utterly off the rails. To go begging and pleading, to throw himself at the mercy of Jessup's people and still hope to make the original exchange ... yet, he knew Grassal was right, that he was out of options for helping Lilly, so Amadeus pulled himself to his feet.

Everything hurt, and he felt weak from blood loss. He removed his shirt, held one side in his teeth, and used the knife to cut his shirt into strips. He wrapped one around his forearm, and used another to dab at the blood. He wasn't good, not good at all, but he had to keep going. The lives of those he loved depended on it.

He removed the phone and severed thumb from his pocket and held the thumb against the screen to unlock it. The location feed showed that a group had come up the river in boats. He was ninety-five percent certain this group consisted of Jessup's goons, and maybe even the man himself. The boats were now stationary at the docks, five kilometers to the south, beyond the direction they'd come.

The thought of walking even a hundred meters made every

part of him hurt. Amadeus slumped back down, and sent the following message to Grassal.

"It's too far."

At first there was no response, but then through bleary eyes Amadeus saw his friend's thumbs moving in reply.

"I'll help. Turn off the attack drones."

Amadeus opened up the phone again and found the control dashboard for the defense drones. Eventually, he figured out how to add himself as an authorized user, with his voiceprint as the authentication token. This done, he issued a command: "Hold fire." The dashboard showed that the command was acknowledged.

"Good to go," Amadeus sent to Grassal.

He heard something crashing through the forest nearby, then a subluminal stepped out of the bushes, arms raised in a semi-circle. It was the size of a rhinoceros.

"That's one of mine," Grassal thumbed.

Amadeus just stared as the creature lumbered toward him, powerful shoulder blades rising and lowering with each bear-like step. The creature's morphology was like most of those from the first wave. All of the creature's eyes were fixed on Amadeus, tracking each of his steps.

The subluminal stopped just in front of Amadeus. Amadeus looped Grassal's tow rope through two of his own belt loops, so that just in case he fell unconscious from lack of blood Grassal wouldn't be left behind. Then Amadeus climbed onto the creature's back and held on as the creature—Grassal's puppet—dashed away, crashing through the undergrowth, the defense drones trailing along behind it.

There were notches of raised flesh to hold on to, nothing as convenient as spines, but enough for his one good hand. Amadeus had begun to slip down the creature's side. He had nearly fallen off when one of the creature's claws pulled him back on, and positioned Amadeus so that he was laid across the creature's back like a sack of flour on a donkey.

Amadeus fought to remain conscious, focusing his energy on Lilly and how she and Su Min needed his help, while also trying not to think about what could have happened to her. But most importantly, he thought about how he would give up anything to help her. She wouldn't like it, but he would deal with that later. Because he was certain there would be a later, if only he could pull this off. There had to be, or all of this was for nothing.

Amadeus rehearsed the speech, about how he needed just one more thing out of their exchange, and he'd turn over everything else willingly.

Some time passed, and eventually the creature slowed to a stop. Amadeus looked at Grassal, whose thumbs were sending the message: "Getting close. Ready?"

Amadeus replied that he was ready, but that he needed to make this offer on his own two feet. So he got down to the ground, stood, nearly fell, then got his balance. He checked Ross' phone, which showed a cluster of men less than half a kilometer away. All he had to do was get close enough. They'd know who he was.

He instructed the defense drones to follow at one hundred meters, stomped Ross' phone on a rock, then threw the severed thumb into the dense undergrowth. Shirtless, one foot in front of the other, wounds wrapped in bloody bandages, Grassal trailing behind him like a balloon, Amadeus put one foot in front of the other. Soon, through ears partially deafened by recent gunshots, he could hear the murmur of men nearby. A few more steps, and he could see them. Amadeus staggered toward them. One of them saw him and alerted his companions. They all trained their weapons on Amadeus. There were at least thirty of them.

Just before he passed out, he managed to choke out the words: "Where is Jessup? I want to make a deal."

36

Bodies pressed against her as the human viruses continued their lumbering course through the forest's thick undergrowth. Subluminals slunk alongside them. In the purple and white light cast by the k-storm, Lilly was able to pick out Su Min, still entangled in the other virus.

The biological funk of unwashed bodies, decay, and disease filled the air around her. Given the way the clothing of the other humans was faded and tattered, she guessed they'd been out in the rough for at least a couple of weeks. Their faces were unhealthy, gaunt and drawn. Beards grew wild and scraggly on the men. Everyone's hair was tangled and full of dirt, leaves, and sticks.

Lilly called out to Su Min, who responded in a voice much stronger than Lilly would've expected.

"I am okay. It is just a little bit," Su Min said, then paused. "A little bit difficult to breathe."

"Hold on," Lilly said, then weighed their options. As she did so, all the animals of the night, chittering insects and screeching monkeys and who knew what else, fell silent. Lilly listened. She heard nothing but the sound of footsteps, the swish of clothing, and the muttering of the afflicted.

The wide leaves parted, and a white man of medium build with copper-red hair emerged. He was trailed by others. They all walked in step, either a well-trained group of middle-aged marching band members, or a single organism, orchestrating the various humans that made up its body like so many meat puppets.

"We are Bigogli," the red-haired man said. He spoke with a dozen voices from one mouth.

"What do you want?" Lilly asked.

"Bigogli wants what humans want. Bigogli wants the nightmare to end. No more k-storms, no more rifts. Removal of the cancer from our home."

"Cancer?" Lilly said.

"All information that caused this cancer must be destroyed," the man said. "Humans must forget what they have learned."

"How does Bigogli know all this?" Lilly asked.

"Bigogli is one, but Bigogli is also many," the man said, then motioned to the people in the human virus. "Their thoughts ... inform Bigogli's thoughts."

"Then you know that information can be copied."

The man cocked his head and tilted his body forward, as if leaning in to hear a quiet speaker in a noisy restaurant. "There is a key. The key must be destroyed. This makes the information ... impossible to read."

Lilly said nothing, only stared at the man.

"Roland Jessup is our common enemy. The one who started this. We would see him die."

"I can't disagree with you there. But let's back up. You said there is a cancer. Where does the cancer grow?" Lilly asked.

"In the Luminance. We must remove it and ensure that it will never grow again."

"And what is it?"

"Humans, and anything that creates their presence in the Luminance."

Lilly said nothing, and even though they had a common enemy, she did not intend to cooperate with them, mostly due to a mixture of stubbornness and spite.

"How can the key be eliminated?"

Lilly remained silent.

"Tell us, or you will join with Bigogli, and we will know anyway."

"No."

With that, the subluminals started toward her, in no hurry, their eyes neither malicious or hungry. Lilly felt every hair on her body stand on end, and her senses amplified what was going on around her. Disgust sat on her tongue, bitter as powdered alum.

With two subluminals only a few feet away from her, she listened. Over the quiet of the hushed jungle, in the space between the occasional mutters of the afflicted and the soft whoosh of rustling leaves, she thought she heard footsteps. At first, the subluminals closest to her showed no apparent interest in the sound. Then, without warning, some of the subluminals that surrounded the red-haired man peeled away and dashed off into the woods.

The first gunshot rang out, then a dozen more. The subluminal closest to Su Min dropped. Inky-black fluid oozed from a hand-sized hole in the side of its body. Lilly recognized the reports of high-caliber rifles. There were so many it sounded like a fireworks show.

Each time more subluminals left the main group, there would be more rifle shots, followed by silence. Whatever, whoever was coming their way was apparently very good at killing subluminals.

Lilly wanted to do something, to join the fight, whatever she could, but she couldn't even move her arms, could barely move her head, except enough to crane her neck. All she could do to those around her was pinch and bite, which helped her not at all. Whatever had become of the individual humans that made up the human virus, harming their bodies would do no good. She'd already seen what happened when you took out one part of the human virus: nothing. She had killed a man, no, not even a man, a boy, a teenager, and she'd gotten nothing but never-ending, gnawing guilt for her trouble.

Lilly felt things shift around her. The human virus lurched forward and began to roll. During the initial lurch of movement, there was just the slightest decrease in the pressure on her limbs. Propelled by hands and feet, the virus made a full rotation before Lilly felt that reduction in pressure again. This time, she was ready for it, and she pulled a leg free from the bodies that had held it. She felt hands upon her, trying to pull the leg back in, but she kicked and thrashed with her free leg, and in this way she evaded their grasp.

Again Lilly reached the top of the rotation. This time she jerked one of her arms free, then the other, and finally her other leg. Now she was able to move around inside the human virus, in a room with walls and floors of bodies, from which extended hands that tried to grasp her. Through the gaps in the walls, Lilly could see Su Min, who was doing the same thing Lilly had done, and who had at least one hand free.

"Keep doing what you're doing," Lilly said. "We'll get out of this."

As soon as she spoke, one of the subluminals that hadn't run off into the forest began to track alongside the human virus as it rolled from the clearing into the wood. The rifle shots were closer now, and Lilly thought she smelled the metallic tinge of blood, though in the dim light it was hard to tell which human had been shot.

The members of the human virus began to shift, as if receiving an instruction from an invisible stage director, and changed into something more cylindrical, like an arthropod that walked on dozens of hands and feet. Lilly guessed the shape would allow them to traverse through the thick jungle with greater ease. Lilly was almost able to squeeze through a gap in the formation, but then the gap closed, and she was again stuck, this time with her torso halfway out of the formation. The subluminal on the ground watched her with all of its eyes.

Maybe now wasn't the right time to remove herself from the human virus.

There were more gunshots. Something warm and wet sprayed her arms, and she looked up to see one of the humans, an elderly woman, bleeding out from a hole in her neck.

The subluminal that had been watching her began to shake and spasm. Its body went stiff, then collapsed onto the ground, as if the life had gone completely out of it.

The cylindrical-shaped human virus continued its march through the forest. With the one remaining subluminal gone, Lilly pulled herself free. She was now ten feet off the ground. She considered trying to jump down, but she couldn't risk a bad landing. They did, however, pass close enough to the thick branches of the surrounding trees that she was sure she'd be able to reach out and grab one.

So, she did.

She grasped the branch and held tight as the human virus continued on, making no response to her exit. This left her with two problems. The first was that Su Min, still entangled in the other human virus, was being carried away. The second was that she was dangling about fifteen feet above the ground. Lilly pulled herself closer to the tree's trunk, ignoring the spider webs that stuck to her face as she shimmied across the branch. Her fingers throbbed from the exertion, but soon she reached the trunk. There, she found a foothold, which gave her hands and fingers the rest they needed.

Lilly surveyed the scene. Su Min was still struggling to pull herself free from the human virus. Bigogli's avatar and the other humans were nowhere to be seen. Continuing her descent, Lilly guessed that they were busy with the attackers.

Six feet above the ground, she came face to face with a green snake, its head nearly the size of her hand. The snake regarded her, then pulled its head back as if preparing to strike.

Lilly let go of the branch and fell to the ground. She landed on her feet then rolled. The soft duff of the rainforest floor absorbed the worst of the impact.

She got back up and started after the virus that carried Su Min. Some of the virus' members were dead, bleeding from one place or another, but the virus did not eject them. Su Min was halfway up the virus' left side. One arm was free. Lilly considered trying to pull her free, but she heard a voice, and she hesitated.

The voice spoke in Spanish, but despite the language difference, Lilly knew the clipped, efficient words of a soldier when she heard them. She allowed herself to hope that somehow the Mexican military had decided to take up the fight.

There were more gunshots, followed by the keening screech of a group of subluminals. The virus, Lilly realized, moved toward the screech's source. Lilly didn't like where this was going, so she made her decision.

She took off in a dash, easily catching up with the ambling human virus, then climbed up the side of the virus, toward Su Min's hand, using clothes, legs, arms, whatever she could to gain a handhold. As she climbed, other hands reached out for her, trying to pull her in. She fought these off, and soon she had Su Min's hand grasped in her own. Through the break in the bodies, Lilly found Su Min's face. They locked eyes, Su Min nodded, and Lilly pulled. After a brief struggle, Lilly had pulled Su Min free to the shoulder.

The human virus stopped moving. When it did, its members closed in, like a finger trap that became tighter as it was pulled taut. Su Min let out an exhalation and her eyes went wide. Lilly realized that the people around her were crushing Su Min's chest. She didn't have much time.

"I'll get you out," Lilly said.

More hands grasped at Lilly, nearly more than she could keep free of. Still, Lilly grasped Su Min's hand again. The woman's grip was growing weaker, and Lilly knew her oxygen would be running out.

With both hands, Lilly pulled at Su Min's hand, grunting

with the effort. Su Min came out just a little bit farther, gulped in a gasp of air, then the human virus began to pull her back in.

Lilly didn't let go. She gave another tug, and Su Min's other arm was free. Now Lilly grasped her other hand, braced her foot against somebody's head, and pulled her the rest of the way out. They each held the other's hand as they clambered down the side of the human virus, fighting off grasping hands along the way.

Yet, as soon as they'd moved away from the human virus, Lilly heard footsteps moving fast through the jungle, followed by the unmistakable metallic *click-click* of a pump shotgun just behind her.

"Don't move."

"Couldn't you have come a little sooner?" Lilly asked.

An object flew through the air and landed on the ground before her. Lilly's shoulders tensed. The object bounced twice then rolled to a stop. The dead eyes of the red-haired man stared at her from the severed head on the ground.

The speaker, a man, stepped forward. He was flanked by a man and a woman. All had weapons.

"That one won't be bothering you anymore," the man said. "But now it's time to come with us. Maybe you'd like to see Amadeus? Mister Jessup is very eager to talk with you both."

37

Amadeus had stayed conscious just long enough to hear one of the men say, "We'll help you." The next thing he knew, a hand was shaking his shoulder, and a voice was saying, "Wake up, there's someone here you'll want to see."

He opened his eyes, shifted his body, and heard something crinkle. Through blurred vision, he saw that he was lying on a plastic tarp. The morning air was hot and every part of his body hurt, but when he looked down, he saw that someone had tended to his wounds. Grassal was tethered to a nearby tree, as serene as could be. With his good hand, he touched his money belt and felt that it was empty, which meant they'd taken the drive with the data. They'd still need the key he held in his head to decrypt it, so at least he had that small bit of leverage.

Three of Jessup's people accompanied two familiar figures down the path that led to their present location. Both had black hoods over their heads. Amadeus' heart both rose and sank. But he'd made this decision, and he would face the consequences on his own feet. He stood up just a little too fast, and his own wooziness, combined with the k-storm's lingering effects, nearly sent him tumbling face forward. Still, he got to his feet and managed to say, "Lilly?"

"It's me," Lilly said.

"I'm sorry, I didn't see any other—"

"Don't talk," a man said, just before pulling Amadeus to his feet and binding his wrists with plastic handcuffs. "We're going on a little trip."

Amadeus was unsteady on his feet, but he could walk. Lilly stared straight ahead, jaw set, her expression inscrutable. Amadeus listened, heard rustling leaves, the swish of fast-drying fabric, and the sound of footsteps on forest duff. They descended a slight slope and came to a place where trees towered overhead, blocking out the morning sun. A warm wind blew over Amadeus' face, and carried upon it the stink of subluminals.

Amadeus looked over his shoulder and caught just enough of a glimpse of Grassal to see that his friend's thumbs were motionless. If there were subluminals about, they weren't his, or he wasn't telling.

Not far away, a branch cracked, then another. Some of the men began to mutter. A wailing shriek rose up from nearby, which was followed by a spatter of gunfire.

Amadeus took a step toward Lilly. One of his captors grabbed his arm and jerked him back.

"It's under control," the man said.

Not far away, a person screamed, something howled, and the precise *tat-tat-tat* of automatic weapons fire drowned it all out. That sounded like the defense drones. He mulled calling out for help, but that thought was interrupted by something strange happening in the air around them, like a heavy blanket had been laid down over everything. All the light blossoms blinked out of existence, and Amadeus realized that gravity had returned to normal.

The gunfire stopped, and a boot kick to his backside urged him forward. Amadeus spent the rest of the walk trying and failing not to think about everything that had gone wrong, and how much more wrong things were about to go.

Eventually, they reached a sandy riverbank, where the air was redolent with the smell of decayed aquatic plants. Sunlight shimmered on the rippling water, upon which floated two motorized catamarans that had been tied off. Their captors loaded Lilly, Su Min, and Grassal onto one, while on the other, there was only Amadeus and three men.

Amadeus examined each of their faces in turn. He didn't know any of them, but they all had a haunted look about them, like they were about to do something they knew they shouldn't be doing, yet they were so far in, so deep, that they would do it anyway, because sometimes that was what men did.

The boats powered up and began to carry them down the river. The motors were loud, running on marine diesel, yet despite that, Amadeus heard the occasional rifle shot. They had only been on the river for a couple of minutes when Amadeus felt a hand on his shoulder. Amadeus turned to see the hand's owner staring at him out of big, damp, wide-set eyes.

The man gave him an almost-apologetic smile that didn't reach his eyes and said, "Make this easy on us both. What is the key for the data?"

Amadeus shook his head. "I'll only give it to Jessup, no one else."

The man gestured at Amadeus' bandage. "Hey, we patched you up, we saved your friends from the psycho virus people. Something could happen between now and then. Show some gratitude, my man."

Amadeus remained silent, and the man must've taken his silence for ingratitude, because he frowned again just before throwing a right hook that caught Amadeus on the jaw. The force of the impact was followed by an explosion of pain that washed over the left side of his face. Everything went blurry. He moaned, then put up his arms in something approximating a defensive stance.

A part of him just wanted to flee from the pain and retreat into some other place inside himself, a place far, far away from all of this. He ignored that part and listened to the part that told him to duck.

Amadeus ducked. The man's fist sailed over his head. From a crouch, Amadeus dove toward the man. The man staggered, once, then wrapped his arms around Amadeus' midsection. Amadeus landed a few punches in the man's side, then the man twisted his body and dropped to the ground. Amadeus was pinned. The man punched Amadeus in the head several more times then released Amadeus and got to his feet. Vision doubled, thinking muddled, blood streaming out of his nose ...

Amadeus got back up.

The man laughed, handed Amadeus a towel, then said, "It's not even fair. We'll talk later."

38

Grassal didn't know what was going to happen to his friends, but they were at least out of immediate danger. Right now he had other things to deal with. All the while he'd been helping Amadeus, the Observer had continued attacking him and killing new arrivals. Maintaining the adapter caused him to feel vulnerable and distracted, so he had to let it close, at least for now.

Grassal conferred with the humans within his body in search of a solution. With some input from a man with a background in mining, he began to visualize a cylinder with a drill at the end, almost like a tunnel boring machine. He converted a small piece of himself into a raw object, just like the cube that had started everything. Soon the object had grown—that was the best way he could think of to describe this process—into a drill made of light, collecting energy and mass from the world around it. He set the drill spinning then sent it down into the fog below.

Grassal followed the drill until he was up against the solid perimeter of the Observer. His drill followed the instructions he'd given it, and its tip was spinning in a blur of light and motion. He could monitor its progress if he really focused on it, but then Suki said, "I'll mind the drill and notify you if it breaks the surface," and he didn't have to.

"First class," Grassal said.

The tendrils still attempted to stop him, to constrain him, but his snippers formed a ring around him, and several of his members focused entirely on running the snippers. Cody found that after they destroyed one tendril, there were a few vital seconds where they could capture the severed tendril and absorb its energy into Grassal's supra-entity, thus growing his stores.

"Continuous improvement and refinement," Tommy said, "is the mark of good engineering. We might beat this thing yet."

Grassal watched as his constituent members worked, coordinated in their efforts but otherwise independent, on fighting back tendrils, operating the drill, and analyzing likely weaknesses. With his own attention freed up, he and Tommy focused on creating more tools: wedges, levers, hammers, saws, lathes, anything that could conceivably penetrate the impenetrable.

Tommy, and sometimes other constituents, gave him suggestions, and he set in motion the intentions that would create the object, starting with raw matter and then manipulating it with his will until it became the tool that he had imagined. Each tool he created spent a small part of himself, but he was still so full of energy, practically bloated with it given they could collect it from the tendrils, that he could afford it. Once a tool was made, he dispatched one of his constituents to operate the tool, and for the most part they did so.

"We've breached it," Suki said.

Grassal sent an instruction to pull out the drill and drive a wedge into the breach. The wedge descended just a little ways into the Observer. The compressive force was too great, however, and the breach closed around the wedge. Yet, since this wedge had once been a piece of himself, and the wedge was now within the Observer, a small piece of his mind was now inside the Observer.

Grassal became aware of a new symphony of sensations, of anger, frustration, and disbelief, and a host of other emotions that were both alien and familiar. Grassal imagined that the wedge inside the Observer was a pufferfish, all spines and barbs. He then tried to imagine the wedge expanding outward, but it wouldn't grow; the force of the Observer was too strong.

"We've got another opening," someone said. This breach was a fissure nearly equal in size to the one they'd already opened up. That was progress but, given the sheer size of the Observer, this wasn't anything more than a scratch. That wouldn't do. They needed a different approach.

Two of Grassal's constituents shoved another wedge into the fissure. Grassal followed this by visualizing a tool—something between a jackhammer and a pile driver—that he used to drive the wedge deep into the Observer, which responded by sending out more tendrils. Grassal created more objects to defend his core against these.

"This isn't working," Tommy said. "We need to think a little bigger."

Grassal knew Tommy was right. He conducted a conference with his constituents, during which he sent out a call for suggestions, and with their input an idea began to take shape. Grassal's body began to grow tendrils of his own, and each one divided, one after another, four, eight, sixteen ... Once he had the pattern, it was a matter of willing each tendril to divide into two more tendrils, and soon he had 4,096 individual tendrils, each with just enough intelligence to act independently but not enough to start a rebellion. He would've divided them once again, but he didn't trust that he could control them. Even this was pushing it.

At the end of each tendril he grew a long, needle-like appendage, and unconstrained by mechanical limitations, he caused each of the appendages to spin with a high rate of speed. Just above each of the needle-drills, he formed four anchors, like harpoons.

The tendrils snaked out in every direction, and he was spread farther than he'd ever been before. He still relied on his existing snippers, and some new ones, as many as he could make, to fight off the tendrils. Some were destroyed, but enough remained that he was able to cover a large part of the Observer's surface like some kind of alien face sucker.

"We're ready," the voices of his constituents said.

Grassal drove the tiny harpoons into the Observer. In most places, they stuck. Grassal spun up his needle-drills and plunged them into the Observer's hard outer layer. Everything around him quavered, and Grassal was sure he heard the sound of thousands of voices, of one voice, gasping in agony and fear. The needle-drills penetrated. Grassal opened up their shafts and soon the Observer's energy began to flow into him. Grassal drank it greedily, feeling himself grow stronger as the Observer began to thin.

The energy he drank contained stories, memories of things he didn't fully understand. The first was a memory of being floating and swirling, free, drifting through a black void for an unimaginably long stretch of time, searching and seeking and ... waiting. Another was a memory of a great being, something larger and more powerful than the Observer by several orders of magnitude, its size just about the distance from the Earth to the Sun. Just the thought of such a being filled him with dread, but he wasn't ready to fully appreciate that fear, because there were interesting details to examine, the details of an agreement, a contract—because everything in this place was a contract—that the Observer would act as a bastion against incursions of outsiders into the places beyond the Luminance. That gave Grassal pause, but he forced himself to focus.

The Observer was growing weaker now. All its tendrils had retracted, and the core of its being had shriveled down to something small and weak, though still far stronger than any Luminant supra-entity had been. Nevertheless, Grassal continued to siphon off everything it had until it was nothing but a desiccated husk. Grassal considered killing it, but then Grassal thought of the history of peoples he'd learned, how one group came to dominate another, leading to centuries of hatred and animosity. He knew he had work to do, he could be here for a while, and the last thing he wanted was some kind of colonial war of attrition. He would need Luminant help, and he didn't think killing their god—if that was the right word—would help him in this task. None of them—human, Luminant, Observer— had asked for this.

And so, instead of killing it, Grassal created a new containment unit within himself, something with thick, reinforced walls. He stuffed the Observer inside, closed off the ingress and egress points, wove a protective layer of energy around its outside, and finally deposited it into a prison deep within itself.

Exhausted and victorious, Grassal sent a message to the humans within him that they could disband and take with them as much energy as they wanted. One by one they detached and peeled away. Together, they rose out of the fog and back to the surface, where thousands of Luminants floated, anticipatory and glowing a shade of faded red that indicated something just below the level of abject terror. Beyond them flickered dozens of white pillars, disturbances, new arrivals who would have to be calmed, coaxed, and sent home. The thought of all the work before him filled Grassal with a sense of weariness.

"The Observer awoke," Grassal said, sending the words out as a mixture of both sound and meaning. "But now it sleeps again. None of what you fear has come to pass. We will start sending our people home and bringing yours back. We will honor the contract and fulfill our obligations."

With that, some of the humans separated into groups of three or four. Grassal knew without asking that they were off to help the new arrivals. When they'd been within him, they'd understood both the task that lay before them and the means by which they would accomplish it. Tommy, with Grassal's help, had trained them well.

Grassal spun up a torus around him, his largest yet, and

created an adapter. Inside, he opened not one but two apertures. The apertures were close together here in the Luminance, but Grassal estimated that on Earth they would be hundreds of miles apart. Soon he saw normal Earth stretching out before him. Silver threads flowed through both apertures, into the Luminance and back out again. They were almost like water, seeking a path downhill.

His torus was now the size of a small city, and he began to conduct the threads, pulling subluminal threads back, repelling the threads of new arrivals before they could manifest here as a disturbance. Soon, he found his rhythm, and the work proceeded apace. Those he sent back first—the newest of the new arrivals—were confused and scared but willing to listen to a friendly and confident voice. Grassal sent them home, one after another, following the same procedure he'd used with Deshondra.

Yet, each traversal took enough time that a queue had begun to form. Since Grassal already had two apertures, he tried sending to both at once. The first time was a little awkward, but nothing too far beyond what he was capable of. Tommy gave him some input, and Grassal then realized that he could batch up the returns to send as many as ten at a time. If Grassal wasn't also focused on bringing back Luminants, he could do more, but he had a contract to follow, after all.

"Can you try something for me?" Tommy said. "There's a hypothesis that I haven't been able to test until now. The test should only take a couple of minutes."

Grassal agreed and Tommy sent him the instructions, which seemed easy enough to follow. Through one aperture, Grassal focused his attention on the first non-biological object he could find, a stone about the size of his hand. Within the stone he thought he detected the slightest traces of energy, of life even, albeit ancient energy and life so slow-moving as to be nearly undetectable. Extending himself through the first aperture, Grassal enveloped the stone with an ephemeral appendage then, with a heave, caused the stone to travel through an invisible tunnel. A few seconds later, he saw the stone through the second aperture, hundreds of miles away from its original location.

"It's real," Tommy said. "Teleportation. I've ... we've done it. But we'll work out the details later. For now, let's just get everyone back."

Grassal sent twenty more people home, drunk on the implications of Tommy's words, on the possibilities of being at the forefront of a new era in human progress.

Soon he was so focused on sending back the next batch of ten humans that he didn't see the attack coming from either front. One moment, he was pushing a group of threads through the aperture, the next moment the thing he'd contained inside himself was creating some kind of connection to a supra-entity —Donald, Grassal realized after it was too late—that rose up from the crowd of Luminants around him.

Within seconds, he was being eaten from within while being assaulted from without. He felt dozens of tiny holes grow inside himself, and then the supra-entity was upon him, filling these holes with tiny tendrils. The other humans formed a supra-entity which threw itself upon Donald. They even managed to partially consume it, but not before Grassal lost the connection to the group of ten human threads.

Ten lives, lost. Ten humans, dead. Because of him. He knew they were dead because their threads had been severed when the apertures slammed shut. And still there was the gnawing sensation, originating in the container where he'd housed the Observer, of hundreds of tiny mouths eating away at him from the inside.

This was what happened when he tried to make things right.

39

The rest of the trip down the river passed without further questions or beatings. Amadeus spent most of the time using the towel to stanch the blood that streamed out of his nose. Eventually, the river emptied out into the ocean. They moored at the same dock where Ross had left his yacht. The crashing of waves filled the silence that had previously been occupied by the boats' motors.

The other river boat was docked there was well. North and south along the coastline rifts—bright, shimmering, and strange even in the morning sun—rose into the sky. Nearby, glimmering light blossoms of nearly the same stuff blinked in and out of existence.

Squinting against the blinding sunrise, he looked around for Lilly and Su Min. They were being led off the boat onto the dock. Physically, they looked fine, and they weren't handcuffed, though two of Jessup's men had a hand on each of their arms. Amadeus couldn't find Grassal. He scanned the surrounding area and saw, about twenty meters away, a man floating out above the water. The man was upright, so that meant it wasn't Grassal, but with the sun behind the man, Amadeus couldn't make out who it was. The air above and below the man shimmered. One of the goons lifted Amadeus and tossed him off the boat onto the dock where he landed in a heap. He started to stand but a strong hand pushed him back down. This indignity was followed by the sound of a familiar voice.

"Hey now, don't hurt the poor kid, he's under our protection," the voice said. "Amadeus, it's good to see you again, little fella."

Amadeus' skin prickled as he realized who and what was floating out on the water: Roland fucking Jessup on an invisible fucking boat.

"I'm happy we could help your girls with their little predicament, but I'm as pleased as punch that you decided my offer was a good one. Since we're all together now, maybe it's time to give the stakeholders a demo? This really is a fine piece of technological craftsmanship, and I'm excited to show it off."

Jessup pulled some kind of control pad from inside his suit jacket then keyed something in. The surrounding air began to hum, Amadeus felt something in his stomach lurch, then all the blossoms of light disappeared. Amadeus looked north and south. The rifts were gone.

Jessup hadn't been lying. The Rift Mitigation System was real. Roland Jessup could stop rifts.

"Do you like cruises?" Jessup said. His own invisible boat was bumping against the dock, and up close Amadeus could make out the vessel's outline from the shimmer of cloaking paint. Jessup stepped onto the dock. "I hope so, because we're going to take one. You, me, the rest of the gang? We'll all get together, maybe grill some tuna steaks, and catch up on old times. There's someone at my place that I really, really think you'll want to see. It'll be a nice reunion, all of us together. Maybe we can even find a way to sort out our differences."

Amadeus didn't blink. Instead, he said, "I've got what you want." He'd managed to get to his feet, though he was still unsteady. "Let's just do the exchange and everybody goes home."

"Now that you've seen the Rift Mitigation System, you know that it works. But the terms changed when you asked for my help."

Amadeus shook his head.

"Help that I willingly and graciously provided."

"You don't want to do this," Amadeus said.

Jessup raised one eyebrow and waited for him to continue, as if he were genuinely curious to learn why, exactly, he shouldn't want to do this. Amadeus, for his part, remained silent, and met Roland Jessup's gaze with the hardest stare he could muster.

Jessup said, "Your people will get their hands on a Rift Mitigation System before it's all said and done. And there is a real need for them, because the rifts aren't going away on their own. Give me the key."

"Rift Mitigation System first."

"Amadeus, I think you're misunderstanding the gravity of this particular situation. I mean, the metadata thing was cute, and I'll admit that we did check it out, but this is real life-and-death shit we're talking about here, so—"

Jessup stopped, his eyes suddenly predatory and keen.

Amadeus sniffed the air, caught a whiff of subluminals, then something else. It was ... vanilla. If she'd been here, then—

Just beyond the bow of the invisible boat, an explosion sent a spray of water, fire, and wooden shrapnel into the air. Amadeus dropped to the dock and covered his head. A few beats of silence passed, then there was nothing. Amadeus looked up to see that a section of the dock had been reduced to flaming wreckage. Close to the blast zone, one of Jessup's men lay sprawled face-down, blood running from his ears and eyes.

"What a fucking waste," Jessup said.

Amadeus' own ears rang, and his body ached from the compressive force of the blast. His vision was a little blurry, but he could still see, and some motion on the shore caught his attention. Through squinted vision, he saw the defense drones emerging from the woods.

Amadeus found Lilly, caught her eye, nodded to the drones, and raised his eyebrows. Lilly nodded in assent. Then, as discreetly as he could, he put both thumbs before him, where Lilly would be able to see them, and entered the pattern for, "Mine."

Lilly nodded again then leaned over and said something in Su Min's ear, which went unnoticed due to the confusion from the explosion.

When Lilly finished speaking, Su Min sprang to her feet and performed a silent, nearly splash-less dive into the water. Still, she wasn't unseen, and one of Jessup's goons ran to the edge and fired a couple of shots into the water.

That aggression against a tagged and trusted member of the T-SOC was enough to cause the defense drones to open fire on the men on the boat. Two men dropped.

Under the cover of the defense drone's fire, Lilly sprinted across the deck toward Amadeus. Jessup turned in time to see her coming and called out to one of his men. The man lunged toward Lilly but just missed her.

Jessup grabbed Amadeus by the neck of the shirt, pulled him in front of his body like a human shield, and put the barrel of a pistol to Amadeus' temple. The defense drones stopped firing. Lilly hesitated.

"Go, Lilly," Amadeus said, but Lilly didn't move. She was looking at something along the shoreline. Amadeus followed her gaze, and saw no less than a dozen figures emerging from the dense foliage that grew along the shore. From among them, a familiar figure stepped forward. Eva looked supremely confident, and before she spoke, she took a long drag off her vaporizer and blew out a cloud of vapor.

"That's enough," Eva said. "You've got twenty-two rifles trained on you, Jessup. Let them go, and stay where you are."

"Yeah ... that's not happening," Jessup said.

"The rest of the dock is wired with explosives. If you don't do exactly as I say, then ... *boom*," Eva said, pantomiming an explosion with one hand.

"And kill our mutual friends?"

"It's sad, but they're making a terrible mistake, and I can't let that happen."

The hand that wasn't holding Amadeus released. Amadeus considered running, but was dissuaded by the pistol that was still pressed against his temple. He did manage to crane his neck just far enough so that, in his peripheral vision, he could see that Jessup was entering commands into the control surface he held in his free hand.

"Eva, you've got to—"

It was too late. A glowing white orb began to grow in the middle of Eva's group. Soon it had enveloped them all, along with the murderbots. Thirty seconds later, Jessup entered another command on his control surface, then the glowing orb blinked out of existence. Everyone and everything that'd been within the orb floated motionless one meter above the ground.

"Portable B-gate. Cool, huh?" Jessup said. "But no time to admire the craftsmanship. We have places to be."

With one hand, Jessup guided Amadeus onto the boat. Lilly, however, thrashed and struggled and had to be dragged aboard by two of Jessup's remaining goons. They deposited her beside Amadeus and ordered both of them to sit on the deck. When Lilly sat down, she entwined her fingers in Amadeus'.

The deck beneath them rumbled as the boat's engines roared to life and carried them away from the dock, leaving the rift and the shore behind them. Soon, Jessup stood over them, hands on his hips, hair slightly mussed. Amadeus thought he looked like someone who'd just won a bunch of money after a booze-fueled night at the horse track.

"And so we begin the endgame," Jessup said. "Tell me everything you know. Give me the key and Lilly might walk away from this. There's no need for the Jones family to end here."

"I don't believe you," Lilly said.

"You don't have to. I believe in myself, and that's enough," Jessup said. "But maybe, just maybe, if we spend enough time together, you'll see that what we've built is ... something beautiful. What you're seeing is the emergence of a new age of man. And I have laid down the foundations of a new order, one where the will of strong individuals stoke the flames of destiny's forge. Does that sound right? I'm still refining my messaging. Maybe I need to hire a better publicist."

"You're a fucking nut job," Lilly said. "There's no way ..."

"That's quite the potty mouth," Jessup said. "Manuel, I've heard enough of this young lady's foul language."

As Jessup spoke, Manuel—the same man who'd beaten Amadeus bloody on the river boat—rummaged through a storage container, pulled out a roll of duct tape, and then proceeded to duct tape both of their mouths shut.

Since he hadn't killed them yet, that might just give them the time they needed ... though to do what, Amadeus wasn't exactly sure. Their plan had gone off the rails about three stations back.

Their mouths taped, Manuel grabbed both of them by an arm and dragged them toward the bow. At least, Amadeus thought it was the bow. With everything covered in cloaking paint it was kind of hard to tell. He could, however, almost discern the outline of the boat. It looked to run about the length of half a football field.

Eventually Manuel, with the help of a couple of his fellows, duct-taped their arms and legs to metal deck chairs. He then began to run a scanner over their bodies. The scanner beeped when it passed over the place where Dr. Kongsampong had injected the location beacon. Manual shook his head as if disappointed, then removed a knife and slashed open Amadeus' arm. Amadeus screamed while Manuel fished around with what he later realized was a large magnet. Eventually, the man found what he was looking for, threw it over the side, then— with surprising gentleness—cleaned and applied a dressing to the wound he'd just inflicted.

Only the searing, throbbing pain prevented Amadeus from losing consciousness.

40

Grassal felt the power that had coalesced within him draining away like water from a leaky bucket. Replacing that power was darkness, fear, and confusion. The Observer was pulling him apart from the inside, while Donald hammered at him from the outside, weakening his firewall, consuming every last ounce of his focus. He felt distracted, assaulted, infected, like the Observer was a virus that had found a particularly agreeable propagation medium within his body. Every molecule within his form stung as if he'd rolled around on a carpet of wasps.

Some of his objects still remained. Grassal tried to set these to work on his attackers, but there were too many attackers and he could only control so many objects with a single mind. He watched some of those objects that weren't under his control being destroyed by other Luminants.

Grassal needed to replenish his energy, but the remnants that remained looked thin and wispy, and a quiet voice in his mind warned him these remnants were unhealthy, that if he touched them, never mind consumed them, he'd be infected by their sickness. Even the flow lines in the area, all of which had previously been regular and predictable, now seemed sickly and corrupted.

Taking a quick survey of the area, he saw that the other humans had fled—Grassal couldn't blame them—but Tommy,

Cody, and Suki had remained.

"I need you all to join with me, and it's your choice, but understand: if I die ... we all die," Grassal said.

None hesitated. All of them joined with Grassal just before Donald drove its body against Grassal's firewall. Grassal resisted, shifting some of his rapidly dwindling energy forward toward the point of impact. This left an opening on his flanks, and some Luminants who were not part of Donald's supra-entity took the opportunity to attach themselves onto his body like so many ticks.

Most of his objects had by now been destroyed, but some remained, and the minds that had joined him helped pick up the slack. Tommy, Suki, and Cody deployed a cluster of drills against Donald, which left Grassal free to fight off the virus that the Observer was causing to propagate within him. He focused on it, trying to understand it. After some exploration, he realized that the Observer had found a weakness within him, a place that was hollow and empty and full of sadness, and had used that as its initial foothold, a petri dish filled with a warm solution of weakness in which it could multiply, causing something within himself to fester and grow rotten.

Grassal tried to close it off but doing so was like poking around in a raw wound. The Observer had identified his weakness, exploited it, and if left unchecked would use it to destroy him. Grassal knew it. He also knew that he shouldn't have tried to make things right. This was what happened when he tried to lead. It had happened with the Admiral, it had even happened—if he was being honest with himself—when he'd agreed that Amadeus should seek out help from Holden Jones. He could've told Amadeus to lay low, to wait for this all to blow over. Instead, a woman at a bakery had been murdered, Holden Jones had been murdered, Claudius Owens had been murdered, all because they were trying to set things back to right.

Grassal felt more of himself being whittled away from inside and out. Tommy, Suki, and Cody were calling out to him but he wasn't listening. They needed his help, but he knew it was too late. They were as good as dead because of his actions and his choices. One of his drills fell, then another. His own Luminant body was being decimated. Some pieces of it floated away from him, only to be consumed by other Luminants in the area, scavengers attracted by the death cries of wounded prey.

Then Grassal noticed something approaching fast from the north. It was large, at least four times the size of Donald's supra-entity. On closer inspection he saw that the form was composed of hundreds, maybe thousands of individual Luminants. Another supra-entity coming in to finish him off.

But instead of attacking him, it latched onto Donald and began to fling away Donald's constituent Luminants one by one. When this began, some of the smaller, individual Luminants that had been feeding on Grassal darted away.

Immediately, the pressure on Grassal was relieved. The Observer continued to gnaw at him from the inside, but freed from Donald, Grassal was regaining his ability to fight it off. His resolve was fortified when he heard a familiar voice in his mind.

"We assist allies. We fulfill obligations, as will you." The voice belonged to Filipe.

"You heard it," Tommy said to Grassal. "We made an agreement, and we have a duty to honor it."

"Everyone is going to die," Grassal said.

"On a long enough timeline, sure, but it doesn't have to be today. Grassal, you're down, but you're not out, so get back up."

"I ... don't know if I can."

"You have to. That memory ... You saw it for a reason," Tommy said. "That wasn't just a random flashback to your shitty childhood. Search your heart. We'll work on the Observer for now."

Grassal let go, placed his trust in the others, and began to examine a part of his life that he'd blocked out so long ago. Now more than ever he needed to see things as they really were, not through the filtering lenses of time.

He remembered how he'd felt when he found all those medicines in the bin, how it meant that his mother really was sick and that she really did need him to look out for her. And he really had wanted to help her, to do the right thing, and so he called the doctor who'd spoken to him in shitty Spanish, and that call had set off a chain of events. First the visit from a social worker, then a visit from the police, and then coming home to the aftermath of a raid by Immigration and Customs Enforcement—his neighbor had filled him in on the details— that had seen his mother whisked off to some detention center. He remembered Tommy telling him he'd filed emergency custodial paperwork for Grassal and days later that his mother had been put on a flight back to Guatemala, back to the little pueblo where their family lived, and that he'd be able to visit her after things settled down, and that in the meantime he could call her whenever he wanted.

Grassal realized that somewhere he'd decided that he was a victim, and that his mother—with her schizophrenia and inability to keep her immigration paperwork in good order—was responsible for his difficulties. He'd believed that a victim, someone like him, could not lead. A victim couldn't stand up for themselves and others, and if they did, bad things would happen, because victims were weak and subject to interference from external forces. There were forces out there beyond his understanding and control—current events confirmed that with a cruel certainty—and even the best-laid plans could be destroyed through no fault of one's own.

But, Grassal realized, if anyone was a victim, it was his mother, a victim of genetics, bad decisions, and a harsh system that had lots of need but little love for *limpiadoras* with paperwork problems. Everything else that'd happened to him wasn't victimhood, it was just life, which sometimes went to shit and you did the best you could in the face of that. The notion that he was a victim, that he was defined by his victimhood, even if he'd learned to live with it, was the weakness. Somehow, the Observer had found and exploited this weakness.

With this realization, a change came over Grassal Delgado. Each particle of his body began to vibrate faster. Every molecule within him began to tingle and pulse. The internal thought-stuff of his body fortified itself and became as strong as any stone. The insidious virus that had been consuming him stopped its forward march. Grassal created a new containment unit outside of his body then began to retch and heave the virus into the containment unit until he'd expelled the poison and sealed it inside.

"Is it out?" Tommy asked. "I—you—we—whatever—feel different."

"It's out."

He could still sense distant disturbances, but now his perception of them was different. Before, sensing disturbances had been like trying to observe them through smoked glass. Now, he could see, feel, hear, even taste them. At first he didn't understand how he could sense them with such precision and clarity, but then it came to him: he was connected to the flow lines, and the flow lines were connected to everything. They weren't just random forces that ran through everything around him. The flow lines were a network that connected every part of this world. Before, he'd traveled along them like a leaf on a fast-moving stream. Now, with nothing to stop him—no Observer, no degenerate weakness within him—he could become a part of the stream.

"Accept this responsibility," Filipe said, "and you will be forever changed."

Grassal did not hesitate. "I know."

With that, his body began to spread throughout the network. Soon he sensed every human, every Luminant, and every disturbance. Where there was a human or Luminant in the midst of an accidental traversal, Grassal directed their thread back to the right place. Where a disturbance was beginning to form, Grassal quelled it and absorbed the disturbance's energy into himself, leaving behind only the natural state of the Luminance. That, Grassal realized, was how he could quell the Earth-side rifts.

There were a few places where disturbances had been quelled—not by him—but what was left behind was toxic and repulsive, so much so that even the flow lines routed around these areas. Grassal would deal with these later. For now, he focused on finding his friends.

Grassal didn't need to create a torus anymore, not since he'd become a part of the network, but he still needed to create adapters to open apertures to connect to normal Earth, and this he did now. He watched as several silver threads—including one of his own—snaked through each of the apertures then converged at a single place where there was water in all directions. He saw his own body as well as other humans nearby. Amadeus and Lilly were among them, but so was Roland Jessup, and some men he didn't recognize. All seemed to be floating on water, and at first he was confused, but soon he detected the distinct sheen of cloaking paint.

Grassal put it together: Amadeus had asked for Jessup's help rescuing Lilly and Su Min, Jessup had accepted, and now Jessup had reneged on their initial agreement. This stung even more because—now that he could quell disturbances—there was nothing Jessup had that they needed. Grassal wasn't exactly sure what he intended to do, but he needed them to know they weren't alone, and that he was going to do everything he could to end this, once and for all.

Thus Grassal began the endgame.

41

The wind buffeted Lilly's face and she took deep breaths through a stuffy nose. Her body ached from the metal of the deck chair to which she was duct-taped. She turned to Amadeus. He looked pale, weak, and afraid. She caught his gaze and blinked out a message in Morse code.

"I love you. Be strong."

He responded with the slightest nod of his head.

As morning turned into afternoon, Lilly felt the fear and adrenaline drain away, replaced by a bone-deep exhaustion. She thought of Su Min and prayed that her friend had managed to escape. She prayed that Grassal would find a way to do what needed to be done. But mostly, she prayed that she would end the life of her enemy, because that was all that mattered. Still, a revenge fantasy could only provide so much energy, and with nothing but immobility, fatigue, and a vast gray ocean before her, she drifted off to sleep.

When she woke, a wall of thick fog roiled on the horizon before them. Soon the fog was so thick she couldn't see farther than five yards. Just when she'd begun to question whether she was losing her vision, the fog began to dissipate and she could see a great, shimmering wall that climbed into the sky. While she wasn't exactly certain what this was, she knew it was some kind of large structure, and that it—like this boat—was completely covered in cloaking paint.

She heard some mechanical sounds, and as the boat began a course that would take them directly into the shimmering wall, a man peeled the duct tape from her mouth then placed a black hood over her head. She felt their boat's motion slow, then stop.

Some minutes later, someone cut away her bindings. She was pulled to her feet and a hand on her elbow guided her somewhere. While they walked, Lilly heard the constant low rumble of machines and smelled machine oil and ozone and the aftermath of welding work. Many of these smells she was intimately familiar with, because for a good part of her childhood, her playroom had been a fabrication shop.

She was guided down what she guessed was a corridor, a guess she based on the way the sound of her footsteps echoed around her. Careful listening revealed to her that there were only two sets of footsteps, her own and the man who was leading her. Her heart sank as she realized that Amadeus had been directed somewhere else. Lilly didn't think that being split up in a strange place—especially in his current state—would be good for his well-being. Lilly resolved that her second order of business would be finding him, the first being killing Roland Jessup.

Eventually, they stopped. She heard the metallic click of a door latch, followed by the squeak of a hinge. A hand shoved her forward, removed the hood from her head, then closed the door behind her. She heard the distinctive *ch-clack* of a deadbolt being slid into place.

Everything was dark. Lilly blinked a few times, then with bound hands outstretched before her, sought out a light switch. The air around her smelled like diesel, cat piss, and decayed food. The walls were cool metal, covered with what felt like a thick layer of paint. Her fingers found a metal box with a switch in the middle. She flicked it, then there was light.

She was in a cabin. There was a cot with rumpled sheets and a little desk. Discarded food wrappers—candy bars and soda bottles—lay strewn about the floor and the desk. A crate lay open on the floor, and Lilly peered inside to see spools of multi-colored wire. Lilly had thought that this bastard would travel in style, but here she was in a dingy man-cave surrounded by garbage, kind of like the bunker, only worse. Trapped again.

Yet, for some reason, those food wrappers filled her with hope. At first she couldn't figure out why, but then it came to her: these people were sloppy, and sloppy people made mistakes. All she needed to do was survive long enough for them to make a mistake that would give her the opening she needed.

While she felt certain that she would kill Jessup, she was beginning to realize that this wasn't just about killing the man, it was about standing against everything he and his fascist pals represented: greed, control, the blatant worship of strength. If Jessup had his way, the right for an individual to simply exist would be under his control, as if he were some kind of god. Maybe the Rift Mitigation System was worth saving, but maybe it wasn't. Either way, she had faith that there was another way ... there had to be.

A part of her knew it was utterly insane to feel so confident when, in all likelihood, these people intended to kill her, probably within the next few hours. She was nothing more than a carrot to hold out before Amadeus.

That they underestimated her, Lilly decided, would be their undoing.

Lilly raised her wrists to her mouth and began to gnaw on the plastic cuffs, a secret squirrel escaping from her cage. Yet, the best she could do was to remove a little bit of the hard plastic at a time, and the work was slow. When her jaws needed a break, she rapped on the metal walls on either side of the room. The only response was the rumble of hunger from her own stomach.

Over the next few hours, she gnawed away enough that she was able to pull the cuffs apart. With both hands free, she began to pilfer through all of the boxes and crates, pushing aside cables and electronic components and various metal things that she couldn't identify. She wasn't searching for anything in particular, but the longer she searched, the more frustrated she grew, until she finally vented the frustration by kicking the nearest cardboard box. The box tore, its contents spilled out, and among the screws and fasteners and connectors lay a utility knife. Lilly smiled, picked it up, and slid it into her pocket.

Satisfied, she sat down on the cot to rest. She had just closed her eyes long enough to visualize Roland Jessup tumbling into the sea when someone knocked on her door. The knock was followed by a male voice that said, "Come out, time for talking."

Lilly heard the deadbolt slide open. Half-expecting a trap, she tried the door. It opened into a corridor with metal walls painted white with cheerful green accents. Manuel waited in the hallway, one hand on the butt of a pistol. Amadeus stood behind him. His face looked utterly defeated and dejected, but there was the suggestion of something else there, just the slightest glint in his eye.

"I think," Amadeus said, "we should have an open mind about this and listen to what Jessup has to say. Will you do that?"

Lilly took a step forward and threw her arms around him. After their embrace, she grabbed one of his hands, then using thumb and pinky entered the code for "bullshit." She raised her eyebrows to indicate a question, and he responded with the slightest nod of affirmation. Lilly felt the corners of her mouth tick up in the hint of a smirk.

"Follow me," Manuel said, sounding almost apologetic as he led them through a labyrinthine maze of hallways and corridors, past doors that opened to—she guessed—rooms like the one she had just been in. This, she realized, had once been a normal commercial ship, maybe a container ship. Along the way, she picked up new smells, of salty ocean air and something sharp and metallic. Finally, Manuel opened a door that led outside and ushered them through.

Lilly hesitated, because through the door appeared to be nothing but the vast blackness of open ocean at nighttime. No, not exactly blackness, she could see some moonlight glinting off choppy water, but still.

Manuel saw her hesitation and said, "You won't fall in. Watch." He stepped through the threshold and appeared to be floating just outside the door. She looked closer and saw just the faintest shimmer of cloaking paint beneath the man's feet. He slapped his hand on something solid. "Holding the handrail helps."

Ignoring every warning flag presently being waved by her reptilian hindbrain, she stepped through the door and out into the blackness. Amadeus followed close behind. He was unsteady on his feet, and she couldn't tell if it was due to injuries or fatigue or something else.

One hand on the handrail, she scanned her surroundings, trying to take in as much as she could, to cement the shape of the vessel in her mind. The shimmering outline stretched almost as far as she could see in either direction. She guessed that the water was at least forty feet down.

Manuel led them along the deck for a while. She and Amadeus moved slowly, despite Manuel's urgings that they must come quickly. Soon they began to ascend stairs, and up three levels they went. All this time Lilly searched for the blurry outline of a lifeboat, or a bridge, or anything that might help her if she was able to turn things around.

They reached the top of the stairs and now that Lilly had a better view of the sky, she could see a red-orange blood moon hanging low above them. She looked around for other details but couldn't see anything on account of the cloaking paint, and the overall effect was profoundly disorienting. Maybe that was the point, or maybe excessive stealth was just standard Super Villain 101 stuff. Whatever. Until she had about a thousand years to get used to the paint, she'd be at a disadvantage.

Manuel reached the top of the stairs and Lilly noticed that

even he double-checked his footing. It pleased her to know that she and Amadeus weren't the only ones who were off-balance.

Amadeus—true to form—stumbled when he reached the top, then recovered, then collapsed to his knees. Lilly bounded up the remaining steps to the top, where three separate things competed for her attention.

The first was two floating bodies. One was Grassal—sans headpiece—while the other looked like a homeless man. No, not a homeless man. Beneath the beard growth, long, scraggly salt-and-pepper hair, and shabby clothes, Lilly recognized Tommy Brunmeier. The second thing was Roland Jessup, who stood beside the recently deceased President of the United States, the latter looking quite alive. And the third was a rift, rising from a wall of fog and into the night sky. She blinked a few times, holding onto a vain hope that this was merely stress-induced vertigo. However, the rift remained where it was, a few kilometers away. The darkness surrounding the rift shimmered with k-storm blossoms.

Lilly helped Amadeus to his feet, and he asked, "What is this, Jessup?"

Roland Jessup smiled and spread both of his hands out. "Why, this is a reunion! Look at us, all together at last. You, me, even the former president here has graced us with his presence. This will be even better than the time we all got together for your little speech in DC." Jessup's eyes—cold, predatory, and gleaming in the strange lights of this night—flicked from Amadeus to Lilly then down to her wrists, then he frowned.

"Sorry about the zip ties. Fuzzy handcuffs might've been better, but you can't exactly expect same-day delivery out here. You know how it is."

"What is this, Jessup?"

Without taking his eyes from Lilly's, Jessup said, "Is he okay? He's repeating himself."

Lilly said nothing.

"Okay, okay, cards on the table. I want two things from you.

The first is the encryption key, which you've already agreed to provide, and the other is a nice-to-have. You want this all to be over, yes? You want your dad back, Amadeus?"

Lilly furrowed her brow.

"I want your dad back, too, because, well, reasons. And you're going to tell me how to make that happen. So, first the nice-to-have ... how did Grassal reunite Deshondra Lewis' mind with her body?"

Amadeus just stared at him, eyes wide, nostrils flared. A vein bulged on the side of his forehead, which glimmered from the sheen of sweat that had formed there.

Roland Jessup smiled wide and he said, "You can talk to him, can't you?"

Amadeus' left eye twitched, just enough to give it away.

"I knew it, I knew it. Just the other day, I said, 'Manny, I bet they're talking to Grassal somehow.' Manuel couldn't believe it, because that's just how he is, but I was right. So ... how do you do it? Is it that thing he had on his head? I'd try the one he was wearing, but it seems to have had its circuits overloaded. Thankfully, Lilly was kind enough to bring a working model along for us to reverse engineer, so I suppose we'll find out soon enough."

"Fuck you," Amadeus said.

"Amadeus, what's with the attitude? We're old pals, and *you* came to *me* for help. And I do want to help. You and Lilly here did the right thing, because I think that—deep down—you understand that Securaux has a solution to humanity's most challenging problem."

"You're just trying to land another contract," Lilly said. "By profiting off a crisis that you created."

"That's never been conclusively proven," Jessup said. "There are lots of questions, lots of questions. No one is certain how the rifts came to be."

"It's not just that," Amadeus said, then pointed at Jessup. "Even this Rift Mitigation System you came up with ... it's a fix for a problem that you caused because your shitty demon gates didn't work right."

"Who do you think built them?"

Amadeus reeled backward, his head shaking from side to side.

"The rifts didn't start until after you started deploying demon gates," Lilly said. "Most scientists agree that—"

"That correlation doesn't equal causation," Jessup said. "By that logic, maybe the rifts started when Amadeus was accused of his father's murder."

"You pushed that story," Amadeus said.

"My point stands. Correlation is not causation, and sometimes scientists are wrong. The truth is, there's so much chaos in the world right now that nobody really knows anything … except that the Securaux Rift Mitigation System will become a piece of critical public infrastructure for every government on Earth. Right now, the world needs experience, competence, and expertise. We certainly can't let a bunch of lazy bureaucrats or argumentative scientists run such an important operation, can we?"

"Nobody will deal with you," Amadeus said. "You are a war criminal. An official, on-the-books war criminal."

A wry grin spread across Jessup's face. "That's only partly true. Thanks to someone I like very much calling in some favors —which I deeply appreciate—we've already got our first long-term customer lined up, don't we, buddy?"

Jessup slapped the late-not-late President on the shoulder. The President, for his part, looked profoundly uncomfortable. Even he knew this was a shit deal, and he'd been a president known for making shitty deals.

"Seriously?" Lilly said. "You are the picture of incompetence. You let Takun overrun your gates, you released more of those … things than anyone could handle, not to mention all the—"

"That's a feature, not a bug," Jessup said. "Those creatures were training. I gave men a sense of purpose." He waved a hand then made a mock-spooky face. "Protect your homeland, fight the big, bad inter-dimensional monster salivating at the prospect of tearing your precious children to ribbons. All that, though, it's just a sideshow. The real thing is the control of and protection against rifts we can provide. War criminal or not, I'm the only motherfucker around who can do it."

Finally, Lilly figured it out. Roland Jessup wasn't out for mere self-preservation, and it wasn't just money he wanted, though that certainly helped him achieve his aims. She should have seen it. It was right there in his personal history.

Roland Jessup wanted the power to control the world around him. He'd lost his daughter and wife because he was powerless to stop what had happened to them. Everything else, Lilly realized, was built from that. Given enough time and the right opportunity, if she could determine just the right place to crack his foundation, then perhaps she could bring the whole damn thing crashing down.

"Tell me how you talk to Grassal, and tell me how he can bring people back," Roland Jessup said, "or I will kill Lilly, and Grassal, and your father, too."

Or she could just slash his throat.

Before Lilly realized what she was doing, she pulled the utility knife from her pocket, extended the blade, and dashed toward Roland Jessup.

She was just about to drive the blade into his jugular when a cracking pain spread across her shoulder. She hit the ground on her side, and all the wind was knocked out of her. She couldn't breathe. Her mind registered something—a knee—pressing into her back. She realized the knee belong to a man beneath a cloaking cape. The man removed the knife from her hand. Lilly caught her breath, bucked, then rolled out from beneath him.

Amadeus threw himself at the man, sending him sideways, then Lilly scrambled back to her feet and prepared for another charge. A gunshot cracked in the air, and four more people appeared from beneath cloaking capes and positioned themselves between her and Jessup.

Jessup placed a pistol against Grassal's temple. "Well?"

Lilly noticed the pistol didn't shake at all. He thought he was still in control. "Fuck you, Jessup."

"I like you, Lilly, I really do. You're strong and scrappy, but you have a very foul mouth, and it's offensive to those around you."

With that, Jessup nodded to one of his goons, who stepped forward and pistol-whipped Amadeus. Lilly heard a sickening thunk as heavy steel hit the side of his head. Her own stomach lurched when she saw Amadeus' eyes roll back in his head just before he collapsed to the metal deck.

"Maybe you need some more time to consider your options. I really want to make this work for everyone here, but my patience is growing thin, very thin." To the four men who'd appeared, he said, "Take them downstairs."

One of the men pressed a gun into her back, two more lifted Amadeus, and thus they all journeyed deep into the bowels of the ship and eventually into a dark room that reeked of subluminal.

"Lights come on in five minutes," one of the men said, "but you'll wish they hadn't."

The lights came on and Lilly screamed despite herself. The creature—inter-dimensional demon, Takun, sub, id, whatever—gazed at her through hundreds of eyes, each one of them tracking her every movement as she scooted toward the back wall, dragging Amadeus over with her. Yes, there was thick glass between her and the creature, but the glass wasn't that thick. She expected it to begin pummeling the glass at any moment.

With nothing else to do, she took a longer look at the creature before her. It was big, at least three times the size of Vaskulo. There was the characteristic mottled gray-and-black skin, four legs that rippled with muscles. Short, black, needle-like spines rose from its back. And, she knew, every last bit of its body had manifested out of the ether, a result of whatever the observer—in this case she had no doubt it was Roland Jessup himself—had expected to see.

Lilly tried to swallow, but her throat was dry, worse than the worst cotton mouth she'd ever had. Her hands shook and her palms were damp. She nudged Amadeus, but he remained unconscious, a little stream of drool running from the side of his mouth. Besides the smell of ammonia and oil, she caught the acrid scent of her own fear-tinged perspiration.

The subluminal opened its wide mouth, exposing rows of sharp, jagged teeth, and emitted a shriek that made Lilly's blood run cold. She did not want to be here, she did not want to face this beast, and the worst part was she had to do it alone. Still, she had to do it, and the creature was either going to kill her or it wasn't.

With that thought in her mind, she got to her feet and approached the glass. Those eyes—yellow, watery, jittery, bloodshot rectangular-pupiled eyes—tracked her every move.

There was nothing to do but stare right back. Her stomach threatened to eject its contents, but she forced it to behave, because she wouldn't show any weakness, not to the creature, and not to whoever might be watching them.

Without any warning, the creature threw itself at the glass of their cell. Something metal crashed and rattled. Lilly did not step back, barely even flinched. The creature's face squished against the glass, and if the only thing between her and Amadeus wasn't a glass pane two fingers thick, she might've thought it comical. Except that she was barely able to think about anything. All her awareness was focused on the monster that watched her, and none on her racing heart, or the sheen of sweat on her forehead. The monster dragged its talons down the glass, causing a high-pitched, almost-painful scratching sound, as if the creature enjoyed the effect it had on Lilly.

But of course it did.

She reminded herself that this one could be like Vaskulo,

fully sentient, conscious, possibly even able to communicate. Lilly stared into those yellow eyes, took a step toward the glass, and before she knew what she was doing, said, "I'm the queen of all wild things. Who are you?"

The creature did not respond.

Still keeping part of her attention on the creature, she studied her surroundings. There was not one but two doors to their cell. One had an electronic keypad lock. That was the one through which they'd come in. The other door could be opened from the inside by means of lifting a metal bar. If she chose to, she could lift the bar, and walk right out ... and into the chamber that held the creature. This, she decided, was not a coincidence, but one of Jessup's fascist strength things, albeit a downright perverse one.

As if summoning a djinn from a bucket of shit, a familiar, haughty voice crackled over a surprisingly sub-par audio connection.

Mistakes, she thought. They would make a mistake, and she intended to find it and use it to get her people out of here.

"Hey girl, it's your pal Ro—. I just wa— — hello, now that — — nasty T. He's quite the specimen, isn't he? We haven't — — — awhile. Just something to — —— . And you've probably figured out by now that —— —— isn't dead, and neither are —— —— because you have — —— —— potential. Teamwork, Miss Jones. We — — — same thing here. We all —— — — ——." A pause, then, "Well?"

Mistakes. Roland Jessup should have killed them by now. That, she decided, would be his mistake. Now, she just needed a little more time.

"Why are we down here?" Lilly asked. Answering a question with a question was always a good way to stall. She imagined him smiling on the other end, enjoying himself, judging her, trying to guess what she'd do next. She intended to make that difficult.

"And do you have —— aggressive?"

On the other side of the glass, the creature paced, never taking its eyes off of her. Lilly decided to try a different tack.

"I'm sorry for assaulting you," Lilly said. "It's the PTSD, and it's, well, let's be honest, it's your fault." Her mouth felt gross as the apology came out, but the silence, the extra time was worth it.

"What, say again? These intercoms, they're —— ."

She repeated herself. Saying the apology was only half as bad as last time. That troubled her. How depraved could one person get?

"Tell me how you communicate with Grassal." Now the radio was perfectly clear.

She could feel the truth on her lips, but if it came out, they lost that much more leverage. She tried and failed to understand how he hadn't figured it out yet.

"I hear crazy stuff in my mind when Grassal is around."

"What kind of crazy stuff?" Roland Jessup asked.

"Images, Roland. It's like ... I can see Grassal in my mind's eye, like he's standing right there before me."

"What does he look like?"

"A guy in a banana costume, about four feet high," Lilly said. "With these cute little boots and—"

"That's enough."

As soon as the connection ended, the creature began to slam its moose-sized body against the glass, again and again. The metal floor vibrated with the shock of the blows. Lilly's muscles tensed.

When the creature wasn't slamming its body against the glass, there were stretches of silence filled with only the hum of the ship's diesel-electric engine. During one of these stretches, she heard glass crack. Her eyes shot to the source of the sound. A little white fissure had appeared near the upper left corner of the glass.

That was how it would get in.

One crack, then another. And then, it would be over.

Her shoulders slumped, her head tilted slightly, and she felt ... pity for the creature. She thought of how it was locked in here alone, separated from others of its kind, and probably beaten, tortured, and abused.

It was then that she realized her own mistake. She'd always blamed the subluminals for what they were, had hated them without understanding that they—just like her—were victims of their circumstances. Su Min had been right—they couldn't help being what they were any more than an oak tree could help losing its leaves in the winter. They'd been dragged far from their home and forced to become something unrecognizable, not unlike her.

It was a long shot, but this realization gave her a new idea. Recalling the way her mind had recoiled when Vaskulo had attempted to reach out to her—when she had vigorously rejected its attempts, just before it was murdered—she relaxed, and remembered the way the creature had spoken to her. She could never recreate the words vocally, there was a multi-dimensionality to them, each word almost a harmonic triad, sometimes major, sometimes minor, transmitted in even triplets. Remembering their ethereal quality, like plucked strings shrouded in mist, she shaped the sentences she spoke in her mind.

I'm sorry for what he has done to you, Lilly thought. The creature slammed into the glass again. The crack spread.

He hurts you. Others hurt you. Everyone fears you.

One more, and the crack was as long as her arm. Some broken bits of glass tinkled onto the floor. After throwing itself at the glass one more time, the creature began to pick at the fissure, exploring the crack's rough edges with the point of a sharp claw. Lilly drew herself up, and took a step toward the glass, where she stared into the creature's yellow eyes without blinking once.

I'm not afraid of you now.

The creature stopped.

You were not given a choice.

A wave of vertigo washed over her. Everything sounded like she was in a vast, metallic hall where sounds echoed again and again. Something large and alien slunk about the periphery of her awareness, a cloud of gas rippling and curling against the walls of her mind. She imagined letting it in, allowing herself to trust it, but it was such a vile thing ...

The creature slunk back, a growl rumbling from deep within its quivering, unnatural guts. It knew. Somehow. It knew. And so, she controlled her thoughts. Her thoughts did not need to control her. She sent another thought.

We are allies. We share enemies.

The creature slapped the wall, again and again. A basketball-sized hole had appeared. The creature had its claw through. It pulled at the glass, trying to widen the mouth just enough so it could slither through and end their lives.

I knew Vaskulo. We were ... friends.

Opening a little hole on the periphery of her mind, she attempted to capture the sounds of Vaskulo when it had tried to initiate contact, the patterns of its speech, the interweaving harmonic layers, the color of the tones. At first, she couldn't get the sonic qualities quite right, but then—unbidden—the strains of Verdi's *Requiem* flowed into her mind. She then imagined Vaskulo's words merging with the music. Immediately, the creature stopped, stepped back from the glass, and then—to Lilly's relief and surprise—lifted two arms in that peace gesture they did, revealing its belly to her, not once, not twice, but three times.

Lilly felt the creature around her, not as it looked, but as it was, like fog moving slowly through the air. She had a sense of being ... larger, as if she had a new capacity to manipulate the world around her. She was about to explore this sensation, when a liquidy rumbling sound echoed off the walls of her mind, and she heard the creature's voice in her mind for the first time.

Tried preventing work. Tried destroying work. Destroyed human minds, destroyed human bodies, destroyed Takun minds. Forgot own name. To no end. Bigogli has failed.

Lilly's guts twisted as she gazed upon the creature that had controlled people and subluminals, the creature that'd tried—in its own way—to stop Jessup's work. It must've known all along what Jessup was trying to do, and if they had only been—

I hate him. Please use me.

Bigogli then spread itself prone on the floor, as if it had gone limp. At first she only stared at it, then she began to explore that sense of expanded awareness, letting her mind reach out as far as it would go. She felt a slight, tingly fluttering sensation somewhere far beyond her fingertips, as if something had clicked into place. And with that, she caused a single, knobby claw to rise. As she raised and lowered the creature's finger, she began to get a sense of the power she controlled. But it was still awkward, and she needed more time to get the knack for it. Locked here in the cargo hold, that seemed to be the one thing she had.

She persisted and soon she could raise not just single digits, but one arm, then another, then Bigogli's head. All the while, she did her best to send thoughts of understanding and acknowledgement. Bigogli responded with thoughts that were somewhere between acceptance and resignation. The more that she moved the creature, the less she needed to move her own body, and soon she was able to control the creature with only her thoughts and will. Once she had enough control over the creature to do so, she had the creature destroy the most obvious cameras—there were three—on its side of the glass.

Eventually, she learned how to make the creature do almost everything she needed it to. While doing so, she developed a plan that, while certainly not foolproof, was probably their best hope. As she practiced a flying leap that she estimated could take down at least four men, Bigogli—who had been otherwise silent during her training—filled her mind with the following words.

Someone comes near, someone comes soon.

This, Lilly thought, was going to be interesting.

42

Grassal followed the silver thread that led him to his body and—through an aperture he'd opened—saw that it floated on a shimmering, nearly invisible surface. Tommy Brunmeier's body floated directly beside him. Two soldiers stood nearby, a man and a woman, rifles held at the ready. Their eyes scanned the area, but there was nothing to see save the light blossoms from the k-storm.

Grassal said to Tommy, "Last chance. Are you sure you're willing to do this?"

"Yes ... but let's run a couple more tests, just in case."

Grassal opened a second aperture at a location that was close to the first one in Otherspace, but several thousand miles away in normal space, at a place he knew well.

At first, the connection was shaky and tenuous. Grassal was still getting used to being able to see and sense in multiple places at once. Nevertheless, he persisted, focused his mind, and soon the connection solidified. Yet, he was still afraid that he'd screw this up, just like everything else he'd done, and that his test subject would arrive at the planned destination as nothing more than a pile of viscera.

Grassal marshaled several of the k-storm blossoms together, creating in normal space an adapter the same diameter as a tree, twice as tall as a person, and shaped roughly like a pea pod. His target, the man who was nearest to Tommy's floating body, noticed the adapter, and both he and his companion raised their rifles, for all the good it would do them.

Grassal struck, directing the adapter to envelop his target. The feeling of a human body within the adapter was disorienting, but Grassal held on, keeping the man fully encased in the adapter, and propelled him from one end of the normal space torus to the other. Along the way, however, Grassal noticed that something had happened to his payload. When he deposited the man at the exit point, the man's body had been reduced to a bloody mess of gore.

Grassal immediately realized his mistake: the behavior of his own adapters, just like B-gates, were affected by the expectation of the observer. As squishy and weird as it seemed, if he expected his transportees to become gore—as some small part of him had—they would become gore. If he expected them to survive, then they would survive.

All this had occurred in the flash of a couple of seconds, though to the woman who remained, it would've appeared that her companion had been enveloped in a pea pod of light before vanishing. She was currently swinging her rifle from Grassal to Tommy then back to Grassal, as if one of the two immobile, floating bodies had somehow caused her companion to disappear. She wasn't wrong.

Before she had a chance to do anything further, Grassal engulfed the woman with his adapter. While he did so, he imagined that she was hale and healthy and standing in a parking lot in Stamford, Connecticut.

Certain that she would be okay—even if she deserved worse—Grassal initiated the transit. A few seconds later, he deposited the woman exactly where he'd intended. Through the aperture, he could see her looking around, still swinging her rifle.

And just like that, he'd done it. He'd just transported a human from one place to another. To celebrate, he used his adapter to remove the rifle from the woman's hands and then transport it back to the place where he'd picked her up, right beside his and Tommy's body.

In Otherspace, Tommy's Luminant form glowed with the colors of excitement and questioning. Grassal flashed satisfaction and success, explained what had happened, and together they shared in a small moment of triumph.

"I'll send your body first, then you right behind it," Grassal said.

They embraced, two bodies of light smashing together, creating a spray of color and light in the world of darkness that surrounded them.

Tommy seemed to want to say more, but he allowed Grassal to focus his attention on ensuring the transit would be smooth. Grassal imagined and expected that Tommy's body would arrive safely in the emergency room of Mt. Sinai Hospital in Manhattan.

Grassal closed the aperture, pulled his adapter up and away from Stamford, then reoriented it in a southwestward direction. The NYC megalopolis passed below him in a flash, and then one node of his mind was in a hospital emergency room, looking at an empty bed.

"Here we go," Grassal said, and began the transit. Tommy's body levitated above the bed.

"I guess ... I guess this is goodbye," Tommy said.

"It's never goodbye."

Grassal collected the silver thread that flowed from Tommy's physical body into Otherspace, connected it with Tommy's Luminant form, and began the transfer. Seconds later, Tommy's consciousness re-entered his physical mind and his body dropped onto the bed. Grassal maintained the connection long enough to see two things happen. The first was that Tommy was blinking his eyes, which indicated that the transfer had done him no apparent harm. The second was that his presence was observed by someone who could give him medical attention, in this case a nurse who gazed wide-eyed at the man who'd suddenly appeared in a hospital bed.

That task accomplished, Grassal returned his attention to the ship and began to search for his friends. Unlike Stamford and NYC, Grassal wasn't familiar with the lay of the land, and he would have to search one area at a time, so he began to move his adapter through the various parts of the ship, across the decks and onto the bridge, opening and closing apertures as he went. On the bridge he found men. Unsurprisingly, they appeared disturbed by the presence of a giant, glowing pea pod. One of them put a call into a radio. Through his adapter Grassal could see the electromagnetic waves emitted by the radio.

Grassal left the bridge then began searching a lower level when a wall of blackness slammed into him. Every part of him that had been connected with this area of normal space was severed. There was no graceful shutdown, just ... nothing. He pulled all of his attention back into Otherspace, where he felt sick and disoriented. He wasn't sure what exactly had happened, but he guessed that they'd activated the Rift Mitigation System.

He collected himself and tried to form a new adapter, but the ability to create a connection wasn't there, not right now, not with conditions around the place where the Rift Mitigation System had fired such as they were. Farther from the ship, the flow lines were healthier and he could create a small adapter, but that was out over the open ocean, far from his friends. He tried tunneling into the location, but the Rift Mitigation System had left a barrier almost as impregnable as the one that had previously been maintained by the Observer, and—for now—Grassal was shut out.

His friends needed him, but he couldn't help them, not right now. The tortured screams of other new arrivals reminded him that there were others here whom he could help.

This was it, then. He couldn't help them right now. He had a job to do and he knew how to do it. All he could hope was that Lilly and Amadeus could do theirs.

But that didn't mean he wouldn't keep trying.

43

Amadeus was in the midst of an unpleasant dream about being in a room overrun with rabbits when one of the rabbits hopped over to him, wiggled its nose, and drove its little teeth into the side of his neck.

He woke with a gasp. Every millimeter of his body vibrated with energy. The pain in his mutilated hand was nearly gone, but the side of his neck throbbed like the aftermath of a wasp sting.

Manuel leaned over him, a wide grin spread across his broad face.

"Amphetamines," he said, then held up an empty syringe for Amadeus to see. "You need to be awake for this." Manuel strode over to stand with his two companions in front of a half-opened door. All three held rifles.

Lilly's back was against the same wall he was presently leaning against. He bounded to his feet, noticed that he felt like he had springs on his shoes, and started toward her when a thud drew him up short. He turned his hyper-focused gaze from Lilly to a subluminal on the other side of a clear wall that was full of cracks. The creature emitted an ear-piercing shriek, then again threw itself against the most damaged section of glass. This time the front half of its body crashed through, and it started trying to wiggle its way through to their side. Something about its movements seemed uncoordinated though, as if it was unused to its own body.

"Well?" Manuel said. "Give us the key, and tell us how you're talking to Grassal. The truth, and no more bullshit. The truth, and you can walk right out this door."

Without a second thought, Amadeus tried to say, "Morse code," but his throat was so dry and his tongue so thick, that all that came out was a moan. The inability to speak startled Amadeus so much that he staggered.

By this time, Lilly had slid one arm around his waist. She pressed her forehead against his. Her eyes were wide, his were wider, but she kissed him on the lips, then whispered in his ear, "Trust me, and distract them on my cue. Now whisper something in my ear."

"If this is your choice, say your goodbyes," Manuel said.

Amadeus just managed to whisper the words, "I love you."

A second passed, then another. The corners of Lilly's mouth twitched up in a smile, then, in a voice that scared him in its volume and intensity, she said, "Get the fuck away from me." She pushed him, he staggered, and she pointed to the door. "Go on, go stand with your friends. Fuck you. I'm done."

Confused and hurt, Amadeus stepped backward, moving toward the men by the door. He heard one of the three men laughing at him.

The creature pulled itself the rest of the way through the glass, drew itself up, looked around the room, then stalked toward Lilly.

Amadeus' racing heart stopped in his chest.

"It'll be over soon," Manuel said, then gave Amadeus a pat on the shoulder. Amadeus shuddered at the man's touch.

The creature situated itself so that its backside was between the door, where Amadeus and the men stood, and Lilly. A second later, it pounced upon her. Lilly began to scream, but it sounded ... fake.

Trust her.

Then Amadeus understood. Amadeus gave his best war cry then, using every bit of his amphetamine-powered 70 kilograms, threw himself at Manuel and managed to knock the man onto the ground. This diverted the attention of the other two from the Takun, and that was all that it took.

The Takun sprang, impaled both of the standing men with its claws, then began to tear their bodies apart. Warm, wet fluid splattered onto Amadeus.

Below him, Manuel struggled to free himself, but Amadeus—wide-eyed and full of drug-induced strength—kept the man on the ground until Lilly and the Takun loomed over them both.

"Where is Jessup, and where is the cooling system?" Lilly asked, her voice pleasant, as if she were asking for nothing more than the location of the bathroom.

Manuel shook his head back and forth. "He's insane. My family. He'll ..." Manuel was shaking his head back and forth, as if full of indecision. Finally, he said, "I told him not to underestimate you."

"We're here to kill him," Lilly said. "Your family will be fine."

"His office. Second deck, L3. The cooling system has a circulation pump that runs off the ship's generators, and that—"

He did not finish, because the Takun plunged a claw into his eye.

Amadeus looked up at Lilly, a question on his face. Lilly helped Amadeus to his feet, then pointed to Manuel's field vest, where one dead finger was curled around the pin of a grenade affixed to the vest.

"Well done," she said.

The room smelled of shit and ammonia and bile and all his thoughts were jumbled together. The Takun stood just behind Lilly, docile and terrifying. Amadeus tried to get his breathing under control, because he really wanted to speak. After a couple of failed attempts, he finally managed to croak, "How?"

Lilly gazed at him through dilated pupils, tapped the side of her head, and said, "I changed my mind."

The Takun mimicked her movements exactly.

Crouching, she carefully removed the grenade from Manuel's vest, along with another she found on his person, and stuffed them into her pockets. She then handed Manuel's handgun to Amadeus, and took his blood-splattered rifle for herself. She ejected the magazine, nodded, and pushed it back in.

"Amadeus, this is Bigogli."

"No."

"Yeah. It is. We've reached an ... understanding, and Bigogli agreed to help us. So, to L3?"

"He could've been lying," Amadeus said, pointing to Manuel's corpse.

"Bigogli says he wasn't."

"You trust it?"

"Yes." She held his gaze, then said, "Are you ready to kill Roland Jessup?"

"I am. For your father."

"For my father," Lilly said.

"And for Gravity, and Janette Nguyen, and for every other person he's harmed."

"Altruist," Lilly said.

They left the room. Bigogli scouted ahead of them, down long, narrow metal corridors, past doors Amadeus hoped stayed closed forever. Soon they passed through a machine shop and entered the main engineering room in time to see Bigogli fling a mutilated person into the spinning propeller shaft. The body wrapped around the shaft and flopped a few times before sending a spray of gore into the air.

Amadeus examined the system in the room, looking for anything that might suggest a generator or a cooling system. After a few minutes of studying the room, his eyes settled on power cables and steel conduits that ran up and out of the engineering area. Amadeus followed the cables to their source and soon arrived at a control system built into a large green metal panel.

The system didn't look like standard equipment for this kind of ship, mostly because it was about ten years newer, and used flex screens to provide terminal readouts from several subsystems. He studied the readouts. One line of output showed temperature readings. He clicked for details and a schematic appeared on the screen. The send and return pipes flowed from this room, through the ship, and into two more unlabeled rooms.

"These pipes could lead to something," Amadeus said, "depending on which way you go."

From the rear of the control system, Lilly said, "There's something here that looks even better."

Amadeus stepped around to find Lilly pointing to a red lever. The lever label read, "Emergency shutoff."

Amadeus smiled and Lilly pulled the lever. The lights dimmed. Somewhere nearby, machinery groaned.

"That way?" Amadeus said, pointing in the same direction as the groan.

Lilly closed her eyes as if recalling a detail from a memory, pursed her lips, then opened her eyes and nodded.

They followed Bigogli, who tracked the pipes down a set of stairs, around a corner, and onto a catwalk that led over a row of generators. Amadeus knew they were generators because they were labeled as such. Each was about the size of a washing machine and each shared the same central shaft. In the middle of the catwalk, a ladder led down to a service panel that allowed access to the central shaft.

Behind them, a door opened. Lilly crouched. Amadeus followed her lead. Bigogli bounded toward the door. Amadeus heard a meaty tearing sound, followed by a thump. He then pointed to the service panel and said, "Looks like a good place for a little concussive maintenance."

Lilly glanced at Amadeus' hand, smiled, and said, "I got it."

She climbed two rungs of the ladder and opened the service

panel. The whirr of the generator's drive shaft reverberated off the metal walls around them.

Amadeus moved down the corridor, as far as he could go and still see Lilly. He nodded at her.

She took a deep breath, pulled the pin, and set the grenade just inside the panel. She closed the panel, climbed the ladder in one fluid motion, then dashed toward Amadeus. Together they turned the corner and covered another five meters before the grenade went off. Through the ringing in his ears afterward he could hear the furious clank of metal beating against metal as the broken shaft continued to turn.

The lights flickered and dimmed then they were plunged into blackness.

Amadeus cursed while he reached out with his uninjured hand, trying to feel for the nearest rail.

"Hold on to me," Lilly said. "I ... can find our way. Ready?"

Amadeus grunted and found her shoulder. The ship lurched, and began to tilt to one side. Amadeus moaned. The ship tilted back to the other side then leveled out.

Lilly started off at a jog. He couldn't see anything, but he kept right with her. She led them around one turn, then another, and yet another, all the while moving through sheer blackness. The din of the broken propeller shaft had faded, and twice he heard gunfire, but the shots were muffled by the walls between them.

Red emergency lights came on at the same time an alarm began to bleat. A door lay before them. Bigogli opened it and stepped through. There were some gunshots followed by the sound of men screaming. The screaming stopped and the alarm filled the air, along with the sound of stretching and compressing metal, which meant that a k-storm had formed around them.

"Keep going," Lilly said, and stepped through the door. Amadeus followed behind and saw the remains of a computer and electronics lab. Three doors—not counting the one they'd entered through—led out of the room. A man with terrified, darting eyes stood with his hands over his head. Amadeus raised his pistol and aimed it at the man.

"Where's Jessup?" Lilly said.

The man, who was barely any older than Amadeus, quaked with fear as his eyes darted from Bigogli to Lilly to Amadeus and back. Lilly waggled her gun at him and raised her eyebrows, perfectly indicating her impatience. Finally, the man pointed to the door in the middle.

"And the cooling system?" Amadeus asked.

The man pointed to the door directly behind him.

"Take us there," Lilly said.

The man shook his head.

"That was not a request," Lilly said.

Bigogli leaned in toward the man, putting its face directly in front of his. The color drained from his face and a wet spot formed in the front of the man's trousers. Amadeus thought that the man's knees were about to buckle, but after a moment he pulled himself upright and seemed to come to a decision.

"Follow me," the man said, his tone slightly imperious, as if he was trying to salvage what remained of his dignity. The man led them down a hallway, which was lined with clear holding pens, each of which contained one of the faceless hominoid subluminals that he'd once seen streaming out of an Ubermart distribution center. The creatures threw themselves at the glass as they passed. Each time, the man flinched.

"I'll never get used to that," the man said.

They entered a room which was full of circulation tanks, the tops of which were uncovered. Steam rose from some of the tanks. Pipes—the same ones Amadeus had been trying to follow earlier—rose out of the water and ran in at least four different directions.

"Shut it down," Amadeus said.

The man shook his head. "I ... he'll ..."

"I'll kill you," Lilly said.

"I'm already dead," the man said, "but I have a family ... he said that if I'm not strong, if my performance isn't—"

"You won't have anything to worry about once we're done," Lilly said.

The man sighed, hung his head, and began to enter some commands with a keyboard. A few seconds passed, another alarm began to blare, the water began to roil, and soon the surface was covered in bubbles. The room felt noticeably warmer. The liquid in the tanks began to glow, as if a giant lightbulb at the bottom of each had just been switched on.

Amadeus pointed to a large blue pump, one he suspected forced water from the cooling tanks and through the supply lines.

"Hey," he said, pointing to the pump. "For good measure. Just like before?"

Lilly looked at the pump, removed the other grenade from her pocket, and nodded. To the man, she said, "Where is Jessup?"

"His office, maybe? L3," the man said.

Lilly caught Amadeus' eye and smiled, pleased with the extra confirmation of Jessup's location. "Lead us there," Lilly said.

The man stammered out an objection, but Bigogli moved closer to him and gingerly placed one long claw on his chest.

"This way," the man said. "But with the power out, it's only a matter of time ..."

"Time for what?"

"Until the backup power on the locks fail. I told him failing open was a bad design decision."

As if to underscore the point, a chorus of mournful shrieks and whoops rang out not far from them, back toward the holding pens.

"Bigogli says that they can hear but will not listen," Lilly said.

The man pointed to the door, and just after everyone had passed through, Lilly walked to the pump, pulled the pin, set the grenade down, and dashed back through.

"Go, go, go," Lilly said.

They ran, the man in the lead, Bigogli behind him, and Amadeus and Lilly behind Bigogli. Lilly kept looking back over her shoulder, sweeping the corridor behind them with her rifle. The grenade's report was a dull, metallic thud, just one more sound in the cacophony.

Their path led to a steel door with a locking wheel. The man turned the wheel, then pulled the door open just far enough to let in some light.

"It's Davenport," the man—Davenport—called out over the blaring alarm. Bigogli shoved the man aside, pulled the door open, and bounded into the room beyond the door. Amadeus heard about a dozen gunshots, then nothing except the alarm and the wild shrieks of the faceless subluminals.

Bigogli finished its dark work and rejoined them. It was covered in the blood of men, but black fluid also oozed from several gunshot wounds on its body.

"We're clear for now, but there'll be more," Lilly said. To Davenport, she said, "Well?"

Davenport swallowed and stepped through the door. The remains of three—maybe four, Amadeus couldn't tell—men lay scattered about the floor.

"Up and over," he said. They passed down another corridor, stepped outside, and ascended two flights of stairs that led to the main deck. Outside, the night wind whipped at their clothes, waves crashed against the hull, and k-storm blossoms filled the air. On the port side, a few kilometers away, a rift had formed, rising up into the night, and the blood moon was reflected in the water.

They followed Davenport across the deck to the starboard side and came to a set of stairs that led back down into the ship. Before descending, Amadeus surveyed the water on the starboard side and was pretty sure that he saw the lights of several ships in the distance. He caught Lilly's attention and pointed.

"You think those are—" she said, but was cut off by the sound of gunshots, followed by the animal shrieks of dying men. The shrieking stopped and was replaced by the salacious din of the faceless subluminals.

They descended a flight of stairs, passed through a door, and entered another long corridor. Unlike the other parts of the ship, this section had faux wood paneling and carpet. Modernist artwork hung on the walls.

"It's just down the hall. Good luck," Davenport said, then turned and ran back in the direction they'd come.

"Let him go," Lilly said.

Bigogli was nearly too large to traverse the narrow corridor they followed, and its spines scratched against the faux-wood walls as it trailed behind them. The k-storm's gravity waves were causing the walls themselves to expand and contract, as if they walked through the breathing lungs of some great beast. Behind them a man—probably Davenport—screamed.

"This one," Lilly said. She pointed to a sign on the door that read simply, "Administrator." They both readied their weapons.

"I love you, Lilly Jones."

"I love you, too, Ami. Let's finish this."

Just then, the first of the faceless Takun descended the stairs. Bigogli readied itself to fight with its back to its attacker.

Amadeus started to grab the door handle, but Lilly caught his hand.

"Let's knock. Let him think he's in control. Trust me on this."

Amadeus nodded. He'd trust her. He always had, and he always would.

She knocked twice, then a third time. There was no response. She knocked again, louder this time, and from inside came a familiar voice whose smooth timbre cut through the bedlam around them.

"Come in," Jessup said.

Lilly opened the door and stepped inside, Amadeus behind her. Jessup sat in an overstuffed leather armchair. One hand held a revolver, which was aimed at Lilly, while the other hand rested on the shoulder of a child-sized doll which was wedged beside him in the chair. The doll appeared to be made out of scraps of clothing.

"Close the door behind you," Jessup said, indicating the door with his revolver. Lilly did as he asked.

"Seems a fitting way for all this to end, doesn't it?" Jessup said, his face a half-smile that barely hid the naked terror behind it. Amadeus knew that look, because he felt it, too. "We might as well drag your boy out for it." When neither Amadeus or Lilly moved, he said, "He's in the storage locker over there."

"My father?"

"Gone. I don't know where, and I can't explain it."

Amadeus' heart sank.

"Go on, get him," Jessup said. "I'm not going to shoot anyone unless somebody does something stupid. There's no point. Your people will be here in a few minutes. Well done, I suppose. Assuming they can run cleanup without destroying every fucking thing on this ship, they'll get their Rift Mitigation System. But we ... we won't be around to see them, thanks to your profoundly stupid decisions. That said, we can at least be civil with each other as we face the end."

Amadeus decided to take him at his word. He crossed the six steps to the storage locker and opened it. Grassal was crammed inside, still looking as placid as ever.

"We had this shit"—Jessup pointed a finger at Amadeus—"that *your father* helped me build, totally under control. It was all good in the neighborhood. And now? Poof. It's all over. We're about to be torn to ribbons by inter-dimensional demons. And even though I kind of hate you two for what you've done, I still admire your strength and determination. I ... underestimated you both."

Outside the door, several subluminals shrieked as one. Amadeus felt a wave of emptiness in his stomach, because he suspected that was a victory cry celebrating the death of Bigogli.

"So, my unwelcome guests, since we've all got an estimated life span of about one minute—and I feel that maybe you owe me the courtesy of one last question answered—do you have a big revelation for me?"

"There are some things you can't control," Lilly said.

Something began to beat against the door.

"Also, it was Morse code," Amadeus said. "That's how we communicated with Grassal."

Jessup nodded, as if satisfied with that explanation, then the metal door broke off one of its hinges and a subluminal began to pull itself through.

Amadeus, Lilly, and Jessup all opened fire. At the same time, a dazzling, pea-shaped latticework of light appeared in the room. The shape enveloped the subluminal and then the subluminal was gone.

Amadeus blinked, trying to process what had just happened, and only then noticed that Jessup was aiming the revolver at him. Lilly raised her rifle. There was one flash, then another.

A split second later, a searing geyser of pain erupted in Amadeus' chest and he was knocked backward onto the floor. There were more gunshots, then Amadeus saw Roland Jessup collapse into his chair. Blood oozed from a hole where his left eye had been and drain out onto the doll.

Above his own head grew a brilliant white light, which was momentarily blocked from his view by Lilly, who leaned over Amadeus and placed pressure on his right pectoral muscle. Tears welled in her eyes, and some strands of hair fell in front of her face. He tried to reach up and brush the strands back, but he was too weak to raise his hand. The light grew brighter and brighter and even though Amadeus tried to hold on, the blinding, brilliant light was the last thing he saw before consciousness slipped away.

44

A chill hung in the air of the late spring morning, two months after being whisked from Roland Jessup's ship, and Lilly had almost reached her destination. Before her, the Rockies stretched out like a rough gray sea, frozen in time. She was aware of every footstep she placed on the scree below her feet, not only the way her feet felt on the small, loose rocks, but of the crunching sound they made.

So many sounds made her jump lately—a loud voice, the cry of a circling hawk, a slamming door—but the crunching of rock thankfully wasn't one of them. The nightmares and lack of sleep made things worse. The years of counseling that stretched out ahead of her promised to provide some relief, but she knew that healing would be a long and arduous process. She smiled as she thought of Dr. Kongsampong, who had admonished her to maintain her focus on the present moment. She tried to do that, but she couldn't help but think about tomorrow, which she expected would be one hell of a day, and the day after that, which should be better. Tomorrow, however, was for other people. Today, though, was devoted to something all her own, something that she should have done a long time ago.

Almost there now, the cool wind lifted her hair just enough for her to notice, but not enough to make her jump, to make her think something was about to spring out of nowhere, throw itself on her, and begin the end of Lilly Jones.

No, that kind of thinking wasn't helpful, and she shut it down, just like she'd practiced with the therapist. She returned her focus to the present moment, to the scree crunching under her feet, to the songs of the mountain chickadee and western kingbird, to the weight of the urn she carried in her hands. But the weight she felt, it wasn't just that of the urn, it was the weight of her father, of living with the legacy of the decisions he'd made, and how she chose to deal with them.

She'd done what she'd set out to do. Jessup was dead, but others were, too. What she'd done, she'd done not for her father, but for herself, because there was a rage within her, it had always been there. For months, she'd had something to focus it on. Now, that was all behind her, and the rage, according to her therapist, served no useful purpose and could become self-destructive, and she should seek closure.

Three days had passed since she'd returned to the bunker in search of that closure. The lonely hours she'd spent sorting, cleaning, and inventorying had led up to this walk and its singular purpose. Soon she reached her destination and stopped, her feet inches from the edge of a sheer cliff face.

Lilly ran her hand over the mahogany urn she'd carried up the mountain, feeling the smooth contours of the wood grain underneath her fingertips. She unlocked the hasp then took a step toward the cliff's edge, remembering the last time she'd been here, at a funeral for a man who hadn't been dead. Then she opened the lid and flung the ashes out over the cliff. She watched them twist and scatter on the breeze, disappearing over a stand of scrub pines.

"Goodbye, Daddy," she said, then sat down on the scree and let the heaving sobs run their course. Just before she stood to go, she noticed a hawk riding currents of air. She watched it for a while, smiled, and said one more prayer for her father's immortal soul, in the hopes that it too would be free to glide through the air of whatever place it found itself.

Eventually, she returned to the bunker, cried all evening, and fell into a dreamless sleep. Early the next morning, she took a perfectly uneventful flight from Denver to DC.

She gazed out the window of the Silver Line Metro car she rode into the city while Verdi's *Requiem* played through her earbuds. The closer the train carried her to the station, the more people stepped aboard, as if coming close to a center of power caused suits and briefcases to accrete in the train like calcium to limestone.

Her stop arrived, and she followed the crowd along the wide sidewalks of First Street, and up the steps into the Dirkson Senate Office Building, as if this was just another normal day in her life, and not one in which she laid out the facts of the matter for one of the most important events in modern history. No one fully understood the implications yet. But her follow-up testimony would be a part of the record. At least they'd given her time to prepare, not like the first time, whisked from the flaming lair of a madman into a busy hospital emergency room, picked up by two police officers who'd responded to a report of a white, flaming mushroom, and finally turned over to a pair of moderately befuddled Homeland Security agents.

Inside, a guard ushered her to a wooden desk in a conference room. Her attorney said to the committee chairwoman, "Thirty minutes, and no more. As you can see, Miss Jones is undergoing a very challenging time in her life. I request that she not be put under any undue strain or forced to answer anything she does not wish to answer."

"We'll abide by your terms," the chairwoman said. Ice cubes tinkled as she took a sip of water from a glass, then said, "Miss Jones, one last time, where is Grassal Delgado?"

"I've been wondering the same thing about the late-not-late president. Last I saw him, he was getting backslaps from Roland Jessup."

"That's the subject of an ongoing inquiry and is not relevant to the matter at hand."

The chairwoman was one of the late-not-late president's biggest boosters, but had been strangely silent on the whole matter of his recent resurrection. The chairwoman scowled and said to an aide, "Omit that from the record."

Lilly's attorney leaned in close and whispered, "Please behave. This will be over before you know it."

The chairwoman said, "Again. Where is Grassal Delgado?"

"At a top-secret location, several hundred feet underground."

"We already know that, because we put him there, and you know that's not what we're asking."

"He—the thing that makes him him—is not in this space," Lilly said.

A holographic projector she hadn't noticed before began to play a scene that showed a large pillar of white light that flowed from the ground to the sky.

"Then how do you explain this?" the chairwoman gestured at the image. "This is from Boston two weeks ago. Our sensing data indicates the presence of the same physical phenomena that was detected when you were returned from Jessup's boat."

"I've been in Colorado. I don't know anything about that," Lilly said, then nodded to Dr. Kongsampong, who was seated at the table with her, but appeared to have fallen asleep. "Maybe Dr. Kongsampong can provide you with a more thorough analysis of Grassal's current state of consciousness than I can."

"Miss Jones, we just need to know: how can we talk to him?"

"Again, I don't know."

"Your previous testimony indicates that you communicated with Mr. Delgado."

"I did communicate with Grassal," Lilly said. "We coordinated on a plan to bring matters to a ... reasonable conclusion. We did what we had to do. But I haven't been in contact with Grassal since."

"It seems to me that you lured Roland Jessup to you so you could kill him before Mr. Brunmeier's JDSC associates arrived. That was a very bold plan."

A burst of laughter escaped her mouth and filled the room and Lilly didn't give a damn how she sounded.

At the same time, her attorney stood up and said, "There is no evidence that my client killed anyone, and even if there was, your assertion is immaterial to this hearing."

"At least tell us this: do you think he will stop?"

"Do you want him to stop?"

"Miss Jones, this is gravely serious. As far as we can tell, Grassal Delgado alone is responsible for the cessation of all rift activity. Billions of people are placing their safety and trust in one man. What happens if he decides not to continue quelling new rifts?"

She looked from one gray bureaucrat to another, meeting each of their eyes. "Protect his body, and do not deploy the Rift Mitigation System, and be patient."

The rest of the meeting was a rehash of the same questions, worded differently, because they had so little trust that a critical system could be run by one person who worked for free. Lilly said as little as possible, and afterwards her legal representation team fed her a steak dinner. She needed it, too, because she'd forgotten to eat breakfast. She'd always assumed you couldn't get good steaks in the East, but life had proven her wrong yet again, and she lost herself in the act of eating.

Lilly only realized she was making "mmm" noises while she ate when she noticed Dr. Kongsampong was grinning at her. Then Lilly felt a little guilty enjoying this, while Amadeus ...

"Today was a good day," her attorney said. "You gave them just enough to keep them busy for a few more months, and just enough to reassure them that—"

Her lawyer droned on, and Lilly focused her attention on the exceptionally delicious sautéed wild mushrooms. Outside the restaurant after dinner, a small press gaggle awaited them, and the lawyer tried her best to fend them off. One man, though, Lilly recognized immediately. The purple hair was gone, and he'd lost the anachronistic thick-rimmed glasses, but that unmistakable air of a hack still lingered around him.

"Lewis Braxton?" Lilly asked. "You look almost presentable."

"Good to see you, too. How are you holding up?" he asked.

"Is this on the record?"

"Maybe."

"One day at a time, that's all I can say right now."

"Are you ready for tomorrow?" he asked as she tried to pull away.

"Hell fucking yes."

"You know I can't print that."

Lilly graced him with a smile, turned her back on him, and headed for her hotel. There, she had a sleepless night, undermining her efforts to prepare herself. She was excited, there was that thrill of something long-awaited about to arrive, and she had waited long enough. No one would blame her if she thought it a little unfair she'd had to wait this long to see him, but still ...

The next morning, four police officers and her attorney escorted her through a shoulder-to-shoulder crowd that lined the entrance into Walter Reed Medical Center. As she snaked her way through the crowd, she noticed a couple familiar faces, some people she thought she knew, or who might have been famous. They didn't matter. It was all very overwhelming for her, and though the propranolol her doctor had prescribed did help with situations like these, she was ready to strike. She didn't think that instinct would be going away anytime soon.

One person she did recognize in the crowd was Tommy Brunmeier. She caught his eye and he tried to wave, but the handcuffs made the gesture less like a greeting and more like an awkward hand flap.

Smiling slightly, she strode through the hospital lobby and into an elevator. Four police officers and her attorney rode up with her. All gave her plenty of room. Nobody wanted to be the person who bumped Lilly Jones.

The elevator arrived at its floor and she strode out first. This hallway was lined with a mixture of more police officers and people in poorly tailored suits. There were doctors and nurses as well, but they were there only to watch the spectacle. Until now, it was just the bureaucracy standing in the way. And her testimony yesterday had been the last part of a deal to make this day happen.

Of course she was ready for it.

She walked through the crowd and they began to clap. She felt herself blush, which kind of aggravated her, but she nevertheless acknowledged the applause with a slight tilt of her head. Eventually, she reached the end of the crowd and came to the room, her destination. She pushed open the heavy door and there was Amadeus, standing on shaky legs. A walker was nearby, but he wasn't using it. She ran to him, threw her arms around his shoulders, and that was that.

It felt good to be home.

45

A success notification percolated through the hundreds of worker nodes that Grassal was currently coordinating. The last of the new arrivals—at least those who'd wished to return to normal space—had been sent home safely. With that task complete, he now had only one goal: protect both worlds against the formation of new rifts. Eventually, he intended to begin work to create the Transportation Guild, but he had needed to dam the floods before he started building bridges.

The worker nodes were overseen by the Luminants who had volunteered to aid in his efforts and the new arrivals who'd chosen to stay for a tour of duty. All of the worker nodes reported back to him on the status of the disturbances they were monitoring and controlling. Even now, a k-storm was trying to form in west Texas, but a group of worker nodes had dispatched themselves to the Luminance side of the area and had the event under control.

When he'd started this work six months ago, coordination had been demanding and complex, requiring his complete attention. Since then, however, he'd tuned the systems and trained the worker nodes to be semi-autonomous and self-organizing. Now, he finally felt like he could let go of the reins, at least a little bit.

Grassal thought about the events that had led him to this

point, how he'd gone from a scared, cannibalistic outsider to usurper to inter-dimensional operations manager. He thought of Filipe's words: "Accept this responsibility and you will be forever changed." Grassal had accepted the responsibility, and one of the changes was replacing his desire to return to normal space with a will to fulfill the duty to stay in the Luminance and make things right.

He'd learned to control both himself and the new world in which he'd chosen to live, and had managed to save Amadeus and Lilly from a bad situation in the process. It'd all been closer than he would've liked, and Grassal would've preferred a little bit more of a cushion—he wasn't a seat-of-the-pants kind of person, especially when it came to mission-critical things—but he'd done it.

Since then, he hadn't given himself much time to think about the future, but now that the last of the new arrivals who wished to return home had been returned home, that future was here, and he would play a significant role in shaping it. To do this right, he would need help from smart people who could build things and keep them running. But most of those people were in normal space, and to get their help, he would have to trust that his own systems could run themselves, at least for a little while, while he sought them out.

Grassal received a non-urgent connection request from Filipe. Grassal opened the channel and greeted the Luminant.

"Congratulations are due," Filipe said.

"Thanks. I never could've done this without your help. You ... believed in us, in humans."

"Mutual aid illuminates the lines forward."

"Mutual aid," Grassal echoed. "We can't change the past, but we can shape the future."

"There is something on your mind."

"There is. Two things, actually. Personal affairs that I need to put in order. But I'll need to leave the Luminance for a little while to do it."

"Then do it. Now is the time."

Filipe was right and Grassal knew it, so he left Suki—his most trusted and capable operator—in charge of coordination for the day, then prepared the electro-Luminant machinery that would allow him to create an avatar on Earth.

A few minutes later, he manifested in the Mission District of San Francisco, hovering just outside the kitchen window of the apartment where he'd thrown that damn jar of pickles. Even now he remembered the acrid, vinegary smell that marked the end of one chapter of his life and the beginning of another.

He tried not to peer inside, because that would be a little creepy, but when you could see in all directions and through solid walls, it was kind of unavoidable to see her sitting at the kitchen table, a guitar in her hand. As Lucretia strummed, ribbons of brilliant light flowed out of the guitar and bounced around the room.

Grassal had never seen music before, at least not while in this form, and he spent a couple minutes just outside her window basking in the sound and vibration. All too soon, she finished the song, wrote something on a notepad, then picked up a cup of coffee from the table and lifted it to her mouth.

Unwilling to put this off any longer, he manifested just enough physicality to tap on the glass, once, twice. Lucretia looked toward the window, and when she registered the glowing humanoid form outside her window, her eyes went wide. The coffee cup in her hand began to shake.

Just before the cup slipped from her fingers, Grassal extended an ephemeral appendage through the wall and steadied it. Only a trickle of the warm liquid ran down the side of the glass. Grassal said, "Hi, Lucretia."

"Grassal?"

"It's me."

"You're ... a ball of light."

"Life has taken a turn for the strange. I just ... I never got to properly apologize for what happened, for what I did to you."

"You were sick. I didn't know it at the time. I do now."

"But that doesn't mean I didn't do you harm. I am deeply sorry. What happened, what I did ... it's something I'll regret every day for the rest of my life."

"Apology accepted and appreciated, but I've made my peace with it."

"You always were very understanding of peculiar circumstances. If there's anything I can do ..."

Lucretia smiled a sly smile that filled Grassal with longing and—momentarily—made him question his decision to stay in the Luminance and protect humanity from its own stupidity. "Actually, maybe there is. We have a big show tonight. Could you make an appearance? Everybody's wondering and speculating about you, and if you could be there, at our show ... do you have any idea how much that would raise our profile?"

"It's the least I can do. Just give me a time and a place."

She told him when and where he needed to appear, then there was nothing else to say.

That evening, Grassal found himself at the Fillmore Auditorium. The first song had already started. Bright ribbons of sound filled the air, traveling through the hall like shimmering, rainbow waves. Grassal's body buzzed with anticipation and he realized that he was nervous.

The Interstellar Sisters finished their second number. Zella gave a hand signal which dimmed the lights in the hall, which marked the customary moment of silence for everyone who'd been lost during the Emergence. The silence ended, Lucretia started the riff that kicked off the third song, then Grassal caused a brilliant flaming mushroom to blossom ten feet above the drummer. The flaming mushroom resolved into Grassal's humanoid form. As far as public appearances went, this was the first time he'd deliberately allowed himself to be seen, and Grassal realized—a bit late in life—that maybe he had something of a flair for showmanship.

He looked out to see thousands of faces staring back at him.

Each one wore an open-mouthed expression somewhere between disbelief and awe.

"Ladies and gentlemen," Lucretia said over a drum break, "give it up for Grassal Delgado."

At first there was nothing, only the silence of disbelief, but soon the crowd erupted in applause and cheers, buffeting him like a strong wind. Even though he'd always told himself that he liked to be the guy in the shadows lurking behind the curtain, maybe it was okay to step out front every once in a while.

Grassal remained for the rest of the concert and through the encore. When the show was over, he met Zella and Lucretia backstage, said a goodbye that had a lot more finality than he would've liked, then traveled to his last destination, an old New England mansion that nobody wanted to tear down, but nobody wanted to add on to, either. In days past it would've been called a sanitarium, but now its name—the Summer Reach Care Facility—was sanitized and neutral, without all those negative connotations.

Grassal searched the mansion. Each human had its own unique energy signature, not unlike a fingerprint, and now that he could sense them, he could also muster them up in his memory. Tracking her down was simply a matter of scanning all the energy signatures in the area and comparing them to the one in his memory until he found a match.

He found his mother in a room on the third floor. She sat in a rocking chair that faced a window. She was more gaunt than he remembered, but her eyes seemed a little less haunted. He supposed that was an improvement, though he wouldn't know until he talked to her. Even though he was in a glowing humanoid form, when he entered the room her eyes gleamed with a flash of recognition, and her face broke into the same wide smile he remembered from the good times—there were a handful—from when he'd been a small boy.

"Is it really you?" she said in Spanish. "I thought the government took you away from me forever."

"It's me. I just wanted to say that I'm sorry for how things turned out. I never told you that, because I never realized it."

"My son, how could you know? They did not want you to know about me, that I knew the truth. That is why they locked me in here after your friends made it possible for me to come back to America."

"Ma, this is the best place for you. You're getting the care you need, and you're safe here."

"Safe? None of us are safe."

"What do you mean?"

His mother just gazed at him with those wide, intense brown eyes. She'd always been intense, but this was something else, and a current of fear pulsed through him. She stood from the rocking chair, took a step toward him, and raised a hand to his face. He willed his face to be solid, and her hand rested on his cheek. Eventually, she spoke.

"Something wicked is coming, something awful, bigger than you can imagine. I know about the monsters, the ones that you fought, but those were only the heralds. People think that the worst is over ... but I know better. I have seen horrors from beyond this world, and I can tell you that the worst is yet to come."

Epilogue

Stamford, Connecticut
Five years later

Amadeus attacked the wisteria with an electric trimmer. The damn vines grew and grew, and today's assault was only one battle in a long campaign. He'd rather not do it at all, but it needed to be done, and with the birthday party over, he thought this was as good a time as any. The twins were asleep, Lilly had to take a call with her agent, and the ache in his back wasn't too bad today. Still, he needed to be careful not to overdo it. He had a doctoral thesis to defend next week, and the members of the physics department wouldn't cut him any slack, lingering bullet wounds notwithstanding.

Su Min, her husband Lee Jong He, and their three-year-old twins had flown in from Seoul for his and Lilly's twins' birthday party. His aunt Annie and uncle Mark had come, and even his father had made an appearance, though his government handlers had limited the duration of his attendance to one measly hour, since the terms of his sentencing allowed for little deviation from his work at the research facility.

But the party had gone on well past the twins' usual nap time, and the resulting screaming fit from the one-year-old celebrants had sent everyone out the door, propelled by understanding goodbyes.

Because neither set of parents were quite ready to reveal their children's secrets, the party had been a deliberately small affair. There might be more twins like theirs, but if there were, no one was saying anything, not yet. At this point, only the party's attendants, two pediatricians, and one geneticist knew about the Brunmeier twins' condition. Even now, the geneticist's words about their children echoed in his mind, somehow drowning out the trimmer's whine: "The traits are dominant. In a few generations, your descendants will likely be a people apart."

He finished the largest vine at the rear of the house. His back had begun to complain, so he turned off the trimmer, set it down, and wiped the sweat from his brow. He thought about things for a few minutes, but was interrupted by a chime that was triggered by the motion sensor Lilly had installed at the end of their driveway not long after they'd moved in.

Amadeus' first thought was to dart inside through the back door, pull the curtains, and monitor the vehicle and its driver—assuming it had one—from inside the house, close to everyone who mattered. He stayed outside, however, and soon heard the sound of an old gasoline vehicle coming down the driveway a little faster than he would've liked. There were children around, after all. That line of thinking soon turned dark, and he began to scan the yard for other threats more dangerous than wisteria. He looked for hints of movement in the nearby woods. He imagined gunfire tearing through walls, penetrating the soft flesh of Lilly and the twins and—most cruel of all—the way the bullets would sail right past him, leaving him to live the rest of his life without them.

But those were the old instincts, the same ones that occasionally caused him to wake screaming in the night. Lilly had the nightmares, too, and that's why they slept in separate beds and never let the children sleep with them. Night terrors were nothing to mess with. Therapy and counseling had helped, though there was only so much that could be done.

Amadeus walked from around the back of the house to watch the car—a turn-of-the-century Honda Accord—cross the remaining distance from the driveway to his house. Amadeus couldn't see the driver's face for the car's high beams.

The car skidded to a stop about twenty meters from their minivan. The driver's door opened and a middle-aged man stepped out. He wore stained, baggy jeans, dirty sneakers, and an ill-fitting plaid shirt. No, Amadeus realized, he wasn't middle aged, just prematurely bald and poorly groomed. The clothes were wrong, and he was uglier, somehow, but Amadeus still recognized the guy who'd assaulted him on his graduation day in what seemed like a different life so long ago.

"You fucked up my life, Brunmeier," Davy said. "You have no idea how bad."

The quaver in the man's voice and the wild look in his eye told Amadeus what Davy had come here to do, and all that Amadeus had to prevent that was an electric hedge trimmer. Maybe, if he was fast enough ... he cursed himself for leaving his sidearm inside. Ever since they'd moved in here, he and Lilly had taken to wearing one, because doing so helped them both feel a little safer. Now that he needed it, the only thing he could defend his family against was an aggressive shrubbery.

"You have no idea how bad," Davy repeated, then reached for something behind his back. Adrenaline surged through Amadeus' body. His muscles tensed and he was just about to charge when a rifle shot cracked, sending a spray of dirt up onto Davy's jeans.

From behind him, Amadeus heard Lilly say, "That's your only warning. You have five seconds to get the fuck out of here. Five. Four."

Amadeus smiled and thought about how lucky he was to have someone like her.

At three, Davy still hadn't moved.

At two, he reached for the gun again.

At one, the air around them rumbled, there was a bloom of brilliant light, and Davy disappeared, leaving only the sound of the motor running, and the bark of some neighborhood dogs.

"You okay?" Lilly called out.

"Fine," Amadeus said. "You remember the Davy from UConn I told you about?" He turned to see Lilly leaning out the living room window, his father's M4 carbine still pointing to the place where Davy had been.

"That was him?" she asked. "I expected somebody ... bigger."

"Now that you mentioned it, I did, too."

The summer crickets resumed their chirping, and Amadeus just stood there, not quite sure if he should get back to work or not. Before he had decided, Lilly stepped out of the front door and onto the porch.

"The kids still asleep?" Amadeus asked.

"They slept right through it."

"Small miracles. I guess he'll be here in—"

The air just a few meters away, in the front of the lawn, near the old red oak tree, began to blossom and glow. There was a mushroom of light, and Amadeus heard a familiar, booming laugh. The light resolved into a humanoid form.

Grassal.

The form looked mostly like Grassal, but it was also utterly alien. Instead of a physical body—that one was in a secure, undisclosed location a couple hundred feet below the earth— this body was a swirling form of blueish-green light, a mannequin made from the aurora borealis.

"As of today, that guy is officially banned from gate traversals by the Transportation Guild," Grassal said. "Maybe he'll reflect on some of his poor life choices during his walk back to civilization from the Mongolian Steppes."

"Thanks," Amadeus said. "It's been a while, buddy."

"I've been busy. I know you have, too," he said. "Hi, Lilly. Getting enough sleep?"

"It's never enough," she said.

"Can I see them?"

"Come on," Lilly said, leading the way inside. Grassal followed her through the front door, not that he needed to do anything so pedestrian as use a door. Amadeus pulled the door closed behind him and stepped into the foyer, where cheerful balloons dangled from the ceiling. Late summer sunlight filtered through the window, illuminating the motes of dust that hung in the air.

They all climbed the stairs, went down the hall, and stopped just outside the door to the twins' bedroom. Despite the glowing, ever-shifting form of his appearance, Grassal made no noise whatsoever as he glided into their bedroom. Lilly put an arm around Amadeus' waist, the way she sometimes did when they would stand at the door and just watch their babies sleep.

The twins—Janetius and Claudius—were in their cribs. Janette was still asleep, but Claudius was trying to pull a plush rabbit from his mobile. He noticed his visitors and turned to gaze at them with bright, green eyes. When he saw Grassal, Claudius' smile grew wide, revealing two bottom teeth that had just come in.

"Unka Gwassa!" he said, then threw himself over the crib rail —the ability to do so was a recent development—and toddled over to Amadeus, arms outstretched. Amadeus bent down, picked up his son, and hugged him tight. Grassal reached in and stole Claudius' nose, then created a giant, glowing nose in the center of the room. Claudius squealed with delight as he reached out for the nose, which disappeared with a flash when his hand passed through it.

"He's happy to see you," Lilly said. "And I am, too. But really, where have you been? Are the new volunteers ready?"

"Mostly," Grassal said, "they're first-class. The latest group's been on rift mitigation duty for three months now as a learning exercise, and they've performed perfectly ..."

"You did train them, after all," Amadeus said.

"But ..." Lilly said, prompting Grassal to continue.

"But I still have no idea what I'm doing, and neither does anybody else. Everything's held together with bubblegum and duct tape, and we're all in over our heads."

"Sounds like parenting," Lilly said.

That earned her a booming laugh from Grassal.

Claudius began to squirm, so Amadeus put him down. He tottered on legs as steady as any one-year-old could manage. When he reached Grassal, he stuck his arms up in the air, then reconsidered and caused himself to levitate upward so that he was eye-level with Grassal.

Grassal wove light for him. Claudius giggled, then began to grab for the strings of light, moving them this way and that, collecting great handfuls of them. He flung one handful at the stuffed dragon in his crib, which caused the dragon to fall over. Amadeus also grabbed for the light, but his hand went right through it.

"From our perspective, you're doing great," Lilly said. By "our," Amadeus knew that Lilly meant the general human perspective. "Except that we're in the dark about what you're doing."

"That's kind of why I stopped by today," Grassal said. "There's ... something else out there, something bigger than the Observer, and I'm planning an expedition to find out what. It'll be a mix of Luminants and volunteers. I've put it off as long as I could, but with five separate groups of volunteers capable of running both rift mitigation and transit operations, I've run out of excuses."

"So, one last reunion before you go?" Lilly said.

"I just wanted to see those babies one more time before I leave. They're beautiful, as always."

"Thanks," Amadeus and Lilly said in unison.

Amadeus said, "It doesn't have to all be on you. You've done your part. There's no shortage of volunteers ..."

"But this is on me, and I can't let this go wrong. Even if that means ... well, no matter what it takes. That's why we're still working on the universal rights charter, and that's why we're taking our time to finalize the contract with the Luminants. Everyone has to benefit, especially the Luminants. It's their dimension, after all. We're just a bunch of interlopers."

"One way or another," Amadeus said, "it's good to see you. Come back soon."

Amadeus smiled and felt the first welling of tears around his cheeks, but told himself he wouldn't cry, because this wasn't an ending, this was just an interlude. There was more to be done, and he would be doing it, taking part in it, but on his own terms, in his own way. And though their lives might've taken vastly different paths, they were still friends, brothers, and would be forever linked, no matter what dimension or life stage they found themselves in.

Janette had woken up and begun to cry, so he scooped her up and held her in one arm.

"I will, buddy, I will," Grassal said.

They embraced, to the extent that one could hug a glowing mass of particles, and Grassal was gone. Amadeus looked from Lilly to Claudius to Janette and back to Lilly again. Here he was, with his little family, the life he and Lilly had built. They were together, they were safe, they were home, and no matter what happened, he knew that they would be okay. After what they'd been through and what they'd done ... Whatever the universe would throw at them, Amadeus knew they could handle it together. His story was now their story, and they would write the next chapters together.

With that thought on his mind, Amadeus met Lilly's gaze and smiled.

Afterword

Thank you for reading *Reunion*.

We've come a long way together, and I appreciate all the time you've put into this series.

While *Reunion* concludes *The Emergence,* I have more exciting book projects planned for the future. Join my readers' group at sethmbaker.com/signup/ and I'll let you know what's happening.

If you've enjoyed the journey—and I sincerely hope that you have—please consider supporting my work by leaving a quick review on Amazon or Goodreads or sharing this work with a friend.

As always, thank you for your time and patronage.
Seth M. Baker

Acknowledgements

This book exists thanks to the diligent efforts of beta readers Amberlee Venters, Marcus Bell, and Madison Drake; copy editor Celestian Rince; the team at Deranged Doctor Design for the fantastic covers; and readers like you. Any errors are my own.

About the Author

Seth M. Baker has worked as a software engineer, international English teacher, freelance writer, and pizza delivery man. He's been making up stories since he was a kid.

He grew up in West Virginia, USA and has traveled extensively. His earliest memory is of a wildfire consuming the hill behind his house.

He lives in a misty Appalachian valley with his wife and sons.